The Eight Heroes of Old

Tommy Kent
The Time Warden

A Novel

Joe Cordova

Copyright © 2024 by Joe Cordova
All rights reserved.
No part of this publication may be reproduced, distributed, or transmitted in any form or by any means, including photocopying, recording, or other electronic or mechanical methods, without the prior written permission of the publisher, except as permitted by U.S. copyright law.

ISBN - 13: 979-8-340960-29-0
ISBN - 13: 979-8-3304-6654-2

The story, all names, characters, and incidents portrayed in this production are fictitious. No identification with actual persons (living or deceased), places, buildings, and products are intended or should be inferred.

To Kacey Cordova, my wife and biggest fan.

Tommy Kent
The Time Warden

…When time calls…
…a hero will come…

Prologue: Last Will and Testament

Humanity, as it once was, exists no more. Social bonds connected people. They led to acts of charity, communication, construction, and creation. But, the bonds have eroded. What remains is a world of isolation, self-interest, and destruction. Those who don't rank their own survival simply perish. The grandest of structures have crumbled to dust. Roads have withered. Now, humans dwell underground, far from each other. Small packs of survivors persist, but nothing significant.

In a bygone era, sunlight pierced through the clouds, nourishing the Earth. Lush plants and trees flourished, and the melodious songs of birds brought a sense of peace.

Even those who had lost their eyes could still sense the Creator's gifts. They could feel them in the warmth of the sun or the songs of the birds. Or so I've read. I yearn for the beauty of those days. Now, only darkness prevails, and humanity's former glory is but a distant memory.

Great cities have been reduced to rubble, and technology has become a relic of science fiction. The only sounds that break the silence are the harsh winds carrying storms of ash and sand. There's no rain nor snow, only thick, impenetrable clouds, painting the sky of dust and gray.

Hope, the Creator's greatest gift to humanity, now exists solely in history books, or what's left of them. I've unearthed these old volumes that chronicle the legends of great heroes, created by the Allfather, chosen by time, to face these perilous evils. These heroes rose to the occasion, each with their own stories and struggles, some from the unlikeliest of places. But in this world of darkness, those days are gone. I wish I could have seen it with my own eyes.

But alas, where is the hero who could have prevented this descent into chaos? I can only surmise that they failed and took the last remnants of hope with them. Perhaps not. I haven't lost hope entirely. I've learned from these historical texts how to manipulate magic and time through an intricate machine. My last efforts have left me battered and frail. My time here is at an end, but my hope rests with my sons. I've armed them with the necessary tools and knowledge, only they're still young. Dearest Tommy and Jimmy, I wish for a better life for you and your mother.

I know my time is running out. I'm uncertain how much time they may have. But, if there's even a glimmer of hope left in this world, it's in both of them. This is all I can do. Goodbye, my sons. Goodbye, my wife. Until we meet again…

Joe Cordova

1 Father's Mission

Darkness loomed over the sky. Thunder and red lightning clashed, while fierce winds rattled the doors of a shed in a desolate field. Not far from this shed stood a dilapidated house, both structures at the mercy of decay. They were unfit for habitation, but in these grim times, there were no better options.

Inside the shed, two voices, young and soft, rang over the clamor of howling wind and the banging of the shed doors. The sounds of welding tools rattled against the rampant commotion. Sparks shone through the cracks in the walls. A boy, no older than ten, was constructing a machine capable of altering reality.

"Just need to place this here and weld that there," Tommy mumbled. He was a small boy, looking like he hadn't had a proper meal in months, while his hands ached to lift a wrench. His attire was a patchwork of salvaged clothing, with the only recognizable item being a pair of goggles that his father had discovered amid the ruins. "Jimmy, can you pull the rusty lever over there and start turning the red valve?"

"But Mom said you weren't ready yet," Jimmy argued. He was a spitting image of his mother but shared the same misfortune in clothing as Tommy. His hair was darker than his brother's but held a similar charm.

"It's nearly done, don't worry. I've read the books Dad gave me, and it should work. Now, go ahead and pull it," Tommy reassured him.

"But I don't think it's calborted right," Jimmy remarked, struggling with the large words used.

"You mean calibrated," Tommy corrected, lifting the darkened glass from his eyes. The sparks settled as he finished his welding. "Look, you've seen what this can do. It's all set. I followed Dad's instructions as best as I could. Trust me," Tommy said with encouragement to his younger brother.

Jimmy hesitated while covering his eyes with one hand and the other on the lollipop of a handle. He pulled the lever, as his brother had said, completing the final step in their father's notebook. As Tommy predicted, a massive, circular machine came to life, with coils and lights aligned precisely with a sketch in a handwritten book left open on the floor. A swirl of light radiated from the shed, visible for miles, while a slight magnetic field tilted nearby metal objects.

"Don't look at it, Jimmy!" Tommy warned, descending from the machine after adjusting a few valves. "It's too bright! I'm going to put on my gear and go in!"

"I'm not so sure." Jimmy's voice wavered as he replied. "Mom said you're still too young. What if I can't bring you back?"

Tommy embraced Jimmy in a firm clasp. "I have to do this, Jimmy…" Tommy shed a small tear but wiped it quickly before Jimmy would see. "It's what father dreamt of… I have to do it for him. Anyway, You're smarter than me, Jimmy. You can figure it out if needed. The time is set: to a thousand years in the past. The last time anyone saw a hero. Almost an eternity ago. I'll be there. Trust yourself…" The machine sputtered and gurgled. The light burst into erratic flashes. The machine teetered on the brink of collapse. "I have to go now; we may not get another chance."

Tommy donned his father's old leather jacket, a handmade piece not intended for such an endeavor. But regardless, he rolled up the sleeves to fit his small stature. Covering his eyes with his welding goggles, he braved the machine and vanished into the circle of light as his silhouette diminished.

Jimmy, unsure of Tommy's fate, called his name and offered a small prayer for his brother's safety. The light emanating from the shed caused disturbances outside. Dark clouds gathered overhead, the winds intensified, uprooting dead trees nearby. Jimmy sensed something amiss and decided to turn off the machine for his own safety. He worried about the attention it might attract.

The violent winds, coupled with the machine's strain, placed it under immense pressure, leading to its deterioration. Valves started turning over their safety thresholds, and the gate overheated. The coils burnt out. The bulbs shattered. The fuse box shorted. This caused the whole machine to implode.

In that moment, Jimmy reversed the lever ending the machine's rampage in disrepair. There was no way for Tommy to return through it. Jimmy stood there in disbelief, on the brink of tears, hearing his mother calling for them.

Emily, a mother so caring yet with a face daring to confront the harsh world, rushed into the shed, seized Jimmy, and hurried back in the direction of their home. There was no time for questions; she knew that Tommy must have stepped through the machine and must trust in the hope that he would return. There was no time for grieving, only the urgency of ensuring Jimmy's safety. With a determined swiftness, she pushed herself to the limit, as malevolent howls of horrific creatures echoed in the distance, closing in on the remnant of her family.

The display of light amazed Tommy as it scintillated, surrounding him with different colors. He removed his goggles. Although the light was bright, it was not harmful to his eyes. The vortex worked wonders around Tommy and flashed his life before him. He was able to see into his past; he saw his father standing before him as a child, smaller than he was now. Flashes of Tommy's last birthday with him filled his mind, along with the day his father died. Rewatching those memories soothed his heart. But a new amazement of light kept coming, revealing more of his life until the day he stepped through the portal.

Time came to Tommy like a book upon a podium which he could read like a well-written text. The book had no illustrations, but it filled his mind with vivid images as if it were alive. Turning page after page, he could learn everything humans had learned, from their first days to their last. It was all there for him to discover.

Tommy felt no anger nor despair, emotions he had known his whole life. He felt an unexpected surge of happiness and hope. While he felt this peace, he continued to read the Book of Time. History's forgotten fragments unfolded before his discerning eyes. He understood every question immediately. But he didn't get the one he wanted most: What happened to the heroes? and searched for the answer that eluded him.

Something felt wrong in his gut. Darkness enveloped him, extinguishing the light in an instant. It faded to black, then to nothing. The images in his head were gone. Time had lost him, and he felt like he was falling, falling with no end. Centuries passed by him and through him. He felt his age as he grew older and older. He felt the cold hand of death. His body withered away. Then, he lived again. From infancy to old age, he lived through the ages again and again for eternity. He was in an everlasting cycle of life and death, from dust to dust. The endlessness stole every memory from him, leaving him feeling lost and defeated. The madness took all his hope. Despair filled his heart.

This void of time caused desperation. Desperation became determination. Ever conscious, he split from his body, his soul forever bound outside of time, but the link to his body was his mind. He soon found the ability to control his body like a marionette and to manipulate time. A welcomed gift in this desperation, eons of learning was now his.

From that emptiness came life, and from that void came darkness. Out of that darkness, the light returned, flashing even brighter than before. An amazement of yellow and white filling his eyes with immaculate beauty and wonder. Through the light, a voice called out to him in a soft and comforting tone yet shook his very core.

"Tommy Kent," the voice spoke, warm and maternal, etching it into his consciousness.

It was overwhelming when he realized how he had even forgotten his name was Tommy. For what felt like thousands of years, he could not remember it because he had lost it. He had almost forgotten his whole existence. But, the voice saved him from that endlessness.

Tommy could not speak, but his heart projected his words as if he could.

"Who are you?" Tommy asked.

"I am the Lady of Light, Tommy."

He did not recognize her voice, but it was so soothing to hear. He had not heard another voice for a very long time, not even his own. It was almost familiar as it reminded him of his mother. He tried as hard as he could to remember her, but he could not see her face in his mind. He couldn't remember her name, nor his brother's. He lost all sense from the time he was living.

Tommy surveyed the veil, his spirit soared untethered in this realm. Behind the illuminated woman stood a figure. He tried as he could to make out the details, but in his heart, he knew his father was watching him.

"Don't lose focus, dear Tommy," she spoke again. "And do not lose heart, your father is with you."

"I don't understand," Tommy replied. "What does this mean?"

"Time has chosen you. Fulfill your obligation to be the world's next hero. You know what you must do."

Her elegance enchanted Tommy to the point where he could no longer respond. Never in his life had he witnessed something so remarkable. It would have brought tears to his physical eyes. He didn't wish to leave her sight, but the Lady of Light faded from him as well as the silhouette of his father. Tommy basked in the essence of that light and felt at peace as he tried to focus on the words she spoke.

It was then where he remembered his father and the strong hands that held him for the last time. He remembered his efforts and the small notebook he wrote. It was then he could now understand what his father needed him to do.

Hero? Tommy thought. *How could I be? I don't even know where I am. I don't remember.*

Tommy conflicted with himself as he tried to piece together his thoughts. He did not know where to start or what task was set before him. He tried to retrace his thoughts back thousands of years. His spirit could still feel every death. He recalled each time until it dawned on him. *The heroes!* His face lit up with a childhood excitement he didn't know he had!

Tommy spent what would have been years learning all he could about the heroes of old. He took the Book of Time and read every page down to the very last detail and period. There were eight that had saved the earth and eight times the world had been in dire need.

What makes me special for being the ninth?, he wondered. *Could I possibly be the tenth, and the ninth died in failure?* His world had been in shambles all his life, and for what he had been told, a little short of a thousand years. *Why wasn't there a hero to save them from that fate? Why now?* he continued to muse. *Why did time take so long?*

In his pondering existence, he now realized that time was irrelevant to him, and he had the chance to change it. If the fate of the world was up to him, then he would have to find a place to start. He looked at all the heroes and then to the most recent, Marcus Steel, The Possessor. The last hero was there, in the current year. He watched Marcus with all his struggles and eventually his success.

But why would Marcus be the downfall if he saves the world? Tommy continued to ponder. He investigated further to see where the events twisted in the darkness. Tommy saw horrid things. The creatures that still haunted him and his family devoured the lives of innocents. He doubted himself as he could not face that threat. Their evil eyes pierced through him. Even in the vortex of time, he could hear their bloodthirsty howls.

Tommy closed the book and looked away. He ran his phantom hand over the golden cover and the smooth leather that bound it. He wished he could touch it because of how beautiful the artwork was; it mesmerized him. Never in his time would something like this be allowed to exist; time erodes all.

As he ran his fingers over the book, it let off little sparks in every direction. The book responded by opening. Tommy found the same sparks coming from the pages of time as he manipulated his fingertips over them. The sparks were so bright and hot; he feared the book would be set alight, but instead, time pulsed like a heartbeat. It had a rhythm that flowed out of the pages like harp strings.

Tommy felt bewildered by the malleable time strings. They could be pulled and stretched, unlike any other substance. Buoyant and resilient, they returned to their original form. It did not matter how they were manipulated. At first, the novelty amused him. Swinging the strings around, coiling them up, and bouncing them on the floor like a rubber ball. But, he remained oblivious to the chaos his actions caused.

It wasn't until one of the strings broke that he caught a glimpse of something in the reflection of the shattered strand. The world's moving parts shone through the light of the fractured ends. They revealed history in a distinct light, diverging from his past recollections. He saw the repercussions he was inflicting on the world and feared the consequences. To prevent further destruction, he placed the strings of light back into the book and watched as they reformed, restoring the natural order.

Tommy resisted the urge to meddle with time again. But curiosity soon won out. He resumed playing with the book and strings, learning to alter them in reality bending ways. He reshaped time into forms, from spheres to an ooze. He observed the changes in historical events.

At first, he made changes at random, but Tommy eventually began to discern patterns. He realized how to manipulate time, mastering the technique. He pushed and pulled the pages and bent the light. He ignited sparks in every direction. It was like a child coloring with crayons. Despite the childlike enjoyment he experienced, he remained focused on his purpose.

Tommy toyed with every era of time. He altered them until he understood how time could bend, allowing him to change it at will. With his confidence fortified, he undid every change he had made. He adopted a stern resolve to tackle his mission head-on. He realized that time was now under his control, and he envisioned himself as the most vital hero in history. Tommy saw the world's dramatic and catastrophic fate, including the fall of the last hero. He tried to fix the situation. But, every attempt to fix one problem led to a new one. Tommy decided to invest time in learning.

He wanted to understand the complex nature of time manipulation before trying again.

Placing his hand over the pages, he found that they consistently reverted to their original state. He felt frustrated. He doubted himself. He struggled to understand why his efforts only made things worse. Even when Tommy tried to start his interventions earlier, he twisted time. He pulled and stretched it without success. In vexation, a tear appeared on a page to an unintended outcome. He tried to recreate it without methodical motions. Stepping back, he observed the devastating consequences of his actions, the lives he had ruined to secure his own future.

Tommy turned away with a heavy heart. He pondered and questioned whether it was worth the suffering he had caused. His quest for control over time had taken a toll. He was starting to see that he caused the world's turmoil.

Why am I the one chosen by time to do this? Tommy thought. *Is this some cruel joke?* He gazed down at his perpetual body. He saw that eons were passing through it, yet he remained a forty-year-old man with no signs of aging or rejuvenation. *That's interesting,* he remarked. *Time doesn't affect my body anymore either.*

Alas, his efforts were in vain. Time was a singularity. Despite his ability to bend it, time always regressed to a single timeline. While many possibilities could exist, only one remained relevant. Tommy's quest to change the course of history seemed impossible.

In his despair, he questioned if he could only affect change in the time of his own birth and for those living then. His attempts to peer into the future were met with failure, as the era he had left behind had not yet been written. It was a disheartening realization for someone gifted with control over time.

Tommy thought about these challenges for thousands of years. In this existence, he discovered how to re-enter his own body. The discomfort he felt as he became corporeal once more had him shuddering and grimacing. His body, before frozen in time, began to ache as it experienced sensation and memory.

Memories that had been elusive from his spiritual consciousness rushed back. And Tommy found himself overwhelmed by emotions. He yearned for the warmth of his mother's skin, the sound of his brother's voice, and the sensation of the cold wind on his face. In the conflict of these emotions, Tommy felt lost and unsure of how to proceed.

Tommy had been distracting himself with endless pondering and toying with the void of eternity. Yet, he longed for companionship. He knew that he could not control humanity's fate. It lay in the hands of those who could save it.

I'm going to need help. Lots of help. Now I understand, Tommy thought. He began working on mastering time entry again. But, it was a painful process.

With unwavering determination, Tommy focused all his might, and a portal opened for him. He descended through swirling purple lightning and smoke, expecting to land on hard earth. Instead, he found himself on cool and clean ground, surrounded by damp grass after a light morning shower. The sun's brilliant rays washed over him, and he took his first breath of fresh air. The overwhelming beauty of the world around him moved him to tears.

He marveled at the sweet air and clear skies, a stark contrast to the world he knew, which had been plagued by ash and cold. The simple pleasures of life, like the warmth of the sun on his skin, were now a revelation to him.

Tommy took refuge under a nearby tree, relishing both the cooling shade and the welcoming light of the sun. He noticed fruit that had fallen and decided to taste it. The flavor was bitter with a foul hint, but he cherished the experience as a rare delight. He looked up at the tree's branches, seeing ripe and fragrant fruit above. He used his arms to climb, digging his fingers into the bark. Soon, he rewarded himself with a fulfilling snack. He closed his eyes and savored the taste, smiling for one of the first times in his life.

While the luxury of eating the fruit led to a painful gut, Tommy had no regrets. He understood that he needed to refocus on his mission. Calming his mind, he concentrated on opening a new portal. Walking through it, he found that entering and exiting time had become second nature to him. He explored various periods in history, seeing the construction of pyramids, moments when heroes were called to act. He even attempted to forge fellowships. But, of these experiences all lacked authenticity to him. Yet, he never lost sight of the wonder of feeling the sun's warmth on his skin, a sensation he had longed for.

Back in his own time, the sun had never graced the world. Cold gripped the age as Tommy shuttered in his memory, but sunbeams enveloped Tommy in warmth. In this instant, he understood what he lacked. The gentle crash of waves on a beach. The caress of a non-burning wind. The clear skies above him painted a picture. The world was unaware of the tragedies it would soon face. But, these were all abstract thoughts to those living within Tommy's age. He rationed the conflicts waged by humanity. They bickered among themselves, and the web of lies seemed so trivial.

Tommy felt more prepared than ever for his mission and the calling that time required of him. With a clear destination in mind, he set forth to gather the help he needed. But, fear still gnawed at the corners of his mind, causing him to doubt his ability to face the impending threat alone.

He couldn't forget the faces of the creatures he had encountered in the distant future. Hellhounds, always on the hunt, starving, left an indelible mark on his memory. Their growling faces and malevolent stares haunted him. He tried to confront these memories, but the haunting images forced him to look away.

Determined not to let fear control him, Tommy clenched his fist and began planning for the victory he envisioned. He understood that it would not be a solitary endeavor. Instead, he believed that time would once again call upon heroes to fulfill their destinies. Tommy never wavered from the feeling that they would play a key part.

"This was my father's plan right from the start," he muttered to himself. As he spoke, Tommy donned his brown overcoat with deliberate care. Through his travels across time, he acquired many things which held no value to him, not like his goggles and coat. The fabric, worn but sturdy, settled around him like armor against the coming trials. His gaze shifted to the welding goggles that once belonged to his father, their surface scratched and weathered. With a reverent touch, he picked them up and secured them around his neck. They were more than a tool—they were a piece of his father.

Joe Cordova

"I am going to assemble the eight heroes of old." With steadfast resolve, Tommy embarked on his quest to unite the heroes, knowing that only together could they hope to face the impending darkness and save the world.

2 Shadow and Thorn

A city that was as busy as ever, lived with a constant motion. Everyone had some place to be and were getting there by whatever means. Cars were honking, subways were shaking, and legs were walking. The city teemed with people as crates of fresh newspapers arrived at a store. In bold letters read the headline: *He Lurks in The Shadows and Brings Justice Again.* The world felt safer and was in a great incline for prosperity.

"Hey Lena, can I get one of those papers?" Marcus asked while standing in line for the checkout.

Lena, giddy as always, had patience that matched Marcus. As she helped one of her best customers, she grabbed the newspaper and handed it over with a familiar nod. Her warm hands, calloused and dry, were a testament to the years spent tending to her beloved store.

"Yeah, sure thing," she said with her raspy voice, legs just hobbling to the counter. "They never have a story about anything else. Our hero is always the front cover, but sometimes I wish they would put a different story on the front."

"People really like having a hero in their time, I guess," Marcus replied. "Don't you?"

"I know he is the current hero and having one living in our time is a good thing, but…"

"Yeah, I know," Marcus said. "He isn't like other heroes."

"Can he really be a good guy with that? that…thing?" she asked while ringing up his items, she gave the total and handed over the bags.

Marcus looked at the paper and read a few lines down. "Yeah, I think he is." He smirked.

"Just don't go throwing my things around my store, Marcus." She spoke with mocking humor, saying, "You know, ghosts scare me. Anyways, take care now, and be safe out there."

"You too, Lena!"

Marcus left the store and made his way down the sidewalk. It was a normal day in New York. The sun was bright with little forecast. It was breezy, which Marcus was thankful for wearing his gray sweater and jeans. Marcus wore his new shoes with ease, matching his stride. He tried to distract himself by taking in the city's great scenery. Deep inside his head, he heard a voice that was dark and haunting.

Marcus, just a few blocks down from here... it said in a drawn-out tone.

"No, we will be late to meet Diana, you know we cannot miss this."

I can feel the evil within them Marcus, as can you, you need to stop them.

"No, we don't have to, and you listen to me now."

Oh, come on! Last night wasn't enough for us, and you know it.

"This is the city that never sleeps, cut me a break, we will get our chance. We cannot save everyone; I learned that lesson far too many times. It's time I start saving myself."

People stared at Marcus walking down the pavement. He looked like he was talking to himself, moving his lips with a loud conversation. He appeared engrossed with his own world. He gestured his hands as if he was stressing points only he could hear. They avoid him, parting with wide berths. Parents turned their children away and tried not to make eye contact. The air did create a small calm around him when they understood it was actually the hero of their time. Still, many of them found the situation creepy.

"This is not how I want my day to go," Marcus continued to say. "You've gotten me into enough trouble already. You also know, we have time frames where we are allowed to work, it's just not now."

As I am bound to you, I must obey, but just so you know, I sense something is coming. It's not good for you or me.

"What?" Marcus paused for a second but carried on as the voice grew silent. He arrived at a park near his apartment. There, under a tree, his wife had placed a blanket. She was reading a book. Her light brown hair flowed in the breeze and was stunning for Marcus to see. He could stand there and watch the rays of sunlight compliment her beauty. Taking a deep breath and calming his nerves, Marcus walked forward.

"Hello, Diana," he said while he approached. His heart raced as he saw her. Her hat almost hid her face, but her hair did the rest, tussled by the wind. He wanted to say more, but he slowed himself and waited for her to respond.

Tell her she looks good, the voice in his head said, trying to tease him.

Diana tried to speak, saying "Hello," before Marcus interrupted.

"Shut up!" Marcus shook his head. He realized the face Diana was giving him was already not a good one.

"Sorry, Diana, I didn't mean that for you."

"I figured," Diana replied in an unamused tone, exhaling whatever good feelings she had. "I saw you in the news last night."

"Is that so?" Marcus said, taking his seat near her, but still keeping his distance.

"A bank robbery near closing time and you just come in and save the day."

"Ironic, huh? That's how it all started," Marcus tried to say, but something was on Diana's mind, and he could tell.

"But do you have to be so ruthless to those guys?"

"I don't want to start off like this." Marcus paused. "Anyway, you know sometimes, I cannot help it," he said, trying to change the subject with a concerned look on his face. "How was your stay with your mother? Is she doing well?"

"She is doing fine, a little tired of me, I'm sure. Dad has gotten better with his condition too. He is in therapy and his doctor upped his medication."

"I'm sorry, Diana. I should have been there for you. I know how that day was for you. It must have been so scary."

"We all wish we could have done things differently, but at least everything is better now. Almost everything," she said with a roughness in her voice.

"It's good to see you again, Diana." Marcus gave a half smile.

"It's good to see you too, Marcus," she smiled back.

Marcus noticed the hesitation. She seemed to think for a second about holding his hand. But, instead, she picked up the lunch she made for them to share and handed it to him.

"I made this, your favorite," she said, posturing a warm and sincere reply.

Marcus took it, thanked her, and unwrapped a well filled sandwich. He took a bite and looked at her hand that was missing her rings. It wasn't unusual as they hadn't held them in a long while, but every time they would meet, Marcus always had to check. It stung him to see nonetheless, but he always held out for hope. Fixating for too long on the thought, he almost choked when she spoke.

"I have missed you, Marcus," Diana said. "It's been a long time."

"Our bed is still there. I kept the apartment just the same as when you left. If you are ready."

"I want to…" Her pause left Marcus with concern, "I still love you, but I still think we need more time. Maybe perhaps by late summer or fall. If you can keep yourself under control."

"I know, it's not me you have to worry about, but I've been keeping him in check. We have a schedule now and he is content with that."

"I know," she said with sadness. "I still cannot get over what happened."

Marcus took a big bite of his sandwich.

"I miss waking up next to you," Diana said. "And I miss the breakfasts you would make for us. I still can't get pancakes that good," she spoke with a tinge of longing in her voice.

"It's hard," Marcus said. "How's Phantom? I miss that cat."

"He is fine, still cuddly!" She smiled.

They exchanged half-hearted smiles. Both were too timid to speak their minds. Diana looked at the man she once loved. Her feelings were faint, and she wanted it to work, but the pain was still too much. Marcus gazed at Diana, but his eyes fell short in discouragement. He wanted to reach out and take her hand, but he knew it was still too soon.

"You know, Marcus," Diana finally said to break the silence. "I'll talk to our counselor and see if it is a good idea to move in, but until then. I wish you all the best."

Marcus had the faintest hint of hope as he nodded.

"But don't rush into anything. I don't want to pressure you," Marcus responded.

Marcus and Diana said their goodbyes and Diana left. Marcus decided to stay a bit longer gazing over the water. It was almost quiet.

Here he comes, the voice said.

"Who?" Marcus replied, confused, but the voice didn't respond.

Marcus began to realize everybody around him stopped moving and he himself was quite slow. Ominous fog blanketed the grass of the park. An ill wind turned the river's waters. Before Marcus' eyes, a purple vortex appeared. It had gray smoke and a shadowy figure that walked through.

"Hey, D, what is that?" Marcus asked.

The voice stayed quiet.

"He cannot speak to you here," the figure said as he stepped into Marcus's front view.

"And why not? Who are you?"

"Because I don't let him," Tommy said as he was now visible.

"I don't know who you are, but a purple vortex like that doesn't just come out of nowhere!" Marcus roared. He did not know who was in front of him, but he did not back down if it was a threat. Trying to move, Marcus found himself powerless as he was separated from the voice's power.

"I am Tommy Kent," he said, making a formal introduction. "I require your assistance, Marcus. Yes, I know who you are, and I know what you can do."

"Yeah, well. I don't think so," Marcus replied. "I don't do anything without my partner's advice."

The vortex closed behind Tommy as they both stood in a weird place, frozen in time.

"I need you to not listen to him for one second and let me explain."

"If you know who I am, and what corruption I bring, then why should I trust you? How do I know you don't want this power for yourself? I see a lot of guys who would kill for it!"

"I've been watching you your whole life, Marcus. I know everything you have done. You are a hero like me. I cannot say anything that would convince you to trust me, but I can show you."

Tommy waved his hand and filled Marcus's mind with images of Diana and all the good times they had together.

"Your wife," Tommy said with a calm tone. "She is very beautiful, and I know you two are experiencing some trouble right now. But you and Diana will be just fine. I know this because I'm from the future."

Marcus' mind became clear, and he saw Tommy still standing before him. He wiped the drool from his mouth.

"You're making this up," Marcus responded. "And I'm not having it. Let my friend go, and then maybe we could talk!"

The demon that was bound to Marcus was snarling like a wolf from outside the wall of purple light.

"You have heard it too. The voice in your head. The one that told you who you are. Time always calls for a hero. You have heard the call from the Lady of Light."

"What do you know about this? Who are you really!?" Marcus shouted.

"I am the new hero, and I tell you, your time is not over."

"I've already saved the world once, and you can see, the world is at peace."

"Yes. You have and you will again. This is not your story anymore. It's mine. Time has chosen me. I'm not going to talk to you in some riddle. In my era, the world has been ruined, and everything humans have built, destroyed. The land is a chaotic waste."

Tommy fine-tuned his new outfit, including the cuffs on the brown overcoat he'd made during his travels. He appeared well mannered in front of Marcus but had an awkward appeal.

"My father gave me everything I needed to succeed," he continued. "I built a time machine with the help of my brother at the age of ten. Since that day, I have not been able to return to my time and have been trapped. I lost my mind, and at the end of it all. I heard it; the voice that had chosen me, the Lady of Light. She gave me my ability to traverse time so I may try to mend the world before any of this could happen."

"So, if you are the hero, why can't you do it yourself?" Marcus questioned angrily.

"I've tried, but it always ends the same."

"And with me, it'll be different somehow?"

"Not just you, all of us. All of them. The heroes. I need them all."

Marcus still could not wrap his head around the story told to him, but Tommy knew every secret Marcus had. He saw Marcus in every moment in his life where he stumbled, so he used that to help convey to Marcus his intentions over the next hour. Tommy explained everything, holding back a few details Marcus need not know; the whole fate of humanity needed him.

Marcus felt astonished at all the secrets he knew about him and certain events in time. But something was still eating at him, as he desired more answers.

"This is crazy. Insane even! I don't even know what to think. Are you sure you are from the future? Cause you'd be like, really smart, right? Also, if there is time travel, then where are the other time travelers? Why hasn't anyone stopped Hitler?"

"They always ask about Hitler." Tommy sighed. "I'll tell you. Surely you believe Hitler and the whole Nazi regime was bigger than one person, right? And if you were to kill Hitler someone else would just have taken his place."

"Yeah, but still, no one tries?"

"Well, if you killed Hitler, and stopped him, there wouldn't be a need to go back and stop him. But what if I told you Hitler was the time traveler trying to stop a bigger threat. Now that story about being bigger than one person would make sense. Hitler was the least destructive outcome."

Marcus just looked at Tommy, dumbstruck and in disbelief.

"I'm just messing with you, Marcus," Tommy said with a great laugh.

"Why would you say that?" Marcus said in disgust.

"When you've been around as long as I have, you develop a very dark sense of humor."

"Dude. That's not even cool."

"The sad reality is I am the only time traveler. There are no more, have you not heard a single thing I said. The future is ruined. There is nothing left."

"Surely, there is something," Marcus said. "You had enough to make a time machine, and how was that possible if you really had nothing."

Tommy didn't respond, as it just reminded him of his father and the dedication he put into his work. Tommy was caught in his own thoughts, while Marcus was left to wonder, just watching Tommy stand motionless.

"Tommy?" Marcus asked, as he snapped his fingers in front of his face.

Gaining consciousness, Tommy waved his hand and time resumed like normal, people began to move, and the wind passed through the trees. Marcus found himself feeling dizzy.

"Take it easy, for a second, Marcus. You'll be fine. But your body just went through a speed shift. Think about it like when your heart beats enough times to cycle blood through your body for a week, in the span of a second. You'll be fine, but for an ordinary person, it could kill them."

Marcus caught his breath for a second while the shadow returned to him.

Finally, so we're kicking his ass, right? the voice said. *I can't wait to devour him!*

"No! We talked, and he is okay," Marcus said to himself. "You can sense it, too, right? He is a hero."

"You sure about that?" the voice replied.

"Why, what do you know about him?"

Go on, believe him, the voice said again. *It won't hurt me.*

"What aren't you telling me?" Marcus asked, continuing to talk to himself.

"It's quite all right," Tommy interjected. "He won't like me no matter what you say, and he will try to turn you against me. There is some good in him. You may not know, and he surely wishes not, but yes."

Silence him! the voice told Marcus. *He enrages me!*

"Don't worry," Marcus reassured. "I'll keep him under control, but just so you know. As long as he doesn't trust you, I will still have my doubts. Any funny business and we won't hesitate to do what is needed," Marcus said to Tommy.

"All right," Tommy said with an odd cheer after just being threatened. "Let's go! But first you might want to dress a bit cooler. Where we are going will be a little warm."

After a quick change of clothes, Tommy opened a new gate to travel through, a portal of purple and gray, just like the vortex Marcus saw him step through. Tommy handed Marcus a helmet that almost seemed to come out of nowhere.

"Put this on," Tommy said. "I was able to build this while you were changing. It should allow you to travel in the void for at least a while. It's dangerous there, and I cannot guarantee anything. I've never seen anyone leave their time other than me. Don't touch anything. Don't look at anything. And do not, I mean do not! Don't you dare look into your future! Seeing your future will drive you mad, and you could lose yourself."

"Okay…Okay," Marcus responded, annoyed by Tommy's over-exclamation. "I have no desire to see my future anyway. But I do want to know. Are we getting the others in order? So, I take it we are going to the Cactus, huh? Do you even know where to find him? Some say he is still alive somewhere in this age but has returned to nature."

"We will find him. And yes. I'll take you there now. But his sleep cannot be awakened. Returned to nature, he has and will remain. We need to find him before he does. Right when he first returns to rest."

"Find him? Why at that exact time? Can't we just take him from any point in time and put him back to that time? And why do we have to find him, can't we just view him and see where he goes then get him? It sounds a lot easier than trying to look for him in mountains covered in them."

"First off, time view does not work like that. It's more like reading a book, you can open to chapters and view their lives, but once you start you cannot skip ahead like watching a movie. There is no fast forward. You watch someone's life from start to finish in real time. For me it doesn't matter, but for you. I don't think you have two-hundred years left in you. Do you know how old the Cactus is?"

"Almost two…" Marcus started to answer but was cut off by Tommy.

"Almost two-hundred years old. I do not want to spend two-hundred years viewing a Cactus grow up. I'm impatient. As funny as that sounds."

"So, you're just lazy," Marcus said.

Time is irrelevant to me, the voice inside said with a chuckle.

"Well, if you say so..." Marcus agreed and they both entered the portal Tommy had opened, right in Marcus's apartment. The swirling thunder and gusts of wind from the vortex turned Marcus's apartment to shambles.

Marcus took one last look of his place, shaking his head while taking a leap of faith. It could all be a ruse, he thought, but it was too late to stop now.

Lights flashed before Marcus' eyes as colors surrounded and passed him. He could see life and death. The mundane people did not strike Marcus as much as what he saw next; his father working, staying diligent in his labors. Papers cluttered next to a familiar lamp emitting just enough light as not to wake his slumbering family. Marcus could feel the frustrations of his father and his anxieties. Wanting to reach out, Marcus wished he could only tell his father that everything would be all right.

Tommy put his hand on Marcus's shoulder. "Your father, Marcus. He is proud of you," he said in the most comforting tone he could manage. "He did everything he could for you."

"I know. It wasn't his fault. I've come to terms with how everything ended. His life's work... Can we move on?" Marcus wiped the tear that was beginning to form on his eye and tried to make a joke to break the emotion. "Hey, maybe we could see who assassinated Kennedy?"

"You're sure one for conspiracies, aren't you?" Tommy chuckled. "That's too far back. Maybe another time, but I'll spoil it now. It's nobody important."

Take a peek, Marcus, the voice taunted him. *Look into what this guy hasn't told you. See what secrets he keeps!*

Marcus debated if he should see what the voice was telling him, but in a moment it all flashed before them. Finally, all the colors passed, and darkness surrounded them.

Ahh the void. My home, the voice again told Marcus, *Well, did you see? Did you see what he may be hiding from you?*

"We're here," Tommy said.

The vortex opened to a blistering sun that was blazing above. Stepping into the land, the shrilling buzz of cicadas filled the valley. Heat was reflecting from the earth, radiating in waves of illusion. Dry grass and desert brooms scattered all across the hills and rocky mountain sides.

"Welcome to Arizona, in the heat of the Sonoran Desert!" Tommy said with more enthusiasm to play games with Marcus. "It's quite hot here at 102 degrees before noon."

"Heat just seems to fall short of an explanation!" Marcus said, feeling the anger of the sun. "Why did we have to come when it is hot? I'm already starting to sweat, and we have only just arrived. What year is this anyway?" Marcus replied.

"1979 in the middle of June. Right here in the…" Before he could finish, Marcus let out a quick yell of pain, and a few choice words.

"What the…!?" Marcus yelled, looking down at a ball of quills jabbing into his leg.

"A cholla!" Tommy exclaimed!

"A what?"

"Choy-ya," Tommy said, annunciating the word. "Teddy Bear Cactus, I was about to warn you. Watch your step. These little guys will hurt!"

"Yeah, no kidding!" Marcus took out his pocketknife and pried the thing off. "Okay, let's make this quick. I already don't like being here. There are a lot of them!"

Marcus looked around at how many cacti there actually were. Teddy bears, paddles, weird ones with long spikes, and the tallest of all, the saguaros that fill the land, covering every hill.

"The Cactus was a saguaro, right?" Marcus asked. "Those are the tall ones, and there are still hundreds!"

"Yes, but your friend will be able to find him for us," Tommy replied.

Marcus and Tommy go on searching. Walking over hills, hills, and more hills, as the sun was baking them in their boots. Their water depleted at the end of their forty-five-minute hike. Both exhausted and dripping with sweat. Finally, they came upon a group of saguaros standing tall and having many arms.

Wait... the voice said to Marcus. *I sense something. Old magic, as old as I am.*

"Can you tell which one?" Marcus replied.

"No need," Tommy said. "Show yourself, shadow. Let him know, you are here."

Clouds gathered over the hill they were standing on. The sun's rays almost felt distant. Marcus's shadow pulled itself from the ground and stood behind him in a chaotic form. Its face as empty as death and a stare so cold it would blow through you like a winter's breeze. The shade detached from Marcus and hovered above. The energy given off by the Possessor would strike fear in even the bravest of men.

"It's about time I met you face to face," Tommy said to the shadow.

In a dark, deep, and twisted voice, "Tell me, Time Warden, do you fear me? Do you fear what lies outside your vision?"

Tommy stared him down with no intent on answering. All sounds had faded from before and the shade from the clouds was a much-needed break from sun as Marcus gave off a sigh of relief.

The ground shook with great intensity and the wind changed direction. Amidst the tension between the two, Marcus, caught in the middle, looked over and saw that one of the saguaros was beginning to move.

"Behold, Time Warden," the shadow said. "The Desert Sentinel, I don't think he will take too kindly to my presence here. Are you sure you are ready to deal with it?"

"I must," Tommy could only say under his breath.

3 Welcome to the Future

"Whoa! This thing is huge!" Marcus said while taking a few steps back. The magic that brought this thing to life was ancient and forgotten. The same magic that granted Marcus and Tommy their powers. Marcus felt the quakes on the ground as it took its first step.

The Cactus, now awakened and alert, took notice of Tommy and Marcus right away, but was more directly drawn to the dark shadow floating above. He did not like the evil Marcus controlled. He swung his large arms in a wide arc, trying to hit in is elegant fighting style against the shadow.

Marcus' knee took quite a hit smashing into rocks as he dodged the Cactus's attacks. The shadow fought back, pushing like a poltergeist, and pummeling the Cactus to take a stance.

Tommy was in awe at the creature as the Cactus stood tall, eyes as black as charcoal, and skin rough and full of spikes. It had many scars on its two legs and around its arms.

"This thing must be at least thirty feet tall," Marcus said, picking himself up.

"Thirty-seven feet and three inches, to be exact," Tommy said. "Hello, my friend, we come to you, and we are not your enemies! We are friends!"

The Cactus took a moment to stare at Tommy, but began his ginga, swaying his arms and legs, preparing for another attack.

"This Cactus had practiced in the arts of capoeira. It's a sad story, actually. He…"

Marcus grabbed Tommy and they tumbled over in time, missing the jagged rocks of the desert floor. Spines whizzed past them. They braced for another attack from the menacing Cactus.

"Yeah, I don't think we have time for a history lesson," Marcus shouted at Tommy.

"Well, this is why you are here," Tommy replied, brushing the dirt off himself. "We need to convince him."

"It doesn't look like it speaks or has any interest in doing so."

Marcus sent the demon to fight the Cactus and tried to defend Tommy. The demon, even in this form, did not stand tall enough to compare.

The Cactus's swings and dance proved to be more difficult for the shadow to fight. Ancient magic protected the Cactus from the demon's claws, giving it every advantage. But the shadow smiled, snarling with anticipation of the next attack. D had never fought a foe such as this, but it mattered little. Every adversary would fall to him in a matter of time.

In the middle of casting some time spells to slow down the Cactus, Tommy switched up his tactics. "Can you hold him?" Tommy asked. "Time spells seem to be of little use, it can brush them off because of how old he can live. I can try something else."

Marcus understood the demon's plan right away and pressured him to subdue the Desert Sentinel. He worked with the demon's power of mind control to take possession of the Cactus. The demon entered the creature's body. It cursed the light in the soul of the saguaro. But, it twisted the ancient magic, breaking it down and turning it sour.

"Not too much, D!" Marcus shouted. "We just need to hold him." The demon could read his thoughts and felt his sorrow. But, like everything else, he fell under his control.

"He is strong. If you are going to do something, do it quick!" Marcus shouted, gritting his teeth.

Tommy showed the Cactus a vision from his past. He beheld vivid memories of those he learned to love intertwined with vibrant images of what is to come. "You see this, we need you. We are friends. We are heroes just like you!"

"This is just bizarre; how can we talk to a plant? How can it even understand us?" Marcus questioned. "My control over him is about to break!"

Tommy stepped towards the Cactus and placed his hand over him. He traced the scars, then spoke in a soothing tone, "Release him." He will trust us."

"All right, D, let him go!"

Taking enjoyment from the Cactus's suffering, D refused Marcus's call, even exiting the Cactus as it fell to one knee. The demon continued his torture.

"D, that's enough!" Marcus shouted, and with that, his shadow listened, dissolving into the recesses of his mind.

The Cactus, as if he was taking a deep breath, felt relieved. He nodded his head as he was more sentient than he looked. The saguaro too was once chosen to be the hero of his time and knows his job will never be over. He heard the Lady of Light's call and knew he had once more part to play in the fate of the world.

Marcus stepped forward. Clenching his fist, he turned his head upward, trying to meet the face that was high above him. "Look, uhm, big guy. I know this doesn't make sense," Marcus said under his breath. "I'm talking to a giant plant. This doesn't make sense to me." He turned back and continued. "I'm sorry about what my friend did to you, but we need your help. I hope you can still trust us. There are others and we will need you to help us with them as well. Don't be bothered by the demon. He is under my control, even though he is evil."

The Cactus knelt down to Marcus and looked at the face of the shadow that hid behind his shoulder. He didn't feel fear, but looked in anger at it before gazing back at the one who controlled it.

Marcus witnessed the two in the standoff and watched as the two almost looked to be conversing with each other. Marcus nodded as the Cactus smiled at him.

Marcus's voice seethed as he spat out Tommy's name. "You need to pay more attention; you were almost crushed!"

"I do admit, I get so lost in my own fascination. I just lost my place in time," Tommy replied. "This creature is just so amazing! This was the hero right before you, Marcus."

"I actually didn't think he was real, to be honest," Marcus said. They don't teach much of this one in school, you know."

"That's too bad! He is the most interesting one!"

The Cactus looked towards Tommy and nodded.

"Well now, shall we get going to the next hero?" Tommy continued.

"Next hero? We just got one, and I am still trying to wrap my head around this," Marcus said.

"Marcus, the whole world needs our help, and you want to slow down? There isn't a moment to waste!"

"But you are the Time Warden, right? Isn't time irrelevant to you?"

"And what do you want me to do? Go back and wait inside the time vortex until you are ready?"

"Well," Marcus stumbled with his words. "At least let me get something to drink, I'm thirsty!"

"Like a coffee? I know you like coffee, Marcus."

"No, not like coffee. I do enjoy it, but not when it is over a hundred degrees outside! I want something more refreshing."

"Don't worry, Marcus, we will get you your drink, but we have to save Arnold first. I will need your help again and I know you have experience with a certain type of energy."

"Umm, yeah, the False Hero…" Marcus replied.

"I know how the story goes!" Tommy snapped, interrupting Marcus. I have always been curious about nuclear energy and if your friend's power would translate."

"Nuclear!?" Marcus said with a tremble.

The shadow spoke up about how it would try.

"Great, where we are going is basically a large nuclear reactor about to explode!" Tommy said eagerly!

"It's not a nuclear reactor," Marcus replied.

"I know. I said it was *like* a nuclear reactor. But, the energy is unstable. We will need you to fight off the radiation. Or, have your pet do it. Cactus-Man will grab Arnold and pull him through."

The demon snarled at the thought of being Marcus' pet.

"Okay?" Tommy asked as he got a feel of the Cactus's understanding. "Perfect! Make sure our faces don't melt and Cactus, I am not sure how much you understand, but just grab him and go, got it?"

"I'm not so sure about this," Marcus replied. "I find you too impulsive. Isn't there another way? Why do we have to go there?"

"Because that is where he was. He died in service. He was the only hero to die saving the world...There is no other time."

"Yeah, I know."

"So, you know, if we take him from his place in time before he completes his task. He may not ever be able to."

"There are risks, I suppose. Can we really change the future like this? All this time stuff really doesn't make any sense."

"It does if you are insane!" Tommy laughed.

"Well, let's hope I don't get to that point."

"So, we know our parts. Cactus, here, take this and put it on. I believe it should fit you," Tommy said, reaching through a portal and pulling out a large trunk. It was a suit he made to protect the Cactus from the void.

"Here take this as well," Tommy said while he handed the Cactus a helmet. "When you reach the professor, slap this on his head and pull him through. We don't want to scramble his brains. He is a very intelligent man."

Tommy stepped aside. "Are we ready?"

The two of them both nodded.

"Perfect!" Tommy grinned, opening the portal through a beam of light. On the other side was a room made completely from metal with a core reactor in the middle. The heat inside made the desert feel like a vacation, but the heroes persisted.

Warning sirens wailed, echoing through the large room. Red lights whirled and came in flashes, illuminating the room. At the base of the reactor was a man. His arms reached out and his hands burned on a large machine as it overheated. He was screaming in agony and the whole structure had begun to crumble and fall apart.

Marcus stepped through as the man fell back. The room was hot, but it didn't bother the demon as he began his work. D's protection was like an aura that kept the radiation away from the two. Marcus was focusing on controlling the demon, shielding them from the rising radiation.

"Qui êtes-vous?" the man asked, looking in confusion, then fear as the giant Cactus stepped through the portal. "Que suis-je!?" He tried to stumble away as the Cactus picked him up by his collar and put the helmet on his head. Then, he dragged the man as he tried to scramble from the giant sentinel. But, the Cactus's spikes made him stop fast.

"Trust me, this is better than the alternative," Tommy said to him as he came through.

"Où suis-je? Où...? Où...? Je...?"

"Calm down," Tommy said as he watched Marcus walk back through the portal. "You are safe now."

"You speak English?" the man asked in confusion and trying to catch his breath. He turned back and watched as the portal closed. "It was my duty to stop that machine from destroying humanity! Take me back!"

"Take it easy, Professor Arnold. The world is safe now thanks to you and your efforts." Tommy walked over to examine Marcus. "See, you did fine!" he said before closing the portal.

Marcus helped the man off the desert ground, pulling him away from a nearby cholla Cactus.

"Did I die?" Arnold asked.

"Far from it, Arnold," Tommy said, turning back to him. "Professor, welcome to the future! 1979, in fact. A great time to be in!"

"There is time travel in the future? And humanoid plants? C'est remarquable! I have so many questions! Do all plants walk and talk in the future?"

"Only this one, but he doesn't talk," Marcus replied. "He is a hero, just like yourself."

"A hero? I was chosen, but I don't consider myself a hero."

"We all are heroes, Professor, just as time has chosen," Tommy added. "But time calls for you once more!"

"Time… Yes. As my duty. I just… where are we?" The professor seemed a bit anxious, but almost ready to act. He shook his hands as they burned with pain.

"Please, you suffered horrific burns," Tommy said. "And radiation damage, let us tend to that first. I believe Marcus can help."

"Hello Doc, my name is Marcus Steel."

"I'm not a doctor," Arnold corrected. "Just a professor, and I am not sure how you can help with this."

He raised his hands that looked awful and blistering. They had already begun to swell from the core and leak putrid ooze.

"I can't, but he can," Marcus said as the shadow appeared from behind him. He worked his twisted magic on Arnold, repairing his damaged cells and restoring him to health.

"That is truly a remarkable skill," Arnold said in wonder as he looked at his new skin. Not only did he heal his hands, but also every injury on his body. "It's a bit frightening," he continued, adjusting his glasses. "How did you obtain this power?"

"It's a long story," Marcus replied.

"Gentlemen!" Tommy interrupted. "Shall we get going, once again? Time is very important. And it is time for us to go!"

"I know you're the warden of time," Marcus said, annoyed. "But, you don't have to speak like that."

"Do you not find my puns amusing, Marcus?" Tommy laughed. "I'm sure one of the heroes will."

"Professor," Marcus whispered to Arnold. "Just so you know. I have strong beliefs he has lost his mind. I'm not entirely sure he knows what he is doing."

"I'm going to need a little more time to take everything in," Arnold said, inhaling a large breath. "This is just too much to process." He looked over the valley as he stood on the tall mountain. "This place. It doesn't look like France to me. Are we in Africa somewhere? Or Maybe Mexico?"

"Sorry for the culture shock, but we can discuss things once we take you to your friend," Tommy said.

"My friend?" Arnold replied as he tried to piece things together. But, the desert heat was not very welcoming. The sweat on his forehead made him not want to stay there any longer.

Marcus watched Arnold's astonishment seeing Tommy in action for the first time. The portal the Time Warden created cracked with small bounds of lightning. The smelly fog putrefied the air but had a strange sweetness.

The air from the other side was much cooler, as they tasted the sweet aroma carried by the breeze. It was twilight in the area. The sun's light was about gone. The cold autumn night was a shock after the heat they were feeling.

Arnold looked at the front of an upscale mansion, although it was not maintained. The forest surrounding the mansion made it feel very secluded in the quiet greenery. Crickets chirped in the grass and birds flew through the trees.

The portal closed, causing the light to fade, and leaving them in the dusk. The front door was near as Tommy invited the heroes to follow him as he walked up the steps. As he was about to knock, he turned to Marcus.

"How much do you want to bet she asks about Hitler?"

"Tommy, not this again!"

"Who is Hitler?" Arnold asked, studying Marcus's face for clues, searching for a hint in Tommy's smirk.

When Tommy knocked, a voice from the inside began yelling about privacy or something. It grew louder as the man came closer and more frustrated by Tommy's constant abuse of the knocker.

"Who is it at this hour?" a voice from the other side said.

Tommy kept knocking as they waited. Marcus stood behind Tommy and Arnold behind Marcus. The Cactus was too large to come close to the front door. As they gathered on the porch, the Cactus looked at the dead flowers in a garden bed and took pity on them. He bent down and brought them back to life.

"Good job, Prickly-Man," Tommy said with a smile. "Keep doing that. You will have to stay outside anyways."

"This creature is amazing," Arnold said and took out a small notebook to record the beauty. He smiled and asked questions that fell on deaf ears. As he was finishing speaking to the Cactus, the door opened.

The brass hinges creaked. The sound ruined the allure of the well carved oak door as it swung open. The harsh, grating noise overshadowed its intricate beauty. It was a heavy door indeed, as the smooth motion took it away. A man stood there and asked who was there at this late hour.

"Please, she does not want to be disturbed. Whatever you are selling," the man said, hiding behind the door.

"Marlon?" Arnold asked. "Is that you?"

"Professor Laurent?"

Arnold stepped past Marcus and Tommy. He went to shake the hand of his great friend, who was once his student and assistant.

"This does not look like my home," Arnold said.

"This isn't your home; we are far from it! We are in Pennsylvania!" Marlon said with his curiosity through the roof. He had so many questions for Arnold but kept his composure.

"Where?" Arnold continued to ask.

"In America! How are you still alive? Where have you been?"

The two rejoiced, still shaking hands. Two decades had passed since Marlon last laid eyes on Arnold. The years had not been kind to Marlon either. His wrinkles disguised his face, but he still had the red Scottish hair.

"They saved me!" Arnold pointed back to Tommy and Marcus. "They showed up at the last second and pulled me out of the reactor room. Is Christana here with you? How did you get all the way over here? America?"

Arnold began to think, and realization came over him. "This isn't 1932, anymore, is it?" He asked.

"No. It's '51..." Marlon said as he saw Arnold's face. He had not aged a day since he saw him.

Arnold, now looking at his friend as the dark had hidden most of his features, saw him as much older now. Gray had invaded his hair, and his eyes were weaker than before.

"It had only been a few minutes since I saw you," Arnold said.

"A few minutes? It's been years!" Marlon said, baffled. "What are you talking about?"

"Is she here? She was so distraught. I almost felt like I wasn't making the right call."

"Professor..." Marlon said with a very ill voice. "She isn't who she once was. She isn't the same girl you left all those years ago."

With a great sigh, Arnold let out a bit of his grief. "You weren't lying about time travel," Arnold said as he turned to Tommy.

"No... Things are about to take place, and I will need all of us."

"Us?" Puzzled, Arnold reached into his pocket and pulled out a pocket watch. "How much time do we have?"

Tommy turned to Marlon and asked if he could put some tea on for them.

"I will do so; I will go to Christana. She is in her studies. She doesn't like to be disturbed at these times, but she must see you!"

"So, is she?" Arnold asked Tommy. "A hero? We would not have come if she wasn't, I feel. I doubt we would make a trip just for me to see her."

"You are, in fact, correct. We can discuss this later."

The group of them moved to a common room as they waited for Christana to make her way down. Marlon came down first and alerted them she would be ready in a few minutes. Marlon made his way down and lit a fire while putting a kettle on the stove.

It was a good while before Christana made her way into the common room. She was dressed well, and she came down the stairs questioning who was disturbing her at such hours.

Marlon had withheld the information that Arnold was among the guests, as he thought it would be a good surprise for her. He also did not quite know how to tell her and figured it would be best just to let her see him herself.

Christana did not like company. This was especially true when she buried herself in her studies. Although, it was more looking at old photos and reading literature from times long ago. She stayed true to her passion and what kept her heart from falling apart. It was a sad outcome for a hero, now living her life as a hermit, cut off from the world. She saved it, but it was a world not for her. Her world died a long time ago.

Wooden steps whispered. Her beige pumps clung to the gain. Silk folds of her gown cascade down her body in a fluid motion. Tommy rose from the plush couch. He fixed himself and walked to the bottom of the stairs to meet Christana. He stepped forward and reached out his hand. His smile was wide but meant well as he saw her unamused face. He recoiled his hand, nervously trying to think of a solution. Sweat beading upon Tommy's forehead, despite the cool environment.

"She looks upset," Marcus remarked carefully, whispering to Tommy. "Be vigilant with your words."

"We have him," Tommy spoke to Marcus, trying to ease his nerves. "I hope he is enough."

4 Reunited again

Tommy stood in front, patiently waiting for the hero's descent down the stairs. He kept his hands by his side. He looked to Marlon, as he began the greetings.

"Ms. LaValle," Marlon spoke up. "This is Mr. eh..." He paused for a moment. "I don't believe I caught your name."

"Kent, and we..." Tommy said before Christana interrupted him.

"I don't know what you want, but I do not welcome you here," Christana said. Her accent matched Arnolds as they were both strong. Even being away from France for so long, she never lost that part of her, even if she wanted to forget.

"You must leave," she demanded. "I am busy, and I do not wish to partake in any conversation with you."

"Ms. LaValle, please. I am a time traveler from the future to save this world from disaster," Tommy said, trying to plead with her. He lowered his hand trying to assure her, but Christana cut him off.

"If you were from the future, then why didn't you stop Hitler?" Everyone could read the pain in her eyes. This question affected her the most as it intertwined with her story, bringing her pain and loss. It appeared Tommy could have prevented all her problems if he had answered it with the right words.

Tommy turned to Marcus and smiled. "They always ask!"

"Christana?" Arnold questioned as he stepped forward and placed his hand on the side of her face. "You're so old now. You're as old as me."

Christana stumbled to find the right words but ended in silence. The shake of her head displayed her refusal to believe her eyes. Her posture radiated defiance, screaming rejection. She tried to rationalize it, but she was brought to tears.

"Marlon am I seeing a ghost?" she asked as she took the hand of the professor.

"I could not believe it either, Ms. LeValle," Marlon replied.

"This is not possible. It just isn't." She then embraced Arnold, and decades of emotions flooded her heart. "I've missed you so much! I thought you were dead! I thought I lost you on that day so long ago! I've...You... You don't know the things I've been through!"

"You did lose me," Arnold responded, pulling himself from her. He still felt strange about seeing her, for now he knew. "As I am told. I was meant to die that day. But they saved me and brought me here."

He looked her in the eyes. They held a color like the morning sky. He could still see the young woman he left all those years ago.

"The way you screamed at me. I know how you feel. How you felt. It wasn't safe for you!"

"I would have stayed with you!" Christana replied.

"You loved me. I know that now. Someone doesn't cry like that over just a friend. I surely thought I was going to die, but my sacrifice for you would have made it worth it. But Christana, how could I ever have acted upon those feelings you had for me? I know I was too blind to see what it was you felt. I should have known."

"None of that matters, now. Tu es ici! Avec moi!" Christana looked towards Tommy to ask. "If you can travel time, why bring him now and not sooner? The world could have used his brilliant mind." She stared Tommy down for answers, even letting go of Arnold to confront him.

"It wasn't the right time. The world needed you and all the trials you faced," Tommy responded, his voice measured. "I did not bring him here for you. We need you. The world needs you again,"

"What are you talking about?" Christana asked.

"The world needs you to save it once more."

"I've already played my part. My mission was a success. I thought." She was taken aback for a moment as she had come to the realization of who everyone was. "You're all heroes too, aren't you?"

"Yes," Marcus said. "We all have another part to play in this. Including you and the Professor, although I still am not sure if I can trust Tommy, my dark half doesn't seem to trust him."

"Your dark half?" Christana asked with a bit of fear.

"You'll meet him eventually…"

Marlon stepped in to say the tea was ready. He guided them back to the den. It was well-furnished and decorated with paintings of Paris and the French countryside. They all sat down and began discussing the events that led them to this point and what darkness loomed up ahead.

Around the cocktail table, Tommy answered all the questions they asked and the plan for the next hero. Tommy informed them they had a bit of time to catch up before they moved on, explaining he planned it in his schedule before making another joke about time. He knew exactly how much this would mean to Christana.

All were now aware of the darkness before them. As least as much as Tommy would convey. He left out names and important events. But still stuck to the importance of their help. They had all fought that same evil in a way, so it wasn't unfamiliar to them. They all sat for hours discussing other things, current events, and even what life is like in the future. Even though the evening grew late none of the heroes felt like putting their heads to rest.

Christana sat by Arnold, her chair adjacent, and her hand holding a delicate porcelain cup. The tea was hot as they sipped it, catching glimpses of each other's eyes.

Arnold fidgeted, his gaze falling on his former assistant. He had a hard time adjusting to her transformation. She went from being a former student to now a hero. It was even weirder for him to see her as the same age, but he accepted her hand when she laid hers on top of his. He was thinking back to the mission he recently completed. He remembered the misery on her face as Marlon dragged her away. In that moment, it was a spark he felt.

After a few hours, Tommy noticed Arnold holding Christana's hands. She was telling him about her life since he left. He smiled to himself like he planned it this way, as he knew Christana's whole story. Her part read so well he could actually feel her emotion through the pages of time. He desired to ease her lingering sorrow.

Tommy also watched Arnold and laughed to himself as he wanted to shake things up for the man. He had everything he wanted right in front of him, even though he never realized it.

The fire was crackling as Marcus stared into it. He remembered his encounter. The evil he defeated was now a part of him. He could gaze into the fire without blinking or even touch it now without getting burned. He wondered how he would fail to defeat anything before him. He faced doubt before but was always able to overcome it.

The wind struck the windows, making them rattle. Outside, the Cactus peered in through the frosted glass. He watched the heroes gathered around the small table, their faces lit with warmth and camaraderie. He longed for friendship but was content with being outside, knowing his presence was still valued.

As the muffled laughter reached his ears, the Cactus felt a sense of belonging wash over him. He stood tall and steadfast, blending seamlessly with the trees, embracing his role as the silent guardian of his friends.

Marlon, whose curiosity was streaming about Tommy, counted the heroes he met on his hand. Before this point, he was one of the only people, if not the only one, to have met two heroes. It even brought him a bit of fame a decade ago. It helped him publish more of his studies and, eventually, a book he and Christana wrote together. It was to facilitate her to move on from the war, but to no avail.

In Marlon's excitement and pleasure of meeting more heroes, he asked Tommy about the future. He asked about the events of the other heroes that come after Christana. After Tommy answered every one, something bothered him. But, he was almost too afraid to ask. The world was still recovering in this era, after all, but regardless he asked Tommy. "So, you really are from the future?"

"Yes, as I've said, and with my stories, you should believe me by now," Tommy replied while enjoying his first sips of tea. Taking it with two sugars, he delighted in answering any question Marlon asked.

"Why didn't you stop Hitler?" Marlon asked.

Tommy sighed as if it were the millionth time he had heard that question.

"Who is Hitler?" asked Arnold.

Later in the night, after the fire had died out, and smoke rose into the flue, and the teapot was empty, Christana made arrangements with Marlon to set up rooms for the heroes to rest. Tommy told them the next day they had more time traveling to do, said his goodnight and went upstairs, guided by Marlon with Marcus in tow.

Tommy had his own room, a cozy space complete with a warm bed that stayed unused and pictures of a man in a well-worn military suit; much older than the current time period. Tommy saw a photo album and began looking through it to pass the time, looking at the images he peered into the era in which they were taken.

Marlon led Marcus to his room. It was nothing fancy and quite smaller than the rest. But, at least it had a fireplace if he wanted to sleep warmer. It was a cold night and Marcus still could not rest well. His companion was not disturbing him, but he had a gut feeling, things were not going to work out. He looked out his window. It faced towards the lone driveway that led into the forest. He saw the Cactus outside standing still. The moon, now full in the sky, shined its light over the courtyard. Images of his wife back home flooded his mind. Things were rough between them at the moment, but he still held on to hope. He was concerned for her safety and tried to fathom how far away he was from her, not just in distance, but time as well.

Time travel did not sit well with Marcus. *Maybe that is just as they were supposed to be,* he reasoned to himself. Maybe Tommy was wrong to do so, but he could still sense the Lady of Light had touched his soul. He questioned if he was to be the hero of his time. *Why would he need the help from the other heroes? There are too many questions that need answers,* Marcus continued to muse.

Back in the den, Christana didn't want to let go of Arnold's hand, but exhaustion nearly had him. For everyone else, it was a normal day. But for Arnold, the events were still too baffling to him as he displayed his turmoil.

"Arnold?" Christana shook him gently, trying to keep him awake. "Marlon has a room ready for you." She wanted to keep the conversation going, but her heart sank knowing Arnold would fall asleep soon.

"We can talk more in the morning, Christana," Arnold said with a smile, head back and eyes shut. "It's been a terribly long day for me."

"Let's get you back upstairs," she said, nudging him with her tenderness. She wished they could be more but thought perhaps the professor was right and they weren't meant for each other. She helped him to his room and watched him remove his shoes and overshirt. "Have a goodnight, Arnold."

Arnold said his farewell as she closed the door. "Maybe I was too harsh on her," he tried talking to himself. "I have too much responsibility." Arnold let his mind toss back and forth and his eyes shifted him asleep.

Once morning had arrived, Marcus made his way downstairs to find the others were already up. Tommy greeted him and said Marlon had made them breakfast. Marcus thanked Marlon as he watched the expert toss of crepes in a pan.

"Not at all a Scottish breakfast, but it was Arnold's favorite," Marlon said to Marcus. "Tommy tells me you're something of a breakfast connoisseur."

"He said that?" Marcus replied, trying to stay modest. "I dabble." Marcus took his plate with fresh berries and cream and went to the heroes to listen as Tommy was making them laugh with his stories.

"Marcus, come join us!" Arnold said.

"I'm going to step outside if you don't mind. I didn't sleep well. I might just need fresh air."

Upon stepping outside, Marcus found the sight of the courtyard enchanting. It was a perfect place to enjoy his breakfast. Flowers of white and gold danced in the wind. The air changed his mood in a moment, taking a big bite of his crepe.

The Cactus had rid the place of all the weeds. This gave it a lush blanket of grass and encouraged more flowers to grow. But, the cold autumn would kill them anyway. The Cactus showed off the restored flower beds with excitement to Marcus. He even tore down the destructive vines growing on the mansion.

"You really are the keeper of nature," Marcus said. "I'm still not sure if you understand me."

The Cactus stood there staring.

Excusing himself from the laughter, Tommy followed Marlon and stacked the breakfast plates high. While the coffee pot sat half empty, Tommy and Marlon continued their conversation. "I'll get this place cleaned for you, Christana," Marlon said, watching her ascend the stairs. But Christana didn't seem to be in the mood. She continued on her way, Arnold following behind to see if he could assist.

Christana pulled the trunk from under her bed and brushed off the dust. It contained her medals and other mementos from the war, but also, inside was the rifle she used in service.

"I'm going to need this. I haven't used it for a very long time," she said.

"You were an excellent shot, much like an Annie Oakley of your time," Arnold said, proudly.

"Just like father wanted," she replied, rolling her eyes.

"You enjoyed it," Arnold reasoned, trying to understand her.

"I enjoyed time with you and learning. He never wanted me to be the way I am now. He wanted to spend time with me. He enjoyed it."

"It was the path that was given to you."

"I went to war to die, not to save."

"Well, it was lucky your father trained you so well. Now, you are here."

She took the rifle to clean it. She took out oil and an old rag to polish it and set it upon her desk.

"I'd like to be alone," she said, not even giving Arnold a look.

"I understand," Arnold replied. "I'll go back downstairs and see if Marlon needs help with cleaning."

As Arnold walked back to the common area, he met up with Marlon and struck up a conversation with him right away.

"I'm glad you have taken care of her for so long," Arnold said to Marlon.

"After you had... Well... After she went back with her parents, I went to your estate. It became so much, I had to sell it. She did not take that well. After everything was settled, her parents came to me looking for her. With everything that happened, she left for America. Later, she joined the army..." Marlon paused before speaking again. The next statement weighed heavily on his heart as he spoke. "The whole world was at war... It was horrible...The things we saw. The events that took place. Be glad you died back in your time."

"Is that why she was so upset?" Arnold said. "Why did she ask about..."

"Arnold, you have to understand, her parents were in France when everything was taking place...If it wasn't for her, we would have lost everything. But she...She did. Just like the day I hauled her away. The screams that haunt you, also haunt me, and I had to hear it twice."

Arnold watched as Marlon recalled the terrible memories. He motioned his hands, imagining himself back in that moment, holding Christana as she wept. Marlon looked at his hands as if they were filthy, like he caused it himself.

"You've missed so much," Marlon said with an uneasy tone.

"I had no idea. I can't imagine her suffering," Arnold sighed. "I know she missed me; I can see it. Her eyes are weak. There isn't the fire that was once there, so bright and eager to learn."

"Now that you are here, I believe it can still come back."

Marcus took in the whole atmosphere. The garden smelled wonderful in the sunlight. He heard the birds chirping and the wind through the grass. Indeed, the Cactus astonished Marcus with his actions. The demon did not like the smell, nor cared for the sight of such greenery.

The Cactus seemed proud of what it did and before long, the rest stepped outside.

"Our next target is the Golden Tiger from China 1586 After Dragons," Tommy said to them. "I have given you all the equipment you need to traverse time. I will go over the same rules. This will be following the defeat of Jiao Long, the East Dragon, as you all may know if you learned any history."

"I studied him a lot! He was very peculiar. I wish I could have done it in person," Arnold said.

"Well, now is your chance because we are going. Get Ready!"

"Au revoir, Marlon, take care while we are away. I hope we shall return!" Christana said.

The portal opened and one by one they all stepped inside, not knowing what was to come. Christana's eyes glittered from the light, seeing the time vortex take shape. She was the most willing of the heroes so far, even if it was to spend time with Arnold, more than Tommy's motives.

Marcus went through last, but before he could take his first step, the shadow on his shoulder stopped him. "You are right to have fears," D said. "If he betrays you, I'll snap his neck." Marcus shook his head and walked through.

An open field greeted the heroes with tall grass, and a small farmhouse. The mountains beyond stood tall and full of lush green trees. The smell of freshness filled the air like none of them had experienced before. It was free of smog or the smells of production that polluted the air in their time. It was of a simpler era.

The breeze was no cooler than the air before but welcomed them all the same. It was as refreshing as cold lemonade on a summer's day. Even the air smelled like lemon zest and fresh tea. Arnold could see the tea trees growing in front of the house as the breeze carried that sent all the way to them.

"This place is so wonderful! I have never felt at peace quite like this before," Arnold remarked.

"Ah yes, like being back home," Christana responded.

"Don't get too comfortable. I'm not sure how he will react to us being here," Tommy said. "The Tiger is fierce, just be aware, he may attack."

"If I don't stop him first," Marcus said with great determination.

"I don't want a fight. We have to be convincing without a struggle," Tommy continued. "I have never met him nor know what he is really capable of doing. Some say he moves like a shadow. Others say his aggression is unmatched."

"I prefer not to fight either," Arnold said. "I just want to understand his powers."

They approached the old house and saw a man in poor clothes tending to his livestock. The chickens were following closely as he threw the feed on the ground while the goats grazed on the grass outside of their pen.

The man turned his head around to look at the strangers approaching him. His eyes gleamed a menacing glow like that of a cat, orange, and piercing.

The heroes all stood still unsure of what to do, but the man could smell them from where they were. He felt a disturbance that disrupted his time and the flow of magic in the air. Everyone watched before their very eyes, the man transformed. His skin grew fur like a tiger, but with a golden glow in the sun, and claws that were like jagged metal or glass. He stood on two feet. His head was well above the nearby chicken coop and cast a golden shadow in front of it.

The Tiger called out in Mandarin, asking them who approached. The growl in his voice was frightening, even Tommy took a step back out of fear. It echoed through the field, as the wind fled from his roaring voice.

Christana tried to catch Arnold. She was afraid he was making a mistake by moving forward. But the professor stood his ground. He looked at the beast in amazement, meeting his childhood hero. His fascination got the better of him as he walked forward and began to speak to the Tiger in the native tongue of China.

5 Fire Amongst Green Serenity

Arnold's Mandarin wasn't flawless. And he had occasional pronunciation slips. But, he could still have a small conversation with the beast. The professor tried to explain who they were and why they were there. But, Arnold was so amazed by the hero that he was awestruck. The fur was almost blinding in the morning summer light while the wind caught it, shimmering it even more.

Jin's voice was unlike any other, deep with a subtle growl. His sharp teeth glinted. His outstretched claws could grasp a large watermelon. The Tiger then turned to Tommy and spoke. "In my meditation this morning I felt a change in the wind. I knew you were coming and prepared myself. Time is calling for me once more, isn't it?"

"You speak English?" Arnold blurted out, his surprise evident, though he quickly realized he should step back and let Tommy take the lead.

"I'm Tommy Kent. this is Marcus, Arnold, Christana, and our friend the Cactus."

"You're all heroes," Jin replied. "I could sense it as soon as you entered my realm."

"How did you know?"

"I could smell you, and I could hear you. Every word."

"Exceptional hearing too!" Arnold exclaimed! "You are by far my favorite hero from history. I learned a lot about you!"

"You are the third hero to stop the evil threat, and you weren't the last. We need you now," Tommy tried to explain.

"You desire to take me away from here? My home? As a hero I am destined to stay here. To protect the earth from further threats."

"That's why we are all here," Marcus replied. "The future needs us all."

"No, I believe not. Exclude me from this matter. I perceive a magic within each of you, a magic that should have vanished ages ago."

"But…"

"Enough!" Jin roared. "I wish not to help in your time, you may be heroes, but you lack discipline. I can see clearly."

"You want to know about discipline? I have more than enough to show you!" Marcus said in rebuttal. The shadow grew behind him showing his true form.

"I knew it. The darkness never hides for long," Jin scoffed.

As tensions escalated, the two squared off, ready for conflict. The Cactus saved Marcus. He pulled him aside and confronted the Tiger like a barrier between them. Without him, things would have spiraled into chaos.

The Cactus had a natural spirit. He stared past all the physical realms to the spirit of the tiger that gave Jin power. With a calm and determined demeanor, the Cactus met the Tiger's gaze. His eyes, reminiscent of wisps of smoke, met the fiery intensity. He could not speak, but the Tiger understood. Jin could feel the spirit within the Cactus and transformed back into a man.

Jin cooled down, taking a deep breath. He listened to his thoughts. "Jade seems to like this one."

"Who is Jade?" Christana asked.

"That would be the spirit of my lost tiger. She guides me now, but it seems you have a guardian of nature on your side, far from the destruction I faced."

"That's where you get your powers. The legends were true," Arnold said, fascinated by Jin. He walked over to offer his hand or bow. He was unsure of the right gesture for respect, which left him a bit awkward. "Do you shake hands with foreigners or is it all right to bow?"

Jin bowed first to help lead Arnold to do the same. "Forgive me," Jin said, walking past the strange professor to Tommy, who he recognized as the leader of the group. "I tend to lose control sometimes. It's a wild instinct."

"I know a thing or two about losing control," Marcus added. "It does take a lot of discipline."

Christana approached Jin. "You know just as much as I do, that you must help. Like you said, instinct."

The man looked at the Time Warden. "I can't help you."

"Please, you don't know what's at stake," Tommy pleaded.

"I'm sure it's no different than the evil that tested me. If you are the hero, you can do it yourself."

"Jin, if I may, let me explain. I am the Time Warden. I was blessed by the Lady of Light with the task of saving the world, but I can't do it without your help."

"This would go against everything I believe. Everything I have learned."

"But you are a hero! Can't you feel the call?" Christana asked.

"In my past, I had companions like yourselves, but they suffered under our trial, as I still do. The wildness grows stronger every day, and my aggression grows. I would be detrimental to you."

"The power of the tiger is strong," Tommy intervened. "But I've seen you control it. Stay on your path as a hero and answer the call. It's what your wild side calls to."

"I'm sorry, I can't. Now, leave me. Go back from where you came and let me tend to my animals."

Marcus tried to intervene, but Jin unleashed an intense roar with all the force of his breath.

"Come on, Marcus," Arnold said, tugging at his sleeve.

The rest of the heroes went back into the grassy fields to await Tommy. As he stood there, Jin kept his growl and stance. Tommy shook his head, giving one last word.

"I thought better of you, Golden Tiger. The history books spoke of your legendary honor."

Christana consoled Tommy as he came back to them. The grass was knee high hiding grasshoppers within. They jumped from blade to blade as the heroes walked together.

"I failed," Tommy said. "To the next hero, I suppose. We will have to continue without this one…"

"There must be something we could do to convince him," Arnold said. "I can't believe a man of his honor would be afraid. We all know the risks. What would keep him?"

Jin listened to the heroes in their woe but chose to ignore it. He finished throwing the feed for his chickens and decided to step inside his home for some shade.

It was cozy enough, but not a place for a man to live out his days. The village nearest lay a week's journey on foot, three days by wagon without rest stops, yet Jin had to exist under these conditions.

His guilt churned his stomach while the spirit within beckoned his adventure. He clutched his hands summoning his wild spirit free.

"I can't Jade," Jin spoke to the tiger's spirit as it was the only company he had. "I can't go through that again, I'm not strong enough…"

Like a playful cat, the geist played with the scroll upon his hearth knocking over so it rolled onto the ground. Picking it up, Jin read to remind himself of the words from his old teacher.

"Jade…" Jin sighed.

The heroes discussed leaving, but Tommy was just kicking the grass watching the bugs fly. Arnold was intent on staying until Jin could leave with them. But, Marcus argued they would need to leave to get something to eat.

"We can't stay any longer," Tommy said, opening a portal. "We've wasted too much time already."

"Are you sure?" Christana asked. "We could hold out hope for a little longer."

"That won't be necessary," Jin said, walking towards them, dressed, and well fitted for an adventure.

The portal snapped shut as Tommy looked back with a cleaver smirk. "I knew you'd join us."

Jin walked over to them, gave his best bow, and set his stance to signify his enthusiasm.

"What made you change your mind?" Christana asked.

"What kind of hero would I be if I give up? You are given weaknesses to overcome. It's the only way to grow. I'll try my best to keep the beast from harming any of you."

"Doesn't anyone else feel the chills?" Tommy asked.

"How is it you speak such perfect English?" Arnold asked, cutting the good vibes, as his curiosity got the better of him yet again.

"It was a gift. I have been blessed. When time called for me, it was when Jiao Long invaded my small village. I had a small tiger, Jade... I found her alone in the bamboo forest as I was going to the market to sell some pigs. I raised that tiger. I loved that tiger. She died to save me from his merciless invasion. We were left to die, but at that moment I heard the call. The same one all of you experienced too. Our spirits united, man and beast. I gained knowledge, and I gained strength."

"And you used it to save China," Arnold added.

"And the world," Tommy replied. "Jin Chen, protector of your time."

"Oh, that reminds me!" Arnold said, turning away from the group and walking deeper into the fields.

"You can feel our spirits? You know what is in our hearts?" Christana asked. "That is a special gift."

"It's not a gift I was granted for being a hero. I gained it through meditation," Jin replied. "By connecting to the Allfather."

"Well Jin," Tommy said. "I promise I will explain everything after we assemble the rest."

"How many are there?"

"Three more. Come quickly now, oh and put this on!" Tommy said to him while handing him a very curious helmet.

"Professor!" Tommy called out, "We don't have time for your studies. We can do that later!"

The professor put a small gadget into his coat pocket. He had used it to measure. He wrote down his findings and returned to the others. Tommy's portal burst forth, threatening to snatch the paper from his grasp.

"Walk through the portal," Tommy said. "This time going to Germany in the 1850s."

"I was hoping for more of an explanation," Jin muttered under his breath."

"Don't worry," Marcus said to Jin. "I still don't trust him much either. But I can feel it in my heart. It is what I need to do."

"As do I."

Marcus stepped through the portal as Tommy waited for Jin to make his decision concrete.

This was all very strange for Jin. He encountered people with bizarre attire and unfamiliar technology. As skeptical as he was, he still stepped through and followed the rest.

The famous emporium of Hanover stood before the heroes. They entered a night scene with softly glowing cobblestone streets. The cold winds without rest carried the smells of the city, pleasant, but bitter, and the refreshing taste of the river.

"Mr. and Mrs. Gensen's Great Porcelain Emporium," Tommy said. "I would have loved to come to a place like this as a kid. Heck, I still *am* a kid!" Without hesitation, Tommy ran inside despite the closed sign and leaving the other heroes behind. His eagerness was overbearing.

"I don't understand," Jin said, confused by every word Tommy said.

"It's a lot to unload for sure," Marcus said.

"What is this place?" Jin asked, trying to read the words upon the building to no avail.

"A toy maker lives here," Arnold said.

"But it was more than that," Christana added. "Fine China and porcelain. He makes everything. I have a few teacups from him that still survive. They are really expensive."

"Goodness, the teacups we used back at your estate?" Arnold asked.

"I keep them on display. I've never used them."

"Maybe we should if we ever get to have tea together."

Marcus cleared his throat to help get Arnold back on track.

"As I was saying, he built toys for the orphanage and the children living there. He always preached about how magic was still in the world. It was all around us, and we could still use it if we just believed and only if we just had a pure enough heart. I based my research on the theory that we could possibly use machines to harness the residual magic around us. Fascinating, I tell you. Why I just…"

"Arnold!" Christana said, breaking him from his rant.

Adjusting his glasses, Arnold continued. "Through those beliefs, his toys would come to life and play with the children that didn't have much company. He kept a few for his own, however, and would regularly go into town to get supplies. It was one day when he did not return, the toys within the emporium became worried. They created their own doll using the old man's best suit and pants. They gave him hands of steel and a head made of porcelain. That doll then went on to become the world's next hero. He is known in history as the Porcelain Man."

"Truly a remarkable story," Jin commented.

"Are we going in after Tommy?" Marcus asked.

"It's late and Gensen was a very old man. He would be in bed by this hour, I would assume," Arnold said.

"Maybe it would be respectful to stay outdoors," Jin added. "Let Tommy handle recruiting the new hero."

"Sure is taking a while," Marcus said, annoyed and bitter.

"I could take a look," the demon said to Marcus."

Not long after Marcus spoke up Tommy came out with the Doll in his arms. Sadness overcame his face like moments before when Jin had rejected his invitation. He held up the Doll, limp and drooping over his arms. Tommy carried him out like he had saved him from a fire.

"What could have made it come to this?" Tommy asked and he exited the emporium, "We were too late, my friends, he's dead…"

6 Brewing Trouble

Disheartened, Tommy gave in to his emotion. He fell to his knees, sobbing and hiding his face in the Doll's jacket. The other heroes gathered around, Christana even trying to console him. "Can't we go back to a different time to get him alive?" she asked, looking into the Doll's eyes. "It's a bit creepy looking."

"No, this will have to do," Tommy said, trying to hide his grin.

"What are we going to do with an inanimate doll?" Marcus scoffed.

The Doll abruptly swiveled its head toward the heroes, nearly startling Christana into a panic. She screamed bloody murder, punching a hysterical Tommy.

"We came up with that while inside!" Tommy said, while trying to catch his breath. "We thought it would be funny! Well, I guess I came up with it. He cannot speak, much like our Cactus friend over there."

"Are you kidding me?" Marus exclaimed, motioning his arms to add to his dismay. "What is with you? You are trying to get us to save the world, but you are playing pranks?"

"What's the point in saving the world if you're not going to have fun along the way," Tommy replied, brushing off Marcus's tone.

"I agree with Marcus, I don't find this amusing," Christana replied.

"Calm down. Besides, he is playful too. And very friendly," Tommy reassured Christana.

"Yeah, it's an oversized toy," Marcus said.

The Doll gave Marcus a rather sad gesture, even though its face did not change or give any expression.

At this point, they noticed Jin and Arnold were missing. They walked a short distance down the road, surveying city streets, not too far.

Tommy went back inside to talk with the old man while Marcus stayed with the Cactus and the Porcelain Man.

To Jin, things were so different over on this side of the world. The buildings and the culture were not like home at all. He had been all over China, but never outside it. He enjoyed all the different smells and sights to see. His amber eyes helped him see clearly in the dark.

Arnold followed him, still engaged in conversation. Arnold had been to Germany before. It was where he was called to save the world. But this time felt different. There was a certain peace to this place.

"All these heroes are so special," Arnold said. "It makes me feel so inadequate."

"What do you mean?" Jin asked.

"Well, you have your powers, and Christana's has hers. And Marcus, if I had the power he carries, my trouble would not have been so difficult. It would have been so easy to save the world, but time granted me a different gift."

"I still don't understand," Jin continued to question. "The Lady of Light doesn't make mistakes nor does our prophecy make jokes. We are given our powers to assist us."

"Buh oui, but mine are so contradictory to my beliefs, I mean look for yourself." Arnold grabbed a stone from the street. It turned to dust in a matter of seconds right before Jin's very eyes. "I am meant to create and build things. I have always desired to advance the human race. I tinker with my gadgets, and I have even won a Nobel Prize for my inventions." Arnold gave a sigh as he blew the dust to the wind.. "My gift…" He paused before speaking again. "I destroy things. In my hands they crumble. Hardly a power when we have a fierce tiger and a demon… a time traveler."

"It sounds like you have more gifts than you allow yourself to see, Arnold," Jin said. "I'm sure there is a reason."

"You don't need any other gift," Christana called from behind as she caught up to them. "Your intelligence is nothing to hide. That is also part of your gift."

"I suppose you're right, Christana," Arnold agreed and smiled at her.

"You were the only man capable of overcoming your struggles. It wasn't Marcus, it wasn't me. Time chose you."

"Believe Christana," Jin urged. "You have an incredible talent. Be proud of it!"

They continued to walk on the road, taking in the fine scenery. Jin and Arnold were much alike, they were more about a simple life. To keep to themselves and be more fascinated with learning. Jin was still trying to gather his own thoughts but remembered his sacrifice. He wondered if he could do it again.

"We have the Doll in our party now," Christana said. "I came over here to tell you, so we will be leaving soon. There are just two more heroes we need to find."

"Christana, do you remember?" Arnold said, staring into the distance.

"Remember what?"

"Do you remember leaving France and seeing Germany for the first time?"

"Oui, bien sûr!"

"What a time that was. Cities like this one will be destroyed. What a shame. It's a shame I cannot do anything about it now. Before it happens. So many lives lost…"

Christana realized the professor had changed and had embraced his role as the hero. When he was called, he did not doubt, he did not fight it. It was not in his nature to be a man of duty, but he filled those shoes so well and gave his life for the people. When she took his hand, no reply was needed. They simply knew something just had to be.

They all walked back to the shop with the living quarters at the top, where the others waited. Their next destination was tenth-century England, a time of dragons and great evil. This was the era of Sir Owen, the Crystal Dragon, who brought peace between them. Tommy was busy explaining everything to the Cactus and the Doll, who made good listeners. Marcus strode restlessly, his steps tracing a repetitive path.

"Do we have to leave just now?" Arnold asked. "I do not wish to go just yet as I have a small favor to ask."

"What would that be?" Tommy considered as he listened.

"There is so much literature in this era. So much art and other things that will be lost before my time. I wish to take a piece of it."

"No, Arnold, I cannot let you take things from here. It would be too dangerous," Tommy replied.

"Please, all I ask is just for a little knowledge. Take me to the library in Berlin."

Tommy paused to think for a moment.

"Please! There is something there I think I could use!"

Christana looked at Tommy and nodded in agreement. She acted as if there could be something worthwhile. Tommy felt conflicted about letting Arnold do as he wished because he was anxious. It was an emotion he was hiding from everyone under his cool and comedic demeanor.

You can feel it too. I know you can, the voice said inside Marcus's head. *He is hiding something. You can feel his fear. His distress.*

Marcus tried less to pay attention to the demon possessing his mind as he was now beginning to trust the time warden. Even still, the demon that he kept chained like a dog in his mind, was right. He could feel something stirring in that man's head. He could sense all the discomfort like tangled knots.

Let me into his mind. Let me see, the demon said to Marcus.

Marcus reluctantly agreed. He let the demon slip into the mind of Tommy as he was debating with the others. Almost immediately, the demon returned to Marcus in agony, dazed and confused. It could not focus and refused to respond to Marcus's questions as he tried to calmly speak to him, hiding his words from the others.

Tommy turned to Marcus and caught him in his panic argument with the shadow. By Tommy's distraction, the rest of the heroes noticed as well.

"Are you okay, Marcus?" Christana asked.

"Yeah," Marcus said, stuttering. "Just bad thoughts."

MADNESS! the demon cried out in Marcus' head. *All madness. There is not a single cognitive thought in his mind!*

"What does that mean?" Marcus tried to ask the demon.

"Marcus, are you sure, you seem pale?" Arnold inquired. "Just take a seat."

They put Marcus on the steps before the door to the house. Marcus seemed really confused, but he came to shortly, just dizziness fading away.

"I'm all right," Marcus wearily said.

"Well, we cannot travel as such," Tommy said. "Marcus, stay here for a while. Ask if the old man will let you stay at his house for the night." He then glanced at Arnold. "I suppose in the meantime, I will take Arnold to the library he wishes to visit."

"Génial! I am most delighted!" Arnold replied. "Let us go immediately!"

"I'll stay with Marcus," Jin said.

"The Doll and the Cactus can stay too," Tommy added. "We will be back in the morning."

Christana, Tommy, and Arnold all left in the portal Tommy made. With a gust of wind blowing back, they were gone.

Meanwhile, Marcus and Jin knocked once again on the old man's door and asked if they could stay for a while. The old man welcomed them into his home and gave them simple stew by the fire. His workshop was filled with various pieces of fabric, buttons, and wood, but more importantly, porcelain where he crafted Doll heads among many other things.

Jin reached into his satchel and retrieved some tea to make for all of them as he listened to the old man who was soft spoken and very kind. He had many dolls on display all over his workshop giving creepy stares at Jin as he brought water to boil over the range. He could not feel at ease with all those eyes upon him, alive or not.

"I knew Tommy was a good fellow as soon as he stepped into my home," the old man said. "Very charismatic and funny. Very much in touch with his inner child." The old man looked at them. "It is very rare these days." He took the tea from Jin as it was handed to him and sipped it as steam rose.

The aroma filled the room. Tea from fresh leaves like this is very difficult to come by in this area. Anyone who would drink it would have to be of royalty or very rich. It was pleasant for all of them. Marcus still preferred coffee, but he accepted it, nonetheless.

Jin sat quietly so as not to disturb anyone. He was using his time to meditate and focus.

Marcus, admiring all the work the old man had accomplished, was taken aback. There were so many dolls and toys he made. "This is incredible, Mr. Gensen," Marcus said while sipping on his tea and taking a liking to one doll in particular. "You don't find generosity like this back where I am from. It is very rare. Everybody is just too involved with their own lives. They don't care much for strangers. It is very disheartening."

Marcus thought of his home back in New York with the busy streets and tall buildings he never cared to appreciate. People lived with busy schedules. They pretended to like others for their own gain and played the same game to climb. But, Marcus was different. His whole life he was inspired to be like the heroes of old. His only desire was much like the old man's, to help others, especially the people that needed it most. Marcus was able to live that dream. He was contemptuous of what he accomplished. Even though he was skeptical of Tommy at first and didn't trust him, in his heart he knew people were in danger. He felt like all he wanted to do was save them. He risked everything going with Tommy on this journey and hoped to know if he made the right call.

"You know, my wife and I never had any children of our own," Mr. Gensen said. "We never could. But she died young. I was but a simple man, heartbroken, and grieving. I knew my time was not for a while. So, I created these dolls. They kept me company, but mostly they gave me something to focus on. I still had more to give to this world."

"That's beautiful, Gensen," Jin added. "We should all be like you. I suffered a great loss in my time. Sometimes that pain can create the most beautiful of things in this world."

They settled in for the night, and after the fire went out, they were all lying in their beds.

Christana, Arnold, and Tommy stood before the great library of Berlin. Being the first to ascend the stairs, Arnold was quick to call back to Tommy who stayed behind.

"Hurry Tommy, there is so much to learn!"

"That's okay," Tommy said to them, "Go on without me, I have other matters I wish to attend here in this city. I'll be back shortly."

They didn't understand but left Tommy to his own business. Christana took the hand of the professor and led him in through a window she noticed was left open.

Tommy took to the outside in the cold cobblestone street. He gazed up at the moon, and wondered if he would ever see his home again or his mother, or even Jimmy.

"I hope those dark creatures don't get you, Jimmy." Tommy sighed. "I'm going as fast as I can."

But Tommy's thought sank deeper. He knew Marcus tried to investigate his mind. Distrust may be forming in the group, and he could not let that happen but could not explain things to them just yet, not fully at least. "Would they even understand?"

His mind was still too scrambled. It was madness for sure but could not see either end to the knot that it had become. He could not unravel the mystery behind it, it was even lost to him. He was courageous, for sure, but very uncertain, even as knowledgeable as he was. As long as he had lived, he still felt like a child. Tears were brought to his face as he doubted himself. He was not sure how to lead a group of such talented individuals.

Most importantly he thought of his father and what he might do. "Would they understand? I'm just a boy. Maybe Jimmy would have been a better pick to be the hero."

He wondered where he was. If he was safe. If his mother was safe, but his memory was still clouded in shadow and couldn't look past where he left. The future was just as uncertain to him as anyone else. That uncertainty is what gave him such fear. It gave him great anxiety. Tommy stood still just trying to make peace with himself. He still held on to hope as it was the only thing he had left.

Candles burned low, as Arnold and Christana looked through all the books that had been kept in the large library. Page after page, the professor studied, looking for answers hidden in the text. It was like a puzzle to him, solving it would take much effort. Luckily for him, his assistant was just as such. The moment they had was just like it was all those years ago. She loved watching him study and was infatuated by the way his mind worked; it was fascinating to her. He would become so immersed in the work that he did.

Arnold's mind was like a steam engine, all the gears turning. The books were like rails, taking him where he needed to go.

Christana watched as the candlelight flickered off his glasses. It took her back to the very same scene as a young assistant to him in his studies. She would sit and watch him for hours, helping with whatever request.

Christana poured Arnold a glass of water. He didn't even thank her, he was so focused, he didn't even notice. He was on the verge of something. Putting one book down, only to pick up another. He would have loved to have these books in his time as his work required it. Pulling his greatest invention from his pocket, he acquired the data from a small device with a dial. It read the essence of magic, residual or upon a person, even containing the potential to harvest it. He did everything he could to stop it from getting into the wrong hands. Looking at it, he wondered where he went wrong.

Aside from his distraction, Arnold wanted to know if it was possible to predict catastrophes and potential heroes. These last manuscripts were destroyed later by those who sought to end the heroes. Only wanting the magic for themselves. Arnold thought it would be possible to even tap into that magic, just as the old man did and use it to create something good for humanity. Checking the device in his pocket, he made some calculations and wrote them down on a scrap parchment.

"If I could get these findings back to my study for comparison, then I think I could have something here!" Arnold declared. "There are certain spots in history where the magic fails and or is at its weakest. That is where evil is able to slip in. The magic is usually strongest right when a hero is awakened." He took Christana's hand and showed her.

"Regarde ça, you see here. The magic has been becoming weaker and weaker as heroes emerge. I believe that is why heroes come sooner and sooner throughout history." Christana followed his hands as he marked some of the points measured with other dates in time. "Look!" he continued as his excitement grew, almost proud to show his assistant his findings.

"This is great, Arnold, but what will this have to do with us right now?" Christana asked.

"Well, you see, this could mean, eventually, we may never have heroes again. Just as Tommy described, Marcus is the last hero. Why did it take one thousand years just for a hero to emerge in Tommy's time? Why that long? Isn't it supposed to come when the threat begins?"

"I see, this could mean, the magic is lost, or the hero failed."

"Was Marcus the hero that failed? As Tommy said, the villain comes in Marcus' time. He was there."

"Must we warn Marcus?"

"This is not his part. This is not his story. Something happened during Marcus's time as the hero. I would need to do some studies over there in his time. I need to see just what happened; I would like to take this machine to measure the magic present there too."

"I feel like something really bad is going to happen. I almost feel like the magic from the world is fading. It felt so much stronger where Jin was. Back in my time, it feels almost weaker," Christana added.

"Exactly. The first hero comes at the end of the 8th century, then not until 1121 we have the next. The Tiger nearly five hundred years after that. Then a little over three hundred years later for the Doll."

"Then we come back-to-back, not even one hundred years later."

"Magic is dying…" The silence was heartbreaking with this realization. "The whole thing is falling away from where it was. We have to tell Tommy."

"There is something else, isn't there?" Christana asked, almost frightened. She was clever and could always tell when the professor was hiding something.

"Just as the charts show, not only is magic fading, but the darkness is growing too. An evil is taking its place."

7 A Mother and Son

Jimmy tried as he could to shut off the portal. It was making all sorts of noises, from whirls to sparks, to almost explosive. The winds outside shifted and turned harsh. It cut through the barn and blew the doors wide open. Sparks flashed from the machine and set fire to parts of the decrepit place.

Jimmy took action to put out the fire. He could not let the place burn down. As soon as he had it under control, his mother came rushing it.

"Tommy went in!" Jimmy screamed, knowing full well of the boundaries his mother had set.

She warned them not to be fooling with the machine again. But there was no time to scold them. Her instincts were strong. She knew it was only a matter of time before

Tommy took it upon himself, but glancing around, she knew he had left them.

Emily grabbed Jimmy; he was light, skinny and almost starving. She lifted him and ran for the house. There was no time to worry about the machine. Whether it was destroyed or left to burn out did not matter. What mattered was getting to safety.

In the distance, she could already hear howls. They were deep with despair and as chilling as the night. The sound pierced the ears of Emily and Jimmy, tormenting them as they tried to flee.

Jimmy was in tears at this point. His panic and worry made Emily more afraid for Tommy. But, what she saw behind them on the way home was even more terrifying.

A hound with the face of the most defiled of creatures. Its fur was dark as night and teeth resembled twisted roots. They snarled before rushing, every step leaving only fire and ash. These Hellhounds hunt their prey and rip them to shreds. Their breath black like smog, poured from their mouth like exhaust from a large truck. Their eyes blazed with a fiery red light, resembling rubies. The Hellhounds made their way through the wasteland down to the home.

Emily, almost dropping Jimmy, continued to run as fast as she could. If anything, she could have Jimmy run and use herself as bait for the wolves, but it was not much further. The Hellhounds closed in on her. She kicked up dust with every step. *Faster! Faster! Faster!* she thought.

As they reached the door to their house, Emily made a last effort. She closed it in time before one of the hound's mouths took hold. Out of breath and exhausted, still, she got up to secure the heavy steel locks and shut them tight. She could still hear the banging on the other side. The relentless hounds now knowing there was someone inside, would not give up the hunt. The beasts circled the house trying to find a way in.

Emily put Jimmy in a safe room through a hatch that led down into the basement. Once secure, she grabbed a loaded gun and double checked to make sure it was ready. It was the shotgun her husband would use to scavenge. It was old and made of scrap. It felt like it would break if mishandled.

She held it up, shaking with fear, not sure if the hounds would find a way in or not. She knew she could not defend against them, even with the weapon she bore. She could feel her heart in her throat. She stumbled, almost dropping the gun because her hands were now greased with sweat. The howls outside became so haunting, Emily could feel the color leave her face. A small prayer was said.

The Hellhounds, smarter than average wolves, knew they had an easy feast. The beast at the door was clawing against the metal. The sound alone ripped Emily's eardrums and sent shivers down her spine. Alas, the door held from the attack, but the Hellhounds were cunning and hungry.

One of the dark creatures at the door began hurling and gagging. Emily had known what this meant as she had seen it before when a beast would dry heave and roll its eyes back. A putrid slime came from the Hellhound, the acid from the stomach eroding a hole in the door. The hounds gathered and soon, more followed in the same act.

The door's integrity would not last, but Emily was not sure what to do. She debated either taking a stand or going further down into the bunker and wait it out. The hounds would not capitulate. They would dig until they could feast upon them and chew until there was nothing more than bones and rags.

Her breath quickened and heart was in pain. Her knees shook and almost gave up their strength. The sweat was now in her eyes, burning, as she tried to rub them clean. She could see the face of one of the beasts as its teeth were gnawing through the hole. Emily raised the gun, crying and begging it to go away. As if they listened, the wolves became distracted from something else, far in the distance.

Most of the creatures gave chase to the new hunt, while two attempted at the door. Outside, Emily heard a motor and knew this could be her chance. She checked with Jimmy, comforting him one last time before shutting the hatch tight. After making sure it was secure, she turned back to face the hounds.

Dirt was flying in the air on the small hill nearby. A man on a motorcycle was revving and spinning the wheel. He looked beaten and weary. His clothing had almost as many troubles as him. All that he knew was to save Emily and her sons. He rode forth drawing his weapon from its holster as the Hellhounds, ghastly and fearless, gave chase. Coming to a stop, the man took aim at the advancing demons. He would need a very steady hand and sharp eye to take a shot at this distance with his worn pistol. He took in a breath and squeezed. Some of the Hellhounds flanked, so he had to make his shots quick.

The Hellhounds were ever more threatening in death as in life. They took forms of flames and showered the field in wicked rays of light. Shockwaves rang out and craters dug deep into the earth.

The man kicked his bike and sped to avoid the flank. The beasts then came in every direction to disrupt the rider. He avoided every attack, but his bike could not take any more strain. Nor did he have the fuel to keep avoiding them. This was his last stand. He reloaded and took aim once more. Three Hellhounds were rushing at him as he sunk another bullet into the skull.

Emily struck the hound as it pushed its head into view. Her efforts made little impact, and it persisted in forcing the door. This beast was massive and used its weight, bursting and bending the hinges and locks.

The second hound behind it was snarling and biting the air as it grew impatient. It took hold of the first creature's legs and ripped it to shreds. Blood dripped from its mouth as it bashed the door that was on its last hinge. The unholy thing took steps back before rushing it again.

Emily, with her only chance before her, placed the end of the gun outside the hole and fired. The explosion kicked her backwards as flames engulfed the house. A mis of toxic fumes and loss of breath had her coughing out both her lungs as she struggled for breath. The disappearance of the door compromised the safety of her home. As strong as she was, she made her stand, rushing to grab Jimmy to carry him out of the blaze.

"Mason!" Emily shouted as she saw him still engaged with the last of the evil creatures.

The beasts overpowered Mason and threw him from his bike. The Hellhound clamped its teeth onto the bike and sent it crashing. Mason rolled on his back and fired his last round. Broken metal impacted the ground as if it were raining, and Mason became burned from the close explosion. The last Hellhound lay behind him. But, before it could get up, Emily, with her last bit of strength and courage, obliterated it.

The last explosion echoed through the valley as ash began to rain. Mason stumbled to his feet. He gingerly grasped his handgun, wiping the blood from his lip.

"Are you all right?" Emily asked, limping over to him.

"Me? Are you?" Mason replied, coughing as much as she was from the ash. "I saw lights and the wind became too violent. I just had a bad feeling."

"Yes! We are fine. Most of us."

"Where is Tommy?"

"He is gone," Emily choked on her words.

"I'm sorry."

"No." She coughed. "Not like you think."

Mason responded with a puzzled tone, "Where could he have gone?"

"It worked! He did it! The time machine, he was able to..." She flinched in pain grabbing her side. Hues of purple cascaded down her side, and crimson smeared her brow.

"Tell me later. We cannot stay here." Mason took her in his arms. "We have to trust in him now."

"I know. I'm concerned. He is just so young," Emily replied.

"He will be all right," he told her, taking Jimmy from her arms and helping her walk. "Looks like your place is no longer safe. Come back to my safehouse. You're welcome to stay."

Emily agreed with hesitation. She took his hand out of the safety and concern for Jimmy. But her gut twisted like it was swallowing her heart.

Night was almost indistinguishable from day. The clouds overhead darkened the whole vicinity from any light. The earth had become so cold. Emily, Mason, and Jimmy stumbled back to his quarters, drained. He shut the steel doors, their surfaces marred by rust, and fortified them with an old oak table, which settled into place with a satisfying clunk.

The cellar smelled of old compost but stayed pleasantly warm. Mason cleared spaces for his new guests and placed wood in a small crevasse on the side. It had a small chimney that went up to the surface. His hands were rough and cracked. The thought of having lotion or oil to soothe his hands was a luxury only in a dream.

Rubbing his hands together as sparks ascended into the flue, he watched the fire come to life. His burns ached as he felt the heat. But, in these hard times, enduring such pain had become an inevitable part of life.

The crackling of the wood brought comfort to Emily and Jimmy. Mason called them over to sit by the fire and put two stools in front of it.

Mason then took a quilt and wrapped it around Jimmy. It was heavy but sitting next to the fire made Jimmy very content staring into it. The light reflected in his eyes as he recalled the scene before his brother.

"I don't have anything fancy to offer you. Just stale water, but I can warm it over the fire," Mason said to Emily.

"Yes, please. That is more than enough," Emily's voice whispered. Her mouth was parched, and her cracked lips felt like sandpaper. Her head throbbed with more than the pain from her wound. She rubbed her arms, then her legs, trying to ease the chill that had settled deep into her bones. She shuddered as Mason removed his jacket and placed it around her shoulders.

"Sorry, that's all I have for now. I can go up and grab another blanket in a minute. I just have to wait until it's safe," Mason said while comforting Emily. "Your husband," he started but was quickly interrupted.

"Don't talk about him. Not now. I just want to rest."

He left her to contemplate and confine herself. Mason then turned to Jimmy, still looking at the fire. "You know you were really brave today."

"I wasn't. I was scared," Jimmy mumbled.

"Just because you are brave doesn't mean you can't feel scared. It means you can take a stand, that is true bravery."

"But Tommy...I'm not sure. It seemed like things went wrong."

"Don't worry. Tommy can take care of himself now."

"Mason, please, just let him rest." Emily told him as exhaustion overcame her.

"I'm just trying to ease his mind."

"I know. It has been a difficult day…" Emily sighed. She hid her face behind her shoulder. Gaining composure she continued. "I should have been watching them more closely… I should have…" Her lips started quivering. Her eyes shut holding back the tears that wanted to burst out.

"Don't blame yourself, Robin set…"

"Stop!" Emily's tone displayed her frustration. Her voice was enough to silence all the noise in the room. Even in her turmoil, her resentment towards Mason shone through. "I told you…I don't want to hear it from you. Please just leave us be." Emily's thoughts reclaimed her mind as she ignored Mason. She thought of how she could have done better with Tommy to keep him from such dangerous endeavors. She knew Tommy would sneak out while she was sleeping. There wasn't much she was able to do. She tried locks and discipline. He was just like his father. He was ambitious and never listened.

Mason motioned to leave, stopping at the door to his room. He didn't face Emily, but his frustration made it clear he didn't want to talk to her either. "You know I tried to save him. You cannot hold that against me."

"Goodnight, Mason…" Emily said with a stern Mom voice.

Mason felt troubled by his anger and unrest. But, after Emily's intense stare, he closed and locked the door tight. He was friends with her husband, Robin. During stable times, good enough to get by, Mason and Robin had an amicable relationship. Yet, life in these times would never be easy, and when Robin's family was in peril, Robin came to Mason for help, he found none. He thought of that day when he turned his back on his friend. It was the only man in this world who wouldn't stab him over a rat carcass.

"What would he know?" Mason reasoned with himself. "Robin was always out trying to gain new knowledge from the old world. He was a fool to think his machine would work." Mason thought of every time they went out in search of answers. Robin would bring back books to fill his mind and parts to build that contraption.

"All was for nothing," Mason mumbled those words the day Robin died for that machine. "He could have survived like the rest of us." Mason laid down in his bed, taking off his boots and let the pain of his body pulse over him.

"Maybe it wasn't all for nothing," Mason assured himself. "He taught Tommy all he knew. And perhaps it did work after all." The words of Robin echoed in his brain. "Maybe there could be more to life than this."

Robin, the strong man that he was, always had a cheerful side to him, even in the bleak chaotic landscape.

Scavenging for food was his hobby, not just a means to survive. But, he had to venture further each time. Progressively becoming more dangerous. His scavenging was less about food and more about the artifacts he found. It came to a time when he would embrace an idea too far-fetched for Mason to continue to help.

The last time Robin ventured out into the darkness, he knew the risk was too great, but he had no choice. His family was almost wiped out. He believed in his machine more than in finding food.

Mason remembered that day very well when Robin came to ask for him to accompany him. Thinking Robin had lost his mind and weighing the risks to a mythical machine, Mason declined. He let Robin face his fate alone.

Robin did return, but not alone. He suffered severe injuries and fled to Mason's door, pleading entry. Mason did not answer. He heard the wolves outside but would not dare to open the hatch to his shelter. He stood by the door listening to Robin's cries with his guilt sinking further into his soul. By the time Mason opened his door, it was far too late. Robin's wounds were too great and a few days later he succumbed to his injuries.

"How could Emily ever forgive me for that?" Mason mumbled in his half-conscious state. The weight of his choice crushed his spirit as he replayed the scenario in his mind. Opting for Robin from the outset, he realized, would have ensured their safe return.

Mason tried to look after the family, but he questioned the time machine. He did not believe Robin created such a thing, but seeing it now and how Tommy left, twisted his stomach to knots.

On the other side of the door, the fire beset Jimmy. He remained in silence. The day's events still flashed before his eyes. The brightest of his memories were of Tommy entering the vortex of light.

"Jimmy," Emily, mustered the strength to call out to him. Her voice was soft and rasped from the dry air, and it struggled to carry very far. "I know what you are thinking. I forbid you from going to that machine again. Do you understand?"

"But..." Jimmy whimpered. His heart sank into his belly, worried about Tommy's return.

"I said, no!" she coughed up. "I'm sorry. I cannot lose you too. We don't know if Tommy even made it through or if he is alive and now that we are alone, we have to stay together. It's too dangerous."

"Yes, Mom..." he said with a frog in his throat.

Mason walked back into the room with a silent step. He overheard, but avoided Emily's dead stare. "I forgot the blankets. I think it's safe to get them now," he said, excusing himself as he climbed the ladder. After a moment,

Mason came back down with the fabric in hand, sat them next to Emily, and excused himself again.

Feeling the crack in her bones, Emily rose to make sure Jimmy would have a comfortable place to sleep for the night. She was so overused and weary. Her eyelids struggled to remain lifted. She laid next to the fire and fell sound asleep sharing the blanket with her son.

Jimmy could not rest, however. He had nightmares of Tommy and could not get the image of him begging for help out of his head. Jimmy tossed and turned, distressed. But, his young mind could not understand all that was happening. When Emily turned over and pulled the blanket from him, he knew it was his chance.

He arose from his makeshift bed and sat next to the now smolders that remained. He investigated the embers and soot. The soft glow was comforting to him. He took a deep breath in and began to sob to himself.

"I failed you, Tommy," he cried. "I do not know what to do. I don't know how to save you."

You are smarter than I am, Jimmy. I know you can find a way, Jimmy imagined Tommy saying.

The words were lifelike in his head as if he heard it in his ears. It sent shivers down his spine. Jimmy examined his sleeping mother and spoke her name. Silence followed. She was still resting and from what it seemed, exhaustion had her under a spell. So, Jimmy took a step towards the door.

He kept an eye on his mother as he made his way out of the room. He looked over and saw the hatch leading up to the surface. It wasn't a high climb, but for him, it may have been a challenge. He put his barefoot on the cool iron ladder. He seized the first one and stole up to the hatch, attempting to rotate the wheel. It was too tight for him.

"Don't open that!" Mason whispered. "Come on Jimmy, what are you thinking?"

"I... I..." Jimmy almost started crying but was silenced by Mason. "I just wanted to get back to the time machine."

"You can't do that. It's dangerous out there. What did your mother tell you?"

"I know, but... But... I..." The words were lost to Jimmy. He climbed down and sat on the floor.

"The hounds could still be out there. They will rip you apart. What would your mother think?"

Jimmy mustered the courage to say, "Tommy needs my help!"

"Jimmy, go back to bed," Mason said with pity. "You cannot disobey your mother. Go to bed or I will tell her."

Jimmy slipped into the distance with stealthy footsteps. His lips were quivering, and eyes rubbed raw. Jimmy's heart was like a thorn bush. He never felt so heavy. With Mother always on guard, it was already tough to sneak away, but now he had to worry about Mason as well. He knew it was dangerous, but he felt a sense of duty to his brother.

Mason called to him, keeping his voice quiet. "I'll help you with your machine. Just don't tell your mother."

Jimmy looked back at Mason and nodded. A small whisper from his lips, "Thank you."

"You will have to be patient. Your mother will not like me helping you. It will have to remain a secret. Now, go to bed. You will need your rest."

Jimmy went back to his small bed, his mother turned and asked if he was fine. Jimmy observed her unawareness, then responded with a brief nod. She brushed his forehead accepting his answer. He closed his eyes with a smile on his face with hope restored.

8 Ignition

"In earnest, I do not feel fatigued," Jin said to Marcus. He had his head back while sitting in a wooden chair. A set of blankets lay on the floor for him, but it sat undisturbed.

"Yeah, me neither," Marcus replied. Jin had given him the sofa to sleep, but Marcus was only laying back twiddling his thumbs. The cushion was inviting. Marcus was overdue for the kind of nap New Yorkers are never able to have. But, his eyes remained open, looking at all the knickknacks and assortment of doll decorations.

"In all honesty, I awoke a few hours ago. Then we came here, and it was night."

"Yeah, I'm not sure Tommy really has any sense of time," Marcus said, letting his frustration leak into his words. "He just thinks 'oh it's nighttime, these guys must sleep.'"

"How does a warden of time not have any sense of time?"

"He doesn't need sleep. He is always awake and frankly, I don't think he realizes how humans live anymore."

"He doesn't seem very serious."

"Not at all," Marcus continued, sitting up from his position. "Ever since he came to me, he has had this demeanor like a child."

Jin stood from the chair and peered out the window. The full moon bathed the city in a silvery glow. It created enchanting shadows that highlighted every corner like an oil painting. The night was clear, and the light was crisp. Elegant flowers bursting with blue and white lined the roads. At the end, a bridge to the east led out into the countryside of green grass and small plowed fields. "This place truly differs from my homeland. It appears almost darker, with the night feeling so sinister."

Jin could tell by Marcus's perplexed face, he hadn't the slightest clue of his words. "Tell me Marcus, what do you know about Tommy Kent?" His expression shifted from annoyed to a more irate tone.

"I don't know anything. All I know is that he said we have to save the world. He did not want to tell me anything more than that. The first day I met him, he spoke to me for nearly an hour and within that time, I really only understood he needed help. His rambling is bonkers."

"I don't understand the meaning of *bonkers*."

"Right… It just means silly or it's out of control. Again, he assembled most of the heroes and sat down to talk, but he only gave the same rambling speech he gave me. I think the others were too distracted by each other to really care. And the Cactus doesn't talk, so he's no help."

"You know more than that. What are you trying to hide? Is this a trick you wish to play on me?" His eyes flared a fiery orange. It was as if he was about to shift into a feral form. He held the windowsill with force, his nails sinking into the wood grain.

"Yes…" Marcus said but answering too soon. "No…I mean…Yes and no…No and No…"

"Marcus? You're perspiring!"

"Well, not me. I'm not intimidated by you. He is just nudging me."

"Yessss, Marcus, tell him," D urged as he shifted himself in a controlled movement to peek over Marcus's shoulder.

"By the great dragons above, what is that thing?" Jin asked.

"I am the darkness. I am the anger in man's heart," D replied. Its eye glowed yellow and mocked Jin by making its teeth like a tiger's.

"And you made an ally of this... thing?" Jin responded, gearing up the growl in his voice.

The Doll rolled across the floor and hid behind Jin. He took refuge behind his satchel, and he raised it to cover his face. He pointed at the demon, urging Jin to take caution.

"You know this thing?" Jin asked the Doll but received no answer.

"That's enough, D!" Marcus scolded. "Not exactly. I was to save the world from him. He ended up saving me." Marcus looked down at his hands. "This thing is a part of me now. But the Lady of Light instructed him to follow my orders."

"And he listens to her?"

"He has to, he can't disobey."

"What does this *D* know about Tommy?" Jin said, loosening his grip upon the wood. "Tell me!"

"When Tommy first took me through time. I saw a glimpse of the future. It is horrible. Worse than I have ever seen. I saw his future. It's shrouded in darkness."

"Can we trust him?"

"I'm not sure. D doesn't seem to." Marcus met Jin by the window to have a gaze at the night sky. He took a deep breath and relieved himself of his stress.

"Just like the therapist said…" Marcus mumbled to himself, continuing to take deep breaths. "He doesn't control you…"

"What are you saying?"

"I'm talking to myself. I have to keep in control. When I get angered, it's easier for D to control me. He wants to be free. I can sense it. I must always focus on my emotions." Intaking another smooth breath, Marcus released it slowly. "I haven't brushed my teeth in days…" he said to himself again. "Never mind me."

"Marcus, you are losing focus."

"I was hoping you would forget."

"What offense has D committed to stir such great anger within you?"

"The demon looked inside Tommy' head."

Protruding from Marcus' shadow, D spoke with a snarl. "It was blinding with pain!"

"D said there was only madness in his mind."

"Marcus sugar coated it. Like a living nightmare. Even I would have a hard time possessing him." D swirled around the room before also peering out the window with Marcus.

Jin gave them space, taking the Doll to sit it down on the chair as it was still frightened by the shadow. "That doesn't ease my nerves."

"I don't think we can trust him, Jin," Marcus said, staring at the moon. Before the incident, Marcus had always been a morning person, but the night was his nature now. D eased his way out of sight and remained within Marcus's shadow. He could feel the call of the darkness. He could feel the stress of the night and what was in store for them. Turning to face Jin Marcus continued, "I know he is hiding something from us. Why won't he tell us? He just expects us to come along despite not giving us any real reason to."

"It's the calling. I feel it, can't you?"

"I can feel it, but not the same way as before."

The Cactus, disturbed by the noise inside, walked towards the window. Jin saw him peering inside, listening to Marcus' rant. His sad expression made Jin feel as queasy as he looked.

As the conversation died, the Cactus returned to standing still, out of place in a country like this. Most passersby kept their distance from him and the thorns that adorned his skin. The neighbors were not accustomed to such plants but knew Mr. Gensen well and thought it to be one of his imports. Yet, he bore one flower on his head, despite all the conniving and scheming. The pedals reflected the cold light of the stars.

The Doll broke his stature upon the chair, to find himself a comfortable spot upon the coat rack. His arms wrapped around the hooks and let his head hang. He wanted to sleep through Marcus and Jin's conversation.

Jin knew it as he watched the curious toy uplift himself to get away. Jin felt the guilt of his heart twist as the Doll peered back at Marcus staring out the window. He walked over to him and put his cold iron hand on Marcus' shoulder.

"I'm sorry, George. Even for me, you still creep me out," Marcus said.

The Doll shrugged in response.

"I didn't mean to offend you. I don't know how much you understand. I can sense that you do to some degree. I just wish I could know. Uncertainty is my real fear."

"Then don't let it be," Jin said "We can confront Tommy when he returns. We will get our answers."

Marcus looked to Jin, "Do you think so? Will you have my back? What if I am right and he isn't what he seems? What if he is the threat? Maybe he is the reason why we feel like time is calling us again. What if we cannot get back home?"

"I shall stand by your side. I trust you now, Marcus. Not the demon, but you."

"Sorry for putting you through this…but thank you."

"You have a curious way of speaking, Marcus. I don't understand you at times, but it's the manner of how you say it that conveys your message."

An owl perched itself on top of the Cactus. The hoots resonated throughout the field and even called out to the trio of heroes in the room. Jin watched as it took flight. Its wide wings cast a shadow over the window. But soon, it returned with its prey. Jin watched the worried Cactus stand still. An owl ripped apart the tiny field mouse, kicking off the Cactus's flower. The pedals withered as the stem dried. Like shedding a tear, a drop of blood from the mouse ran down his face from his charcoal black eye.

Warm air and the soft scent of pine filled the room where Arnold and Christana sat playing chess. The fireplace gave light to the lounge of the library they now occupied. Fingers picked up a knight and placed it over a bishop. Another hand carried over a pawn and took the knight. The click of the wooden board made every move feel more intense. A cup of tea was steaming on the side table. The chairs rubbed and creaked as the unpolished leather cracked. The player felt satisfied as they clicked on the board, marveling at the queen in their hand. Christana looked at it in amazement.

"It is so well crafted and carved so beautifully," she said, peeking at it in the dim light.

"Ah, I remember a time when I could beat you without breaking a sweat. Maintenant, after five games, I can't even come close. C'est incroyable. Things have changed, n'est-ce pas?" Arnold wasn't afraid to show how astonished he was at how much she had grown.

Christana placed the queen among her collection of Arnold's pieces. Her fingers lingered on the cool, worn surface. She picked up her tea and took a slow, thoughtful sip. The warmth contrasted with the cold ache in her chest. Her eyes drifted to the fire, its flames dancing, yet failing to lift her spirits. On the mantle were portraits of people from history. They stared back at her, with their gazes frozen in time. Among them, she recognized Jin, his eyes filled with a familiar intensity. A heavy sigh escaped her lips as the weight of memories pressed down on her. The faces in the portraits were a poignant reminder of moments and people lost to the passage of time.

"Christana?" Arnold asked.

"You are the most intelligent person I ever knew, Arnold. Tu es peut-être…even the best that has ever lived."

"Please, I am just a mere servant to time. Je ne suis qu'un étudiant de la vie. I just try to help humanity. You have become more so. I cannot gain an edge on you. It's almost like you are reading my thoughts."

"I'm not what you assume," she replied, rubbing her chilled arm. She considered shifting to let the warmth bathe her skin. But instead, her fixed gaze met Arnold's, examining the depths of his eyes. "Intelligence, alas, is not my forte."

The Eight Heroes of Old

"I find that difficult to believe. Why would you even say that? What happened to you?"

"It's my gift. I simply know what move to make. That's all. I am not brave like you are. I've put my studies to rest."

"Why are you saying this?"

Leaning over the chessboard, Christana placed her hand out. She encouraged Arnold to take it. His eyes hidden behind the glare of the fire foretold a warning Christana did not wish to hear.

"I should not have let you go." Arnold's hand dropped into hers as she enveloped it gently. "I've missed this so much. It's just like old times." She looked at the warm glow on his face given by the flame. "If I was what I am now. There would not have been a need for you to… to…"

"Christana," Arnold said, taking her hand completely. "You are saying nonsense."

"I don't want this to end, Arnold. I don't. I'm so glad to have you back."

With a concerned sigh, Arnold moved his chair closer to her, and put his arm around her. "I know now how you feel. You must not blame yourself for what happened. The reason I stayed was because I was afraid…"

"Of what?"

"Christana, this is a blessing we have. A moment in time together. I will miss this too. Do not fret." Arnold sighed again, his mind running from his as he tried to assort the right words, but they all came out too soon. "I've been thinking about this whole conundrum. I will have to return to my time, Christana."

"What are you talking about?" Christana asked.

"I will have to go back to the time I was taken. We all will. I am not meant to be here."

"Don't say that! You cannot say that!" Christana pushed back from Arnold's chair. Her eyes brimmed with determination to refuse any other word Arnold would say. She held his gaze. "You are not suggesting you are going back to die!"

"Christana, it is my fate. My destiny. I will have to go back. You were young. Impressionable. I loved our friendship, but I must apologize. I never meant for you to be infatuated by me. It was not my intent." He tried to console her but was only met with resistance.

Christana's lips began to quiver. A tear shed from her eye and rolled onto her coat. She tried to keep them closed to seal the pain in her face. "Don't you think I know," she replied. "I wish it was anyone but you. I was a silly girl that fell in love. I'm not a girl anymore. I still feel how I did all those years ago. Now, as if my prayers were answered, you're back. Je le ressens maintenant. Je ressens la joie."

"You cannot think you can be so selfish to hold me here. It is my place to die there. I have made peace with that, why can't you?"

"I don't care! I refuse to let you go back!" Her fist pounded on Arnold's chest. She clenched his coat tightly as she wrinkled it. "You cannot leave me here! You cannot leave me by myself!"

"Christana, you understand better than anyone that I must fulfill this duty. Once our roles are completed, we return to our respective places in time."

"I will have no more of this," Christana said, the legs of her chair wailing as she stood. "Arnold, I love you. Je t'aime trop pour assister à ta mort. Not again…Not again." She concealed her lips behind her fingers and brushed the tears as she turned away. Christana dabbed her hand on her coat. Her breath caught in a stifled sniffle. She fixed Arnold with a gaze. It held both sorrow and determination. Her voice wavered, betraying her nervousness, as she spoke. "I don't wish for you to be a memory."

Arnold could not let out another word as Christana was abrupt in leaving. He sat back in his chair to watch the fire, pulling out his gadget to distract from the feelings. The flames dwindled, flickering on the charred log's rim. She only turned back when she was halfway up the stairs. She saw him sitting in his anguish, but she continued up the steps.

Christana sat herself upon a bench, and at that moment, she could not hold back anymore. Like she felt that day, the one that played so hauntingly in her mind. Her heart sank. She felt every beat in her hands as the memory pulsed through her. The loud sirens and flashing red lights. The orders of Arnold to Marlon to carry her away. Even the heavy slam of the steel door as Arnold sealed himself inside.

Her hands were damp from tears. She tried to wipe them away, but the anguish persisted. It crushed the hope she had clung to moments before. *It's not fair!* she thought. The bitter words tainted the fond memories. She understood his sacrifice, knew it was for the greater good, for the world's salvation. But it offered her no solace. She had lost the person who meant everything to her, and the pain surged back with relentless force. She ran her hand along the rough wooden arm of the bench, seeking some anchor in the storm of emotions.

Struggling to catch her breath, her eyes stung with tears, now tinted crimson from grief. The chill in the air mirrored the coldness in her shattered heart. Alone in the darkness, she mourned the loss that tore her apart.

Tommy continued his wandering. Bathed in the silver glow of the night sky, city streets whispered secrets in every shadow. It revealed the true essence of people. It laid bare their hidden fears and desires, which were unveiled under the cover of darkness

Some of the nocturnal inhabitants shunned society. Each had their own twisted and divergent thoughts. They lingered in the darkness, avoiding the tranquility of the day, highwaymen looking for an easy target. This might have unsettled most. But Tommy knew there were far more sinister beings lurking beyond sight. A glance at their direction, and a simple shift of his hand was enough to drive them away. He showed them the darkness within his own head. The evil snarls of the Hellhounds from his distant future. It didn't matter, as the thieves went looking elsewhere.

Tommy stood at an elevated sense of awareness. Dust kicked up behind his back, causing his jacket to float. He used his power to make his pose seem more epic. But despite everything, Tommy retreated deeper into his own thoughts. Encountering the horrors of the dark firsthand still plagued his mind. A glance for those men may have been small. But, for Tommy, monstrous Hellhounds ran rampant in his heart for years. Thoughts raced through his mind like a whirlwind. It was a torrent of faces, lights, shadows, and sounds all swirling together. His consciousness pulled in many directions, spanning valleys and mountains, rivers and deserts.

Tommy followed the moon's path, sensing winter's chill in the air. Each cobblestone step resonated softly. The earthy scent mingled with the shuffle of his shoes.

Eventually, he reached the town's center with the fountain that was the focal point of the park. He bent over to gaze into its tranquil waters. He watched as the water rippled and fell like starlight. The reflection showed a familiar face. It was the young boy he once was. He was contrasted with the image of his father standing behind him.

"Father?" he whispered, spinning around to confront what lurked behind him. But realization dawned swiftly. Looking into the water, his reflection couldn't have been clearer. His features, with defined shadows of wrinkles, resembled his father more than ever. Doubt gnawed at him. *Have I failed my father?* He thought. *I can't face those creatures. What am I to do? I can't fulfill Father's mission or protect my family while they still haunt my past…or is it my future? Maybe Marcus was right about this time travel being tricky stuff.* Tommy's mouth grew a smirk. But its brief sparkle vanished as he reminded himself of the distrust from Marcus. *I should speak to him.*

Tommy turned back to the full moon. Its brilliance filled his eyes. Coldness seeped into his hands resting on the stone. He felt a pervasive sense of distrust, not only in himself but among the entire team. They were like the moonlight, revealing what lay beneath the surface. "They doubt me," he said to himself. "I am not fit to lead this time… I'm still…What lies ahead is too shrouded in darkness, even if I wanted to look. I just have to trust that in the end, it will all come together."

Delving deeper into his thoughts, he saw them as broken glass fragments. They needed to be pieced together to form a whole. They needed unity, strength, and resolve to face the darkness that awaited them.

Enough time has passed, he thought to himself. *Arnold and Christana should be finished.* With a few mental slaps, he stowed his emotions. Motioning his hand, and imagining with clearer thoughts, Tommy whirled a portal and stepped through. He entered the library by the front doors and followed the beacon of light flickering in the other room. Within, he found Arnold sitting in a chair by himself. After confirming that Arnold was asleep, Tommy woke him with a reassuring hand on his shoulder.

"Did you find what you needed?" Tommy asked, beaming a warm smile at the professor.

"Yes! And more so. But we will need more."

"More time?"

"No, more research. I should have been more clear. These books are fantastic. I wish I could take them with me. I seem to have found an old story that…"

"Where is Christana?" Tommy interrupted while looking around. He didn't care much to listen to the rambling of Arnold about a story he himself had read a thousand times.

Arnold took his teacup in hand and examined it for anything left, but his lips remained thirsty. "She is upset," he muttered, setting the cup down and resuming his thoughtful pose: upright in posture, gazing into the fire.

"Why?"

"She doesn't want me to go back."

"Back to your time?"

"Yes. She wants me to stay with her. She thinks we could have a life together."

"And you know better?"

"Of course, I do. I am not subject to being blinded by emotions. I am a rational being. I always have conclusions before I have a question. I am just but a fragment in time, as we all are. Without a doubt, I must return to my time unless I wish to disrupt the order of things." He sighed and stood from the chair. He walked over to the small smoldering fire and extinguished it with the tool beside the bricks. "I am not meant to be here. No matter how much she wishes me to be."

"I'm sorry, she will come to terms with that," Tommy replied and took the kettle from where Arnold was working by the fire. The residual heat within the power was enough to heat the water back to a fine steeping temperature. He added more tea to the kettle but was too impatient to wait. "We live a difficult life as heroes," Tommy said, forcing time to make the tea ready in an instant. "We never really have anything for ourselves…Except maybe tea."

"I know. She knows it too, but it is more difficult for her."

"She will understand. Don't worry, my friend." Tommy drank the tea after using his power yet another time to cool it, then slurped it down without hesitation.

"I have something to confess."

"What's that?"

"She speaks of her emotions, and she isn't afraid to make them known. She is strong in that regard. She knows what she wants, and she knows how to let others know of their mistakes."

"Where are you going with this?"

"This whole time I never knew what I meant to her, but perhaps I did. She had always been my greatest friend, I never saw her in that light, but now I think I am starting to…"

"It's going to be morning soon…We should get going."

"I understand. Forgive me in my rambling state. It's not your concern. But I do have something to discuss with you," Arnold said, cleaning his glasses before returning them to his eyes.

"Save it for when we get back to the others."

"I'll go get Christana."

"I'm here," Christana said walking down the stairs.

Arnold scrambled to get words out, he made half an apology but stopped to change his tactic. In the end, his stumble made him look like a fool.

"It's all right," she closed the distance between them. "Don't say anything," she whispered as she ran her hand over his chest.

Arnold pulled her arms closer and moved his hand around her back. Her eyes held the youthful blue yet sang a familiar song. Christana's fingers memorized the grooves over his cheek as it felt his abrasive stubble. Their lips drew closer as his heart raced. Pulling her in, it felt as though their thoughts had become one. Cool to the touch, the kiss was simple yet ended sooner than either had hoped. Still, their hands remained intertwined, and their gaze never wavered, even as they parted.

Tommy cleared his throat, stepping back and into the fire tool. The large crash soiled the moment, but only by his mistake.

"We should get going," Christana said, taking her helmet in hand and offering Arnold his.

"I believe you are right," Arnold said, holding her hand as he took his helmet from her.

"I'm sorry for ruining the moment," Tommy said.

"Apologies are on us," Arnold said. "We must be more professional. We are still on duty."

"Make no mention of it," Tommy replied while forcing a portal open. "Take those books with you!"

"But these books were to be lost to time. Wouldn't that disrupt the order?"

"I've taken them before, it makes no difference," Tommy chuckled.

Arnold did as he liked. He took a few of the other novels he had not had a chance to read. He adorned his helmet, cherishing Christana's hand in his before walking through the portal with Tommy.

9 Despair

The sun had begun to rise over Hanover and the birds were already taking flight and singing their songs. Upon the door to the emporium, Tommy saw the flower from the Cactus wilted before the doorstep. Like a prolific vision, his heart sank, but knocked on the door regardless. Marcus stumbled through his greeting, eyes half-closed, fighting to stay awake.

"Good morning, Marcus! I hope you had a good rest, are you ready to go?"

"Ready? It's bedtime!" Marcus responded with an aggravated tone.

"Bedtime? I said I would be back in the morning."

"Yes, you said you would be back. But you did not really think we were going to sleep, did you? I was wide awake. So was Jin. We've been up all night!"

"Why did you stay up all night? You should have been sleeping?"

"You really have no concept of time, do you?"

"What? Of course, I do!" Tommy matched Marcus' tone and brought a stern voice to bat.

"Then why do you think we will go to sleep just a few hours after we woke up?"

"Actually, Tommy, Christana and I would like to sleep as well," Arnold added. "I only nodded off in that chair briefly before you found me."

"I don't believe this!" Tommy declared and threw his hands in the air.

Marcus stepped outside pushing into Tommy. With threatening eyes, Marcus continued his aggression. "We are going to sleep!"

"Tommy, we are all tired," Jin said. "You must understand, right?"

"I'm really thinking he doesn't." Marcus looked to Arnold and Christana for assurance.

"Marcus please, you have to just get some rest. You aren't thinking clearly. We can rest if that is what you all really need," Tommy tried to reason in a nervous voice.

"It's not about that anymore. You really don't have a clue, do you?" Pushing ensued with Marcus forcing Tommy into the fields.

Tommy made every effort to escape from his friend, but Marcus backed him into a ditch. While Marcus steamed in his rant, Tommy let out a forceful yell and unleashed a hint of his powers, knocking Marcus to the ground.

"Enough Marcus!" Tommy shouted in retaliation.

"All right, that's how you want to play this," Marcus said, brushing off the mud.

Jin's claws gripped the door frame as he stepped out of the house, following the noise. He watched as Marcus confronted Tommy, asking all the questions they had been pondering for the last few hours. But when Tommy knocked Marcus down, Jin sprang into action.

The wind picked up as the sun's rays burst over the horizon. Christana stepped forward towards Marcus, but the Cactus put his arm in front of her. By this time, Jin was next to Marcus standing in his furious form. The eyes of the Tiger were almost tormenting to gaze into. Jin's paws grasped the sun's glow at their tips. He swooped at Tommy, attempting to seize him. Tommy evaded each attack, sidestepping Jin's grasp.

Marcus stood and pushed past Jin, calling D to bring forth more power, as Tommy began stumbling and tripping over his own feet. The two proved a worthy confrontation.

"Marcus, I will tell you," Tommy tried to reason as his power began to waver. "Now is not the time. You can trust me. I will explain everything, but..." Tommy's words were silenced as Marcus unleashed D to devastating effect.

The world remained quiet. The birds stopped their chirping. The heroes in that moment halted their breath. Like darkness as an entity itself was present, D held Tommy by the throat, lifting him well off the ground. The shadow grew around them and the sun seemed so distant. The demon gripped tighter.

"Marcus, ease up!" Arnold exclaimed.

"I want answers now!" Marcus demanded. "You have no plan. You have no clue. You gathered us all up to die!" Marcus stood behind D, asking all the questions. "Why is it that I am the last hero?"

"Marcus, you should ease yourself," Jin said, his voice reverberating with regret now seeing the demon in person.

"You looked into your future, didn't you?" Tommy uttered with a fainting breath. "Did he show you? I told..."

"No! I didn't...But the demon showed me yours...Let him go, D."

"As you command..." D laughed.

"I saw what comes from your work. You are the cause of all this, aren't you?"

"Marcus, what are you talking about?" Christana asked.

"I saw what he has done. This man doesn't have a plan. He never takes anything seriously. I have seen a part of his life. The part where he tried to save this world. It is all because of him."

Marcus forced the return of his shadow. "I believe he means us harm."

Tommy laid on the ground, his body wracked with violent coughs. His hand clutched desperately at his throat as he struggled to soothe the relentless burning. He took ragged gasps. Each one scraped painfully through his dry, tight airway.

Marcus's eyes turned red, and the demon smiled in his mind. *Tell him Marcus. Tell him how you really feel,* D said in Marcus' mind. *You shouldn't trust him. We have both seen what he has done.*

"Tell them! Tell them you caused it!" Marcus demanded.

Tommy, still convulsing with harsh coughs, looked up at Marcus, his eyes locking onto his. "Marcus," he gasped, his voice strained and broken, "all of this..." He stumbled, another fit of coughing wracking his body. "All of this is your fault."

Marcus, he is lying, D snarled.

Marcus turned his back on Tommy, his shoulders tense. He looked down at his trembling hands. "I don't believe this," he muttered, his voice filled with doubt.

"Marcus. I know it is too soon. Please, let me explain."

"Do you think I am an idiot?"

"Marcus! Just listen to him!" Christana said.

"Marcus, I have something I need to tell you. Something to tell all of us. I believe it is your demon," Arnold declared, his voice steady and grave.

"No, it's not me. I already saved the world in my time. My calling was fulfilled."

Tommy, finally free of his agonizing breaths, stood and placed his hand on Marcus. "You have to listen to me."

Marcus turned to face him. His expression softened as he looked into Tommy's green eyes. They now held a clear, unwavering truth.

"Manson Herald. Do you know him?"

"Yes. What does this have to do with me?"

"Marcus. In your fight against your enemy. You caused a lot of destruction. Because of the circumstances in your story, the people lost faith in their hero."

"But they still cheer for me. My time has been very prosperous!" Marcus tried to explain.

"Marcus," Tommy continued. "This threat is worse than you can imagine."

"Who is Manson Herald?" Jin asked.

"He was a political leader in Marcus's time. He proclaims that the world has had enough of heroes. He persuades everybody to stop putting faith into a false prophecy. They are strong enough to take care of themselves."

"How can he do that?" Marcus asked. "How does that even cause the end of the world as you say?"

Arnold stepped forward. "I have reason to believe you do not make it in your time. I have done some measurements in our travels, and I have done my research. I found that magic is dying. I still have more observations to make. I don't know how to explain it, but it becomes weaker and weaker by the day."

"What does that mean for me? Still, I believe I am powerful enough to stop any threat. It's not like evil can enter the world as long as a hero lives. Right? Isn't that the prophecy? *As a hero lives, the world will prosper, people will know peace, and the world shall see no evil.*"

"Yes, Marcus, you are correct, but…" Tommy intervened, but stopped himself like he was debating in his own mind.

"But what?" Marcus demanded to know.

"But evil already exists in the world. Your demon. You say you control him, but darkness already has a presence, a foot in the door, so to speak."

Marcus fell to his knees, grabbing a handful of grass and clenching it tightly. "So, this is it? You are assembling them to kill me? I am the great evil? Do I turn on everyone like the false hero turned on them?"

The Cactus stepped forward, seized Marcus by the shirt, and lifted him high into the air.

"No, Cactus! Put him down!" Tommy pleaded, desperation in his voice. "Please!"

The Cactus gently set Marcus back on the ground.

"I know you don't like the demon, Cactus, but trust me. We are not here to kill you, Marcus." Tommy, with as friendly of a character as he could muster, assisted Marcus to his feet. "You have a calling. We all do. It's the reason why you all came with me. You heard it in your hearts, felt that same darkness lurking over the world."

"I am sure of it now," Jin agreed.

"And it grows by the day," Arnold added.

"Marcus in your current timeline as it sits, Manson Herald would proceed to convince the world to stop believing in heroes. They all believe in him. They all worship him…But worst of all, he convinces *you* to stop believing in heroes," Tommy said while trying to console Marcus.

"What? How can that be? How could I…"

"You see, Marcus. Your demon has been so ruthless. You kill people just to protect others. You stop the *bad guy* in awful ways. Especially for…" Tommy paused as he rationed in his own mind again.

"Tommy?" Arnold asked. "What?"

"For you, Marcus...it's too much for you. You realize that you should give up your powers and your right as a hero."

"Marcus, is that true? Are you really that brutal?" Christana asked, her voice trembling with fear. "How can he convince a hero to give up their powers?"

"As Manson gains popularity, he gains strength. Even to the point where world leaders name him ruler. On the day of his coronation is the last day of recorded history."

"Everybody?" Marcus asked, stowing the sorrow within himself. "My mom...My wife?"

"I'm sorry Marcus, you all perish," Tommy replied, matching his tone.

"And the demon?"

"He serves the Defier. His allegiance is to him. But he never forgets the imprisonment you had over him."

D's laugh echoed like a murder of crows as it stepped out from Marcus's shadow. "Very good, Time Warden." His teeth, crooked and sharp as razor blades, emerged from the darkness of his face. A dim fire burned in his chest, suffocating itself in its own smoke. "If you think my allegiance isn't to Marcus, then you are sadly mistaken. I am here to help him. The Lady of Light commanded it of me. I serve him."

"I'm sure you do," Jin said, baring his teeth at it.

"You are fearful of me, aren't you, Tiger. I can see into your soul and sense it," D snared.

Jin remained silent.

"Don't worry. I won't hurt any of you. Not unless Marcus commands it," he laughed. "I wouldn't betray Marcus as long as he wouldn't betray me." He sank into the shadow cast by Marcus.

"I still don't believe this," Marcus said with failure under his breath.

"Don't be hard on yourself Marcus. You aren't meant to know your future. It's not your fault. You were just doing what you thought was best as the hero. Manson Herold has his way with words and is very convincing."

"So, why do you need us exactly?" Christana asked.

"Yes, Marcus, what did you mean when you said he was the cause of this?" Arnold asked.

"It's okay, Marcus, I'll tell them," Tommy said. "You see, every attempt I made to save this catastrophe from happening, ended in failure. Time always corrects itself and every timeline returns to the original at some point. Every attempt I make still ends in the world, my time, to be black, chaotic, and desolate. By my hand I see everything that Marcus explains come to fruition. If I kill Manson Herald, someone else takes his place."

"It's bigger than one person," Marcus said quietly.

"Now you see, Marcus," Tommy laughed, helping to lighten the mood. "If I try to convince Marcus not to give up being a hero, it only makes him believe he should even more. Everything I do ends in failure."

"How will this be different?" Jin asked.

"How can we stop this from happening?" Christana added.

"The gifts of the Allfather fade in my time. The reason why I cannot do this alone is that no one believes in heroes anymore. Together, I know we can make them believe again."

"If we unite, then is it certainly possible," Jin replied. "I know my calling."

"It won't be easy. We will still have to stop Manson from taking the throne."

"We can stop him. I won't let him change my mind. I've already had that happen. It won't again," Marcus said with determination. "I'm not a fan."

The Cactus stood tall, his form outlined against the rising sun, granting shade to the group as he stared back at them. The Porcelain Doll walked towards him in appreciation of his great size. The two exchanged a greeting in silence before they rejoined the others.

"We aren't going to put our hands together and say some weird *hoorah*, are we? Please spare me from any of that," Marcus said.

"What's wrong Marcus, don't you have any team spirit?" Arnold laughed.

Tommy joined with laughter that inspired others to do the same. A moment of bonding for certain between the heroes, as they all calmed their nerves together.

"We're all exhausted. Let's get some rest," Christana said with a yawn, rubbing her eyes before heading indoors.

"Christana, wait," Tommy said. "Let's go to a place a little bit more comfortable."

Tommy opened a portal, transporting them back to Christana's mansion. The spacious estate had ample rooms and resources for everyone. Arriving at night ensured they could rest undisturbed by harsh daylight. The mansion appeared exactly as they had left it. Marlon, retired to his guest house, preserved it in flawless condition.

"Go ahead and get some rest. We have another hero to get tomorrow," Tommy said.

The Cactus remained outside and returned to his resting position. The Doll found himself comfortable on the coat rack and let his head hang from the highest hook. Marcus found the same room he had not far from Christana's master bedroom and adjacent to Arnold's. Down the hall, he could see Arnold walking Christana to her room.

"Bonne nuit, Christana," Arnold said before turning away.

As he did, Christana reached out and grabbed his arm, pulling him closer, and kissed him on the cheek. "Je suis désolée pour tout à l'heure, Arnold," she said softly.

He gazed into her clear blue eyes, finding comfort in their clarity. Her soft golden hair and gentle voice were soothing to him. He didn't want to return to his own time; he now understood what he would be leaving behind. Reminding himself that this time together was fleeting, he gently touched her face. Feeling her cold cheek, as soft as snow, continuing to find solace in the winter sky that held her eyes.

"Reposez-vous bien, Christana," Arnold said, his lips moving as slow as could be, wishing to meet hers. He glanced over and noticed Marcus watching them from the doorway. With a heavy heart, Arnold turned and made his way to his room, his footsteps echoing in the old house.

Marcus shut the door behind him and collapsed onto his bed. "Do you realize what's at stake?" he asked D.

"Oh, dear Marcusss, I do. I understand fully. You wish to be with your family. You want things to go right."

"Are you with me?"

"I do as I must, Marcus."

"But are you with me?"

"Yes, Marcus. I will obey."

Marcus flipped the switch on the bedside lamp, settling into the sheets. His room featured a small fireplace, and the demon kindled a fire within it. Familiar with human needs, the demon tended to them as one would a shepherd caring for sheep. D floated in the air like a ghastly wolf's head. Wisps of smoke and shadow surrounded him, bellowing the flames with his breath. He often assumed this form when he did not wish to draw power from Marcus. A vestige of his ancient times.

Marcus slept soundly while the demon kept watch. The demon was bound to Marcus and couldn't betray him. He longed for freedom but knew that leaving Marcus meant solitude.

Jin lit some incense he had packed, discovering a lighter in one of the drawers. He could smell the oil inside it. Like solving a puzzle, he worked it until it ignited with a spark flashing in his hand. Times had certainly changed, and he felt distressed by how the world had evolved. Observing some automobiles outside, this thing called technology seemed very strange indeed. Tonight, he missed his farm and his chickens dearly. He didn't have much, but he had never known anything more.

Placing a cushion on the floor, he settled down and began to meditate. Collecting his thoughts, he entered a Zen state, his nightly ritual that calmed his nerves and eased him into a deep sleep. The beast inside him was restless. It was much like Marcus's own dark half, with a natural instinct for aggression. However, this meditation soothed that side of him, erasing the troubles of his mind. The smoke rose and filled the room, creating a symphony in his head accompanied by the sound of rain.

Tommy sat alone at the table where they had spoken the previous night. He waited patiently for the others to awaken. The hours dragged on. Each tick of the clock echoed in his ears. Impatience gnawed at him; waiting and stillness were not traits he embraced. Tommy shared his sentiment about wasting time, finding sitting idly unbearable. His mind raced with thoughts of the faces he had seen, faces doomed if he failed in his mission. Sleep eluded him, as it always did, leaving him restless.

Growing antsy, he stood and tried to dispel the haunting images by pacing the room. As he paced, he examined the pictures on the walls and mantelpiece. He scrutinized each one closely. Restless, he wandered through the house, taking in the décor until he reached the rooms of the others. Arnold's thunderous snores signaled a profound slumber. Christana's room he avoided, sensing her dreaming presence. Marcus's room was last. Peering through the keyhole, he met the eye of the demon staring back at him. Unperturbed, he moved away and descended downstairs to the front door.

Passing the Porcelain Doll hanging on the coat rack, he stepped outside. Tommy found solace next to the Cactus, which stood peacefully. Though he remained silent, he began to converse with him. The Cactus stirred, regarding Tommy as the little boy he once was. He grew a fruit and offered it to Tommy, the sweetness dripping down his chin. Grateful, Tommy thanked the Cactus and shared more of his adventures with him. In the Cactus, he found a friend, and the Cactus stayed by his side.

Joe Cordova

10 Tooth and Claw

Marlon woke up in his rather large but comfortable bed. It was very early in the morning before the sun broke the horizon. Birds were beginning their early routine the same as he did. He dressed in fine clothing and combed over his thinning hair. It was graying on the sides but kept its red sheen on top and upon his mustache. After fitting his watch upon his wrist and tightening his laces, he grabbed his watering can and began to fill it.

The indoor plants thirsted but they could wait. His small red bird began to rampage inside its cage. Marlon placed feed upon the small dish along with a nut for the bird to play. Once the indoor needs of his plants and pets were met, he adorned his small brown jacket before stepping outside.

The morning breeze was always the nicest to him. He took a refreshing whiff of the pollinated air and was glad to finally receive help with the yard work. He began watering his small garden on the side of his home, appreciating the new flowers. He then scraped the mud off his boots and walked around to the front where Christana lived. To his surprise, he saw Tommy sitting on the porch steps still talking with the Cactus.

"Tommy?" Marlon asked while walking towards the two. "And Cactus? You are back already? Have you saved the world?"

"Well, for you it's just the next day, but for us..." Tommy paused for a minute, stroking his chin in contemplation. "It has been about the same amount of time actually." Tommy laughed while he poked the Cactus, but he stood still in his slumber. "But to answer your question, we have not had the chance. We are just staying here for the moment. I must say, you used to keep this place in top shape."

"I do as Christana needs, but it has been more difficult to tend to everything in recent years." He looked at Tommy with full anticipation. "Is she here?" Marlon asked, removing his worn driver cap.

His rugged face, marked by years of toil and worry, softened with concern. Marlon's hands, calloused from a lifetime of hard work, trembled slightly as he gripped the brim of his hat. He had taken care of her for so long, his protective nature as strong as his broad shoulders. Glancing up at her window, his sharp blue eyes noticed the curtains were still drawn, deepening the lines of worry on his weathered brow.

"She is perfectly safe with me, Marlon," Tommy responded, standing to show his comfort with an awkward pat on the shoulder.

"I do feel anxious. I was certain I would never see her smile again. Her face lit up like I had never seen it before. The professor was never a man for love. He had always been too caught up in his studies, and when he wasn't doing that, he was at the university teaching."

"Well, they certainly are getting along now," Tommy exclaimed. "They are inseparable, but they do make a good team. Without them, I am not sure I would still be here."

"Have you assembled the rest?" Marlon asked, piquing his curiosity. He twirled the ends of his thick mustache, which often got in the way of his speech. He had always been fond of the old heroes. Never in his life had he imagined meeting two, let alone the entire group. He held serving them in high esteem, a true privilege. Marlon, always the courageous type, had faced his fair share of adventures. Now, he was overcome with delight. He yearned for an encounter with the others. His eyes sparkled with anticipation

"We have not had the chance to meet Owen or Gorn. We had to… take a break. But I do have the Doll who Mr. Gensen called George, and the beloved Golden Tiger."

"That's marvelous!" Marlon cheered. "Jin had always captivated the mind of Arnold. Is he inside?"

"There will be plenty of time for that," Tommy joked. "I have made sure to schedule rest in our adventures now."

"And what about this one?" Marlon asked, walking up to the Cactus. He sized up the tall desert sentinel, his eyes wide with admiration. He had never seen such a remarkable creature. "Pretty sharp, you are," he said, as if trying to awaken him from his desert slumber. "Thank you for fixing the garden," he added. He patted the Cactus on the bald spot. His voice was full of gratitude.

The Cactus began to shake, his tall form swaying gently as if imitating a morning stretch. His roots anchored in the rich, muddy soil, securing him firmly in place. Around his feet, the ground was a vibrant patch of overgrown grass and flowers. These blossoms were a striking yellow with mint-colored stems. Yet, they carried no discernible fragrance.

As the saguaro bent down, he seemed to examine Marlon with a curious gaze. The Cactus's green skin shimmered, reflecting the golden hues of the rising sun. He made a surreal and extraordinary gesture. He extended an arm towards Marlon, offering a handshake. Marlon, awestruck, reached out to meet the Cactus.

"What magic makes this creature?" Marlon said in confusion and amazement. "I'm sorry, I do not wish to offend. You are more than just a creature. And I thought Owen was the most remarkable."

"He is one of my favorite heroes," Tommy said. "He knows human formalities very well."

"Is that so?"

The Cactus lacked digits to wrap around Marlon's hand, but it still motioned with him. The timing was perfect. Not too long, not too short. Marlon examined his hand after to see it unharmed as the spikes returned to the Cactus's arm after.

"Tommy, in my future, do I live to see this great hero?"

"Yes, my friend. And your spotlight of fame returns to you. New channels and magazines all want a word from you. They all want your take on a new hero…"

"A new hero?" Marlon asked, drawing conclusions in his own mind. "That would have to mean…"

"You know, this hero is an excellent dancer!" Tommy said, his hand curled up on his mouth, as if he wanted Marlon to take the bait for distraction. Tommy sighed to himself, knowing he may have let a little too much information slip past his lips.

Marlon closed his eyes. His heartbeat slowed as he felt the weight of all the troubles that had befallen Christana.

Doubt gnawed at his mind, but in his heart, he almost knew the truth. As the pain sank deeper, he took a deep breath, and it was gone.

Opening his eyes, confusion struck him as he tried to remember where he was. The first sight that greeted him was Tommy standing before him, arm outstretched and hand wide open.

"I'm sorry, Tommy. I seem to have forgotten what we were discussing. It happens from time to time," Marlon said, pausing to find his words and catch his breath. "Where were we? Oh my, I am winded."

"We just finished our morning jog," Tommy said convincingly. "And we were in the middle of speaking about how great a dancer the Cactus is!"

"Oh right! It's always important to keep fit! Yes, I remember now. That is what got us on the topic of how the Cactus stays fit."

"Of course!" Tommy replied with his cheesiest cheer.

"How did you learn to do that?" Marlon asked the Cactus. "How are you so unique?"

"Do you want him to give you a demonstration?" Tommy asked with a smile on his face and marched himself over to a bench beside the courtyard and garden. "I know he loves showing off. Is this enough space for you?"

The Cactus nodded. His tall form swayed slightly as he began to pace the area. He shifted his feet to feel out his surroundings. Marlon stood nearby, a bit frightened by the sheer size of the saguaro but couldn't tear his eyes away.

The Cactus moved to the center, jumping in place trying to become more limber. Once set, he assumed a stance, one leg back and arms poised for a swinging motion. He began a four-step rhythm, pulling one arm back while gracefully raising the opposite one. With surprising agility, the saguaro's ginga grew to an incredible array of movements. Legs swung upward, crossing over to a handstand. While balanced, spins and twirls kicked in every direction. Limbs disturbed the air, stealing the pedals from the flowers. It was a mesmerizing display of fluidity and strength.

The Cactus kept up the pace, his movements a blend of elegance and power. He motioned for more kicks. Each done with perfect precision. Then, he executed a flawless backward somersault. The spectacle amazed Tommy and Marlon. Their earlier talk about fitness was forgotten in the face of the saguaro's show.

Tommy began clapping to the Cactus's rhythm. His hands echoed the beat as the saguaro continued his fast dance. The perfect blend of both beautiful and lethal power. "While a performer is dancing, they are usually accompanied by a drum along with another assortment of instruments. Clap with me, Marlon!" Once the rhythm was established with their hands, Tommy stomped his feet to add base to the beat.

As the dance reached its climax, the saguaro's movements became a blur of speed and brawn. His final moves were so swift that it was difficult to see the immense master of the arts in action. In one breathtaking motion, the saguaro kicked the head off a garden statue.

The Cactus returned to his starting position, holding the pose for a moment before taking a deep bow. Tommy's claps grew louder, joined by Marlon's hesitant applause. The saguaro's performance was extraordinary. It left both men in awe of the Cactus's skill and elegance.

"Yes, Bravo!" Marlon exclaimed, standing with Tommy. "It was truly an honor to watch you perform. Such talent! What is this dance called? And where did you learn this?"

The Cactus motioned to Tommy. His manner showed pride and a touch of sadness. But, he was clearly pleased to have entertained Marlon so well.

"You see," Tommy began, turning to Marlon, "he had a family once. A human family. They practiced in their garden in front of him while he was still a young Cactus, not yet a hero. Not yet sentient." Tommy's voice softened with reverence. "They would dance and train, and he absorbed their movements, their grace, and their passion. Over time, he learned to dance just like them. When the

Lady of Light graced him, he gained that knowledge. He still practices it in their honor."

"You must bring them a great amount of honor. Thank you again!"

"That was very good," Jin said while approaching them from the house.

"Good morning, Jin!" Tommy said, welcoming him to the garden. "Where are my manners? Marlon, this is Jin, the Golden Tiger as history knows him. Jin, this is Marlon, friend of Christana and Arnold."

"This place is very peaceful. I went outside to get fresh air. Normally, I feed my chickens and tend to my fields early. I hope they are fine," Jin said, concerned for his animals.

"I do a lot of the same, my friend. However, Christana does not have chickens. I do tend to my garden and a lot of the house business of Christana."

By this time, the birds were chirping. The wind was gentle and carried the scent of the new flowers toward them. A soft gust sent petals swirling around the Cactus as it approached. Jin took a deliberate pace towards the towering saguaro. His calm presence stood out against the blooming garden.

"Very interesting dance, you do. What is it called?" Jin asked.

"It's called capoeira, and it is more than just a dance," Tommy declared. "He truly is a fascinating hero, the most fascinating to me, at least. His dance is a form of martial art from Brazil."

"A martial art?" Jin said, turning his head from Tommy to the Cactus. "I wouldn't mind sparring with you. I practice in the arts of fu jow pai. Tiger style kung fu for those of you who aren't familiar with the language."

"He is clearly taller than you, even in Tiger form he is still twice or three times your size," Tommy said, putting his faith in the Cactus.

"I can take it. I always look for ways to practice and better myself. It teaches discipline and patience," Jin replied, getting himself ready and removing his outer layer and garments down to his pants and bare feet.

"I would really wish to see!" Marlon said with over excitement.

The Cactus stepped forward. He was unyielding in his resolve to face the Golden Tiger. He was almost eager to test his mettle against such a renowned opponent. The Cactus lacked deep knowledge of history or other fighting styles. But he presented himself with honor.

"When we first met, Cactus," Jin started as he faced his opponent. "You pulled Marcus back so quickly, it was like you wished to fight against me. Is this true?"

A simple nod was the only response.

"The Tiger and the Cactus, tooth and claw!" Tommy whispered to himself. Like a child, he smiled.

"Is this safe?" Marlon asked.

"We'll be fine," Jin said, letting his beast emerge from his skin. His transformation was like finding a mine full of gold.

The Cactus stepped forward, performing his traditional sign of respect to Jin. They faced each other with mutual determination. Jin took a deep breath, the air stirring around him as sunlight gleamed on his golden sheen. He spread his claws at his sides, in contrast from his human form, the Tiger was well defined. Arms strong as stone as he awakened them. Jin assumed a stance, focusing his claws towards the Cactus.

The Cactus moved with surprising elegance as the Tiger closed the gap. The two opponents were magnificent in their movements, evenly matched in strength and speed. Every swipe from the Tiger was deftly dodged by quick footwork from the Cactus. In response, the Cactus swung his legs like flails at the large cat, executing a frenzy of majestic kicks. Their combat was like a detailed painting. Each move and countermove formed its vibrant colors. It was like a waterfall meeting a rocky bottom.

Jin had never faced a foe so large or threatening, but he relished the challenge. The Tiger tried gaining a foothold advantage, but the agile Cactus rarely kept his feet on the ground. Attempts to gain a height advantage were also thwarted. The saguaro's towering form easily matched any leap. Jin's last resort was to use his unique skill. It was a short-phase teleportation to disorient his opponent. Movement so quick, his leaps placed him wherever he pleased.

Eventually, the Tiger's claws found their mark upon the soft green flesh of the Cactus. But the Cactus was not defenseless. Regret overcame Jin's eyes as he withdrew. He pulled spikes from his paw in frustration with his menacing teeth. This distraction allowed the Cactus to land a blow. It flung the Tiger backwards through the air. The Cactus began a rhythmic sway, his feet, hips, and arms undulating.

Jin twisted his body and tail, landing gracefully on his feet. Despite the fierce battle, he felt grateful for the experience. The blow from the Cactus satisfied the beast within him, signaling an end to the fight. Laughter filled the air as they acknowledged it had all been in good fun. Both combatants had displayed impressive strength, and their mutual respect had deepened.

The Cactus ceased his ginga and performed a bow. To show his appreciation, he grew fruit atop his head and offered a bright magenta pink fruit to Jin. Jin savored the sweet taste that left a lasting fur stain. The Cactus then generously offered the fruit to everyone there. A gesture of friendship and celebration after their lively encounter.

"That was a spectacular show…" Marlon paused for a moment as he accepted the fruit. "It feels strange just calling you Cactus."

The Cactus remained mute, presenting him with more fruit as a hospitable offering

"This is really good fruit! It's delicious, but I cannot take it anymore!"

The Cactus grew fruits not only on his head but also on his arms. He attempted to communicate with Marlon, despite lacking the ability to speak. He gestured with his arms and signaled with his face. But he had limited expression. His scar that resembled a mouth did little to convey the message to Marlon.

"They called him the Capoeira Cactus in his time or the Saguaro Guardian," Tommy began. "He didn't have much of a name."

The Cactus began to motion again. It grew a fruit and gave it to Tommy.

"Curious hero. Are you trying to say you had a name?"

The Cactus nodded in response. He was indeed trying to tell Marlon something.

"Does your name have to do with this fruit?" Jin asked.

The saguaro nodded and was delighted as Jin guessed the first clue. The group pondered for a few moments, trying to unravel the mystery of the Cactus's name. Each took turns guessing, but only continued to dishearten the Cactus.

11 Life on Sunday Morning

Soft light peeked through a crack in the drawn curtains. Christana stayed motionless sitting on her bed. A small wooden desk nestled by the window displayed faded letters tied with ribbon. They were remnants of her correspondence from the war. A worn, leather-bound journal lay open beside them. Its pages were filled with inked memories. They were of battles fought and friendships forged.

A handwritten letter upon the wood. Her sergeant's words were imprinted on the paper of her bravery. The envelope was beside it along with the knife that opened it. Paperclipped to the corner, a vintage phonograph played a faint melody. Its nostalgic tunes weaved through the room like whispered echoes of the past. The air carried faint scents of old leather and polished wood. Hints of lavender mixed with the subtle aroma of freshly brewed coffee from the nearby kitchen.

Christana laced up her best pair of boots, her Sunday shooting boots, preparing to step out. The leather was weathered but tough. The strap had clear signs of wear. The silver buckle was tarnished and dulled with time. As she caught her reflection in the mirror, she saw a woman staring back at her. A girl she did not recognize these days. The pain of Arnold's departure lingered, casting a shadow over her thoughts. She didn't like the person she had become in the following years. The memory haunted her still. It was a weight she carried with every step.

Her long blonde hair draped over her shoulders as she took her rifle in hand and settled at her desk. Taking the polish cloth, she ran it over the metal, which had not seen use in quite some time. The wood of the rifle was dark with hints of cherry. Christana ran her finger over the scars ingrained in the wood. Her gentle palm held her own scars that she wore on her side. She spent her younger years in the midst of France during the tumultuous years of the First World War. She had grown up tough under her father's guidance.

The draft called for her father when she was only two years old, leaving an indelible mark on their family. Though war had been harsh, he returned determined to shield his daughter from harm's way. Every stroke of the polish cloth was another memory of every Sunday morning. Her father held her close. The snap of the bolt and fresh smell of burnt powder.

Christana meticulously cleaned her service weapon. She could almost see her reflection in the polished iron. Once pleased with the restoration of the rifle, she placed it in the sleeve and slung it over her shoulder.

The dark pigment washed down the drain, cleansing her hands. Christana's cosmetics sat organized on a compact tray next to her. She picked up a tube of gloss and applied a touch to her lips. She took a deep breath to compose herself. She walked to Arnold's room and rapped on the door. But silence greeted her. With a slight push, the door creaked open, revealing an empty room with no sign of Arnold.

She descended the stairs. Her footsteps creaked on the wooden treads. She entered the living area where Marcus and Arnold were in a deep conversation. Or at least Marcus was stuck listening to Arnold's rambling.

"You see, Marcus," she heard Arnold say. "I have been studying the effects of magic and the history of this world for all of my life. That is why I am absolutely sure what I said was true."

"What do we suppose we do? We really should make a plan," Marcus replied.

"Well, you see, I believe…" Arnold, catching Christana on her way out, stood and greeted her. "Good morning, Christana. Marcus and I were just discussing matters of what may be ahead. Would you care to join us?"

"Bonjour, Arnold. And Marcus. Good morning. Don't let me interrupt. I was going to clear my head and put in some practice." She looked for something in Arnold's eyes. Pushing the boundaries of the awkwardness that caught Marcus in the middle.

"Enjoy your time, Christana," Marcus said to break the silence.

"Would you care to join me, Marcus?" Christana asked. "If that's fine, Arnold, I don't want to interrupt anything."

"I don't know much about guns, to be honest. The only ones I've seen were the ones firing at me," Marcus said in an undertone.

"I'll teach you. It'll be entertaining at least," she said as she walked to her front door. She stood by it and looked back at Marcus.

"I guess we can save this conversation for later, Marcus. Go ahead," Arnold encouraged. "I'll make myself some breakfast."

Christana led Marcus outside only to find the other half of the group debating and in bouts of laughter. Jin, in his impressive tiger form, stood nearby while the Cactus eagerly handed out fruits. Laughter and confusion mingled in the air as the Cactus offered fruit to Christana and Marcus as well.

They both expressed their gratitude. Christana immediately took a bite and savored the taste. Marcus tucked the small fruit into his pocket for later. The morning was already feeling lighter and more vibrant to Christana.

"Marcus, Christana!" Tommy greeted them. "You just missed the greatest show ever! But we are now just discussing what we should call our friend the Cactus over there. He needs a name."

"Every name we suggested, he didn't like," Jin said. "We tried Pokey, Sagoro, and many others."

"Marcus, he seems to be trying to talk to you."

"We learned about him in school. I was in middle school when I first heard about The Great Saguaro that saved us. His time was about twenty years before I was born," Marcus explained.

The Cactus handed him another fruit.

"You gave me one of them already. I'll save it for later," Marcus said with his annoyed tone.

But the Cactus persisted, pointing and gesturing to the fruit atop his head. He danced and played, like a game of charades.

Marcus pinched his bridge trying to remember the name. "Bahidaj?"

The Cactus lit up with excitement as if Marcus unveiled another clue.

"In the Native American language that's what the fruit were called. In Spanish I believe they went by another name. Uhh...Tuna I believe."

"Tuna?" Christana asked. "What kind of name is that? It didn't taste like fish."

"I don't know. It's Spanish. Hey, Cactus. You had a friend right?"

A solid nod was overshadowed by Marcus continuing to talk.

"Carlos? I believe his name. I don't remember. I remember watching an interview in school where he spoke about the Cactus. He was calling you something... Silly? But in Spanish. What's the word for silly? No wait! He called you Fruity! But in Spanish."

"Yes, of course!" Tommy said while tapping his forehead. "It's been such a long time I had forgotten! It wasn't much of a name, but a nickname! Frutuoso!"

With a final great relief, the Cactus grabbed Marcus's hand and shook it firmly. He then pointed to Tommy.

"Yeah, yeah," Marcus replied, pulling himself from the yanking of the Cactus. "He called you that because of your silly nature. Tommy is right. That's his nickname."

"Yes, not a formal name, but it's nice to have a nickname."

"It's nice to have you on the team, Frutuoso!" Tommy then turned to Christana, noticing her uniform. "Well, you are dressed well, aren't you?"

"I was going to go shooting," she replied. "I'm a bit out of practice, and I am taking Marcus along with me."

"Very well, I will wish to talk to you when you return. I have something very important I would like to ask you," Tommy said. His face was serious for once. His weathered olive eyes spoke of concern, but he smiled in delight as she and Marcus were bonding.

"Okay. When we shall return, I'll be all ears," she said, carrying her rifle by her side as she continued around the house.

Christana led Marcus out back behind the mansion, revealing a property far larger than Marcus had realized. The grandeur of the estate, once magnificent, now hidden by the dense canopy of old trees. The mansion's grounds sprawled. But they were overgrown in places. They still hinted at their past splendor.

They arrived at a small shooting range. Christana had custom built it. It was nestled in a clearing, now covered with pine needles and acorns. Targets at varying distances lined the area. Enjoyment was in favor of the design, more than rigorous training. The range was simple but charming. It had makeshift markers and a few old barrels as obstacles. Christana and Marcus stood side by side, the sun filtering through the leaves above, casting dappled shadows on the ground. The scene was peaceful, a perfect blend of nature.

"Do you mind taking that target out in the field?" Christana asked. "It's not heavy."

It was a medium-sized gong, rusted and marred. Marcus agreed to move it, but making it easy for himself, commanded D to fly it out to the designated spot. It was intriguing to watch the demon glide the gong to its position, three hundred meters down the range. With a nod from Christana, D secured the gong on the post.

Christana set up at a bench and table, arranging sandbags and unloading a case of bullets. She lined them up like soldiers in boot camp. With a wave of his hand, D blew the dust off the bench, ensuring it was clean for Christana. She loaded her rifle one round at a time, each cartridge making a satisfying clink as it slipped into place. Sitting down, she peered through the scope, taking a deep breath. A serene calm washed over her, steadying her nerves.

Marcus saw the determination in her eyes. A fierce concentration that radiated from her. He had never seen such focus, almost losing himself in the intensity of her gaze as he stood off to the side. The child of the wind didn't shiver her spine. But he did feel the tingle. The first boom caught him off guard. It echoed through the clearing. Birds left the trees, cawing and their feathers ruffled in the wind. But, before he could react, another shot rang out.

Lightning-fast, Christana pulled the action back and loaded another round. Boom! The sound bounced and echoed over the hills, followed by the resonant ring of the gong. The rapid succession of shots showcased her skill and precision. Each bullet hit its mark with unyielding accuracy.

"I'm just not as good as I used to be, I suppose," Christana said, sliding back the bolt. She watched as the smoke rose from both ends, as the casing struck the floor.

"You're hitting the target," Marcus replied.

"My groupings are too large. Come take a look."

Marcus sat at the bench and leaned into the scope.

"I have a shot that landed left. Most of my hits were high. I could blame it on my scope. But." She examined her hand. Steady, yet had a faint tremor. "Your turn."

"I'm not sure. It's pretty loud. It did actually catch me off guard."

She persisted, handing him the rounds to load into the gun. Smoke still rose from the muzzle, and the metal was hot. The smell of burnt powder lingered in the air. Christana took another breath in, savoring the familiar odor.

"It reminds me of home and my father," Christana said, reminiscing about the past. "I used to come out here a lot. Not so much anymore." She took another deep breath. "The breath before you take your shot, the calm before you squeeze. It's very relaxing and soothing for the soul. My father taught me that."

"Wow. I never thought of it that way," Marcus mused, taking the rifle in hand. "I've only seen them used to cause harm."

Christana put her hands over Marcus's as he leaned on the bench. She went over the basics of safety and gave him a lesson on handling. Before long, Marcus was loading his rounds into the rifle. He peered into the scope. Down range, he could see the gong. In the middle of it was a red mark of paint. Within the mark were five hits, clustered inches apart. He peeked over at Christana.

"You sure you didn't like your shots? They look like they all hit the mark," Marcus commented, trying to uplift her spirits.

"I used to shoot with precision every time. Now, I find my hands shake…" Christana confessed softly, her confidence faltering for a moment. Quickly, regaining composure, she urged, "But don't dwell on it. Take your shot."

Marcus adjusted his stance. He felt the weight and power of the rifle in his hands. Unlike anything he had handled before. Remembering Christana's instructions, he steadied his breath. He found a sense of calm amidst the tension.

Taking careful aim was more challenging than he anticipated after diverting his gaze. This wasn't like the video games he played back home; this was different—real, tangible. Every slight movement seemed amplified through the scope. He felt his heartbeat upon his trigger finger. The slight pulse twitching the crosshairs. Even finding the gong downrange was a challenge enough.

"Hold it tight," Christana said. "Tight to your shoulder."

Keeping it steady was tricky, but he became impatient. He took another breath and fired. With no echo of the gong, he pulled back the action and loaded another round. Rubbing his shoulder, the recoil reminded him to respect the weapon.

The metal snapped as the bolt rolled closed. His aim faltered again which inspired Christana to assist. Her hands gently enveloped his, guiding with a whisper, "Focus, take it slow. Squeeze, don't pull." Despite the sweat slicking his palms and his mounting nerves, he persisted. And finally, amidst a final breath, a resounding victory echoed.

Christana applauded warmly, acknowledging his achievement. With renewed confidence, Marcus continued, striking the target twice more before setting down the rifle. As he looked at Christana, her impressed expression mirrored his sense of accomplishment tinged with the ache in his shoulder.

"My shoulder is going to be sore tomorrow," he joked.

"You'll recover," Christana reassured, settling back to reload her rifle. Marcus leaned against the post, massaging the newfound bruise, watching as Christana effortlessly hit the target five more times.

"It's like music to my ears."

"So, why did you bring me out here?"

She fired another round, the crisp report echoing through the stillness around them. Placing the rifle carefully on the sandbags, Christana sighed and rubbed her hands, a flicker of hesitation clouding her expression. Marcus, sensing her reluctance, pressed gently, eager for her response.

"It's just I wanted company," she said, but it was an obvious lie.

"Why wouldn't you bring Arnold out here?" Marcus said. "The two of you seem to get along, even more so."

The Eight Heroes of Old

"I just needed to clear my head. I needed something else. Something to take the edge off."

"But me in particular, or just because I was there?"

Snapping more rounds into the rifle, she took her time to respond. "I see it in your eyes. You know just like I do. The pain... The heartbreak..."

"I'm sorry. I don't know what to say. Did Arnold and you get into a fight or something?"

"Marcus, unlike the other heroes, you know what it is to lose someone close to you. Someone you love."

"How do you know what I feel?"

She fired the rifle, more distracted by her aim than wanting to answer. "I saw you staring into the fire the day you came. You had the same expression as me for many nights. That fire can keep you company. You wish it could burn away the emotions and the pain."

"I guess you do," Marcus admitted. "That's some gift you have."

"I had the calling to bring you out here. I had my suspicions, but I know it's true now. I just needed someone who would understand," Christana said softly, her voice tinged with vulnerability.

"You can lay it on me, Christana. It's fine."

"I loved him, Marcus. I lost my whole world when Arnold died. Now he is back from the dead, but he isn't back for me." She fired again; her movements almost mechanical. "I know it's not about me, but I wish you all had left me out of this. I wish you never brought him here for me to see. I would rather still think he was dead."

"Did he say something to you?" Marcus asked, his concern evident, a hint of anger simmering beneath the surface.

"It's not what you think. Arnold is still my friend. He just has a way of stumbling with his words. Sometimes he says things he shouldn't. For a genius he doesn't think sometimes. In our time at the library, Arnold confessed to me that after all is said and done, he will return to his time. We all will. Therefore, he must return to die."

Marcus felt a wave of empathy wash over him. He spun his wedding ring around his finger, a solemn gesture. "My wife and I," Marcus began, his voice catching slightly. "We aren't doing too good." He turned away, unable to meet Christana's gaze. "I know your pain of losing the person you care about the most. It's always when you are okay with who you are. When you are finally not afraid to be by yourself, you find the person you cannot live without. The one that makes you a better you. I don't know what I would do without Diana. I know the day is coming. She can't be mine. A fairy tale. What Tommy said yesterday. It confirms it. She can't handle…the darkness…"

"I'm sorry about your marriage, Marcus," Christana said softly, her heart aching for him.

"Now, I'm making this about me…" Marcus said, wiping the tear he accidentally let slip.

"Please, continue," Christana said, leaving her position at the table and walking to Marcus. "I want to listen."

"We are working things out. I'm not sure they will be okay though. I hurt her. I hurt her really badly. Not just physically, but emotionally too. I would say it's not my fault, but my stow-away's. But I cannot pass blame. It is all my fault. We were happy. But now… I'm not sure if I can mend what I've broken."

"Marcus, you have a chance at least, and that has to count for something," Christana said gently. She took his hand, noticing his wedding ring gleaming in the sunlight like a token of hope. It was black with bands of silver through it and gleamed like the moon.

"Christana. I'm not sure it's that easy. I'm sure there is a way for Tommy to work things out. There has got to be. He is the Time Warden, and he could make it right."

"My mother always wanted me to find someone my age. I was a naive girl, but I fell in love with a man much older than me. Everybody always held me back. I wanted to follow my feelings. Ironically, now my feelings are never wrong. I trust them more than any person alive. My instincts tell me there is no possible way."

"That's harsh…"

"You and I are not so different, Marcus. I knew it was good to bring you out here."

"Talking it out always helps, right?"

"I'm sure Marlon had his fair share of my words. Losing Arnold was difficult for both of us, but we had each other."

"What about Marlon? He is your butler or something?"

"He is my friend. He…Understands me. I brought back more than just scars from the war. Marlon has been my support through it all."

"I want to show you something." Marcus took out his phone, a modern device in this ancient setting. It was on its last bit of power, but he managed to pull up a picture of his wife.

"What is this?" Christana asked.

"It's called a cellphone. Everyone has one of these back in my time. It's like a minicomputer, but more powerful than the ones you have this year. We can store all sorts of knowledge and photos. This is one of my wife," Marcus explained warmly, showing Christana an image of Diana. Her hair cascaded like silk, shaded in tones of umber, and she sat on their couch with a new kitten nestled on her lap.

"Her eyes are like autumn," Marcus said. "This was before everything happened."

"She's beautiful, Marcus," Christana said with a heartfelt voice. "Truly she is. Her hair is pretty!"

"She is the most beautiful person I've ever met," Marcus proudly replied. "And also, the most decent heart I have seen in years."

"That's very sweet of you, Marcus. I wish the best of luck for you and her." Christana handed Marcus his phone. The alert beeped to show low power.

Despite that, Marcus spent the last few percentages looking at photos of Diana. Cherishing every moment, he hovered over his favorite, still amazed by her hazel eyes, and she cuddled their cat.

Christana checked for the rifle to be clear and free of any lingering rounds and placed it back in the case. She dismantled the table and sandbags, placing them in the shed, in the same position that was free of dust.

"If you ever need someone to talk to, I'll be your friend," Marcus said.

"Thank you for this, Marcus. It really helped me," Christana said gratefully, stepping close to embrace him. In that moment, her fears began to dissipate, and she felt a resurgence of confidence. The emotions she had buried deep inside began to surface, finding solace in the friendship they were forging.

"Do you think we will see each other again? After all is said and done?"

"I don't know what the future holds, but I like you Marcus. I hope we do." Once again, Christana led Marcus back to the front of her home. "Let's go see what Tommy wanted."

12 The Calling of a Leader

Marcus and Christana approached the group, their arrival interrupting yet another heated debate. Amidst the chaos of the garden, it resembled a scene ravaged by a tornado. Christana couldn't help but feel disheartened at the sight. The flowers were vibrant the evening before, but now lay trampled. Marlon's meticulously tended lawn was uprooted and destroyed.

As they navigated through the wreckage, Marcus stumbled upon the head of a statue buried in the debris. He lifted it up and showed it to Christana, who regarded it with a discerning look of displeasure.

"Yes, I think I totally could beat Marcus," Jin said, smirking. "The beast inside him lacks conviction."

"You could barely fight Frutuoso, are you ready to go toe to toe with Marcus?" Marlon ranted.

"Of all of us here, I have seen and even felt what Marcus can do. Surely, I would place my bet on him," Tommy said, agreeing with Marlon.

Frutuoso patted Jin on the back with his prickly arms. This offered silent encouragement that Jin desperately needed. His belief in him was unwavering, though his allegiance remained a mystery to onlookers.

"What's going on?" Marcus said now more intrigued than before. "You guys are still talking about the Cactus's name?"

"No, Marcus," Tommy said enthusiastically. "We were just simply talking about who would win in a fight. Our friend Frutuoso, or you."

"We were also talking about me being able to overtake you. I think I stand a good chance," Jin said this with an overly self-assured voice.

"No guys, this is a bad idea. I don't fight for fun," Marcus asserted firmly, his tone carrying a weight of seriousness. He was taken aback by their suggestion. "You don't know what will happen. As far as that goes. I may lose control. I may end up seriously hurting you."

"Come on, Marcus. It's just a bit of fun," Tommy said. "After all, I must thank you."

"Why is that?"

"You helped me settle my nerves. I was going too fast of a pace, and you helped me realize, it was just my anxiety trying to just get things done too quickly. You are right, we need to slow down...I need to slow down."

"I'm sorry, Tommy. I shouldn't have lost control like that. It wasn't right of me, but I guess, good things really can come from the bad." Marcus paused for a moment. "But as for sparring with you guys, it won't be fun when someone gets seriously injured."

"I think you should listen to Marcus. This just sounds like trouble," Christana chimed in her thoughts about this debate.

"Is it that awful?" Jin said, changing his tone.

"Yes. Trust me. It gets ugly," Marcus continued. "Let's just forget about it."

"Well, we should just be glad we have Marcus to back us up in the horrible events we shall face," Tommy said. "We should get going anyway. Where is Arnold?"

"I believe he is still inside," Christana said.

"Very well, could you go get him, Marcus? I have something important I would like to ask Christana."

"Very well," Marcus dismissed himself.

"Christana, if I may, let's take a walk in the garden. The rest of you may stay here."

The group dispersed, each member heading off on their own path. Marcus went to the mansion. There, he found Arnold and the Porcelain Man. They were lounging on the velvet sofa. Christana's best tea sat on the table between them. Its floral and citrus aroma filled the room with a delicate, invigorating scent.

A dirty plate, adorned with a few remaining crumbs from what appeared to be biscuits, lay next to the teapot. Arnold's fingers wandered over his unshaven chin scratching the crumbs. A few strays clung stubbornly to his jacket collar. But he was focused on the Doll across from him. It sat limp in the chair, seeming to listen intently to Arnold's musings.

As Marcus entered the room, George's head snapped up with sudden, fluid grace. Despite its mechanical nature, the movement was eerily elegant. The Doll's fingers could not close around the teacup but lifted it with an uncertain grip. Delicate china threatened to topple.

"Ahh, Marcus, have some tea! Sit down and converse with us!" Arnold said, raising his teacup as an inviting gesture.

"He drinks tea?" Marcus' curiosity piqued as he watched George take another sip. He didn't have an open mouth, and the tea rather just spilled on his coat, but he raised the teapot to Marcus to pour him a glass.

"No thanks..." Marcus said, off put by the Doll.

"He doesn't exactly drink it. He is so fascinating! Most of my research was based on him and the magic that grants him life. Anyway, how did things go with Christana?"

"Well, surprisingly...it helped," Marcus replied. He still stood, taking in the peculiar scene. "She was...focused for sure. We both had a lot to get off our chests. I see you and the Doll are forming a great companionship. The whole group seems to be."

"That the spirit of it. Our group is growing stronger. Yesterday was quite..."

"Yes, I know...I already apologized to Tommy. The outcome is looking better."

"I imagine Christana talked about me?"

"A little bit...Why are you...curious?"

Arnold's stumbling with his words forced him to find composure before speaking again. "I hope I don't hurt her too much."

"She told me. It seems like she was hurt, but we talked through it. It's always been a challenge to talk to people about my problems. They think being a hero is easy and my problems must not be too bad. I especially haven't had anyone to talk about my troubles with my marriage. I can't even think what Christana must have gone through in her struggles. It's like nobody understands."

"I understand to a degree. In my studies, it was difficult for me to find assistants that could keep pace or even grasp some of the concepts I taught. My tougher classes stumped many students. It was like I was speaking a completely different language..." Arnold laid his head back. He rubbed his waking eyes and Marcus could tell he was lost in his thoughts and wonder. "All I wanted was to be able to express myself. Christana was the only one that understood. We would spend late nights just discussing the wonders of this world. The beauty of nature. Wild thoughts and ideas."

"You have a chance to do that all over again. Why don't you?"

"It's not that simple. Once our work is done, we all must go back to our place in time. I wish I could stay, Marcus. I do wish for that. Maybe it would be wise for Christana and me to keep our distance."

"What if you don't?"

"I don't want to hurt her again."

"Why does that matter? You should not keep your heart from her. Don't lose what you have. She is a strong woman. You're lucky to have her."

"I'm a logical man, Marcus. It can't be."

"We are in charge of our own fate. Whatever you decide is up to you. Don't throw that away based on some out of time misjudgment. If we cannot change time, then what are we doing here? Why would we even help Tommy if our world's fate can't change?"

"You make a fair point…"

"Well, Tommy wants us to get going. We are about to head out and go to the next location in time."

"The dragon?"

"The dragon," Marcus said, nodding to assure him.

"They say the great catacombs beneath the earth are home to the dragons. In the historical text, the dragons could be large enough to devour men whole."

"You don't know this, but the hero after Christana, the Cactus. His story intertwines with that theory. In my time, it bled out into webpage after webpage of endless conspiracy theories."

"Is that so? I wish he could speak. I would love to know his story. Have you ever seen a dragon, George? Do you know what they are?"

George, however, had no concept of what a dragon was, and shrugged in response. He finished his tea with a delicate sip, then rose gracefully to his feet. With a precise motion, he gestured to Marcus, indicating he was ready. George reached for his hat, deftly plucking it from the coat rack, and settled it onto his head.

"Very well, I see you are ready as ever," Arnold said. "Let's go to Tommy."

Arnold, Marcus, and George made their way out of the mansion, stepping into the crisp air of the courtyard to rejoin the others. The mansion's grandeur faded into the background as they moved forward, united in their quest, the scent of tea lingering in the air.

Tommy walked along the side of the mansion. His steps light as he admired the flowerbeds Frutuoso had so meticulously cultivated. The blooms looked especially vibrant in the sunlight. Their colors harmonized with the natural hues of the house to exact beauty. The Cactus's arrangement among the flowers seemed purposefully placed, as if he had spent years studying perfect color combinations.

Christana walked beside Tommy, reflecting on how, despite their short acquaintance, she had come to know him as ludicrous and impish. He was always joking, rarely taken seriously. But today was different. Today, Tommy showed a side she hadn't known he possessed. His stride was measured, and his speech clear and methodical.

"Did you know," Tommy began, his voice unusually calm. "That Frutuoso spent years perfecting his craft? The way he blends colors and textures is almost like an art form."

Christana glanced at him, surprised by his tone. "I had no idea you paid such attention to it," she replied.

Tommy smiled, a hint of his usual mischief in his eyes, but there was sincerity too. "There's more to me than jokes, you know. Sometimes, you just have to look a little deeper. I of course made that up. He is the hero of nature. It comes to him naturally."

"Tommy, is there something on your mind? What did you want to ask of me?"

They continued their walk. The sunlight cast a warm glow over the flowerbeds. But Tommy kept distracting himself.

"Christana. I have a very important task," Tommy said and gestured his hands. "My father. All he ever wanted was to write his own piece of history. He wanted to share his side of the story. He wanted a better life for me and my brother. He wanted to make sure his wife was safe."

"What point are you trying to make? Tommy please. If you fear what you need to say..."

"I'm getting to it, don't worry." With a deep breath Tommy continued. "I wish I could have spoken up then. I wish I could have told him not to go. All he proved was he was the wrong man to save our family. He died chasing his delusion."

"Tommy, don't say that. He obviously loved you very much. He wanted everything for you and his family."

"I wish I could have him back. I need to make sense of everything. I am just like my dad. He was silly. He wanted kindness in a world that showed him none in return. I cannot... Marcus was right about me. I've sensed it for a long time, but I am not a..."

"Not a what?" Christana urged him. She placed her hand upon his shoulder to support him.

"Don't think less of me, Christana, but inside, I'm afraid. I can't deal with what's ahead. I can't fight my urges to be childish. I am not fit to lead this team."

"You don't have to be afraid. I was too when my time was called. We are always fit to be the lead in our own rolls."

"Not like this. Marcus helped me realize I am too immature. But for what I wish to ask you. You are the strongest leader of all the heroes. You led a group of soldiers into battle. You know what it's like to suffer great loss. You know what's at stake."

Tommy stopped and plucked a flower from the garden. He twirled it between his fingers as he gazed at its spinning petals. The anticipation made Christana's legs jitter and her skin tingle.

"With your unique power, I think the honor would best suit you," Tommy continued. His expression vacant, the usual light in his eyes dimmed. "I am not much in terms of a hero. I have no good judgment nor anything special about me. I can travel time, but I am not a fighter. I lack restraint and I lack peace of mind."

Christana looked at him, confused. "What are you saying?"

"I'm saying, Christana, I want you to lead this team. I've watched you closely. You have led teams to victory before. You have good instincts." He smiled softly, but there was a depth of sincerity in his eyes. "I cannot lead this team. It's not my place. You're the hero. I am not the hero I am meant to be. I cannot lead them."

"You have just as much part in this story as I. You will lead this team well. I know that for a fact." Her voice trembled. "What if I can't? Time with Arnold has told me much about my own character. I falter. I…"

"Trust yourself. You always have. You know you will. You have everything you need. I name you captain. Captain of the Eight Heroes of Old."

"Eight heroes of Old?"

"Lead them. Bring them together. The group is already coming together. They just need a little more of a push."

Christana was stunned. Her mouth fell open in disbelief. But, in her mind, she knew it was her duty. "With honor, Tommy. I will." She paused and whispered to herself, "The Eight Heroes of Old." A smile slowly spread across her face as she realized the significance of his words.

Tommy watched her, knowing this was what she needed. She was what they needed. In his mind, he knew the job suited her better. It was her calling to be strong. To be a leader.

13 Glass Wings

Marcus, Arnold, and George stepped out into the courtyard. The mid-morning sunbathed the area in a warm, golden light, casting long shadows and bringing the garden to life. Jin, Marlon, and Frutuoso were already settled, deep in conversation. Frutuoso absorbed every word as Marlon poured out his knowledge of tigers, his eyes flashing bright with amazement.

The peaceful murmur of their discussion was soon joined by the sound of approaching footsteps. Tommy arrived; his usual playful demeanor replaced with a rare, quiet intensity. By his side was Christana, her presence radiating a pleasant aura that seemed to brighten the courtyard even more. Tommy's joy was palpable, his eyes twinkling with excitement as he prepared to share their news.

"Everyone!" Tommy began, his voice carrying a newfound weight. "I have an important announcement to make!"

Christana stood beside him; her expression was serene yet resolute. The group fell silent, turning their attention to the pair. The air was thick with anticipation, and even the Cactus seemed to lean in, curious about what was to come.

Tommy took a deep breath, his face serious yet hopeful. "Christana has agreed to take on the role of captain. She will lead the Eight Heroes of Old. It's the term I am branding us."

There was a collective intake of breath, followed by a moment of stunned silence. Then, slowly, smiles began to spread across their faces. The gravity of the moment settled in, and Marcus spoke up first. "Wait, I thought you were going to lead us. I mean, isn't this your time?"

"I understand your fear, Marcus, but I do this out of my own flaws. Christana was born to lead. There isn't anyone better. After yesterday, she and I both agree this is the best judgment we can make. Her instincts are unmatched. You will be our noble leader, won't you, Christana?"

Christana nodded, her eyes meeting each of theirs in turn. "With honor," she said simply, her voice steady. "I will do my best to lead us to victory."

The group erupted in a chorus of cheers and congratulations. All except Marcus, who stood back watching the group surround the two.

Tommy beamed, knowing that this decision was the right one. Christana was exactly what they needed—a leader strong, wise, and ready to guide them through whatever challenges lay ahead. But looking back, he saw Marcus not following in suit.

"What's the matter, Marucs?"

"I don't doubt Christana would be a good fit to lead. I know from the history of her accomplishments, but…"

"But what?" Tommy asked, stepping forward and facing Marcus to isolate them.

With a sigh, Marcus just asked but a single question. "But aren't there nine of us?"

"Good observation, Marcus. But I am not a hero of old, am I?"

"Shouldn't we find a new name then?"

"Do you have any suggestions?"

Marcus shrugged, realizing he didn't actually have a name to propose and preferred not to dwell on it.

"You can feel it, Marcus…" D whispered to him. "Ask what you really want to ask…"

"But Marcus does make a good point," Arnold spoke in addition to Marcus. "Doesn't your power let you have a clearer picture if you can see the future?"

"The future for me is..." Tommy closed his eyes, trying not to imagine the fiery fangs and vacant eyes. "It's a shadow. It's dark," Tommy admitted, a hint of doubt creeping into his voice. "I must admit to you all, I am not a person of greatness. I am but a simple child. I was only ten when I left my home." He paced, trying to find the right words.

"Ten years old?" Christana asked. "It must have been a struggle."

"I am still ten years old in a way. Time stands still for me. My soul and mind have lived through thousands of lifetimes," Tommy explained, looking down at his hands, which seemed to bear the wrinkles of age. "The time vortex is the machine I built following my father's instructions. It should never have worked. I ran the calculations again. It isn't possible. I was given a unique power. But also, a strange set of struggles."

"Don't be doing this because you are running away from your fear," Marcus said. "You must embrace it. You cannot expect to overcome defeat if you fear it. I learned that lesson the hard way."

"I do not wish to run away. But Christana and I share something unique. She is the leader, and I hope you all accept it in your heart."

"Marcus, don't you feel his pain?" D whispered again. "He leads you down a path you don't want to follow."

"Well, Maybe Christana will be different," Marcus spoke to D, but the whole group heard his words and Tommy gladly accepted.

"But you were right. I didn't have a plan. I don't know what I am doing. For once I decided to scrap the plan as it never works. I'm just doing what I feel. I'm just doing what I am called to do." Tommy smiled and looked at Christana. "That is why I made her our leader. She has what it takes and will do far better than I ever could leading this team. In all that I have learned. I am still naive. I lack wisdom. I am childish."

"No need to be so hard on yourself," Jin said. "I was once foolish too. I made mistakes in my life, but you learned before it cost you, I didn't."

"There's a constant worry I can't shake. My mother is back home, and I have a younger brother I left behind. Thoughts of them linger, their faces and voices slipping from memory. It feels like I've failed them, like the hero who couldn't keep his promise. The fear of letting them down weighs on me every day"

"Together, we won't fail," Marcus stepped forward and gave Tommy a stern look. "We have all had our doubts before. We have all faced the same threat. We can do this. I won't let us fall apart."

"I accept Christana as our leader," Jin said firmly.

The Cactus stood and went to shake the hand of Christana, showing reverence as if pleased to be led by her.

George followed in the same way, taking her hand and kissing it with a gentle bow.

"I am so proud of you!" Arnold exclaimed as he walked up to Christana, his face beaming with pride. "If you stay true to your heart, like the young girl I have always known, you will do fine. Tu es capable de grandes choses."

"Merci, Arnold," Christana thanked him, her voice rich with gratitude. She gazed into his eyes. She could see the genuine admiration and confidence he had in her, and it bolstered her resolve.

Arnold placed a reassuring hand on her shoulder. "Souviens-toi, tu as la force en toi. Fais-toi confiance, et nous te suivrons tous. Reste fidèle à toi-même."

"Je ne te laisserai pas tomber. Ensemble, nous affronterons tout ce qui se présentera. Ensemble, nous sommes invincibles."

"Once we assemble the whole team, she will lead us, and she will plan out our whole strategy," Tommy said.

"It will be a team effort," Christana added. "I would like none other than Arnold to be my advisor. He is both wise and talented."

"Ironic that now I become your assistant, isn't it?" Arnold beamed as he grasped her hand in a firm congratulatory shake.

"We are ready, Tommy," Christana declared, her voice steady as she stepped into her new role with confidence. "Let's set out for the next hero."

"Right away!" Tommy exclaimed, his eyes shining with excitement. He stepped aside, casting another portal with a flourish. The winds roared through the courtyard, kicking up dust that stung their eyes and made visibility difficult.

Marcus, raising his voice above the howling winds, asked, "Shouldn't we eat breakfast first?"

"There's no time for that, Marcus," Tommy replied, a mischievous grin spreading across his face. "Besides, you'll want to save room!"

"Save room?" Marcus echoed, puzzled.

"Just get going!" Tommy urged as everyone stepped through the swirling portal.

"Farewell, Marlon!" Christana called out, her voice carrying a mix of hope and determination as she stepped into the unknown.

"I hope I shall see all of you again!" Marlon waved to them as the portal closed, leaving him with a sense of solitude yet satisfaction. He returned to his daily work at the house, still replaying the excitement of their departure. Occasionally, he would shadowbox, throwing a few punches and kicks, a secret thrill he kept to himself.

On the other side of the portal, the heroes were greeted by a harsh, hot wind full of debris. The Doll almost lost his hat, but it was saved by getting caught on the Cactus. The sand burned their skin as they entered a desolate field shrouded in ash. Smoke filled the air, blotting out the sunlight and casting an eerie gloom over the landscape.

Above them, the last of the dragons flew overhead. These magnificent, yet terrifying creatures had horns and scales that seemed to pierce through their own flesh in a grotesque display. Their cries echoed across the dark plain, sending shivers down the spines of the heroes. The sheer malevolence of the dragons was evident in their eyes, a stark reminder of the evil they embodied.

In the distance, a rumbling grew louder, and a cloud of dust signaled the approach of land-borne lizards. The heroes caught glimpses of them. Creatures with pointed mouths filled with ugly fangs and eyes of topaz, ruby, and jade. Each lizard had unique, dirty colored skins, muted and blackened, and their hisses were filled with hatred.

"They are leaving," Arnold said, relief mixing with awe in his voice.

The Eight Heroes of Old

"Today is their last day on the surface," Tommy added, gazing up at the dragons. "The treaty is done. They return to the chasms deep within the Earth."

As the dust settled and the winds slowed, they saw a crowd gathered around a large statue. Peasants and nobles alike mingled in the throng.

On a stage above the crowd stood a man dressed in resplendent armor, adorned with gold enchantments and emeralds lining the shoulders. A silver crown with the markings of the Allfather rested on his head, catching the dim light.

The atmosphere was charged with anticipation and a sense of historical gravity. The heroes exchanged glances, knowing the story that had been told to them since they were children.

Beside the king stood a figure that, at first glance, appeared to be a man. As the heroes drew closer Owen was revealed upon the stage. His figure was defaced. Yet, he also bore a crown not crafted of precious metals. Instead, clear crystals protruded from his skull, encircling his head and growing larger at the sides. These crystals dazzled with hints of cyan and amethyst, and similar formations could be seen growing in a pattern all over his body.

He wore armor akin to the king's and held a sword in his hand. With a reverent gesture, he turned the sword downward and plunged it into the wooden planks, kneeling before the king and bowing his head in honor. The king, with a solemn and serene expression, bestowed upon him the title of royal guard and hero of the realm.

It was now clear the statue behind them was a monument. Large enough to piece the sky, the dragon Azarth turned to crystal. It echoed the same colors as Owen. In the center of the structure, it was like a fire that burned in multiple colors, shining beams of light out the polygonal sides.

Tommy led the group through the crowd of people getting closer to the platform. The monument cast a shadow over the crowd, but the penumbra was like stained glass. Ever brilliant, it blinded gazers and even the faintest light was magnified to beauty. There at last they saw the dragon that stood before them.

"Amazing, isn't it?" Tommy asked.

"We look really out of place," Marcus noted, as people gave them curious glances.

"We are all dressed differently," Arnold added, adjusting his collar self-consciously.

"This is the treaty passed by the Crystal Dragon, is it not?" Christana asked but took Arnold's hand as they continued to stare at the large statue.

Above the crowd, the king declared to all present, he presented his sword and bathed it in the light of the statue.

The Eight Heroes of Old

The glimmer reflected in the crystals, and Owen gave a radiance that instilled awe amongst them.

"Lower your head, Sir knight," the king commanded. "Owen, I grant you the highest honor in the land. You have brought peace to our kingdom. Thousands of lives are owed to you—their families, their wellbeing, all of their homes. Because of you, their souls are saved. By your life, may you bring peace and prosperity to this land. The kingdom is eternally grateful. The Allfather would be pleased! Now rise, Sir Bennet!"

Tommy could see Owen's face; it was riddled with scars, his body marred by burns. Yet when he rose, he did so with a grace and humility that commanded respect. He noted the stare he gave, looking into the distance at the fleeing dragons. Their silhouettes fading in the dust.

"My people!" Owen called out. "This land is ours like the Creator intended, Like the Allfather protected. This statue will be the promise between the creatures beneath the earth and the humans above. As long as it stands, there shall be peace between the two. We will no longer suffer the wrath of those below. As long as I stand, I will keep that promise. Go now and celebrate! Hold your loved ones and honor the dead who gave their lives to defend this country!"

Owen stepped down into the crowd, as they welcomed him with thunderous applause. The people surrounding him bowed in admiration and gratitude. He walked past the heroes, giving them a knowing glance. He saw how out of place they looked, the faces of those who had seen darkness and came through the other side. The king pushed him gently, escorting him towards the castle.

"Why did we come now?" Marcus asked Tommy. "Any particular reason? All these people really make it difficult to speak to him. What if things turn bad?"

"If you just contain yourself, things won't turn bad," Tommy replied sarcastically. "Besides, I did not want to miss it."

"Miss what?" Christana asked.

"Today is the largest feast this side of the world has ever seen. All sorts of cultures join together to celebrate the victory over the dragons."

"That is scarcely a worthy reason to come," Jin scoffed.

"Are you going to join me or not?" Tommy continued as he made his way in the direction of the crowd, following the hungry travelers and citizens of the kingdom.

"Might as well," Arnold said.

Tommy looked up at the ash-filled sky, the dark plumes painting everything in gloom. "This reminds me of home," he said softly.

"The castle?" Arnold asked, glancing over.

"The darkness. The ash in the air. People are very minimal here. For them, they have each other, they work as a community, and shortly, the ash will be clear, and the skies will open again." Tommy looked at Arnold. "In my time, there is no such hope. The people are vile, and as evil as ever."

"That's horrific…"

"Be grateful you still live in a world so vibrant and alive."

As the crowd dissipated towards the celebration, candles and lanterns were lit, casting a warm, flickering glow over the castle. Despite the Cactus standing taller than most buildings, no one seemed to notice him. Hunger may have been the needed distraction. Soon, the pleasant aromas from the feasting hall made everyone less aware of their surroundings. The Cactus had a way of staying undetected, one of his many gifts, blending seamlessly into the background as the festivities carried on.

They made their way deeper into the castle until they reached the feast hall. Tommy peered through a side window as the others kept watch. Music filled the room, a lively band playing for the king and the hero as they sat at a high table, facing the room of nobles. Sir Owen sat to the right of the king as dancers entertained them. The Cactus, too large to fit inside, waited by the door, unnoticed by the nearby guards.

"Marcus, can you get us inside? Make the guards not notice us," Tommy asked.

"Yeah, I don't work like that." Marcus was pretty annoyed by the request.

"Come on, can't you do something?"

"Want me to scare them away?"

"Stop bickering," Christana interjected. "Watch, boys, and you may learn a thing or two."

She approached the guards at the entrance, her strong French accent aiding her efforts. The guards seemed unperturbed by her attire, perhaps assuming it was customary where she was from. Christana played her role flawlessly.

"I am Princess LaValle, the king is expecting me at a table inside."

"Yes, milady. Go ahead," the confused guard said, allowing her to pass.

Christana entered the hall and winked at the rest of the group behind her.

"Amazing," Tommy said, impressed. "Can we just ask?"

Jin seized the opportunity and whispered to Frutuoso before approaching the guards himself. He filled a small woven basket he had taken from a nearby wagon with the fruits from the Cactus. They were plump and bursting with juice.

"Allow me entry, your honorable guards," Jin said, his demeanor calm and respectful, reminiscent of ancient courtiers. "I am Jin Chen, Emperor of the East. I bring gifts of great value. An ancient fruit, only to be eaten by royalty. May I offer them to the king and hero?"

The guards, already disoriented by Christana's entrance, nodded, gaining favor by Jin's accent and demeanor, and stepped aside. Jin bowed and vanished into the building following the scent of the roasting hog.

"It really cannot be this easy, can it?" Marcus exclaimed, his confusion evident.

"Shall we give it a try?" Arnold asked, a hint of curiosity in his voice.

"Why do we even have to ask in the first place?" Marcus grumbled.

"Trust me, they will not allow us in," Tommy replied, shaking his head.

"Forget this! I'll just ask," Marcus declared, standing up and striding towards the entrance to the feast hall. He approached the guards with a determined look. "Excuse me, Guards. I wish to gain entrance to the feast room. Owen is a friend of mine…"

The guards looked at each other, then back at Marcus, their expressions skeptical. "A friend, you say?" one of them responded, crossing his arms.

"Yes, a close friend. We fought side by side," Marcus improvised, trying to sound convincing. "I'm sure he would want to see me."

"Feasting hall is for nobles and lords. For you to enter...Who are you and where did you get those silly clothes?"

"Look. I just..."

"Marcusss," D whispered. "Learn to have more fun!" He protruded from over Marcus's shoulder, staring down the two guards.

Tommy watched with a burst of laughter as the guards fled. "Nice work, Marcus!" Tommy joyfully slapped him on the back. I see your plan didn't go as intended."

"Not funny, D!" Marcus raged.

"Look at them running," D taunted. "You never would have succeeded. Not everyone can enter."

Marcus shook his head, but collected himself. He fell behind the others as they made their sneaky entrance.

The feast hall was alive with the sounds of laughter and music, the scent of rich foods filling the air. The heroes moved cautiously through the crowd, blending in as best they could. Despite their unusual attire, the festive atmosphere made them less conspicuous.

Tommy encouraged Marcus to forget the distraction of D, and Marcus soon succumbed to the sight of the feast laid out before them. Roast pigs, fruit baskets, and all sorts of baked goods filled the table. The smell was heavenly, enticing them all. Inside, they reunited with Christana and Jin. They sat at a table as they were being served.

"This looks like it had feathers at one point, but not anymore. This is tasty!" Jin exclaimed, taking a mouthful of the delicious fare.

They all gathered around the table. The food was too tempting to resist. Everything had a certain elegance, from the laced and decadent pastries to the colorful soups, which became Christana's favorite. Even the Doll was enjoying himself, clapping his metallic hands to the music. Tommy filled his trencher with a bit of everything.

"Come on Marcus, eat something!" Tommy urged!

Marcus was hungry, but he had trouble letting himself relax. He was always twisted up inside. "Come on, Marcus, feast yourself," D taunted him.

Instead of giving in, Marcus looked around the room. He saw people drinking, laughing, and enjoying themselves. The place was alive with entertainment. Actors performed courageous morality tales, and fire spitters wielded torches, spinning them to create dazzling displays. The flash of fire burned through the air, mesmerizing the crowd.

As Marcus scanned the room, he caught the eye of Sir Owen, who stared back at him with a piercing gaze. Marcus quickly turned away and began to fill his trencher with food, hoping to blend in.

Sir Owen excused himself from the king's table and paced down the steps of the high court. Each step made his armor chime as he approached. The fire breathers blew flames around him, the firelight reflecting off the crystals that adorned his body. Owen walked through the crowd, never turning his gaze from their table.

Marcus, sensing the approach, began talking with the others to alert them. Sir Owen drew nearer, his features becoming more distinct. He had emerald eyes and silver hair, his presence commanding the room's attention. The whole table watched in silence as Owen neared, the entire hall falling quiet. The last note of the music faded as Sir Owen reached their table.

"Who might you be?" Sir Owen asked, his voice steady and authoritative. "What are you doing here?"

Marcus choked on his food, trying to speak, as guards surrounded their table, their spears pointed and menacing. Their armor, tarnished and covered in soot, contrasted with Owen's polished suit. It gleamed under the castle's lights.

"I am Tommy Kent. At your service," Tommy said, standing up and offering a deep bow. His clothing was the poorest at the table. Yet, it had an air of humility and earnestness. This contrasted sharply with the great wealth around them.

The king's attention was drawn to Owen as he rose to his feet. Owen stood over the table, peering at each of them with a mix of curiosity and recognition. His mouth fell slightly open as he continued to speak.

"I did not speak to you," Owen said, addressing Tommy. "This one in particular. There is something about him." He pointed to Marcus.

"Sir Owen, if I could," Tommy tried to interject, but was met by the deep stare of Owen.

"Silence! Not another word from you." But Owen turned his gaze from Tommy and surveyed the table. "I dreamt about you. All of you," he said, his voice filled with wonder. "In my dream, the Lady of Light was calling my name. In the light, I saw all of your silhouettes standing before her."

"Well, that makes this easy," Christana said, trying to approach Owen. The guards closed in pointing their spears fiercer than before. Owen drew his sword and put it to Marcus's throat, his eyes narrowing.

"Not another step, or your friend dies."

What is it, Owen? Who are these people?" the king demanded, stepping closer to his knight.

"I'm not certain, but I believe they mean harm to us. The Lady of Light was trying to warn me about them."

"If you could just..." Tommy began, trying to plead his case.

"Silence!" Owen shouted, pressing the sword upon the brink of tearing into skin. "I don't wish to spill blood in this sacred hall. But I told you not another word."

Owen gazed over them again. He saw the Doll limp and falling over the chair, then saw the faces of Jin, Christana, and Arnold. He looked to Marcus and sensed the great evil in him.

At this moment, the king had drawn his sword and held it high to Christana.

Tommy could feel the pressure as he watched his heroes be detained. The sting of the blade was almost apparent in his own mind. The handle was laced in gold just as the king's armor.

Marcus stared down Owen, neither frightened nor deliberate, as Tommy watched, ready for any sign of Owen's intent to strike.

"Stand up," Owen continued to demand. "Face me."

Marcus whispered under his breath, "Not a word, D. No funny business."

"You're missing one. The big one. Where is he?" Owen said. "Do you mean to ambush us? Kill us at a feast of all things?" Owen said. "Who sent you?"

Tommy's voice trembled as he interjected one last time, desperation lacing every syllable. His plea was met with a fierce gaze from Owen, whose eyes blazed with unyielding determination. In one swift, resolute motion, Owen thrust his sword toward Marcus.

But just as the blade was about to strike, a shadow moved with lightning speed. A black hand, strong and sure, caught the sword's end, pushing it back and sparing Marcus from a fatal wound.

Suddenly, the sound of hurried footsteps filled the air as more guards with crossbows burst into the room, their faces set in grim resolve. Panic-stricken civilians fled in every direction, leaving chaos in their wake. Within moments, the chamber was cleared of all but the men-at-arms.

With a sudden, startling movement, D revealed himself to the room. He pushed Owen backward effortlessly, a wild smile spreading across his face. D's charcoal skin seemed almost alive, as if worms writhed beneath the surface like an unsettling dance. Soot and ash flaked off him with every step, leaving a dark, smoky trail in his wake.

"What have you brought here? What is this evil?" Owen demanded, his voice tinged with suspicion and concern.

14 Luster to Shadow

"Owen?" the king asked. "Owen!" He thundered his demand. The hero seemed locked in conflict with the demon before them. The king's sword remained steadfast against Christana, while the other heroes waited.

Sweat dripped from their pores. Jin, on the brink of transformation, felt his claws sharpening instinctively. Arnold and Tommy exchanged urgent signals, preparing for whatever might come next.

"The stable boy turned knight," D mocked. "Have you found your strength? Have you upheld your promise?"

"The darkness…" Owen mumbled.

"I see you know me. It's no surprise," D sneered.

"They have one that isn't with them, Sire." Owen spoke with intense haste. There was a pause in the room.

"Shall we execute them?" the guards asked.

The king, though in his gray years, still possessed steady hands and a sharp mind. He scrutinized the uninvited guests, their fear evident yet tempered by a resolve. He turned his gaze to Owen, the man he trusted most. It was hard for him to believe these strangers harbored ill intent.

Christana, her eyes blazing with determination, locked her gaze on Owen. She unleashed a piercing scream, her voice sliced the air. "We are heroes!"

"Finally, one that doesn't fear me." D laughed, and he slithered back into Marcus's shadow.

"Owen, listen to me! We are not your enemies! The Lady of Light sent us. The darkness you sense in Marcus is not the evil we are trying to defeat. We need your help, not your sword at our throats!"

"Stand down Owen. I wish to hear what they have to say," the king said while lowering his sword.

"You can feel it. The calling. The Lady of Light still has need for you," Tommy said. "You said you had a dream. Listen to Her words. Dreams are very powerful tools used by the Allfather."

Owen, obeying the king's command, lowered his guard and let Marcus free. He slid his sword into its scabbard and stepped near Marcus. Their gazes locked, his eyes probing deeply, before he asked, "If you are heroes, then why is this darkness with you?"

"It's kind of a long story, but he serves the Lady of Light, He answers to me," Marcus replied.

"Listen to me," Owen continued, now facing Marcus again. "I have seen the eyes of true evil. What you harbor is worse than any threat I have ever crossed."

"Then don't look into his eyes. Look into mine," Christana said. "Can you not see the light?"

Owen turned and walked over to Christana. She stood as fearlessly as he did, her eyes meeting his with unwavering determination. "This is my team. We are all heroes, and we have come to ask for your help."

Owen held her gaze steadily. Her soft features and youthful appearance belied her strength and resolve. Her blond hair pulled back, revealing eyes that shone with conviction. "Owen, feel your calling. You know you can trust us," she said, her voice gentle yet powerful.

Owen wasn't the most appealing person to look at, but Christana's gaze was mesmerizing. "You are very beautiful, Milady. Who did you say you were?"

"I am Christana, and this is my accompaniment. Arnold Laurent, Jin Chen, George, the Doll, and of course Marcus Steel and his shadow."

"If I may, this is not how I wished to introduce ourselves, but I do wish to speak to you," Tommy said.

"The world is under great stress and on the verge of peril. Time has called for the heroes once more."

Owen walked back to the king and conferred with him for a moment before turning back to the group. "All of you, stand up and follow me," he ordered.

His armor chimed against his crystal skin, but he escorted Tommy to the door. He waited for the rest to join as he ordered the guards to keep a close formation. The Doll, at this moment, stood and became animate again, causing the king and guards to startle.

"Oh, my dear, it's alive?" the king exclaimed in shock.

"Yes, that is a story for another time," Tommy said.

"Come quickly now," Owen instructed, and the guards escorted them out of the dining hall. Outside, the Cactus was waiting for them. Owen saw him standing still and recognized him immediately. "This thing right here! What is that?"

"Things will only get stranger as we go," Tommy said. "Best I tell you when you are ready to hear it."

They continued on and went to a cathedral in the middle of the city. It had been almost destroyed, and soot covered the remaining intact parts. Owen led them inside, moving broken rubble to reveal a hidden passageway beneath the floorboards. The air was musty and left a lingering taste in their mouths. They descended the dark path, littered with dust and debris. Cobwebs around every corner. The oil lamps went dry.

Frutuoso had to stay outside due to his size. The king ordered some men to stand guard over him. Owen picked up an unlit torch from the wall, breathed on it, sparking it to life. Dancing light guided their way down further into the darkness. At last, they came to a wooden door, rotted and ancient. Owen turned to the rest.

"Here is your test," he said, opening the door to reveal a large room. He lit more torches on the wall, illuminating a stone table in the middle. Large stone pillars supported the ceiling. The room brightened, revealing the table's detailed inscriptions in an old language.

"Tell me. Can you read it?" Owen asked, running his fingers over the carvings and indentations.

They gave it a close inspection. The markings displayed meticulous craftsmanship, chiseled into the rocky surface. Marcus turned to it first as he used D's spell to breathe the dust off the table.

"Can you read it?"

"No," Marcus replied.

"Come on, Marcus. Don't lie to him," D taunted with a faint laugh.

"Don't test me," Owen rebuked. "Can you read it?"

"It is not for me to read," D replied.

Next was Christana. She could not decipher it either, despite her instincts. "I cannot," she said.

Arnold stepped forward. In all his years of studying and learning, nothing was ever recorded like this in any history book. To the full extent of his knowledge, he still could not decipher it. "It is a shame; I am unable to read it."

Jin also faced the same fate. He was a simple farmer with no formal education, reading was already difficult for him in his own language. "No," he said as he stepped away from it.

"The Doll doesn't speak, so I assume he doesn't read," Tommy said. George nodded his head to agree with him.

Tommy examined the table closely. He ran his fingers over the engravings and recited the old words he had come to know, and tried to recall any relevant visions. The stone was ancient, and he flipped through the pages of his mind for an answer.

"Well, can you tell me? Can you read it?" Owen pressed.

Flashes of memories overwhelmed Tommy. He saw the construction of the church, the faces of those who carved the table, and the face of the Allfather. Tommy's muscles failed, and he crumpled, his body wracked with spasms.

"Please help him!" Christana shouted as Tommy foamed at the mouth.

Tommy's visions intensified. He saw his family, his mother smiling at him, her head resting back in a chair as she held his brother. The scene darkened, showing his family in distress, shadows gathering over their home. He saw his brother running in darkness, crying in agony. Tommy then fell through clouds and shadows before landing in a blinding light. He saw the same symbols written before him, encircling like a pattern around the table. He witnessed mountains growing, trees springing to life, and ocean waves crashing into the land. Before him, the birth of the Allfather unfolded, the gift of magic bestowed upon the people. The people received these symbols and then carved them onto the table.

Arnold rushed over to Tommy, placing his hands on him to provide some comfort. "Be still, Tommy. Let it pass," he urged, his voice steady and calming.

Tommy's convulsions gradually subsided, but he insisted on getting up. "I saw it, Arnold. I saw everything," he gasped, struggling to steady himself.

Owen watched with a mixture of suspicion and curiosity, unmoved by Tommy's plight. He seemed ready to let Tommy suffer, a test of their intentions. "Well?" he asked again, his voice cold and demanding.

"It's our creation, and our gift of magic," Tommy said, struggling. "This is the table the Allfather had created. From the very beginning, he had them inscribe the world's knowledge upon this table. Upon this, He blessed his followers with the gift of magic. Upon this table, He planted the seed."

"Magic was given to us by the Allfather to defeat the dragons," Owen continued.

"Yes," Tommy said while catching his breath. "We have all heard the story. I have seen it personally."

"And you saw this?" Owen asked. His eyes narrowed as he became perplexed.

"Yes. It is my gift. I can see through time. Interact with the past." Tommy pushed himself up on his own, thanking Arnold for his assistance. "Why bring us here?"

"Because this is a holy relic, built by the Allfather almost 1200 years ago. Now, it lies in ruin. Not many can read the inscription on the table. Not even me. But my heart tells me what it says. A hero would have known."

"I cannot read it either," Tommy admitted. "I just saw it. I saw the face of the Allfather. A sight not meant for me to see."

"When the dragon's emerged, there was no end to their slaughter. King Richard sent his finest men to find this lost relic. They brought it back here in hopes it would retain enough magic to defeat them. But alas, it was only a table."

"We are all heroes. The ones that came after you. Just as the prophecy proclaimed, when time calls a hero will come," Jin added. "My gift is similar to yours."

"It is our duty to answer the call again. Heroes really don't find it easy to trust each other."

"You really are heroes, aren't you? But you cannot read the table?" Owen asked. "Is there something wrong with your future?"

"Very wrong, indeed," Tommy answered, stepping closer to Owen. "We can discuss more, but we will need to do so over our meal. We are starving. I promise I will explain everything to you.

"Very well," Owen said, extending his hand to Tommy. Owen guided them back to the surface. Upon returning, they found the guards enjoying themselves with the Cactus, who was dancing and handing out gifts.

"What is the meaning of this?" Owen asked, surprised.

"This is very entertaining, My Lord." One of the guards responded. "Some of us were hungry and it just gave us food. Before long we were singing and dancing with it."

"Have the servants prepare another table, one suited for me and my new guests. We have heroes among us. Your loyalty is to them as well as me."

"Yes, My Lord," the guards responded in unison, rushing off to handle the arrangements.

As they walked back to the meal hall, Owen spoke with Tommy. "This place is sacred," he explained, pointing to a small inscription carved above the door. "The Allfather Himself taught us how to prepare food and sharing a table was the most sacred of traditions. This hall was built to honor that timeless memory."

They entered the hall, which was being meticulously restored to its original grandeur. Musicians tuned their instruments. Actors prepared to perform. The king's table was being expanded for the new guests. Candles were lit, casting a warm, inviting glow over the room. The king stood and announced to the hall, "We have new heroes among us. Let us welcome them with open hearts!"

A cheer erupted from the crowd, welcoming the heroes with open arms. The music resumed, more vibrant than before, and an even more extravagant array of food was brought out. Rare wines and a variety of ales soon followed.

People approached the table, requesting blessings from the heroes. Although this custom felt strange to them, they obliged graciously, understanding its importance to the locals.

Marcus and Tommy, however, were focused on their conversation with the king and the hero of this time. Owen introduced the king as Richard Montford. They spoke at length. Soon, Christana joined them. Her presence added a calm confidence to their discussion. Tommy warned of a dire future. He described the harsh lands and their mission's urgency. He recounted every detail of his journey through time and the calling that brought them together.

The conversation flowed for hours as the festival continued into the night. The group devoured the food, savoring the chance to indulge abundantly. Arnold tried the exquisite wine they had prepared for just this occasion. He had them pour himself a glass. It was rich at the very least, but bitterness was overwhelming, as he swished it in his mouth. There were hints of berry and sage mixed with other herbs. The wine was fancy for the time, but not to the choosing of Arnold. He preferred nuttier flavors and drier. It was not as clear as the wine they had in his time, and the yeast left a lingering taste upon his tongue.

"It's a fine wine," Arnold said to Christana. "Not much like the wine we have back home. That is one thing the French have perfected over the last few hundred years."

Christana nodded in agreement but refrained from drinking. The memories associated were too painful, and she chose not to tempt herself. A part she thought best to keep Arnold unaware.

Arnold was no fool to her body language and put the discussion to rest.

Tommy, deeply engrossed in his discussion with Owen, hardly ate. His excitement was palpable. He finally paused when Jin began sharing his own story with Owen and the king, detailing how he became known as the Golden Tiger.

Tommy picked up his iron fork and surveyed the array of foods. One particular item caught his eye. The whole reason for wanting to attend this feast was on a platter before him. He skewered it and brought it up to his eyes for inspection. A rare delicacy in his time. The earthy aroma, rich with butter and spices.

In his dark childhood, it was the only thing they would eat. The only thing that would grow in complete darkness. Unlike anything he had ever tasted and a flavor he had forgotten. He took another bite, and the intense flavor transported him back to those dark days, but in a pleasant way. Like a warm hug from his mother, he remembered her holding him while they watched his father cook. The fond memories that made Tommy completely agree with what Owen had told him before. Sharing a table is a sacred tradition.

Another earthy and buttery bite dripped down his chin. In that moment, surrounded by newfound allies and the remnants of an ancient feast, Tommy felt a renewed sense of purpose. The only thing he missed as much as his family. The taste of the mushroom, richer than any he had ever known.

15 Settling Dust

A soft sizzle over a small, crackling fire gave light that bounced throughout the bunker. The flickering flames cast dancing shadows on the rough, concrete walls, giving the room an eerie, ghostly ambiance. In a well-worn pan, mushrooms were tossed back and forth, their earthy aroma slowly filling the confined space. Though unseasoned, the mushrooms were the only edible remnants they had. The faint smell was a small comfort in the otherwise bleak surroundings.

Emily awoke from a restless sleep, her eyes adjusting to the dim light. She saw Mason hunched over the fire, the orange glow reflecting off his tired face as he diligently stirred the pan.

"They're almost ready," Mason said, his voice breaking the heavy silence. "Go ahead and wake Jimmy. He will need to eat too."

"We're fine, Mason," Emily replied, her voice barely above a whisper.

"I don't want to hear it," Mason snapped, a rough edge to his tone. "I am just trying to help."

"You won't have enough for yourself, but we will make it back to our place and we have a small supply there."

"You don't have to resent me. Look at yourself. You can barely walk. You took a hard hit."

"And you didn't?"

Mason didn't answer. He just continued to stir the pan, his thoughts drifting. The mushrooms were grown in a side room, a makeshift garden he had painstakingly cultivated. His stocks were running out, and this might be one of the last meals he could prepare for himself. Another trip outside would be needed soon to scavenge for supplies. The ash in the soil made it fertile, perfect for growing mushrooms, a small blessing in these dark times. Cultivating them had become an art, each variety unique and adapted to their harsh reality, driven by the desperation of survival.

Mason served two plates of freshly cooked mushrooms, their steam rising in the cold air. It wasn't much, but he knew they needed it, especially Jimmy. He placed the plates on the rickety table.

Emily's resolve wavered as she saw the steaming plates. She knew they needed to eat, that this was no time for stubborn pride. She quietly moved to Jimmy, gently shaking him awake. He stirred, his eyes opening to the sight of the meager meal. She helped him to the table, his small form seeming even more fragile.

Jimmy ate eagerly, his hunger overriding any sense of taste. The trauma of yesterday still lingered, but the simple act of filling his belly brought relief. Mason watched, kneeling beside Jimmy, his eyes filled with a mix of concern and determination.

"Did you sleep well?"

"I did," Jimmy said slowly.

"Good. It's important for a young boy like yourself to get plenty of rest," Mason replied. "Make sure you keep up your strength."

"Just eat up, Jimmy. After this, we will be returning home," Emily said to him.

"Where will you go?" Mason asked. "You cannot think you can return to your home. It isn't safe. Please just stay here. I can keep you." Mason tried to plead with her.

"Mom, why can't we stay with Mason?"

"Just eat your breakfast, Jimmy," Emily said in a soft voice. "I will not discuss this here."

"Very well, but you know you cannot leave. By this time, the Hellhounds will be lurking around your home. It would be foolish to return. With that, you are welcome to stay. Whatever it is at your house you need. Let me go retrieve it for you. I can slip in and out."

Emily excused herself from the table and left to use the restroom. Mason seized the moment, getting up and grabbing a piece of parchment and some ink made from wet ash. Kneeling down again by Jimmy, with pen in hand, he asked urgently, "Jimmy, do you know what you may need for the machine? Try and remember quickly!"

Jimmy thought hard, his young mind racing. Despite his age, he was incredibly intelligent, a trait he inherited from his father. "I think the combustor blew. I saw a few coils explode too," he said, struggling to remember more.

"Hurry, before your mother returns. What else?" Mason urged, his pen moving swiftly over the parchment, writing down symbols and words as Jimmy spoke.

"It might need more of those tiny lightbulbs. I don't know what Tommy called them." Jimmy tried to describe the image in his head for Mason to scribble. "And I will need materials to make a new circuit board. Maybe a few other things. I really cannot say without seeing more."

"Do you know where your dad would get most of these things?"

"He made a lot of them, but most of the things he found were…" Jimmy paused, tears welling up in his eyes as memories of his father surfaced.

"I'm sorry. This is good for now. I will get the things you need," Mason said, quickly tucking the parchment into his pocket as Emily walked back into the room.

He addressed her while standing up. "I'll head to your house right now. Is there anything you need?"

"I can't trust you, Mason," she said with a sigh as she watched Jimmy continue consuming his plate of mushrooms. "But for his sake. I don't know what else to do. Food is all I need. We had a great supply in the bunker below."

"It'll be a while. I don't have my bike anymore. Maybe I can go out and get supplies to repair it later," Mason said, his mind already calculating the journey ahead.

Mason put the list in his front pocket and left. He began his climb up the ladder. Opening the hatch to the bunker, he was greeted by a blast of harsh, dusty air. The old house above did little to keep it out. The feeling of the gritty particles scraping his lungs was one he never grew to tolerate.

The shack, like Emily's, was rundown, its wood rotting and old. Only the stone bricks kept it standing, a lone structure in a desolate landscape. The world outside was decaying, everything succumbing to the relentless march of time and ruin.

Mason stepped out into the wasteland, his boots kicking up ash that covered the ground. The sky was a tumultuous expanse of dark clouds, red lightning crackling ominously across it. The air was foul, every breath a struggle.

His eyes winced as he surveyed his surroundings. He made his way to a locked storage chest beside the house, retrieving a homemade shotgun and a pistol, strapping them to his body. He picked up two empty duffle bags and began his trek to the Kent residence.

He had to be quick and silent and mindful of attracting the attention of wandering Hellhounds. Despite his injuries, this expedition was necessary. He found his bike destroyed in the dirt, parts missing, and severely damaged. Repairing it would be a challenge, but not impossible with Robin's hoarded parts.

Robin was able to build this machine from studying the books he found on his scavenger trips, and pieces of scrap he picked up along the way. The bike was a great achievement this time, and it was lucky for him to even find usable parts. Robin also had a habit of collecting way too many gizmos and other worthless trinkets for surviving these times. Yet, this bad habit would come in handy for Mason.

The house wasn't far. Mason moved cautiously, reaching the doorstep with ease. The door, still in disrepair, bore the scars of acid and explosion. He entered with his gun drawn, methodically clearing each room of any threats before descending into the bunker.

Inside, he found the collection of items Robin had amassed over the years. What once seemed like junk was now invaluable. He gathered the needed items and a few jars of preserved mushrooms, ready to head back. At the base of the ladder, Mason stumbled upon one of Robin's books. He paused, memories flooding back, and thought of the times he and Robin had shared.

"Mason, look what I found!" Robin exclaimed, handing over a book. "I found a place. It was still completely untouched by the hounds." Robin's eyes sparkled with a mixture of pride and wonder.

With a thoughtful smile, Robin handed Mason a thick, well-worn book. Its cover faded, but the title still read: The Fundamentals of Motor Construction. Inside, the pages had detailed diagrams and in-depth explanations. It revealed the intricate art of building motors.

"I found this in a building called a school. I guess a long time ago, people would go there to learn about things to better themselves," Robin continued. "Look at this one! It's like a story of the past. They called it his..tor...y...history."

The Eight Heroes of Old

"What is this?" Mason asked, flipping through the pages, bewildered by the unfamiliar concept.

"It tells about things from the past, about all of mankind's greatest achievements. But look at this page," Robin said as his gaze landed on a page where vivid illustrations seized him.

The page depicted heroes from a bygone era. Marcus and the Cactus stood tall, alongside Christana and Arnold. Owen soared in the background, carrying the Porcelain Doll. At the center was a massive figure. Muscles rippled on him. He bore a sword and wore woven fabric with glowing markings.

"This one looks amazing. His name is Gorn," Robin exclaimed, his eyes lighting up. "He was the one who served the Allfather. It says he was the first hero!"

"Don't fill your head with fairytales, Robin," Mason scoffed, pushing the book away. "This stuff won't help us survive. Don't waste energy carrying these things back."

"I think this is a fine thing to have. I can read these stories to my boys tonight." Robin said while looking at the image closer. "Look underneath the illustration it says here. 'When time calls, a hero will come.'"

"There are no heroes. If that were true, then why didn't they save this world? It's just make believe, Robin, nothing more."

"Well, either way. I find it entertaining. I'll keep them."

"I advise just sticking to finding things to use, not these books. You are barely read as it is."

Robin dismissed the jab and stowed the book to not damage it anymore.

Back in the present, Mason snapped the book shut, jolting him back to reality. He placed it back on the shelf and climbed out of the bunker. Outside, the winds had turned harsher, a dust storm raging through the wasteland. It wasn't going to be an easy journey, but survival was all he knew. He packed everything he had gathered into one of the bags and left it by the front door. He would return to it, but it was too much to carry right now.

As he stepped into the storm, red lightning crackled across the dark sky. He pulled his makeshift scarf tighter around his face. The sand burned any exposed skin, and the goggles Robin had given him were the only protection for his eyes. Step by step, Mason trekked through the ash-covered land, the hike exhausting every muscle. The pain surged, threatening to consume him, yet he pushed forward regardless.

At last, he reached the top of the mountain and saw the school, fully intact and untouched by the beasts. It was a remarkable sight, a relic of a time long gone. The storm had cleared, leaving a view that stretched for miles. There was a certain peace that came with such height, even in a desolate world.

Descending the mountain was easier, though he lost his footing a few times. The school loomed before him. Its two stories were impressive to someone who had rarely seen structures of such size. The front doors had disappeared, and the windows had all been shattered. But inside, it still held many treasures from the past.

Mason moved in swift patterns, finding bike parts and other materials for the time machine. He discovered a supply of parts Robin had gathered, and many of the gadgets Jimmy needed. He decided to eat some of the dried mushrooms he had brought. Their meager sustenance was enough to keep him going.

As he walked through the building, memories of his last visit with Robin flooded back. The glass and debris crunched under his makeshift boots. He remembered how Robin had excitedly shown him the books he had found in the science hall.

"Look at this one, Mason," Robin had said, his eyes bright. "I told you we could find useful stuff here!"

"What is it?" Mason had asked, curious despite himself.

"It shows how to cultivate plants. Look, they used what they called lightbulbs to grow plants indoors where there wasn't light."

"Indoor Gardening?" Mason had read on the cover, skeptical.

"Look, this one is metal work!" Robin said even more excitedly. "We need all of these. We can make tools and perhaps we could find a way to bring plants back!"

"What do we do with plants?"

"I'll show you!" Robin said, taking out a book from his bag. It was old and the pictures faded on it, but it still had a lot of great information.

"They called it a cookbook," Robin said, opening a page to the salad section. "They grew things like tomatoes, I think that is this red one. And lettuce."

"That looks weird."

"It was probably good. We will just have to find out more. Don't you ever feel like not eating insects and mushrooms?"

"I don't think so. There isn't anything else."

"This does not look good to you?" Robin had insisted, showing a faded picture of a salad.

"You can barely see what is on there!" Mason scoffed. "Forget these books! Let's just get what we need. You said you need parts for what?"

"A motorcycle, I believe it was what they were called. I think I can build one with the right equipment. I need something to help me do metal work among other things."

Robin placed the books in his bag. The thrill of discovery fueled his drive. These books, he knew, would eventually lead to the creation of the bike that Mason now

The Eight Heroes of Old

relied on. As he continued to browse the library, many of the books crumbled to dust at his touch, their pages too brittle from age and neglect. The glue that once held them together had long since failed. The spines disintegrated in his hands.

Among the decayed volumes, one book stood out. It was carefully preserved under a layer of protective plastic. Robin's eyes widened as he pulled it out. Its bright pictures and intact pages contrasted with the rest of the library. This book seemed to hold a wealth of knowledge, some of which even the people of the past had barely begun to understand.

Robin tried to read it as best as he could, sounding out the words and marveling at the detailed illustrations. Robin read the cover title, his lips whispering the words as he tried to make sense of them. "Advanced Engineering Concepts. How to Explain Our World with Relativity and Other Physics." Each page he turned revealed intricate diagrams and explanations. They ranged from basic mechanical principles to complex theoretical constructs.

Turning each page, he became more and more fascinated. Each line gave more information and even though it was difficult to understand, he wanted to know more.

"This is incredible," Robin muttered to himself, his fingers tracing the lines of a schematic. "If we could understand this, we could build so much more."

"Mason, look, look, look!" he said, but Mason wasn't there, he moved on to collect other things and lost interest in the useless books. But Robin kept reading.

"Time travel," Robin said under his breath, his eyes widening at the thought. The book claimed it was possible, though it had been merely a theory back in their time. Their technology and understanding had not yet reached the necessary level, but the idea was tantalizing. He could feel his heart race. No other book had given him such a feeling. He ran his fingers over every picture, feeling the imprints of the ink on the page. This book was clearer than all the others; no lines were missing, the pages were still white, and it was easy on his eyes. The words he read seemed almost magical, like the air of a forgotten age filled with promise and potential.

He closed the book and added it to his bag, stepping out of the room only to find Mason running back frantically. Mason pushed Robin, urging him to run. Robin turned and saw a Hellhound not far behind Mason, its mouth drooling as it closed in on them. They both took off running.

Robin had never encountered a Hellhound prowling the school before. The beast coveted them for their juicy meat, and its only instinct was to kill and devour. Mason and Robin evaded it by turning corners and jumping through windows. Their smaller size allowed for a narrow escape from the large creature. With every stumble it made, they gained more distance.

Outside, in the clear, they ran as fast as they could, but Robin's bag was ripping. The fabric was old and couldn't withstand the trauma. Books scattered across the ground.

"There is no time!" Mason said, grabbing Robin trying to force him to just leave them.

"No!" Robin yelled, breaking free. "I need them!"

"Leave them!" Mason yelled even louder.

The beast broke through the doors and fixed its gaze on Robin. Its teeth were itching for a bite. It charged at them, mouth wide open. Robin was determined to keep his books. They meant more to his survival than Mason could ever realize. Robin reached under his garments and pulled out a strange device. He pointed it at the charging demon, closed one eye, took a deep breath, and pulled the trigger. The beast exploded before their eyes, the shockwave throwing them to the ground. The flames nearly consumed them.

Robin was quick to recover, concerned more about the burning pages on his books. Beside them were parts of his broken weapon. After examining them and relaxing after seeing they had nothing more than a few charred edges,

Robin fashioned his shirt into a patch for his bag and placed the books inside.

"What was that?" Mason asked, getting up.

"I made that. I read about it in one of the books. They called it a gun in previous times."

"Do you have any more of that?"

"No," Robin said, gathering another book off the ground then the parts to the broken pistol. "It was my only one."

"This is too dangerous. How did you know that would even work?"

"I didn't." Robin examined the broken parts. "It was just desperation."

"We are not coming here again. It's too dangerous," Mason said, turning around. "Let's just go before any more come."

Robin didn't want to argue. It was dangerous, but the interest in the books would eventually become his undoing.

"What a fool," Mason said, looking around at the claw marks on the floor of the school, matching the marks from his memory. "But he was right. I should have listened."

Mason collected more items and packed them into the bag. It was nearly full. He tried his best to sneak around, wary of Hellhounds. But it wasn't hounds he heard. Voices echoed down the hall. He looked around a corner and saw men scavenging through supplies. Mason quickly turned back, trying to stay hidden. It was no use; the three men heard him stumble on debris. They came quickly, bearing spears and other weapons. Mason stumbled to gather as much as he could. Hounds weren't the only thing to fear.

What were other humans doing here? he thought. Mason had not seen any for years. Most didn't even come up to the surface. *Robin was the only one I had ever known to be brave enough to venture to the surface.*

He rushed to the front door only to be confronted by a feral man with rotten teeth and skin as dirty as his own. They were faster, closing the distance quickly. A spear came close to Mason's face, a near miss. Mason turned to run away, only to find the other men standing before him.

They spoke in a language he couldn't understand, their intentions clear. They were starving, and cannibalism was not out of the question these days. The men were threatening but unsure of what Mason could do. He quickly dropped his bag and raised the shotgun. Before the man could react, Mason fired, sending him to the ground, holes in his chest and bleeding. Mason quickly turned and pumped the shotgun, but the man behind him struck a blow to his shoulder, knocking him down. The other jumped on him, wrestling on the ground. Mason struggled to free a hand.

Finally, Mason managed to pull a knife from his belt and slash the man above him. The struggle was intense, and luck seemed to evade him as the other man began to pummel him. But Mason was determined. With a fierce growl, he drew the pistol from his hip and fired blindly. The shots missed, but the deafening sound terrified the men who had never encountered such a weapon. Mason stumbled to his feet, pointing the empty pistol at them. They didn't know it was empty; they only knew its noise was a harbinger of death.

Mason, holding his bleeding side, breathed heavily. "Now I got you," he said, picking up his shotgun.

The men, eyes wide with fear, turned and fled before Mason could react further. Confused, he realized too late what had scared them more than his gun—the growling behind him. A chill ran down his spine as he knew his doom was near. Before he could turn, the Hellhound lunged, its teeth sinking into his arm, tearing flesh and muscle. The pain was blinding as the teeth seared his wounds, and he was thrown aside like a ragdoll. The beast's attack on the dying man distracted it long enough for Mason to stagger to his feet.

Ignoring the pain, Mason bolted, his broken body protesting with every step. *I'm going to make it*, he thought desperately. He saw the other men running for the front door and hurled himself out a window. The beast, catching the scent of the fleeing men, diverted its attention and chased after them.

The Hellhound quickly caught up to the two of them, violently shaking one it caught within its fangs. The man's torso disappeared into the hound's jaws. Mason raised his shotgun and fired at the beast. The distance made the shotgun less effective, but it caught the creature's attention. Its eyes, burning with a relentless hunger, fixed on Mason.

Mason waited for a better shot, recalling how Robin had taken aim so precisely. Just as before, the beast fell to the gunfire, erupting in flames as it died. They never died peacefully. The other man, tending to his fallen comrade, looked at Mason with a mix of fear and awe. Mason walked past without a glance, knowing what humans had become. He had no interest in helping; they would likely kill him and the others back home if given the chance.

The man stared at Mason, not understanding the weapons or the power he wielded. No one had been curious enough to learn from books like Robin. Robin had dared to dream of a better life, a vision that now fueled Mason's survival.

Mason continued his journey back, hands shaking from shock. Blood dripped silently into the ash. He knew it wasn't his strength or skill that kept him alive, but the gifts Robin had given him. Everything Robin learned from those books was more than they needed to survive. Mason truly understood now just how powerful knowledge was. Despite his bruises, the way back felt clearer. The storm had subsided, leaving a calm path. Days passed as he crossed the wasteland, but confidence grew within him.

Reaching the shack, he bent down to pick up the bag he had left inside the house. Loading the bags onto the bike, he assembled it as best he could and pushed it all the way home. Emily saw him bleeding and panicked.

"Oh dear, you're bleeding!" she said with worry. Despite her earlier indifference, seeing him in this state stirred pity and guilt within her. "Mason..." she said slowly, regret in her voice. "I'm sorry."

"It's fine," he replied, setting the bags down and pulling out the items they needed, especially the jars of food. "I'll be okay."

"Come, let me take care of you. Sit down," she insisted, using a wet rag to clean his wounds. The Hellhound bites burned more than they cut, but the bleeding soon stopped on its own. The wounds were deep, but Mason knew he would recover. It wasn't the worst he had endured. Jimmy entered the room, fear evident in his eyes.

"Jimmy, come here," Mason called, reaching into the bag. Jimmy walked over cautiously, and Mason pulled out a few of the items his father had set aside.

"There's more where that came from. I can get scraps and other metal for you to make the missing parts you need, if you can fix the motorcycle," Mason said with a short smile.

"What do you think you're doing!?" Emily demanded.

"It's just for him. He needs this," Mason explained.

Jimmy's bright face faded as he saw his mother's anger.

"Don't fill his head with false hopes. If you think he's going out there to fix the machine, you're out of your mind. I won't allow it," Emily said, her fury rising. She threw the rag on the floor, staining it red. She picked up Jimmy and carried him to the other room. Mason called out before she left.

"You know we need to do this! We can't leave Tommy by himself."

"Don't make this about Tommy," Emily stormed back after putting Jimmy in the other room and shutting the door so as to not let him hear. She returned to Mason, more furious. "You never believed in him. You let him down. You were always against this before. What's changed? Why should I expect anything different from you?"

"What's changed? It actually worked!" Mason retorted.

"We don't know that! He hasn't come back! He could be dead for all we know, and you want the same for Jimmy?" Emily turned away, emotions finally catching up to her. She tried to bury them, to be strong for her son.

Mason stood, his voice stern. "We can't do nothing. We have to make it work again, at least find a way to bring him back!"

"Mason, you're going to get us all killed!" Emily cried, walking away. "Leave my son out of this!"

Mason sat in the dark, contemplating the weight of his thoughts. His heart raced with adrenaline, and his mind was a whirlpool of restless ideas. Frustration gnawed at him as he paced the room, the faint light from the fire casting eerie shadows on the walls. He knew he needed Jimmy to fix the time machine, even if Emily couldn't see it. Desperation drove him to the pile of books Robin had brought back. One about mushrooms caught his eye, its cover worn but promising.

He flipped through the pages. His eyes ached from the strain. Then, he found it: Ganoderma Lucidum, commonly known as reishi. The art of cultivating this potent fungus was one of the few skills humanities had retained. Perfected even. Over time the desperate struggle for survival intensified. Robin had used it to help them sleep through the long, terrifying nights, filled with the haunting howls of Hellhounds. As Mason stared at the page, an idea began to take shape in his mind.

If he could grow some reishi, he could use it to help Emily sleep. While she was under its influence, he could take Jimmy to fix the time machine. It was a perfect plan—

more than just a means of survival, it was their way out. The urgency of the situation spurred him into action. He began preparing immediately, his hands moving with a determined purpose. Soon, his plan was in motion, and hope flickered in the darkness like the firelight that illuminated his path.

16 The Deep Magic

Owen, Tommy, and Christana walked atop the castle wall in the early morning. The cobblestones, laid with precision, made Tommy feel significant with each step. Though torches flickered along the wall, the sun began to rise. Its rays pierced the dark clouds above, casting the flames into dim relief. Standing on those ancient stones, Tommy felt an overwhelming sense of strength. He leaned over the crenellation, gazing at the battlefield below, where countless soldiers had clashed. The sight weighed heavily on him, a stark reminder of his world's suffering under fire and ash. He feared failing humanity.

Owen joined Tommy at the wall, leaning beside him and surveying the land. The vast expanse of scarred earth stretched out before them, showcasing the recent turmoil.

"This whole land is thankful to me," Owen's words were heavy as his chest heaved. "I can feel the deep magic coursing through me. It transformed me into what I am. The Mother Dragon is now at peace with humans, and we will know comfort again."

"But you feel sick, don't you?" Tommy replied, concern evident in his voice.

"Poisoned almost," Owen spat over the wall, his spittle glistening as it fell.

"But why?" Christana inquired, her eyes searching his face. "What makes you feel this way?"

"All heroes feel this way," Tommy interjected. "It's in our nature to feel unworthy or doubtful. So much relies on us."

"But it is not that. My time called for me," Owen said, glancing skyward. Through the smoky haze, the light was faint but persistent. "I brought peace three months ago to this land, but I could not give the Mother Dragon what I promised. I failed her. She wanted no more death to her children, but I had to end Azarth. There was no other way."

"Evil is in their hearts. They were born that way. It is not your fault. It's only nature," Christana said, putting her hand over his armored shoulder. It produced an unmatched shine. Christana gazed at the shimmering crystals that covered Owen.

"They are beautiful, Owen," she said. "Do they hurt?"

"Every morning," he replied, rubbing his wrists through his sleeves. "They become tighter. So, what exactly do you need of me? Why are all the heroes needed? Does time not call for a hero when one is needed?"

"You were never one to doubt the prophecy," Tommy said. "I've watched you your whole life, constantly devoted to the Allfather. Why start now?"

"I can feel it," Owen said. "The flow of magic through me is dying. The darkness is howling in the distance, and I feel something move over this world that lingers even after the dragons have left. Worse even."

"It's the same darkness all of us face. The evil will of the Defier. His power grew and grew with every passing year. Our friend, Arnold, has made quite a few discoveries. All your stories have been told so far. Mine is still unfolding. Am I up for the job? Can I face this darkness?"

"The light always vanquishes the dark. I shall aid you with whatever you may need. I have always been in servitude."

"Owen, we thank you for your help, but this won't be easy," Christana said.

"We will need one more person to join us. The first," Tommy said, backing off the wall.

"Gorn?" Owen asked. "I assume. He is the only hero before me. The only one I know, but he is not here."

"If you are ready, Tommy, then I shall gather the rest," Christana said.

Christana took her leave after Tommy agreed and left them to their discussion. Owen and Tommy continued to walk along the parapets. He felt great discomfort in Tommy and could only assume it was self-doubt. Owen turned to see the sun break through the smog in the sky. Even for a faint moment, it lit the lone flower in the field. Among all the ash, life was coming back to the Earth.

"If you feel times are bleak and there is no way out, I can assure you, peace can be restored. It's in our blood to do so," Owen said.

Tommy saw the sunlight fade, consumed by the smoke once again. "It's only a small chance, I feel. Can one really change fate?"

"Tommy, how about I suggest something to you?"

"What would that be?"

"Clear your mind. Come with me. I will show you how I spend my time when I am in distress. It is the most relaxing thing there is."

"You mean to fly?"

"You're not scared, are you?" Owen asked, a playful challenge in his tone. He began removing his plate armor, which was specially made for easy removal, with holes in places to let the crystals come through. Owen placed it neatly on the wall, standing now in his garments. He smiled at Tommy before leaping off the wall. A gust of wind met Tommy's face as he glanced over the edge. Owen soared into the skies, his wings clearing the smoke and breaking the darkness. He dove back down to greet Tommy.

"Get on!" he said. Owen's size was massive, even from the high wall, making the climb a daunting task. "I'll make it easy for you!" Owen's voice rebounded off the wall with a rich, melodious tone. He lowered his wing for Tommy to climb. The crystal covered every part of his body, replacing the scales with the sparkle of minerals. His wings glistened, more magnificent than Tommy had imagined. Owen scooped Tommy up and flew with great speed, Tommy holding on for dear life.

"Let's go to a place a little less depressing!"

The dragon flew across the fields, covering distances others could only dream of. Soon, they left the ashen fields and soot-covered mountains behind, finding a place of green and sunlight. The land stretched out in vibrant beauty as far as the eye could see.

"This was the only place the dragons didn't reach. I stopped them before they could," Owen said with pride as he looked over the rich, peaceful lands.

"What was that?!" Tommy tried yelling over the high winds.

"What?" Owen replied.

The Eight Heroes of Old

"I can't hear you!" Tommy continued to yell, but the wind was too strong for speech to carry.

"Never mind, just enjoy the view!" Owen said, soaring even further.

The sight took Tommy's breath away. He wanted more. His heart was not yet satisfied. He carefully stood up and climbed to Owen's head, standing fully on top. From there, he saw all the beauty of the world. Tommy was not afraid. He felt like he could face anything up there. Owen stayed calm, giving Tommy the time to cleanse his soul.

Owen took him back to the castle walls and let him down with ease before returning to his human form. Tommy had never felt a rush quite like that; it was exactly what he needed to clear his mind.

"Our minds are a lot like those clouds, Tommy," Owen said, putting his armor back on. "Sometimes, you just need to break away from them. You can clear them and push the darkness away."

"That's a very good analogy," Tommy said.

"It's a way of life," Owen said, looking up at the opening in the clouds. "Other men will never know what it is like to fly in the sky," he sighed, as if it were a saddening thought.

"My dear, Owen," Tommy said, chuckling. "You will be quite surprised." Tommy could see the bewilderment in

Owen's eyes, and he could not quite catch onto Tommy's words.

"Let's go meet the others. I have a place for us where we can discuss our plans further."

In the royal keep, the king had rooms for all the heroes to stay. Fine wine and cheese stocked them. Designers created elegant rooms to cater to nearby visiting lords. It was still morning, and most of the heroes were awake by this time, all except one.

Marcus had trouble sleeping at night, only to sleep past his waking hour. However, this came with a nightmare he could not shake. He was back at his home in New York. He saw Diana in her room, going about her normal routine. He saw a TV showing Manson speaking to the crowds, proclaiming his great providence. In this dream, he could see the reality that could have been, a life with his wife, not as a hero. It was Manson that controlled his mind, much like the demon did before. This new imprecation left Marcus hurt, the kind of pain that stomped on his heart. It was too much for Marcus to cope with; he longed for his old life.

The demon could see these same nightmares. He saw the path Marcus took. The evil Marcus let grow in his heart never fully left. When the time came, Marcus cast the demon out. He screamed and begged Marcus as he

The Eight Heroes of Old

banished him back to the void. As the demon left, so did the light, and Marcus felt a cold grasp around him, entangling every nerve in his body. Gasping for air, Marcus awoke from this dream. His heart pounded from these visions as if they were real.

Marcus soon snapped out of his confusion, only to find himself back in the castle room. The demon, in a ghostly form, hovered just above him in a smoky haze. The demon did not look amused with Marcus.

"You really would do that?" D asked. "You really would betray me? For her?" He ground his teeth as he spoke, sharing the same nightmares that tormented Marcus.

"What did you poison me with?"

"I needed to see."

"That isn't our future. Not anymore."

"But given the options, you would leave me to the abyss. You would not hesitate to give me up."

"It was just a dream."

"It was more than just a dream, Marcus. I know the intentions of your heart."

"What would you have me do? If that really was the case. Yes, I want Diana back. I want her back more than anything." Marcus rubbed his hand over his eyes, too exhausted to argue with the shadow. It was too early for this, but the demon felt betrayed.

"I know you would. Affection is a curse to humanity."

"What would you know?" Marcus shouted.

Just then, a knock on the door interrupted them, and Jin asked if Marcus was all right. He could hear him from the other room and, as a kind gesture, wanted to help Marcus if he could. Marcus opened the door and let Jin inside, where he set up a mat on the floor and, from his small bag, took out incense. It was almost gone, but he had just enough for a small session of meditation.

"Do you mind?" Jin asked.

"Go right ahead. What are you doing?" Marcus asked as he sat across from Jin on the floor.

"I sensed you were in distress. I want to help you Marcus," Jin continued. He filled the room with a light smelling smoke and rang a small bell.

"I don't think you can."

"Calm yourself." Jin closed his eyes and insisted Marcus did the same. "Marcus, if you don't learn how to control your emotions, and cannot control the beast you have, then it will ruin your life."

"It already has," Marcus scoffed.

"Tell me Marcus, What distresses you?"

"I feel lost. My whole life I spent in doubt. My self-worth is low. I am not the man I promised to my wife. I cannot be the man she loved."

"Go on," Jin encouraged. "Let your feelings flow out of you. Find the storm and silence it."

"I had a dream. I saw just as Tommy said. Was it real? It sure felt like it. I saw myself arguing with Diana and we grew cold. It would never work. I gave up my life as the hero of my time."

"Marcus, don't fill yourself with these visions. Don't let them control you. It was just a dream. Even if this was the path you took, it is not your fate today."

"I let everybody down. It was my job to protect them."

"Just calm yourself Marcus. Let's do some breathing exercises. As you inhale, feel the Allfather's presence with you. Feel the force you are powerless to control, but know he guides you through it all."

Jin continued to coach Marcus, dispelling the clouds that bogged his mind. The distress soon faded, and the darkness inside Marcus was silenced and felt at peace. He hadn't felt it since before everything started. The demon had more control over him than he realized, but Marcus was now able to keep it at bay. A few more minutes into their session, Christana stopped by the room.

"Am I disturbing anything?" Christana asked.

"Not at all," Jin replied. "You are welcome to join us. We are just going over our practices. I use this to help control the beast within. I feel like Marcus could benefit from it too."

"I would, but perhaps another time. Tommy has need of us in the courtyard. I believe it is time to get going again."

"Very well," Jin said, smothering his incense and storing it away.

"Thank you, Jin," Marcus said to him while taking a deep breath.

Christana left to gather the others. Marcus and Jin stepped outside into the brisk morning air. The breeze was a shock, but a welcome one. Owen and Tommy approached them from the gatehouse. Tommy was eager to gather everyone and get the last member for their party. But, Marcus was not pleased with Tommy. He approached him once more.

"Tommy," Marcus said softly. He had a shake in his voice. He was about to ask a question, maybe he did not want the answer. "When you told me about my marriage. You lied to me, didn't you? You told me it would be just fine, but I believe that will not be the case."

"Marcus, please don't do this to yourself," Tommy replied. "You will only find pain when looking into your future."

"Just tell me. I'm okay with it."

"No…" Tommy said. "I'm sorry, Marcus, but you will not be okay. She tries for a while to work it out, but in the end, the darkness is still too much for her."

Marcus looked away to hide his tears that he held back, not wanting to show much emotion. It was painful to hear.

His whole world would be lost, even if everything went to plan. His life would never return to normal.

"Marcus, you must understand. Please don't fret. This is the price for every hero. They save the world, but not for themselves. I know this. I can see all that disheartens the heroes. All your sufferings. I know my fate. I will suffer the same. I believe I will never return to my time. If we fix this timeline, my family may cease to exist. There is a chance I will lose them forever, and possibly, I may go with them."

"The world is ours to save, but not for us to enjoy," Jin said. "I understand... I know too well of this." Even Jin began choking up on his emotions, but he composed himself quickly.

"I will save the world, but not for me. I wish I could see my mother. I miss her. I do feel your pain, Marcus."

The demon stepped out of Marcus, his ghostly form hovering nearby. It always took over when Marcus was in deep pain. This time, he did not smile. He felt anguish just like Marcus. Sharing every affliction, D pleaded with the Time Warden.

"I know my place in this world. Marcus has suffered enough. He wants to be free from me and I will be cast out of this world. My loyalties lie to him, but it pains me to see him suffer any longer. He is the only one I wish not to see harmed."

Tommy walked up to the shadow, his eyes unwavering. "It is his place as the hero. He cannot give you up."

"Is there a way? You are the keeper of time, aren't you?"

"You are a being of intelligence, why are you asking these questions? You know the answer just as much as I do. If we change fate, if it is possible, it will not be for us."

Marcus turned around to face the group. He had shed enough tears in his lifetime. He came to terms with everything he knew.

"It's all right," Marcus said. "I will have to accept it. If I don't then the whole world will suffer. Maybe I am the key, Tommy. Maybe…"

"I doubt it, Marcus. Not to burst your bubble. We all are, but if this plan is going to work, then we need all of us. You are just part of it."

Christana arrived with the rest of the team. Arnold was by her side, and the Cactus was carrying the Porcelain Doll. Owen approached them, looking curiously at the two oddities.

"What is this?" Owen asked. "I didn't get time to meet them, yet."

"That, my good sir, is a Cactus and the other is a Doll," Tommy said.

"A Cactus? Is it some sort of tree?"

"In a strange way, I suppose. If that counts. It's a type of plant. It gives nice fruit and flowers."

"Very curious, and this doll?"

"He's creepy hero," Marcus said. "But his creator was a dollmaker for children."

"And their names?" Owen replied.

"They are known to time as the Capoeira Cactus and the Porcelain Doll because they are a Cactus and a porcelain doll," Tommy said frankly. "I introduce you to Frutuoso and George."

"I hope your stay was…a generous one at least. I do not know what else your kind would be accustomed to."

George and Frutuoso were both delighted to be in Owen's company, their moods visibly lifted. George, overjoyed to finally have his name acknowledged, showed deep gratitude to Tommy. Though Tommy felt a pang of guilt for not addressing it sooner. He realized they hadn't spent much time together since their first meeting.

"The Allfather really has miraculous gifts, doesn't he?" Owen said. "We are living proof."

"Owen," Marcus said, stepping forward. "I can tell, people in this time are much different from people in my time. This place is very strong in faith. Not a lot of people are followers of the Allfather or the Creator. Or even believed magic was a thing. I mean, they believe in heroes and everything, but they do lose sight of things."

"That's a shame," Owen replied. "This magic should not be forgotten. Well... I am ready. The king will allow us to use his command room."

The walk wasn't too far, but it felt like stepping into a different world. The structure, grand and imposing, was finally large enough to house the Cactus. Frutuoso was ecstatic. His spiny limbs quivered with excitement as he rarely had the chance to enter man-made buildings. The hall was a masterpiece of architecture, built with pristine gray brick and supported by sturdy stone pillars. Sunlight streamed through high arched windows as Frutuoso stood in the rays, welcoming them gladly. Banners of various colors and insignias hung around the room. They added a vibrant splash of history and honor to the space.

At the center of the room stood a long, polished table made of dark mahogany. Chairs upholstered in rich, burgundy leather surrounded it. At the far end of the table sat the king's throne-like chair. An opulent piece laced with gold and adorned with a blue cushion, woven with the finest velvet. The chair seemed almost alive, glowing with a regal presence. Owen, with a sense of both duty and privilege, took that seat and welcomed the others to find their own chair.

"Tommy, you had something you wished to share with us?" Owen spoke up, giving Tommy the room to speak.

The Eight Heroes of Old

Tommy took a deep breath, his mind racing with thoughts of Gorn. He knew in his heart that confronting Gorn would be an immense challenge. Gorn was not just a hero; he was the first hero, emerging during an era when magic was at its zenith. In the ancient legends, he would be known as The Viking, the one hero who could withstand any trial. He was said to possess the might of the Allfather and was hailed as the destroyer of magic. His name had echoed through the centuries, becoming a favorite among the people. A symbol of unyielding strength and perseverance. His story, rich and compelling, had the power to move even the most bitter of hearts.

"Maybe it was all just legend," Tommy mused aloud, his voice tinged with a mixture of awe and skepticism. "Maybe everything said and done was exaggerated. Maybe it was all just a myth."

Owen leaned forward, his eyes alight with interest. "Legends often have a kernel of truth," he said thoughtfully. "They grow with each telling, but at their core, they hold the essence of something real. We must be prepared for the possibility that Gorn is as formidable as the stories say."

"You know, we are only missing one more hero—Gorn, the Viking," Tommy said, standing at the opposite end of the table. He wanted to make the most of this moment. His eyes gleaming with the intensity of a battle-hardened leader. He pounded his fists on the table and swung his arms wide, channeling the energy of a king rallying his troops before a great conflict. It was over theatrical, but he had the attention of the group.

"Gorn is a very strong hero. Not one to be taken lightly," Tommy continued, his voice filled with a mixture of reverence and urgency.

"Could you get on with it?" Marcus interjected, playing the role of the perpetually annoyed. He liked things direct and to the point, without any unnecessary embellishments.

"Marcus, just let him have this," Arnold said.

"Thank you, Arnold," Tommy replied, nodding gratefully. "Well, I will get to the point. Marcus was not the first hero I tried to recruit. Actually, it was Gorn."

"And you didn't succeed?" Christana asked. "Why?"

"Well, it turns out he is not fond of magic at all. I, of course, am full of it, and so are all of you. I almost lost my life that day. You cannot reason with him. He doesn't acknowledge the heroes of old because, to him, there are none—just him. His duty was to put an end to magic. The very magic blessed to us by the Allfather. The magic we used to fend off the dragons the first time."

Owen became enthralled by Tommy's words. He knew the tale all too well. The Defier had created dragons to devour creation. And in response, through the Creator, the Allfather came to protect it. The Allfather granted humans the use of magic, as depicted on the ancient table in the room. But the Defier corrupted the hearts of men, turning magic into a weapon against one another. Eventually, the power drained the Allfather of all his life, but he granted Gorn the power to put an end to it.

"Gorn was to seek out and destroy the Source of the magic," Owen and Tommy said in unison, their lips moving in sync. Tommy smiled and continued. "The Source the Allfather put in place a long time ago."

"That would be the end of the Allfather," Owen said. "But his last prayer. With his last bit of magic, granted to humans a prophecy. When time calls, a hero will come."

"Exactly," Tommy said, nodding at Owen. "Gorn took the loss very hard. He swore to end all use of magic. So, when I entered his realm, I was not thrown a welcoming party." Tommy looked around at the assembled heroes. "He will try to kill every single one of us. There is no reasoning with him."

"To him all magic is evil?" Arnold asked, a note of concern in his voice.

"It is his calling. As long as magic can be used, it will forever be tainted to corrupt the hearts of men. Only us heroes, the chosen ones, can wield it," Tommy explained.

"I take it, he especially won't like me," Marcus said. "Maybe I should just sit this one out."

"No, we will need you. We need to subdue him. Just enough for me to talk to him," Tommy responded.

"What's the plan then?" Jin asked.

They all turn to Christana for answers.

Christana sat motionless, burdened by their anticipations. Her gift for knowing the perfect strategy was both a blessing and a burden. "Peut-être que je ne suis pas faite pour ça. How can I fight him?" she murmured.

"Just lead us. Que te dit ton cœur?" Arnold asked.

"Je ne suis pas sûr, Arnold. I don't feel anything. It's like I have been blinded to this." She seemed a bit worried.

"This is very curious," Marcus said, exchanging a look with Jin.

"Perhaps we could be strong enough to hold him," Marcus suggested. "Together, we can try to overpower him, and Frutuoso can help. We could each grab him."

"That could work," Tommy said, pondering the idea. "Just be careful though, he is very strong and won't hold back. Christana?"

Christana sighed, but she felt it was the right call. Maybe if Frutuoso could tire Gorn down while Marcus and Jin pinned him... "The demon..." She hesitated, fearing the very thing they needed to use. "Use it."

Marcus nodded.

"Owen, you can fly around and distract him, try to turn his gaze to you."

"Good thinking, he won't like dragons, I assume," Tommy said.

"And me, Christana?" Arnold said. "I don't feel like I am suited for such endangerment. My powers aren't very useful here."

"Just stay by me. We will be fine."

Christana looked over the room at all the heroes, "I think that is all of us. We know what to do?"

They all responded with agreement.

"All right! We have a plan!" Tommy exclaimed! "Shall we get going then?"

"Now?" Owen said. "Don't you think they should dress for battle?"

"They are!" Tommy looked at Owen's concerned face. "They will be fine."

"Things may be different when we get there. Listen to my commands," Christana said. "Are we ready for this?"

George tugged on the sleeve of Christana. He sat unanimated in the chair before that point. She had assumed he wasn't listening. But the constant plea of George, brought concern to Christana.

"Are you afraid?" she asked. "I'm not sure what you could do. Stay by me and you will be safe."

"Stay with Christana, George. We don't want Gorn to harm that pretty little head of yours," Tommy said. "Are we ready?"

"You don't wear armor?" Owen asked with a puzzled expression.

"We heroes don't really need it, but in the future, people learn to lose it," Marcus said. "A lot will change; you will see soon enough."

"Let's head out. Hopefully when we get there, I will be quick to make any needed changes to the plan. Just as soon as my foresight returns," Christana said.

"Owen, I have this helmet for you," Tommy added.

"I don't need a helmet," Owen responded. Brushing the crystals atop his head.

"It's to protect you from the void. It will fit you by design. Trust me. You don't want to go through there without it." Tommy stood and opened his arms to his team. "Let's do this! One more hero!"

The light shone brightly in the dimly lit room, reflecting off Owen's armor in an aurora of light. He was the first to step through. The others followed, one by one, and were met with an ocean breeze and grassy fields.

There, sitting on a rock, Gorn was deep in contemplation. The light from the portal startled him, and as he turned his head to see the heroes step through, he felt the magic in them pulse like a beating heart. He sensed the demonic presence within Marcus. Disturbed by their intrusion, he stood and took in their images. His pained eyes strained, and his cracked lips took in a breath. He saw each one of them and uttered only one word. "Magic…"

17 Cliffside Confrontation

Gorn stood before the heroes, his eyes cold as the storm that gathered ominously behind him. The smell of impending rain charged the air. The wind whipped his long hair and braids, softly golden and filthy. It flew around his shoulders, giving him a wild and untamed appearance. His thick gambeson, worn and battle-scarred, lay unfettered by the breeze. Scars crisscrossed his face, and his beard was ragged, as though he had seen countless battles.

The aura of strong magic emanating from the group prickled at his senses, calling him to his duty once more. He drew his sword, a weapon of exquisite craftsmanship, complimenting his platemail. Its edge facing the heroes. His fingers tightened around the handle. The silver blade glistened and caught the roaming lighting in its reflection. The intricate engravings of runes on the sword gave it unique properties, imbuing it with unparalleled strength.

"Christana, your orders?" Owen's voice broke through the tension, his tone steady yet urgent.

Arnold stood guard, positioning himself between Frutuoso and Christana. The spines upon Frutuoso pierced outward like a cat's fur showing ferocity.

"Qu'est-ce que c'est, Christana?" Arnold urged.

Christana hesitated, her gaze locked with Gorn's piercing eyes. "I don't know." The admission was almost a whisper, laden with fear and uncertainty.

"What do you mean?" Arnold asked.

"It's like I am being blocked!" she said, worried. "I cannot see. I cannot feel it."

Gorn began to advance, his pace increasing with each step. The ground seemed to tremble under his approach. Marcus, sensing the imminent danger, sprang into action.

"Possess him. Try and hold him" Marcus commanded the demon.

D surged forward, but when he reached Gorn, a blinding light repelled him, purging and banishing his malevolent essence. The demon, now cowed, refused to assist further. Marcus found himself standing alone as Gorn charged, sword raised high. Marcus attempted to retreat, but there was nowhere to go; Gorn's speed surpassed him.

Powerful claws collided with the blade. Jin interrupted the wind in time with his power and might. Tiger eyes blazed with pain and determination. Yet, Gorn's electric gaze bore into him with unrelenting force. Overpowered, Jin suffered a crippling kick, forcing him aside.

"Gorn! We aren't...!" Jin attempted to speak, but another vicious swing cut his words short.

From the flank, Frutuoso leaped into the fray, his movements a blur of agility. Gorn found himself matched by the creature's speed and ferocity. Their battle was a whirlwind of clashing steel and swift kicks, each trying to outmaneuver the other. But Gorn's strength was insurmountable. The Cactus, though resilient, was gradually worn down by Gorn's relentless assault.

In that moment, between the heroes' first deflection, Gorn readied himself again. He whispered words that softly reached Tommy's ear.

"Allfather, I will not fail you."

Christana's voice rang out, desperate and pleading, "Gorn, stop!"

But Gorn was deaf to her cries. His focus solely on eradicating this perceived abomination. Owen, seeing the dire situation, took to the skies. His powerful wings propelled him upward. He unleashed a torrent of fire towards Gorn, but the warrior remained unfazed. Instead, he reached into a pouch and retrieved a glowing stone etched with runes. With a muttered incantation, Owen felt an oppressive weight drag him down. His wings collapsed under their own burden. He plummeted to the ground, the impact shaking the earth and sending a cloud of dust into the air. Immobilized, Owen could only watch as Gorn turned his attention back to the Cactus.

Jin rejoined the fight, now supported by Tommy. Tommy's attempts to manipulate time were futile against Gorn's resistance to magic. A soft blue glow shone from the runes upon his armor. Any spell Tommy cast his was became inert.

Jin struggled to match Gorn's speed and strength, barely keeping pace. Frutuoso, bloodied and battered, staggered back into the fray. His limbs weakened but his spirit unbroken. Marcus, now in control of D, shifted into a shadowy form and leapt into the assault. The darkness of the demon consuming Marcus. Yet, even with their combined might, Gorn remained an unstoppable force. Fueled by an unyielding rage and the weight of the oath sworn to the Allfather.

As the battle wore on, the heroes met their limits. Exhausted and defeated, Marcus crawled away. Jin reverted to his human form, rolling over the grassy field. And

Frutuoso fell, unable to continue. Arnold, at a loss, stepped forward to stand beside Tommy.

Christana, on the verge of tears, could only watch in horror as Gorn's relentless assault continued. Arnold made a valiant attempt to stand against Gorn, but he was no match. Christana's scream at Arnold's near demise momentarily distracted Gorn, allowing Tommy to intervene.

"Please, Gorn, listen to us," Tommy pleaded, desperation in his voice.

But Gorn's resolve was unshakable. "I prayed this day would not come, but I knew the darkness would return," he declared, drawing a small ax.

"I know you see magic as evil. It belongs to the Defier now, But trust me, Gorn, we are not the enemy," Tommy tried to reason, but was only met with more of Gorn's attacks. Tommy evaded using his powers to keep just out of reach. Christana rushed to Arnold's side, her heart breaking at the sight of his injuries.

"I am no fool to deceit. My faith guides me." Gorn's ax burned with a rageful flame, and he cast it forth. The weapon turned black as the soot coated it. The ax danced around Tommy, flying like raven in the sky, and clashing when Gorn made his call. Tommy fell after losing his balance.

The ax continued its fury, swinging rapidly. Setting target on Christana, Gorn charged at her and George who stood beside her. With a final, desperate act, Frutuoso stepped in front of Christana. The ax embedding itself in his already battered body. He stood defiant; his arms held together by the skeleton within. The flowers that once decorated his body, were strewn across the battlefield. As Gorn charged for a final blow, he abruptly stopped, his eyes widening in surprise. He turned to meet what caught his attention, searching for the source of the voice that had reached him.

Gor's eyes widened, displaying shock. He turned slowly and looked back. He thought maybe it was Tommy, but Tommy just lay there looking up and Gorn. Tommy felt sorry for bringing all of them into this. This was too much for them and they weren't ready. Tommy thought maybe he could help them escape, but before he could do anything, Gorn spoke.

"What did you say?" Gorn demanded.

"I said... We," Tommy began weakly, but Gorn cut him off.

"Not you!" Gorn's gaze swept over the fallen heroes, his expression shifting from rage to something akin to realization.

Tommy realized Gorn's gaze wasn't on him but on something beyond him. Turning, he saw the Doll that had come to life, standing resolutely with its hand raised, ready for battle.

"That?" Tommy asked, barely able to keep his eyes open. "He doesn't talk."

"I haven't heard that speech in a very long time," Gorn said, dropping his weapons to the ground.

The Doll stood fearlessly beside Tommy, calm and collected, as it helped him to his feet.

"What?" Tommy asked, confusion etched on his face. "What are you talking about?"

"What are you?" Gorn demanded, looking from the Doll to Tommy and then to the rest of the group. "What are all of you? How do you know that language?"

"Gorn, let us speak to you," Christana interjected. "Let me explain who we are."

"I don't want to hear it from you," Gorn rebuked. "Let him talk. What did you say to me?"

Gorn stood still, facing the Doll as time seemed to freeze for the heroes. Though not the tallest among them, his fierce demeanor gave him an imposing presence. George, equally brave, stared Gorn down. His top hat added whimsy to his already formidable height. Not that he needed help to tower over Gorn.

In the charged silence, the air crackled with tension. The dark clouds loomed overhead. Deep shadows amassed across the precipice where the confrontation unfolded. The distant sound of waves crashing against the cliffs provided a rhythmic backdrop. An almost eerie accompaniment to the standoff.

Gorn's eyes narrowed as he regarded the Doll, its tiny frame belying the courage it exhibited. The Doll's hand remained raised, ready to strike if necessary. It was a peculiar sight: a motionless toy come to life, standing fearlessly against a battle-hardened warrior.

"The prophecy..." Gorn uttered. His lips hardly stirred, yet his entire being underwent a drastic shift. A tear fell from his eye, and he made a hasty motion to clear it from his face. "The Allfather's words had come true. The Lady of Light has blessed all of you."

"That's what we were trying to tell you, Gorn," Tommy interrupted.

"But you think it doesn't talk?" Gorn questioned, his disbelief evident. "If you were truly heroes, how do you not know the Odin Speak?"

"Is he speaking to you?" Tommy asked. He stood up as George positioned himself in front to protect him. "I don't hear anything."

"And you call yourself a hero? The language it speaks is not one you hear with your ears, but one you hear with your soul. The language of the Allfather and those of his followers."

Gorn turned to the others, his eyes widening in recognition. The Cactus and the Doll both spoke this ancient language. It was a language of magic and power, one that resonated deeply within him. With a gesture, Gorn released the spell on the dragon, allowing Owen to regain his strength and normal form. Owen, now free, helped Jin and Marcus to their feet

"I'm fine," Marcus said to Owen as he had already healed himself. As they approached, Gorn helped Arnold to his feet. His wound wasn't fatal. His suit had suffered the most damage.

Marcus could sense Gorn's anger still prevalent and readied himself. He didn't wish to move any close as tensions were building again. Gorn stood still for a moment, waiting as if Marcus may try something deceitful. With Marcus standing behind Gorn, he could only imagine him preparing the assault.

Gorn pulled his second sword with a swift, practiced motion. Drawing the blade made it sing. the rhythmic twang humming through the air, sending a shiver down the spines of those present. In an instant, Gorn pivoted and thrust the point of his sword to Marcus's throat. His movements as fluid as they were lethal.

Marcus froze, eyes wide with a mix of surprise and defiance. The cold steel pressed against his skin, the threat unmistakable. The heroes around them tensed, ready to leap to Marcus's defense, but uncertain of their next move.

Caught in the hand of D, was Gorn's blade.

"It's been a while, Gorn. Is the Allfather still favoring you?" D's face twisted into a wicked grin.

"What are you doing here?"

But D said not a word. His sinister laugh growled as he departed back into Marcus's shadow.

"Easy, Gorn. We all want the same thing here," Marcus played it off. "Don't let him get under your skin. I know what he means to you. He isn't like that anymore. Well, he is worse in a way, but trust me. He is a hero too."

"A hero?" Gorn scoffed. "He should be in the void where he belongs!"

"If you give me time to explain," Tommy said, lowering Gorn's sword. "Tensions are high, but at least you can put your trust in the Doll. His name is George."

"If this be the will of the Allfather, then I will do as I must," Gorn declared, standing tall before the heroes. Though shorter in stature, his presence was imposing. The group formed a circle around him, listening intently as he spoke of his regrets and apologies.

"Gorn," Tommy said, stepping forward. "I have need of you."

"And what would that be? How did you get here?"

The Eight Heroes of Old

"I can explain. I come from the future. We come from the future," Tommy continued. "I have a lot to explain to you, but I believe you may be the most important hero for us." Gorn, still a bit cautious of the situation, walked to Tommy to meet him.

"Can we take a moment?" Tommy asked as they reached the cliff's edge, overlooking the crashing waves below. "This is the place, isn't it? What beauty. I have seen your story, Gorn. I watched you ever since you were a child. I saw how you grew. Your faith in the Allfather is unshakable."

"There is peace here," Gorn replied, taking in the salty breeze.

The heroes overlooked the mighty sea, catching the wild winds of the approaching storm. "You picked a good place to wait. You don't have to wait long Gorn. Can you feel it? I know you can. That is why you returned to this spot. The calling can come again for you. We are all heroes, Gorn. Blessed by the Lady of Light."

"How is this possible?" Gorn asked. "Why are there so many of you?"

"Time is the answer. If I could put this in a simple way for you, I would, as it will not be easy to describe. A thousand years from now, the world faces a great and terrible evil. The same evil you know. A thousand more and the world is plagued with Hellhounds devouring everything."

"How did the world become like this?" Gorn questioned. "Is this why you are here?"

"Yes. The prophecy of the Allfather is true and becomes fulfilled many times after you. Before me, there were eight heroes in total. But the last hero, Marcus, with the demon you know too well, comes a man by the name of Manson Herald. He convinces the world to betray the prophecy and stop believing in heroes. Through their loss of faith, the world of our magic dies."

"Magic? But I ended magic. Did I not succeed?"

"The world has not lost magic. It is very much alive. Your quest was to end it for humans to use it against each other," Arnold added.

"It still exists in our world, but it can no longer be used to destroy humanity," Christana added. "But what is left, creates us heroes."

Owen watched as the heroes spoke to Gorn, coming together to piece the world together for the man. All of their unique experiences paint the visions in Gorn's mind.

"You can feel it. Just like all of us. Your calling is stronger than ever," Marcus said.

"Help us, Gorn," Tommy said. "The world is about to lose faith, but we can restore it. They will need our help. All of our help. Please. I ask you."

The Eight Heroes of Old

"I understand." Gorn said. "If it be pleasing to the Allfather, by my hand this world will be saved."

"By our hands," Tommy corrected.

"The Eight Heroes of Old," Christana said. "That is who we are."

Gorn looked around at them and saw a bit of the Allfather in each of them. He accepted their request to help, showing the feeling in his heart for the call of protecting over the Earth upon his face. Tommy felt hope surge within him; with Gorn, their chances of success had greatly improved.

"The world will thank you once more," Tommy said. "Now, I have to explain everything to you—to everyone." Tommy now welcomed them all to join him. "This will be the time we save our world from its darkest threat. We must have hope. Please come with me."

Tommy handed Gorn a special helmet to help protect him from the void, just as he had done for the others. Gorn examined it closely, unfamiliar with the strange materials and design.

"Don't worry. I found it unusual at first too," Owen said reassuringly.

Though Gorn rarely wore a helmet, he accepted it. He then made his way back to the stone where he had been sitting before, near the edge of the cliff overlooking the sea. He knelt, sword plunged into the earth, and bowed his head in silent contemplation. The other heroes approached, forming a respectful circle around him. Their hearts filled with determination and unity.

"What is he doing?" Marcus asked.

"I'm not sure," Arnold said.

"I am praying," Gorn said. "My works are for the Allfather. I give my mind and soul to him and the works of the Creator. I always do this before I face my destiny."

"That's wonderful!" Christana said.

"Do you not?" Gorn asked, looking at them with a mixture of curiosity and concern.

The heroes exchanged glances, their expressions uncertain. Gorn saw the same questioning faces among them all.

"Have you all forgotten?" Gorn said, a hint of disappointment in his voice. "It's no wonder you cannot hear the Odin Speak."

"I still do," Owen said. "I have devoted my life to the Lady of Light."

"But you cannot speak the Odin Speak?" Gorn continued.

"I cannot," Owen admitted, a hint of shame in his voice.

"Gorn…" Marcus began. "In my time, many people have lost their faith. Or they turn their attention to other things. Devices of their own. They all become too involved

The Eight Heroes of Old

in their own worlds. Many of them believe it just to be fairy tales."

"This is disappointing," Gorn said, shaking his head. "The Allfather is real! He has given us these powers, aren't the heroes proof enough!?"

"Some people just don't want to believe. And because of me, they abandon heroes even more."

"Don't be so hard on yourself, Marcus," Tommy said. "It is not by you. Yes, your story is unique, but you aren't the cause. It is Manson. That is who we need to stop."

"I see," Gorn said. "Hopefully, I can restore these people and for them to open their eyes to the light."

"We shall go at once! We all need to help restore the light. It is our calling," Tommy declared, opening a portal.

The bright light did not deter Gorn as Tommy opened the portal. The swirling energy promised a journey unlike any he had undertaken before. "Let this be our victory!" Gorn declared, his voice full of conviction, and he charged through the light.

"Gorn!" Tommy called after him, watching him fade into the void. He turned to Marcus, shaking his head.

"He wasn't wearing his helmet…" Christana stated.

"No, he wasn't," Marcus added and stepped through.

The rest followed as Tommy waited for the last to enter. He placed a hand on George's shoulder, smiling and thanking him. "I hope I too can hear your words, one day," Tommy said.

George patted Tommy's hand with his cold metal fingers. He looked as if he were smiling more than the synthetic smile on his face. He walked through the portal.

18 Dream Quickly

The weight of the large oak doors groaned on ancient iron hinges. Tommy pushed them from the heavy brass knobs and stepped into the grand council room of the castle. The space was vast. Its high ceilings vanished into shadow. The candlelight flickered. The enchanted crystals in the stone walls glistened. The room seemed to breathe with age and power, steeped in centuries of counsel and conflict. A massive, round table of polished dark wood anchored the center of the room, its surface scarred from the deliberations of heroes long gone.

Outside the narrow, arched windows, the sky was a blanket of ash. The grim pall over the landscape did little to disturb the chamber. An unsettling calm hung in the air.

One by one, the heroes took their seats, their faces etched with the weight of their shared mission.

Gorn stood apart. His rugged beard dusted from battle grime. Armor battered from countless wars. His arms crossed, and eyes narrowed as if in deep thought. His muscular frame, though still imposing, seemed tense. A rare sight of puzzlement crossed his scarred face. He gazed at the table, lost in a silence that thickened the stillness.

"I thought we were ready for war!" he exclaimed, his deep voice echoing off the stone walls.

"You thought we are going now?" Tommy replied, chuckling. "After what just happened, everyone needs rest. Look around, Gorn. We're all exhausted. But I admire your enthusiasm." Handing the helmet over to Gorn, he urged him to not step through the portal without it again. "Your brains could have melted!" With a sigh and crunching joints, Tommy took his seat. For the first time since his departure, he felt exhausted.

Gorn sighed, then took his seat and began pulling thorns from his clothing. Tommy moved to the head of the table. He intertwined his fingers and leaned forward. His demeanor was now serious and determined.

"First off," Tommy addressed the group, his voice steady but filled with remorse. "I'm sorry. I did not perceive Gorn would be this much of a threat."

"I am also sorry," Christana added. The regret was apparent as she spoke but said so firmly. "I failed you all. My powers failed me. I don't know what happened."

"It's not your fault," Gorn interjected, his tone surprisingly gentle. "I felt your spell. But I was protected from it. It's my mother's spell. The runes are carved upon my armor. It protects me from the evil advances of magic."

Christana looked down, her guilt evident. "Am I even fit to lead this team?" she asked, her voice carrying further than she desired.

"You are!" Tommy reassured her. "Don't fill your head with doubt. As Gorn said, it is not your fault." Tommy let the team compose themselves, overseeing each one as they all settled in their spot. "As I was saying. I am sorry I put you all in such danger. I hope you will all come to forgive me. This task is not an easy one."

"We understood the risks," Owen said. "I, for one, will not abandon your side. Even if I should die, as long as it would be for the betterment of the world."

"Same for me," Arnold added, his tone somber. "I was already meant to die, what difference does it make?"

Christana chose to ignore Arnold's statement and continue to listen to Tommy. She did take Arnold's hand however, and gave him a glance, trying not to dwell on the unthinkable.

Gorn observed the group, noting the diversity in their attire and backgrounds. Despite the confusion time travel brought, he found solace in the fact that the core values of heroism remained unchanged. He was curious about their stories.

"I would like to know your tales," Gorn said. "How has the world been in so much danger?"

Owen began, "After your destruction of magic, the last bit of usable magic died with you. The dragons returned. It was worse than before, and our people burned by the shiploads. Their wake left nothing but ash. We managed to kill the smaller creatures, but the larger dragons were unstoppable. Until I found the Mother Dragon. She wished for peace and turned me into what I am. I brought peace to both sides."

"Just as I feared. I believed the dragons would return after I rid humanity of our greatest protection. I had no choice." Gorn responded. "I'm sorry for any harm that has been done to you."

"It was all made right in the end, Gorn. Rest assured," Owen said. "Your story inspired me to continue on my quest. Even when times were darkest. I failed in my own way. I could not uphold my part of the oath I swore to the Mother Dragon. I had to bring harm to her strongest child."

"After Owen's victory," Jin said. "Some dragons traveled east to live among the humans, even giving up their dragon forms. My master was one of them. But so was Jiao Long, they were part of the dragon bloodline."

"The dragon bloodline?" Owen and Gorn asked together.

"Four dragons had made peace with humans and lived alongside them for a time. After years, they saw how the Allfather blessed them and decided to give up their dragon forms and become human. Jiao Long tried to awaken the power of his blood. He wished to be strong like a dragon. With his strength and influence, he conquered most of China. I put an end to him, but at a great cost. I failed all of my friends."

"You had a story as well, George?" Gorn asked the Doll. "A frightful time indeed. I suppose magic never really left our world, despite all my efforts."

George responded in his own way, motioning his arms and proclaiming to all in great gestures of his adventures.

"For all of those who don't understand," Tommy interjected. "Sorry, George, I hope you don't mind me telling your story for you."

George just shrugged and let Tommy continue.

"He was created during a dire time in our history. The fall of the great strongholds on the Earth. A man by the name of Walter Johann had a dark vision. The shards of the magic Source. The very Source Gorn destroyed. The same crystals Arnold uses in his research. They were the very same Source Crystals that caused Marcus's greatest enemy…"

"Get on with it, Tommy," Marcus shouted. "He always does this!" Marcus said to Gorn. "Give the short version, please!"

"Very well. The Source of magic fragmented, and Walter gathered as many as he could, but something was amiss. As much as he desired, he could not control magic. But stories filled the land of a man that could. Gensen, the creator of the dolls. He used magic to bring them to life. When he went missing, the Doll found him! Alive! And he went on to save the day and kick bad-guy-butt!"

"That's not how it went at all!" Marcus grumbled.

George shook his head, as Tommy breezed over important parts of his story.

"Are you saying you couldn't stop it?" Gorn replied to George, feeling the words he was saying. "That's terrible!"

Seeing their confused faces, Gorn turned to Arnold, Christana, and Marcus. "It's a tragedy you cannot understand the words within him. Regardless, where do your stories begin?"

"I was after the Doll," Arnold started. "The Dark Order was created from descendants of an ancient world to harness the remaining magic in our time. They used radiation with magic to turn people into monsters. I am a researcher, a scholar in my field. At a point in my life, I too shared in the idea to harness the residual magic within our world. I dreamed of so many benefits to humanity. But I left that dream when I came to the realization, we should not fiddle with powers beyond us." Arnold wiped his glasses with his handkerchief. "Many died from my foolishness. My research ended up in the wrong hands. At the time, I was a professor teaching at a university. Christana was my aid. I made the mistake of following my dream and my work was stolen from me. We ended up in the middle of the mess, fighting soldiers and mutants. I destroyed the reactor that would turn everyone into monsters. That was the day I was supposed to die," Arnold rubbed his hands, the memory of burns still fresh. "Tommy saved me."

"He was my professor, and I was his assistant," Christana added. "My life took a different turn from that day. I left home. I was self-destructive. I joined the military to fight in a war and by fate, was chosen to become a hero. The same man that eluded Arnold, Stefan Richter, was a German scientist who created machines based on his designs. The evil this man created. He created a device to pull the souls from dead soldiers to release Hellhounds upon them. It was a terrible time."

Tommy's eyes darkened as he recalled the Hellhounds. "Christana and I fought the same threat. In my time, the world is overrun with them, an endless tide of chaos and destruction," he said gulping down the words.

"I could not imagine," Christana said. "The memory still strikes terror in me. That's the end of my story. Tommy told me I am followed by Frutuoso." She motioned to the Cactus to begin his turn, but he stood still as other saguaros tend to do.

"Frutuoso!" Tommy shouted. "Your turn!" he shouted again as he awoke.

The Cactus was eager to share his adventures, conversing only to Gorn in the Odin Speak. He faced many dangers from the same organization from Christana's time, now more advanced and devious.

"Our story begins with the Cactus, actually," Tommy added. "The Dark Order is one of the reasons why magic fades in our world."

Frutuoso spoke of how wicked men had ravaged the natural order. They tore down sacred groves, monuments of peace, and innocent homes. But, only Gorn seemed to understand.

"In their wake, they summoned dark powers with a desire to control the world," Marcus started. "It was a dark time of military advancement." He sighed and calmed his nerves as he looked at Owen. "The Dark Order's biggest achievement was destroying the monument to the Mother Dragon and the Oath of Owen. They wished to destroy the oath between men and dragons to cause an emergence."

Owen's attention was more evident as Marcus said those words.

Marcus looked to Frutuoso and asked if he could continue. After a subtle nod, he spoke again. "Nature was the cost. Dragons would burn everything. The man behind it was a well-respected military leader. We are still unsure of his motives, but the Cactus saved our world from that threat."

"And he knows the fighting style, Capoeira!" Tommy exclaimed with glee!

"Yeah, I still don't understand that."

"It was his family's tradition!"

"Anyway," Marcus continued. "Because of the monuments being destroyed, they were able to summon a demon into this world. The same one I now command. We overcame our foe and now live defending the people from any evil. In my time, there was a false hero. It was my fault how everything came to be. The world suffered because of me."

"Don't give yourself all the credit, Marcus," D laughed, showing himself over Marcus's shoulder. "It was my genius plan. I had an influence over you. I wanted freedom."

"I can't imagine you wanted anything," Gorn snarled at D. "It wasn't too late for you."

"It was, Gorn. The Allfather resented me. Do you deny it?"

Gorn had no words for the demon.

This is where our story reaches its end," Tommy said. "Marcus lost his next battle, but it was not one fought with a sword. It was fought with words."

Gorn found it intriguing. "How does one lose to that?"

"Manson is his name. He has a silver tongue and can bend the will of others. Even Marcus."

"So, what does he do with this power?"

"He makes people forget. He makes them not remember the promise of the Allfather and makes them lose faith in the heroes. They turn their backs on them for a better life promised by Manson."

"And they follow him blindly?" Gorn was furious by this! "How could anyone do that!?"

"It was my fault. Because of me, they lose faith in their hero," Marcus added.

This is where my story begins," Tommy continued. "Manson gained the favor of the people to take power, but his true disguise was working for the Defier. He unleashed a thousand legions of Hellhounds upon the earth. For a thousand years, they devoured every living person. The world became a dark apocalypse. My father remained good and wished for a better life for us. He died with that wish, but I carried it on. I made a time machine and was granted my powers by a miracle of the Lady of Light."

"What an awful fate for this world," Christana said, squeezing Arnold's hand.

"I see," Gorn said. "So, we are here to destroy Manson?"

"Not exactly," Tommy said. "We need a little more than just that. We need to restore people's faith in the heroes. We need to bring hope back to our world. The last bit of magic will die. I was hoping bringing all of the heroes together in one place would help spark it back."

"What is our plan?" Marcus asked

"Christana? Are you able to feel what we need to do?" Arnold asked.

"Yes. I will be able to. My powers don't work like that. I am giving guidance at the moment. We have one day to stop Manson," Christana said, feeling uneasy. "He plans something, but I'm not sure what."

"Manson will be there speaking to the crowds," Tommy said. "We need to stop him. And we need to stop him from taking his metaphorical crown."

"When does he summon the Hellhounds?" Marcus asked.

"Immediately..." Tommy's voice dropped to a warning tone. "Once he takes his place as the high ruler, where all nations bow to this one man, the earth splits and the Hellhounds come crawling out."

"We need to stop him before that happens!" Jin said.

"Can we fight these Hellhounds?" Marcus asked

"No!" Christana said. "They will devour you. And if you manage to kill one, the flames will reduce you to nothing but ash. Even you, Gorn and Owen."

"Can I burn them?" Owen asked.

"They will be unaffected by your fire," Tommy replied.

The demon stepped out of Marcus, the room growing cold as the torches flickered out. "I can kill them. We come from the same place," he said, standing behind Marcus. "The fire is something I can withstand and even protect Marcus."

"Well, it should not come to that," Tommy responded. "We need to make sure it doesn't. If Hellhounds are unleashed, all hope will be lost. It is of utmost urgency. I do not want to see them. Or or or… or hear them. Just don't let it happen."

Christana walked over to Marcus, still afraid of the demon, but continued. "If Marcus could perhaps speak to the people, maybe he could convince them not to turn against us. Is there a way he could speak on the radio?"

"Even better. The technology of the time improves way more than just a radio," Marcus replied.

"The whole event will be televised worldwide. There will not be a single soul who will miss it," Tommy added.

"If Marcus could gain access to the program, then maybe he could speak to them," she continued.

"We will have to get me into that room. Should be easy enough, right?" Marcus questioned.

Tommy looked over at everybody with concern. "Manson will have people working with him. Many will try to kill us. Be ready to do what is needed to stop them. The Dark Order is a secretive organization. They are the evilest of men willing to do whatever it takes to fulfill their mission. Manson has unfortunately risen to the top of their ranks. Whether or not he smooth-talked them into doing as he ordered or followed him willingly... They will kill you if given the chance."

"I may have an issue with that," Marcus responded. "I vowed to never kill again.

"I'll be on my best behavior," D mocked.

Frutuoso and George locked onto every word, grasping the situation's weight. Tommy felt a tingle in his heart as he looked at the Cactus, seeing his wounds from the battle. Exhaustion weighed heavily on him as he struggled to focus on Christana's words. He saw her comforting Arnold, their bond evident. He pitied them, sensing his actions would cause her deep pain. Arnold beamed with satisfaction. Marcus looked exhausted. Gorn was uneasy. Owen was ready for battle. Jin, the most peaceful, was steady in his emotions and breath.

Tommy wondered if he could fix everything, fulfill his father's dream of a better life. He envisioned a world where they succeeded. A garden full of green. His mother's arms. His brother playing. Even his father returning. But it was only a dream. His visions faded back to the dark room.

It's all coming together, Tommy thought. *But why do I feel so horrible? Am I sending them all to their doom? What if this ends up like all the other times? Would we be given a second chance? How do I bring my father back? How do I save my family?* Tommy began spiraling, his mind racing. Sweat beaded upon his brown, but he couldn't move his hand to wipe it. *Not the Hellhounds. Not them... How can I?*

"Tommy?" Christana asked, putting her hand on his arm.

"What?" Tommy said, snapping from his mania.

"Do you think this could be possible?" Christana asked, seeing he wasn't paying attention. "We can speak of this another time. We are all caught up and we can come up with a full plan tomorrow. We should all get some rest."

"Yes, what do you all think?" Tommy asked. "Gorn?"

"This is all interesting. What I think is I will need help understanding everything that was said. You used words I am not familiar with, and the manner of your speech is confusing."

"You may go get some rest, Gorn," Christana said. She dismissed everyone. They all left, staggering away with a slow pace. Christana watched as they formed bonds of laughter, passing around invites for activities. After all the heroes had left, only Tommy and Arnold remained.

"What is it, Tommy?" Arnold asked.

"I don't want to fail. I got a real taste of failure today," Tommy said. "In a flash, I saw everything leave my eyes. The future I desire."

"Tommy, we did not fail. We were still able to overcome Gorn," Christana said, placing a comforting hand on his shoulder.

"There won't be any miracles next time. No hidden surprises," Tommy said. "Is it wrong for me to desire more? I want my life back. The one I never had. I wish to grow up in a peaceful world with my mother, but these dreams have got to pass quickly. Only in short amounts can I do so. It is not my fate."

Arnold spoke in a soft tone to Tommy. "I know you are still a child at heart, but it is okay to dream. All of us did. Every hero had a dream, and just like you, they had to dream quickly. Time does not wait for us. You are special, as it does for you."

"Something is wrong, isn't it?"

"I'm afraid… We are so close…" Tommy covered his eyes, his emotions paid their toll.

"It's fine to feel this way, Tommy," Christana said. "We can change fate. I believe we can. We must." She stood him up and gave him a strengthening embrace. "As much as I know Arnold will have to leave, I can still dream we can be together one day. My love for him is stronger than my mortal bond."

"I realize too," Arnold said. "If I had to return to my time, I would leave Christana broken again. I dream that I too could be with her again."

"Fate is a tricky thing," Christana began again as she broke her hold. Tommy wiped the small tear from his eye. "Some say we have no control over it. Others say our fate is in our own hands. But to change the fate of the world will take quite a bit of magic," Christana said. "Who better to do that, than the Heroes of Old?"

"You are right," Tommy said, thanking them before standing from the chair and taking his leave. "I will be more prepared tomorrow. We can do this. We can change fate." He walked out of the room, his steps resolute.

Christana and Arnold walked from the council room back to their quarters. Their conversation was light and filled with laughter. Their bond grew stronger with each passing moment. Despite the weight of the world on their shoulders, they found solace in each other's company. Arnold, ever the scholar, couldn't shake the idea forming in his mind. He invited Christana to his room, cluttered with notebooks and gadgets.

Would you care to assist me with something?" he asked, his eyes bright as ever when he had an idea.

"Tout ce que tu veux, Arnold!" she replied, agreeing to go with him.

"I have something that is itching inside my head. Something Marcus said."

"Qu'est-ce que c'est?" Christana said, taking a seat at Arnold's table.

"Maybe we can change fate," he said with joy in his words. "I believe we can study this magic that will be left to us. We can use it to give us the best chance to fix our worlds. And maybe."

"Oui?"

"Maybe we could be together."

"Do you think it is possible?"

"If we cannot change fate, then what are we doing here?" Arnold smirked, repeating the line Marcus said to him.

They set to work, collaborating intensely on Arnold's idea. He jotted down calculations, Christana verifying and incorporating her thoughts. They moved in perfect unison, like an unstoppable machine. Pages filled with notes. Blueprints sprawled across the table. And ink smeared their hands. Finally, Arnold believed they had it.

"If we could build this, then we might have a shot!" Arnold said.

"I am willing to try anything!" Christana's excitement overwhelmed her. She tenderly embraced Arnold from behind as he held up the schematic.

"We will have to give this to Tommy. This will amplify his power and give him more control. With this device, it would change our reality. As long as everything goes according to plan." Arnold set them down and turned his attention to Christana. He pulled her arms up around his neck and pulled her closer.

"Given the right moment," Christana responded. "It could work."

"It is only a faint hope," Arnold said with a small smile on his face. "I'm not afraid to dream."

The Eight Heroes of Old

19 Tis the Small One

There was a feeling of peace among the heroes as they emerged from the rooms. Jin and Marcus, eager to explore the city and its bustling markets, set off with a sense of excitement. Frutuoso, in need of restoration, wandered to a nearby water fountain and stepped inside. The cool, refreshing water revived him, healing his cuts and restoring his spikes and flowers.

George watched Frutuoso from the fountain's edge, playing with the ripples. Reflecting on his own perceived inadequacies. In the distorted reflection of the water, he saw only what he believed to be the weakest hero among them—an animated Doll. Merely, clothed and a head, without any extraordinary powers. The other heroes were impressive and unique, each endowed with powers that set them apart. George, feeling small, looked at the Cactus. He had returned to his inanimate form, standing strong against the wind.

With a heavy heart, George walked back to Owen and Gorn, where the two were engrossed in conversation. The Doll listened just an intently as Owen expressed his admiration and fears.

"I've always looked up to you," Owen said, his eyes filled with respect. "I wanted to fill the shoes you had left. It's a big role. When time called for me to be the next hero, I was afraid. I did not expect what I found. I was nothing but a squire, serving under a noble knight. He was a legend. A Dragon Hunter. The king believes he would be the hero. Time didn't work it out that way."

"He was a Skari? What happened to them all? Last I heard from them, they conquered lands unheard of," Gorn said. "The Allfather entrusted us to protect the world. Everything falls into line and time will always call for the right hero to do the right thing. Always. That is just as the prophecy goes."

"The Skari are all gone. They died in the wars of the first emergence. Sir Victor was the last, rest his soul."

"May he find the Forever Light," Gorn responded, bowing his head.

The Eight Heroes of Old

Gorn and Owen walked towards the castle walls. George, unsure whether to stay with Frutuoso or follow them. Owen noticed and invited him to join them.

"I wish to learn the Odin Speak," Owen said, glancing at both Gorn and the Doll.

"It is not something you learn," Gorn explained. "It is a gift granted to you for being pure of heart. I pray every day to cleanse my soul. I keep myself in the grace of the Allfather, and I can still feel his protection over me. It was how my uncle taught me. He was in service of the Allfather for a very long time. I was in the same order that protected the Allfather in his slumber."

Gorn welcomed the Doll to their walk as they both marveled at the structure before them. "We don't have castles like this where I am from," Gorn mentioned. They climbed the stairs of the gatehouse, feeling the cool air as they reached the top. Gorn peered over the castle wall, embracing the calming rays of the sun that had returned after the ash had dissipated.

"Do you feel this?" Gorn asked as he looked at George. But George shook his head and tapped on the porcelain with his hands, giving a saddened expression.

"That's too bad," Gorn said, sympathetically.

"It's a great feeling," Owen added. "You had served the Allfather?"

"I did, for most of my life," Gorn replied.

"What was He like?"

"Strong. Like a father. Old, but wise. But when you were near him, you felt a strange love in your heart. A comfort I can no longer describe."

"Like when the Lady of Light calls?" Owen asked, his spirits lifting.

"Just like it," Gorn spoke in a hushed tone, his voice mellowing as he connected with Owen. The same servitude was deep in both of their hearts.

"Do you know who the Lady of Light is?" Owen asked. "She is shrouded in mystery. Not even Tommy knows who she is."

"I must admit, I do not know," Gorn's tone turned grave as he confessed his lack of knowledge. "As you said. She is a mystery. But her words ring true. When she speaks to you, you know exactly who she is at the same time."

George listened intently, knowing very little about her, but he too had heard the calling of her voice. He walked over and peered over the wall just like Gorn. Owen stood by their sides; arms crossed.

"I would sure like to know," Owen said.

"Do you know the others well?" Gorn asked.

"I have only just met them. It was a complete surprise to me. This whole second calling feels strange."

"Tommy is the strange one. His clothes are even stranger."

"I had some personal time with him. He has endured much in his life, and from what he told me, he is still young at heart, a child, I believe."

"A grown man that still acts as a child?"

"Well, he is a child. It's difficult for me to explain, I do not wish to impose on his own story. Ask him yourself for clarification. But in our time together, he revealed to me his troubles and his doubts. He thinks he cannot do this on his own. His heart falters and will is feeble."

"Is that it? Do you believe his own determination to be false?"

"Yes…" Owen admitted, a break from his emotions shown through.

"The Allfather will guide him. And I will aid him as much as I can."

"He hides his fears behind us," George said to Gorn, his soul speaking truth.

"Maybe that is true, but we will stand strong for him, won't we?" Gorn responded in the same way.

Owen took notice of their communication and waited with patience.

"I won't give up on Tommy," Owen continued.

"Neither will we," Gorn replied. "Now let's find some food!"

Gorn stepped away from the castle wall and led Owen and Geroge down to the king's pantry. Owen watched his great hero, admiring his presence, which was holy and pure. Gorn spoke like a wise old man who had seen more battles than he cared to count but still wished to do better. Owen felt more confident with Gorn on their side and felt the peace that he brought. Soothing like relaxing music after a fulfilling dinner. Owen wished to be like him.

"He is right," Owen said, turning his head to George. "We should find some food, but he is going the wrong way. Shall we?"

George pounded his chest, but still gave the same expression that hinted to his inward turmoil.

"Don't worry, you are just as much a hero as all of us," Owen said to him.

"There is something special about you," George said, taking joy in Owen's remarks. "The Lady of Light chose you for a reason, I'm sure."

"Did I just understand you?" Owen asked, amazed at what he felt. "I can't believe this!" Owen was so overjoyed listening to George, he almost forgot about Gorn. But before they could get moving, Christana yelled from the bottom of the gatehouse. Her voice struggled to rise above the wall's edge.

"How may I serve you, Christana!?" Owen's voice carried further as he shouted downwards.

She rushed up the stairs to both of them. The dust on the steps kicked up with each movement of her foot. It was not the safest set of stairs, but Christana was so excited she did not care for her own safety. Owen and George welcomed her as she arrived at the top. George was more excited to see her, and if he could express emotions more, he would have smiled. Christana was holding the parchment that she and Arnold had drafted. She opened it to show Owen.

"Look at this!" Her voice burst with enthusiasm. "Arnold and I have designed something I think Tommy can use!"

"What is it?" Owen asked, his brow furrowing in confusion. The device was very strange to him. He could not understand the technology before him. It was very detailed but was even more difficult to decipher than the table below the castle.

"In our time, we have what we call computers," she said, trying to find the right words to use to describe it. "Err, it's like…Well. It's unique to use. This design here could help Tommy focus his power. Maybe it could help us ignite magic back. In theory, it could even change fate, and help Tommy rewrite history. We call it a Convergencer."

"Well, this is very strange, but how could I help?" Owen asked, still stuck in confusion. "I still don't quite understand what this is. It is like magic?"

"Well, yes. It is able to harvest magic and use it. That isn't as important as what I would like to ask you."

"Yes?"

"It requires a Source Crystal," she said, her tone changing. "Do you know where we could find any?"

"Do you mean like the ones that cover me?" Owen said.

"Is it possible to take one? I don't wish to hurt you, but… There aren't many of them left."

"Or at all," Owen replied, drawing a knife from his belt. He took from his arm a small crystal, snapping apart without resistance. It did not hurt him or give him any discomfort, but Christana almost felt queasy from it.

"Will this do? If you need more, I can…"

"No!" she said, turning away from the sight. "This will be more than enough."

"They grow back. All the time. The way they consume me is more painful."

Christana nodded her head, knowing full well of Owen's demise.

"In the future, will they claim my life completely?" he asked.

"In a few years, you become completely encased by them," she spoke in a grave tone. "But you are made into the most beautiful monument to your oath. People come from all over the world just to see you."

"That's a comforting thought. What of my father?"

"I don't believe the history books mention him."

"I hope he can manage without me."

"Owen, you are a fine knight. The best the world had ever known. I'm sure your father will receive the greatest of care."

Christana took the crystal and then asked where Gorn was. She needed to ask something of him too.

"He went to find something to eat. We were about to find him before you came."

"Thank you, Owen. Shall we get going?" Christana said warmly as she stepped out, ready to find Gorn. She wandered through the quaint king's court, nestled in the castle walls, with the other two heroes beside her. The buildings were a maze of cobblestone streets. Timber-framed houses with blooming flower boxes lined the roads. The air smelled of fresh bread. In the distance, a blacksmith's hammer rang against an anvil.

Christana soon found Marcus and Jin, as she'd expected. Soft lanterns and the warm glow of a crackling fire illuminated the cozy kitchen of the king's manor where they sat. The aroma of roasting meats mingled with the scent of rich, dark ale. A maid moved gracefully between tables. Her apron dusted with flour. The barkeeper, in his expertise, poured drinks and served hearty meals.

Gorn was there, enjoying a mug of dark ale that complemented his savory roast chicken. Jin swirled a rich wine in his glass, while Marcus devoured his sandwich that he made for himself. Their table was overcome with conversation and camaraderie as they jested about each other's fighting styles. Gorn's laughter, deep and robust, resonated through the tavern, creating an atmosphere of cheer. His good-natured insults were met with quick-witted retorts from Jin. His sharp tongue matched Gorn's banter blow for blow. Even Marcus, though reserved, couldn't help but chuckle at their comradery.

"Gentlemen!" Christana greeted them. "Care if I join you?"

"Of course, you can!" Marcus replied, quickly pulling a stool up to the bar for her.

"How are you paying for this? I doubt you have the current currency," she remarked as she sat down.

"The man over there said we could have anything we liked since we're friends with Owen."

"Is true ma'am. Can I get you anything?" the barkeeper said with a friendly nod.

"Something small, thank you," she responded.

Christana settled between them, with Gorn seated farthest from her. The tavern buzzed with a comfortable hum of conversation and the clinking of glasses. Owen and George pulled chairs to the table and took their seats.

"What are you doing here with us, Christana?" Jin asked. "I thought you would be with Arnold."

"I hoped to speak to Gorn. Arnold and I stayed up all night designing something for Tommy." She shook the schematic that was neatly rolled up in her hand.

Gorn looked over to her, his beard glistening with the foam from his ale. He wiped his mouth and asked, "What would you need from me?"

"Well, if you're interested now, I didn't want to disturb your time. It can wait."

"You aren't disturbing us," Gorn responded. "We were speaking nonsense."

Christana began, unfolding a draft. She displayed the idea she and Arnold had to create a device that could help Tommy. Marcus broke out in laughter.

"What's so funny, Marcus!?" Christana questioned, frustration overtook her.

"It's just. Well. Technology is much different in my time. First off, the machine is huge! Now we have computers much smaller than that. Marcus took out his dead phone from his pocket to remind her. It could be improved on. By a lot, actually."

"I tried to keep that in mind," Christana said as her voice sank with embarrassment.

"That being said, you don't need a power source this big. That would be changed, and the wires could be changed to micro wiring." Marcus took the paper from her and looked it over. "Yeah, this definitely can be better. I built my own computer back in high school. And I am sure once you show this to Tommy, he can help you sort out all the kinks."

"Arnold and I worked really hard on this!"

"I'm sure you did!" Marcus said, trying to calm Christana down. "It's just that a lot of our technology comes from the same device that you tried to protect us from. We use technology and magic together."

Christana was a bit speechless as she wrapped the paper back up. She stuffed it back into her coat pockets, but Marcus began to be serious again.

"I'm sorry," Marcus said. "Maybe that was a little rude."

"We expected your technology to be a bit more advanced than ours, but you didn't have to mock us."

"I know. I'm sorry" he reassured her, "I meant no harsh feelings. What was it you wanted to ask Gorn?"

"Before you completely tore this design apart, I was going to ask, Gorn, would you help in adding your magic to bring this design to life? It would be a simple use."

Gorn finished the rest of his ale, and pleaded for another, downing it in a large gulp before responding to Christana. "I fought to end magic. I was never sure if it was the right call. I fear it might have been, but if you had witnessed with your own eyes, the very evil I did. You would not dare touch those spells," Gorn said roughly. "I watched it turn men vile and do evil things. The corruption it brought."

"We are well aware of your struggles, Gorn," Marcus tried to plead.

"But have you seen it with your own eyes?"

"I have..." Christana responded, her voice deep and strict.

"I went through all that tribulation, just so humans could gain control over magic. My journey was all in vain?"

"Gorn, it's not what you think," Marcus tried to reason once more. "Humans never regain the use of magic, and it is never used to bring harm against each other again. Now, it's only used for good. We have medical advances you would not believe. We build cities powered by it. People live good lives because of the advances Professor Arnold made in his research."

"The good side of magic? There aren't any who use it to harm?"

"Many have tried, but it always ended in failure," Christana added.

Gorn leaned back in his chair, stroking his beard. "What sort of spell were you thinking?"

"Just an enchantment," she said. "Something small. Just so this Source Crystal can be used. I got it from Owen."

"That's a little weird, but okay," Marcus said.

"It will be when the machine is finished," Christana continued, showing him the crystal. It had a magnificent glow and distorted the room with teal light.

"If this is what the Allfather wants. He must have brought us together for a reason. But once this is all finished, I want to see it destroyed."

"Thank you, Gorn." Christana smiled, rolling up the paper. Just then, the barkeeper placed a plate in front of her. It smelled of wild herbs, with a generous portion of meat and vegetables.

"I asked for the smaller portion," she said.

"'Tis a smaller one, ma'am," the barkeeper said.

Christana enjoyed herself thoroughly, joining in the banter as Gorn resumed his playful jabs at the others. Each remark from Gorn squandered with a sharper, more blatant retort from Christana.

Gorn, unused to being bested in verbal sparring, found himself enjoying the challenge. Her quick wit and unyielding spirit left him in awe, a feeling he wasn't accustomed to. His tough exterior, marred by scars, seemed almost to soften in her presence.

As Christana finished her meal and left, Gorn watched her. He was almost mesmerized by her presence and accent.

"Don't even think about it, Gorn," Marcus warned with a chuckle. "She would never."

"I wasn't thinking anything," Gorn retorted, though his eyes displayed a hint of intrigue. "I just never met a woman who wasn't fragile."

"Not one?" Jin asked.

"I met a girl once. Her hair like the golden sunrises we had in Eriksey. Her spirit was strong, yet her skin was soft like a flower. Her name was Eir. But never have I met a woman that could take to blight as Christana does. She is a special one for sure."

"She is our leader," Jin continued.

"I can see it. She is strong."

"I belonged to Rifle Company Platoon Five-Eight-Eight," Christana responded, stopping at the door before leaving. "I served two years in World War two under my sergeant Adam Moore. In those times, you had to be tough. His leadership helped me become who I was meant to be."

"I see. Did you lose someone close to you?" Owen asked.

Christana remained silent.

"She lost more than any other heroes before her…Or after her…" Marcus replied.

"Arnold," Jin said, taking another sip of his wine.

"He died in service," Marcus continued. "Fate has brought them back, but it will also force them to leave. So, Arnold told me."

"We shouldn't be afraid to dream, Christana," Gorn said. "That is when the Creator speaks to us. When we are closest. That is why the Allfather slept all those years. He speaks to us there."

"So, this...device as she called it," Owen spoke again. "She means to change fate. She wants her life with him?"

"More than anything, as I assume anyone would," Jin said.

"That would be powerful magic. To pause someone's death. To change the course of their life. It's the kind of magic you don't deal with," Gorn said with a warning. "She can't. That would have grave consequences."

"But is that not why we are here?" Marcus repeated. "Why should she not at least try for her sake? We are trying to save billions of lives, but one more is too much?"

D imposed himself over Marcus, hovering just behind him, but he spoke to the whole table. "Fate can trick you. Who are you to decide it? Listen to Gorn, Marucs. It can be deceitful."

"And why would you take my side?" Gorn said, raising his voice.

"Fate cannot be changed," D mocked.

"You let this thing speak for you, Marcus?"

"Certainly not. That darkness bends to my will. He will not bully us into giving up the good things in our lives."

"Boy, you better not get under my skin!" Gorn thundered, slamming his mug down on the counter. The bar fell silent as Marcus met his gaze with unflinching resolve.

"I do not wish to disrespect, but we have the power to control fate. I believe it in my heart. Our paths are not set in stone. I have faith in Tommy."

"Marcus! Please!" Christana interjected after far too long. "I'm not doing this for us. We aren't planning on changing fate for my sake. That idea is gone. I have made amends with my feelings. What Arnold and I have is special and I will cherish it until the day I die. But right now, our mission is to help Tommy. That is our only focus."

"I do feel for Christana. I understand her condition," Jin said. "There are so many things I wish I could change. The failures, the crimes I committed. If I could turn it all back, I would, but that time has passed."

"Let's not let ourselves turn to fighting each other," Christana said, inspiring her team. "Arnold and I created this device to help Tommy. That's all. Once this is all over, we will destroy it, as Gorn has asked."

The silence was bleak but broken by Owen speaking up in honor of Christana. Making a toast to her and Arnold's devotion to the team. The heroes shared more drinks around the table, and soon the laughter returned.

20 A New Design

Inside the luxurious confines of the royal keep, Tommy gazed upwards at the night sky. His room was of the highest standard; an elegance saved for only the most worthy of champions. Adorned with plush red pillows and animal skins that covered every inch of the floor, Tommy ignored it all. The walls held priceless artifacts. The air was rich with incense, refreshed daily to keep the room sweet and inviting. The large window showed a perfect view of the moon. Its silvery light cast a serene glow over the castle walls. The night sky was clear, with gentle clouds drifting by and a mild breeze that added to the tranquil atmosphere. Below, the flickering candles in the windows of the hovels created a warm, inviting scene.

The Eight Heroes of Old

Tommy, lost in thought as usual, found his mind racing with images and ideas, leaving him little time to focus. He contemplated the possibility of embarking on his mission alone. Considering whether it was a mistake to involve the heroes in his quest. He had failed many times before but felt a renewed determination to keep trying. "For the first time in my life, I can confidently say, these people are my friends," Tommy told himself. He felt the need to break the silence in his own room, but more than that, he wished to hear those words out loud. "What if I bring harm to them? I can't risk them being harmed. I should just go. I can take them back to their time when I am finished."

His fist pounded his palm with a firm and determined slap. "It wasn't right to get them involved. I shall leave at once!" Tommy declared.

A gentle knock on the door interrupted him mid portal. A faint voice followed, hesitant yet familiar.

"Tommy, are you there? I don't mean to interrupt," Arnold asked softly.

"I was just brooding..." Tommy replied, opening the door. "How may I help you?"

"Perfect!" He said, overjoyed, and stepped into Tommy's room. "Actually, I believe I can help you! What you said to me the other night had me thinking."

"I don't feel much like company right now, Arnold," Tommy said, trying to push him out the door. "I don't feel much like speaking to anyone at the moment. I am...tired..."

"But you don't sleep..." Arnold was, awkwardly still unrolling his schematic. "I thought you would be sitting quietly in your comfortable clothes Owen gave you. You are fully dressed like you were...Are you leaving?" Arnold's surprise was evident, but his quick mind threw Tommy for a loop.

"I..." Tommy could only mutter.

"Tommy, I can tell you are upset, but don't be afraid," Arnold said, adjusting his glasses. "Maybe I could accompany you wherever you needed to be."

"That's okay, Arnold, I wasn't going to be too long. I just needed a breather."

"I may not be the most savvy when it comes to connecting with people, but I do understand when they are lying. You meant to leave us. But why? We just had a major victory and soon we will have our next. You would abandon us?"

"It's not that simple. You don't know what you are talking about!"

"In my time as a professor, I've had many students cheat on their exams, and many have attempted to lie about it. I know how to read your body language, and I can tell you are hiding so much more. Out with it, Tommy!"

Feeling flustered with Arnold's confrontation, Tommy uttered his words softly. "I can't bear to bring harm to you. Christana really cares about me. You do too. It was evident back in the council chamber. Even Marcus cares to some degree, even if he is harsh about it. But for the first time in my life, I have friends. I have lasting bonds with all of you. I'm not about to let any of you get harmed."

"I see it's still haunting you. Friends are important. I know the feeling of not wanting to put them in harm's way. In my trial, I too sent Christana and Marlon away. I tried to at least. I brought them both to a dangerous place out of my own selfishness. I did what I thought was best. Told them to go back to France. I'm glad they didn't listen. I would not have made it very far without them. We can depend on those we love. It's not a burden. Love is a powerful emotion. It gives us courage to fight the hard fight, and strength to do the impossible. Trust in us, Tommy."

"You're right…" Tommy said, collapsing on a nearby chair. "I'm sorry."

"Don't be, Tommy. We all have our doubts from time to time. Now, if you will allow me, I would like to show you something."

After lighting the fireplace to brighten the room, and a few more lanterns upon the wall, Arnold opened the schematic to reveal his plan. "With this, you won't have any more doubts. Christana and I worked on this all night. I believe we found a way to fix our problem."

"What is that?" Tommy said, looking over the paper. Not a single detail was overshadowed. Arnold, a master of technology and design, displayed a perfect image upon the pages. His lines were crips and sharp. The numbering and flow were ever pleasing to see, reminding Tommy of his own father's drawing of the time machine. Everything had to be exact.

"I call it a Convergencer," Arnold said enthusiastically!

"What does it do?"

"Theoretically, it can help you master your power. I know you control time, but the force of will it has on you, as you've explained, can be taxing. To blend timelines takes a vast amount of magic you are not capable of wielding. But this here!" Arnold said with a boastful cheer and finger waving in their air. "You could change an event, and force time around it, resulting in time taking the new path, rather than reverting back to its original flow."

"This design is remarkable!" Tommy said, taking the plans over the light to see them more clearly.

"Well, I used inspiration from the helmet you gave me. That thing is a very interesting instrument. The helmet allows time to flow around us, not through us. I based it on that idea, letting time flow around your new event, then using the magic in the device, blend them together. I hope it goes according to plan. If you could manage to pull the pieces together, keeping the desired parts and discarding the undesirables. Then it would be key in fabricating a timeline that both saves your future and..." Catching himself from his rant, Arnold let Tommy marvel at it.

"This device is...Rather large, I must admit. Arnold, you are the greatest thing our world has lost. Your genius is far superior..."

"No need for the compliments. I'd rather stay modest, if you don't mind. But..."

"Let me finish..." Tommy interrupted. "I would love for you to see the future, Arnold. You would be amazed at everything and how far technologies have come, but this device. The idea is right, but it could be improved tremendously."

"I tried to imagine the technology Marcus would have had and I thought about it having improved a great amount."

"Your design is 1970s, at best."

"Were my calculations that far off?"

"Well, we can definitely make it more efficient in this area," Tommy said, taking Arnold's pen and circling some of the sections. "You did your due diligence, and that will make this easier. Cycles per minute are a little low. If we rewire the device this way, switch this for a microchip, we could amp the power and give it a stronger boost."

"What you did in minutes, Christana and I took the better part of a night. Je suis abasourdi."

"Give yourself some credit. I've lived through countless time loops and I never would have thought of this," Tommy said, consoling him. "You should not be ashamed of your work."

As Tommy's last word fell, another thunderous knock rang at his door. Christana had been calling for Arnold and her voice peeked through the crack asking if he had been by to see him yet. The door was slow to open. Christana peered around and walked in with a saddened step. In her hand, she carried her schematic and in the other, the faint glow of the Source Crystal shined.

"Christana! It's wonderful of you to stop by!" Tommy said. "Arnold was showing me your invention and I couldn't be happier!"

"It needs a lot of work," she mumbled. "I wanted to speak to Arnold about it. We have a mountain of recalculations to do, and the design is far off what it should be."

"Not to worry, Christana, we are well aware," Arnold said cheerfully. "Tommy made it very clear how we could improve."

"But we put all of our effort into it. Marcus even laughed at our design!"

"I'm sure he didn't mean anything from it," Tommy responded, trying to calm her down. "I must admit, both of you have given me something I lacked. Arnold caught me at a rough time, I won't bore you with the details, but...It was good he came along when he did. You have restored confidence in my mission. Let's not waste any more time. I have a feeling, our combined minds will fix it without any flaw."

Christana pocketed her schematic within her jacket and walked to the flame. It was the only light in the dim, stone-walled room near Arnold and Tommy. The castle's grand room, once a place for great warriors and lords from afar, was now repurposed as their makeshift workshop. The handcrafted oak table contrasted with the modern blueprints upon it.

They all gave each other a glance of determination. The preparations began in earnest, with Arnold and Tommy bent over the drawing table, sketching out the new model. It was slimmer and more compact, a testament to their combined ingenuity. Arnold marveled at Tommy's genius.

Christana ran the calculations. Her fingers flew over the lines and sharp edges, stopping to consult her notes now and then. She took in the advice Tommy gave her, nodding thoughtfully as she adjusted her figures. "This has to work," she muttered under her breath. Her eyes darted between the numbers and the scribbled equations in her notebook.

Tommy, sensing her anxiety, placed a reassuring hand on her shoulder. "It will, Christana. We've come this far. We can't give up now."

Arnold looked up from the drawing, his eyes filled with a mixture of pride and concern. "Tommy's right. We're in this together. We'll make it work."

Christana nodded, as she gave a half-hearted smile. "It has to be perfect," she said, "Tommy is dependent on us. We can't afford to fail."

Arnold traced the lines of the blueprint with his finger. "This is it," he said and he embraced Christana.

Christana took a deep breath, her heart pounding in her chest. She shed a small tear that dripped onto Arnold's hand.

"Qu'est-ce qui ne va pas?" Arnold said but let her crumble in his arms. His grasp tightened as she did the same.

Tommy sat in discomfort on his chair waiting out the complicated matter.

"It's all hitting me. The gravity of my mistake."

"What mistake? What are you talking about, Christana?"

But not another word slipped past her lips. She continued to hold Arnold, taking every moment from this time to reflect.

"I know what it is..." Tommy muttered. "But I should not say it."

Arnold turned his glance from Tommy back to Christana. Tommy watched as the inner workings on his mind continued to make connections.

"You were thirty-nine in 1951. By reason, the time of the Cactus, you would have only been in your sixties," Arnold cleared his throat. "Your life ends before that time. It would have to..." Christana shifted in his arms, unwilling to turn her head or gaze at him. "If you were still alive, Frutuoso would never have come to be. As long as the hero lives..."

"The night we arrived at Christina's mansion," Tommy began. "History knows that day well. That night. All of Christana's fears came to haunt her. Of all the darkness she suffered, she could not hold on any longer..." Tommy said, brushing a tear that formed in his eye.

"Arnold..." Christana spoke into his jacket, muffling her voice. "I never meant..."

"You don't have to speak," Arnold replied.

"I need to say something. My pain is...I lost too much in my time. Marlon did everything he could. I was a burden on him."

"We are never a burden," Tommy spoke, fiddling with the pen in his hands. "Especially to our loved ones. They want nothing more than to help. At any cost."

"I'll take you to your room," Arnold responded, taking out his handkerchief for her.

"I don't want to be alone anymore," she said.

"This device will work, Christana," Tommy tried to explain.

"I know it won't be the way I wish. Arnold's life isn't what would jeopardize the flow of time. Just tell me Tommy. Tell me once and for all. Break me of my feelings. Put this wild dream of mine to rest."

"The truth is, Christana," Tommy replied. "I cannot give you the life you wish."

The handkerchief fell from her hand. She embraced the words Tommy said and stood like a stone. She accepted them, as it clearly showed to Tommy.

"I'll take her to her room now," Arnold said, walking with Christana. "We all could use some rest."

"Tommy," Christana said before she left. "Thank you. I won't let my darkness take me again."

"Goodnight, Christana," Tommy responded. But as they left, Tommy mumbled his words. "I won't give up hope on you."

Tommy looked over the design once more. His mind was wild with ideas on how to use it. He anticipated holding it in his hand to gain more insight on its use, but he held on to that idea. Each hero had helped him in their own way.

"I won't give up on you. Any of you," he whispered.

21 Plans

Arnold walked Christana all the way to her room. Their steps were in synchronization and the descending hall seemed like it stretched forever. Christana held onto Arnold's arm, calming her breath as she focused on the passing torches upon the walls. The stone was cold and made for little company as they trampled above it. Their shoes echoed the sound of their movements as they made their way along the dark passage.

Stopping before Christana's door, Arnold held on a moment longer. "I don't want you to be alone." He glared towards his door, not far from hers, but turned back to look upon her disheartened eyes. He took her hand, feeling her soft skin and he danced his fingertips around her knuckles.

The Eight Heroes of Old

With his other hand, he brushed her golden hair behind her ear.

"I'll be fine, Arnold," she said. "You can let me go."

"What if I don't want to say goodnight?"

"We should get to bed." Her eyes were sincere as she dared to meet his. Her smile was weak, but genuine.

"It would be a waste of candlelight," Arnold said.

"Since when have you been the romantic type?"

"I've been doing a lot of thinking on this journey."

"You're always thinking, Arnold. Tu ne t'arrêtes pas." Her fingers became entangled in his as she pulled them up to her lips. "What have you been thinking about?"

"About us. To be honest, I feel lost in this world. But not when I am with you. I feel like I am right where I am supposed to be."

"What else?"

"There are so many things to say. My words race inside my head." Arnold moved his hand about with hers but motioned them towards the handle of the door. Together they opened it and entered the dark room. In the darkness, their eyes still found each other. Their lips met and their hearts beat faster.

"Even without the light, I can still make out your features," Arnold remarked.

Christana felt his heart through his shirt. Her finger, slowly, crossed over his jacket pocket and pulled the small lighter from it. She flicked it alight and set flame to the wicks of the candles. She removed her coat and wrapped it around the felt chair where she took a seat.

Following in the same manner, Arnold removed his jacket and hung it around the back, upon her coat. He sat in the chair adjacent to hers and continued holding her hand. He watched as she bent her elbow upon the table and leaned into her arm for support. Her hand so elegantly uplifting her face. There was not a blemish on her skin nor scar.

"Through all my trials. Through all my misery. One thing still played in my mind," Christana said as she played with the scrap pages she pulled from her pocket. "Do you remember the late nights? Our rendezvous in the park?"

"They were the best times of my life."

"When I was in the army, there were many nights I would gaze at the stars. They reminded me of you."

"We were gazing at them almost every weekend. Like the great astronomers before our time. Such wonder is just out of our reach!"

"I don't want you to leave, Arnold." Christana tugged the candle closer, brightening his face.

"I know, Christana…"

"I meant at this moment. Stay… Just a little longer."

"For as long as you need me," Arnold said, adjusting his glasses.

The next morning, the sunlight peeked into the room and left crepuscular rays in the dust. The sun's warmth wrapped itself around Christana as she slept comfortably in her bed.

A knock at the door, abrupt as the rooster crowing, awoke the two weary heroes. The door crept open, startling Arnold out of the bed. Caught in the sheets that ensnared him, he struggled to find the end of it.

Tommy, who was now caught completely off guard, stumbled to make sense of the scene. "I didn't know the door would open…" Tommy said, trying to catch the latch of the door.

Christana tried to find anything to cover her top, and she pulled her pillow up to herself for decency. "Tommy!" she exclaimed. "I haven't…"

"I'll take my leave," Tommy said, but still couldn't grasp the handle.

Christana tried to reassure him everything was fine, but only sank herself in further.

Arnold pulled himself from the sheets and grabbed his glasses off the floor. "Nothing happened between us!" He exclaimed. "We just fell asleep. That's all."

"I was just coming by to tell you… It's time…"

"We'll be out shortly Tommy!" Christana shouted. "Just leave!"

Averting his eyes, Tommy found the door handled and closed it firmly. "I could have handled that better," he said to himself.

"Arnold!" Christana called out, looking over the side of the bed. "You poor fool!" She laughed still seeing him trapped within the fabric.

Her laugh was infectious as Arnold couldn't control his gut and burst with the same amusement. After freeing himself from the sheets, Arnold picked up his glasses. He straightened his pants and pulled his shirt over himself.

"I'll give you some privacy," he said, adjusting his jacket.

Christana nodded, still covering herself with the pillow as she watched Arnold dress. He let out a deep breath as he exited the space. A mixture of relief and contentment filled her heart as she replayed the night in her mind. She felt closer to Arnold than ever before.

Outside Christana's chamber, where the halls met the rooms of the other heroes, Tommy continued his rattling of doors to wake them. Arnold, with a quick step, caught up to him.

"I'm sorry about all that," Arnold mentioned as he stopped Tommy. "I can assure you Tommy, there was nothing we had done."

"I should be the one apologizing," Tommy said, after placing a hand on Arnold. "You don't have to explain yourself, Arnold." Tommy smiled.

"What's the plan for today?"

"That's exactly it!" Tommy said with a grin. "Coming up with one! I have already told the rest of the heroes to meet in the council room. Owen had the royal kitchen prepare a meal for us. Let's join them!"

As they were speaking, Christana exited her room. Arnold looked over to her in the warm light that filled the room. The large windows streamed the morning sun over her.

"Good morning," Christana greeted them.

"Tommy says breakfast will be served for us in the council room," Arnold said with a rushed voice. "There we will make our plans for what's to come."

"That sounds wonderful." She smiled. She offered her hand to Arnold, and he welcomingly took it.

With an about-face, Tommy led them where all the heroes had gathered. There was more food than any of them could eat, but the room was theirs for the day. The maidens finished pouring a breakfast ale and served baked fish among other fruits, cheeses, and breads.

"Welcome, everyone! And good morning!" Tommy announced. He walked over to take his seat and waited for all others to stop their fidgeting and become settled. "First

I would like to say, I am thankful for all of you being here. It's not just answering the call of time once more. You're helping a friend. I thank the kitchen staff for the incredible meal, and I hope you all feast your hearts out!"

"We are glad to be here, Tommy," Marcus said from his seat to the left of Tommy's. One by one the heroes returned their respects, and their morning meal began.

"I have summoned you all here for time has called once again. The darkness is upon us. Upon the world… We must be ready to fight." Tommy took a moment to stand and pace the table. "This is my story. It is my turn to save this world. I look up to all of you who have served before me. I have had my doubts, I seriously don't know if I can do what I am supposed to do."

"Listen to me, Tommy," Gorn spoke, spreading the ripe berries on the bread. "You have to believe in yourself. Trust in the Allfather. Have Faith. Everything will work the way it is intended."

"Gorn is right," Marcus added. "As I am sure for all of you. At times, we didn't know what was going to happen or how we would find a way to overcome our problems, but time chose us all for a reason, right?"

"I have received all the support I need now. Thank you, Marcus and thank you, Gorn. Your words are taken to heart. I also wish to extend my heart to Christana and

Arnold. They helped me see last night I am not alone. I come from a world where the word help is nonexistent."

"You are far from that place," Christana said, addressing Tommy's solemn attitude.

"I know. And as a part of all of this, I thank you, Christana. I would not have made it this far without you. We also have Christana and Arnold for giving us the key to our whole strategy." Pulling from his pocket, Tommy unrolled the schematic for the device. "With our new device," Tommy started, clearing his throat at the direction of Marcus. "We have made a device that could alter the timeline. I will be able to fix it with the use of my power."

Tommy glanced around the room, his eyes meeting each member of the team in turn. "I really need this to work. I hope for all of us to succeed. I must be ready to face my challenges. I hope you all have faith in our leader Christana. I will now give her the room."

"Thank you, Tommy," she said, standing to speak with a confident grace. "Arnold and I have devised a plan. I believe we can change the very fabrics of reality. We can converge the two best parts of a timeline and unite it to make sure we can fix this problem. As Tommy explained, time is a singularity and always seems to find its way back to the same formation. With this device, Tommy can help lead it. Rough out the edges. I've given it some thought, but once I gain more insight, it will help our plane go along more smoothly. For now, we have what Tommy had described for me."

Tommy unrolled a large, detailed paper. Its edges frayed from frequent use, revealing a meticulously hand-drawn layout of the Capitol Building. The map, marked with dark, precise ink, showed every door and window. "I have witnessed this event hundreds of times," Tommy remarked. "It never gets any easier. But I walked through the doors and buildings a thousand times. From what I can recall, this is the best model we have."

"There will be a TV station broadcasting the whole event worldwide," Christana stated and pointed to a specific room on the map. "We need a small team to get Marcus into that room so he can speak to everybody. He will have to find the right words to convince everyone not to give up on heroes or the great prophecies."

"This will not be an easy task," Tommy added with his firm voice. "As Manson's minions and the forces that serve the darkness will try to stop this from happening."

George was the first to stand, raising his hand in a solemn pledge. "Fearless, aren't you?" Gorn remarked, admiration evident in his tone. "You have a good heart."

Jin also rose to offer his assistance. "We can make sure this is done," he said with confidence.

"Perfect. I believe you are the right people for the task," Christana continued. "You must be ready for any threat that may try to stop you. Do not hold back."

"Be ready for a shock," Tommy warned. His words mellowed with his breath as he spoke sincerely. "The future will not sit well with many of you, but the forces you are about to face will be like nothing you have ever challenged before. Humanity has developed the most destructive weapons. Machines I believe none of you could even fathom."

"What do you mean?" Owen asked. "What would be more terrible than dragons?"

"Machines that mimic their power, but more forceful," Tommy replied, stepping away from the table for a moment. He spoke loudly when he addressed the whole table. "The fears many of you have faced are small in comparison. Humans have learned to fly with these machines. Helicopters and fighter jets, they call them. Think of them like large metal dragons that breathe fire of their own. Or rain a volley of metal, more destructive than a thousand arrows."

"Dragons?" Owen asked, his brow furrowed. "How is this possible?"

"I haven't even begun to scratch the surface." Tommy exhaled, holding on just for a moment before returning to them. "Marcus, before this is over, you will have to bring them up to speed on everything in your world."

"All right. I can try."

"I'm serious. We will only have a day to prepare. Do whatever is necessary."

"I can bring down anything," Owen declared. "Just give the word, my breath will destroy it!"

"I was going to ask you to do this," Christana said. "If Manson uses these machines against us, you will be our only protection. As the others, I assume they will be heavily armed."

"In my time, we have invented weapons of mass destruction," Marcus said gravely. "Weapons that can kill multiple people without even breaking a sweat. Look at Christana's rifle. It doesn't even come close to what they can do now! I don't believe any of you could withstand their power."

"I have faced many things in my time, and I believe I can break whatever power is put in front of me," Gorn said with his steel voice and determined eyes. "Let me at them!"

"Gorn, maybe you don't understand. These weapons are like…" Marcus tried to explain.

"I fought the dark magic, Marcus," Gorn scoffed. "There is nothing more destructive than what I have seen. But by the Allfather, he has never led me astray."

"I hope you are right," Marcus conceded.

"Magic is destructive," Tommy said, agreeing with Gorn. "But do not underestimate your foe. Guns are what modernized the world. It made armor unless. Swords became too slow. But for Gorn, this may be an easy task. I have analyzed his power, and I believe he could be our best foot soldier and hold the front lines."

"Your job will be to walk the ground floor," Christana said, adding to Tommy's words. "Hide among the crowd. Watch for any action that may turn our mission sideways. If that happens, you will be in the middle of it, pulling attention away from Marcus and protecting the people in the audience."

Tommy watched Christana as she gave her final command to Arnold. He felt a sense of pride as he watched her determination flourishing.

"Arnold, you will accompany Tommy," she said. "I will take the high ground to overlook everything. Frutuoso will be by me. Is everything clear? Once all the pieces are in place, Tommy will confront Manson and end this nightmare."

"If I should fail, protect the people. They will need heroes more than anything."

"I won't let you fail," Marcus cried out. "We won't let you fail. We will be victorious!"

"Finally trying some of that team spirit, Marcus?" Arnold chuckled.

"I am depending on you, Christana. Once you feel the change in the flow, give me the signal. I will traverse the void and bring the timelines together, converging the pieces how we need them."

"I can already feel the change. The days don't seem so bleak," Christana smiled at him. "I am hopeful."

"What we are about to do is terrifying. It would be a miracle to pull it off," Tommy added.

Gorn stepped forward, his presence as solid and reassuring as a mountain. "That, my friend, is why you need to believe," he said, his voice vibrant in the dark room. "Have faith."

"I do," Tommy said, running his hands over the wood grain of the table. He felt the cracks and the splinters, like they were small hills and valleys over a distant land. Imagining he was flying at great heights. "I will confront Manson once again. I will bring him to justice."

The table shook, as the goblets atop began to rattle. The papers rolled back up as the room fell silent. The flames on the candles and lanterns spurred to a violent end and the shadow behind Marcus came forward.

"Be warned, Tommy," D said, his stature immediately commanded fear to all present, but they all listened to his words. "You have many things beyond your vision. Things I have seen. Things I know. I am forbidden to tell you, but I must say, I am a part of this team, just as any of you. I will do everything in my power to assist you, but if Manson should succeed. If the Hellhounds are allowed to roam the Earth…"

"You don't need to say anymore, D," Marcus interrupted. "We won't let that happen."

"Let him speak," Tommy said, daring to look into D's eyes, wicked and burning of vengeance. "What will happen?"

"Manson has a true evil about him. He…" D's voice trailed off, the silence that followed was heavy and oppressive.

"What is it?" Tommy asked. "Speak up!"

"I cannot. I am forbidden," D said, his form dissolving back into the darkness that clung to Marcus like a shroud.

"Marcus?" Christana asked. "Is he really on our side?" The concern ran deep in her words.

"He wants to help, but he is bound by the evil that gave him power. He obeys me. Like a servant of two masters," Marcus said. "There are laws beyond ours. Even in the void, there are rules that must be followed. He cannot answer."

"Even by your command?" Tommy asked.

"Even by my command," Marcus replied, his tone resigned but firm.

"We will tread lightly. Just know your goals. Let's not play around. We get what we need and finish it quickly.

"And pray," Gorn added.

"Yes. This is our only chance. Prepare yourselves and pray."

"It will take a moment to build the device," Arnold mentioned. "If I had the right components I could build it in a matter of hours. Assuming all is right with my calculations."

"I ran over the calculations myself. They will be fine," Christana said with a supportive hand on his shoulder.

"Marcus, are you ready to be home?" Tommy asked, with a smirk.

"More than anything! I miss my home and my own bed!" Marcus exclaimed, his voice filled with longing. He dazed off, a dreamy look on his face as he thought of all the luxuries of the present. "New York pizza... Coffee... Oh, the simple joys. You know what, put all of that on hold. I could really use a coffee right now!"

"Marcus!" Christana scolded.

"I'm kidding. Mostly. But I do miss my cat," Marcus continued to muse. "I do wish to see Diana once more. You know, before everything goes wrong."

"Don't be so cynical, Marcus," Christana said.

"I want to hope for the best, but just in case," Marcus replied, his voice fading as his mind began to wonder again.

"Well, Marcus," Tommy said. "Make it the best coffee you ever had!" He pushed time through his fingertips.

Swirls of purple and gold illuminated the room, casting a warm glow. The heroes once again entered the portal, passing through light, then darkness, then light again. The portal swirled behind them as they arrived at the magnificent sight of New York City.

The buildings towered above them, cars zipped by on busy streets, and people bustled about. A breathtaking spectacle presented itself. The city was vibrant, with a slight overcast adding to its charm. Christana's eyes widened as she took in the marvels around her. Arnold stood in awe, amazed by the advancements in science. He knew it would be extraordinary, but reality exceeded his wildest imaginations. Owen and Gorn appeared frightened at first. There were no castle walls or horse-drawn carts. But they soon embraced this new world. This was the world as the Creator intended. To improve and advance in ways beyond imagination. The structures of man climbed to the sky, a marvel to human ingenuity.

Frutuoso, not too far removed from this era, found solace in the city's green spaces, enjoying the companionship of his friends. George, delighted to see children playing at the nearby park, felt a renewed sense of happiness at the sight of their innocence.

Jin walked beside Marcus, offering his guidance. "When you see Diana, remember the breathing techniques I taught you," he advised with a joking tone.

"Thanks," Marcus said with a mocking glance. He then turned his attention back to the cityscape, standing at the edge of the building. He leaned over the side of the wall, gazing out at the sprawling metropolis below. The cacophony of honking cars and distant chatter blended into a comforting symphony. "It's good to be home." A smile formed on his face. "I'd never thought I would miss this big city."

"This is where you live?" Owen asked.

"Almost. I live in Manhattan, the island over there, but it is still a ways away. Diana is completely out of the city, staying with her parents."

"I thought the great wall was impressive, but this." Jin stood by Marcus in awe as the portal closed behind them.

Tommy was the last to step through from the council room. He watched as the other heroes marveled at the great city, before they even landed. Their eyes wide with wonder and disbelief. He lingered behind, his pace slower, his thoughts heavy. As he passed through the portal, he couldn't resist one last look into the void. It was a swirling abyss of shadows and nothing, holding secrets he had yet to uncover.

Something caught his eye—a flicker, a shape barely discernible against the darkness. His heart skipped a beat, recognition dawning on him. He strained to see more clearly, his breath catching in his throat. "Jimmy?" he whispered, voice trembling, and his eyes widened.

22 Bite and Burn

The metal clanged as the hammer pounded it into place. Bolts were tightened with precision. Parts were meticulously set. An old piece of rubber was placed on top of the bike and fastened with makeshift straps. It wasn't perfect, but it was functional.

At last, the engine sputtered to life, flames and smoke belching from the exhaust as Mason spurred it on. Jimmy's face lit up with excitement; he had successfully deciphered his father's schematics and repaired the motorcycle. The heat it radiated was intense but oddly comforting, even in these harsh times.

The low rattle of the engine was unlike anything anyone had ever heard before. It was like a thunderous roar, reverberating through their very beings. Mason beamed with pride at Jimmy. Now, they had a real chance to repair the machine that sat a few meters away in the shed.

Mason turned off the bike. The spinning parts gradually came to a halt, and all the noise died down as the smoke cleared.

"This is truly amazing, Jimmy. You are your father's son, no doubt about that," Mason said, dismounting from the bike. His hands were coated in soot and wrapped in rags. As he lowered himself, his eyes met Jimmy's. "You're doing great work here."

"Thank you, Mason!" Jimmy said with a smile that had not graced his face in a long while.

"Tomorrow, I will take you to see the machine. Hopefully you can fix that too."

"I don't know. I'm scared. Mom doesn't want..."

Mason, trying to console Jimmy, reassured him. "You are right to be scared. She is too. We all have our part to play in this, Jimmy. Your mom would want this. Tommy needs us. Do it for him."

Mason could still feel Jimmy's guilt, but he saw the change in him as he mentioned Tommy's name.

"I know your little heart doesn't know what to do, but any mistake we make can be fixed with the time machine. With it, we can leave this awful place. We can be free from all trouble. We could see your brother again."

The Eight Heroes of Old

Jimmy's eyes exploded with excitement. "Do you really mean that?"

"That's a good kid!" Mason encouraged. "Just remember to keep it a secret. We will surprise your mom. She will be so proud of you!"

"Okay. I'll try," the small boy muttered, trying to hide his guilty smile.

"Now, be good and go get cleaned up. I'll fix us something to eat. And tomorrow we will see what the time machine needs."

Jimmy nodded before making his way to the safety of the bunker. The hatch was heavy, and required Mason's hand to help lift it, but together they opened it. Jimmy stared into the dark tunnel. He did not move or make any effort to climb down.

"What's wrong, Jimmy?" Mason asked.

"Thank you for helping me, Mason," Jimmy responded. "I hope this is the last time I have to go down here. I never liked going down in the bunker."

"I don't either. But just remember what I told you about being brave," Mason said, smiling reassuringly. He encouraged Jimmy to head down, promising he would join him in a minute.

Jimmy nodded and descended the ladder into the vault, still carrying a hint of that rare smile.

Mason turned back to the bike. His hands polished the surface as he wiped away the black smudges that clung to the metal. His reflection, once visible, now twisted and distorted, the gleam dulled by years of wear. No matter how much he tried, the bike would never shine as it once had. The faint reflections it did offer were little more than dark shadowy figures.

Down in the bunker, Mason's steps echoed on the metal ladder. The noise was never calm and had nowhere else to go. Mason entered to find Jimmy, quiet and still by the water. He was not washing or following instructions. The ripples almost seemed to mesmerize him.

"Jimmy don't waste the water," Mason spoke to rush him. "Are you almost finished?"

"Almost," Jimmy replied, whipping the beaded water off his face with the rag hanging nearby.

With a small fire burning, Mason placed the pan atop the flame, adding the farmed mushrooms to hear them sizzle. But also, within ear shot, he heard Jimmy wonder to Emily.

"Do you want something to eat, Mom?" Jimmy asked, shaking her to break her sleep.

Emily mumbled something to him. An indiscernible tone but brushed the small child's hair as she kept herself on the makeshift bed. Her hair covered her face hung gently down as she lifted her head. "What is it?"

"Mom, are you sick?" Jimmy asked.

"No, I'm fine," she replied in a soft tone. Her breath could barely carry her worlds.

"Come get something to eat, Mom!" Jimmy said, shaking her again. "Mason is cooking!"

"I'll be up. Give me a minute." She rubbed his forehead and felt his wet hair. "You're wet." Her eyes opened to see him, as she smiled as her young boy.

Jimmy smiled back. "Yes. I just cleaned myself."

"Good boy…good boy…"

she murmured before drifting off again. Exhaustion overcame her. She hadn't eaten much in days, and her recovery from injuries added to her fatigue.

"Come, let's eat," Mason said, holding a plate for Jimmy and himself.

"What about mom?" Jimmy replied. "She needs to eat too."

"Don't worry. She just needs rest."

Jimmy sat at the table, dancing his fork around the food.

"Do you remember those old books your father would read to you?" Mason waited for the humble nod from Jimmy before continuing. "There is a whole life waiting for us. Have you ever seen the pictures of what this place used to look like? Did he tell you the stories of what life was like?

I know this is all you have ever known, but out there, it will be better."

"I'm worried about her," Jimmy said, looking back at his mom.

"I know, those people in those stories can help us. They can help your mom."

"Mom!" Jimmy cried out. "Come eat with me! Please!"

Emily awoke from her slumber, dazed. She could smell the food cooking and craved it. Halfheartedly rising to her feet, she kept the blanket wrapped around her and met Jimmy at the table. Her broken smile met him as she took a seat. Her eyes were weary, sagging with a beaten purple hue. Her mouth was dry, and her voice cracked with every word she tried to speak..

"I'm here, Jimmy," she whispered, wiping her eyes with her fingers. She laid her hand on her forehead and rubbed it.

Mason slid a plate across to Emily. It was full and had many different types of mushrooms. To them, this was what a variety diet looked like, but all pleasant to them regardless. He then made a plate especially for Emily, not forgetting to use the reishi, as he intended to keep his plan in motion. Mason focused on keeping Emily in this drowsy state for as long as he could. This plight was over Emily's head. It was the brain fog that made her thoughts and reasoning elude her, but either way, it was working.

Mason sat down and they all began to eat their meal.

"Thank you, Mason," Emily said. "I'm sorry, I have not been much help lately. I might be coming down with something."

Mason stayed quiet, uninterested in small talk with Emily or engaging with her. Jimmy spoke up, his words reflected his delight that his mom was finally awake.

"Do you want to play a game after dinner, mom?" Jimmy asked whilst tugging on her sleeve.

"I would love to play a game," Emily said, finishing her last bite. "I may not be able to play for long. I'm still tired." She sighed as the words came from her mouth, but Mason listened as she addressed him. "I'm sorry to place this upon you, Mason, but thank you for watching over Jimmy."

He nodded in response.

"Jimmy, I want you to listen to Mason until I am feeling more rested. He will protect you."

Jimmy looked at Mason and went back to his mother. Confusion clouded his eyes. Jimmy nodded his head in acknowledgement.

Mason watched as Emily used all her strength to play for a few minutes with Jimmy. She had dedication to her child, as Jimmy's laughter filled the enclosed concrete room. But before long, Emily was nodding off. She teetered back and forth before returning to bed. Jimmy's smile faded.

"Get some rest, Jimmy," Mason said, extinguishing the fire. "We will be up early."

Doing as instructed, Jimmy curled up next to his mom and fell asleep. The night drifted past them, only discernible by the eerie feeling that it brought with it. The nightmares came and went, and by the end of them, Mason was up, determined and strong. He awoke Jimmy, ensuring Emily stayed asleep.

"Stay quiet," Mason said to him. "She needs her rest."

They climbed up the hatch and made their way to the motorcycle. Mason kickstarted the bike, which sputtered to life with a rutted babble. The bike spoke in loud roars. The engine spewed smog with powerful thrusts. This bike was unique; no one else in the world had anything like it. Man and metal united once more.

The distance to the shed seemed like a long journey on foot, but the bike could cover it in a few short minutes. Mason sat Jimmy on the bike and held him close as they rode off, kicking up dust and ash. A storm brewed in the distance. Swirls of black clouds mixed with red flashes covering the horizon.

Jimmy jumped off the bike as they came to a halt. Mason examined the bike as it cooled down, radiating heat like a forge. The shed, already in disrepair, had worsened since the portal's last opening. The wind blew the front doors away and tore apart the roof.

Most of the heavy parts upon the machine lay broken and scattered on the ground. All the bulbs and fuses had blown, and the coils remained charred. Jimmy ran to the control panel and opened the circuitry, taking detailed notes of everything inside. Lastly, he checked the generator. It was low on energy, but it might still work.

"What do you think, kid?" Mason asked. "Is it fixable?"

"I didn't know it would be this bad. Tommy knew so much more about it." Jimmy sniffled as he spoke, borderline crying.

"Come on!" Mason said, comforting him. "You are a smart kid. Be brave for Tommy and your mother. Listen, there is nobody in this world that can do this except you. It has to be you. You got this, kid."

Jimmy rubbed his wet eyes, leaving his sleeve soaked.

"You and I both know you can do this," Mason said. He pulled out Robin's notebook. The handwriting of Jimmy's father and all the notes he left in there. Mason recalls one of the last moments with him.

"In this book, Jimmy, your father wanted to do something special. I always doubted him. I made him out to be a fool for believing in such nonsense. But you know what he told me? He wanted to share his own story. He wanted to have a place in time. All the history books he read, he wanted to write his own part. In this book, he poured his heart and soul."

Mason kept flipping through the pages until he stumbled upon the note he remembered. He couldn't read much, but he understood the title: The Last Will and Testament of Robin Kent. Mason took the letter and showed it to Jimmy. "Your dad believes in you."

My dad wrote this for me?," Jimmy asked, amazed by what he had read. His eyes watered soiling the pages as the tears fell. "Why didn't Tommy show this to me before?" he mumbled.

"Everything you need is in this book," Mason said, handing it over completely.

Without hesitation, Jimmy began to write in the blank pages. His scribbling meant little to Mason, but it was enough for Jimmy to read for himself. He recalculated all the damaged parts and was almost finished noting one more thing to check. With steady hands, he opened a secret compartment. Behind multiple screens and embedded in a special circuit board, a faint blue glow illuminated. Inside, Jimmy removed the Source Crystal and inspected for damage.

Remarkable, Mason had never seen anything like it. It was almost too bright for his eyes.

"This was the piece my dad risked his life for. The one that ultimately was why he died," Jimmy said. "That's what Tommy told me. This one is special."

He placed it back in the machine as Mason watched. Mason observed every move Jimmy made.

"I have it all," Jimmy said. "It will take me a long time, but maybe not so long if you help me."

"Is there anything we can do to speed up the process?"

"Take these things back with us. I can fix them at home."

After loading what they could, the team of two made their way back as the storm settled over them. The red lightning feasted upon the sky. Monstrous thunder echoed throughout the valley. The gusts of the wind even rattled the house above as dust sprinkled down in the shelter.

Jimmy curled up with his mother while Mason lay awake. His mind paced. His heart would not cease as he wanted to escape. The crack leading up to a boom in the sky made it difficult to sleep. In his restlessness, Mason peaked above through the hatch. Flames engulfed a lot on the surface as it spiraled in the storm. Ash, dirt, rock, and sparks were carried by in a feeding frenzy of destruction.

The loudest of thunder awoke everybody.

"I've never seen a storm this bad before," Mason said. "Don't let that frighten you. We are safe."

Emily settled back down and fell asleep, but Jimmy rose, determined to face the day.

"The time machine?" Jimmy asked. "Do you think it's okay?"

"It should be fine," Mason said, loading the motorcycle once again. "Fix what you can. I'll be back with the needed parts."

A half day of traveling, and a haul full of scrap later, Jimmy and Mason got to work. They repaired what they could that was broken and cast new metal parts they needed. It was extensive work, exhausting and punishing.

In a few days, Jimmy and Mason managed to get the machine to a partially working condition. Following Jimmy's instructions, Mason pulled the lever and watched the test run ignite the machine. It ran with loud clunks and jangles. It wasn't sturdy, but it worked, nonetheless.

Jimmy pulled wires and soldered them to different areas. Once finished, he flipped switches as sparks flew. He troubleshooted all he could to find the running errors. Fuses became overloaded and fried, and Mason had to be quick to change them. It was dangerous, but neither of them worried about the consequences—or at least, they couldn't perceive any. Finally, Jimmy pushed the final buttons and pulled the last lever. The machine started up. The generator sputtered, giving its last breath. The machine had a strong pull, creating swirls of purple and gray smoke

The Eight Heroes of Old

that engulfed the area. Jimmy peered into the void, mesmerized by its luster and beauty.

Mason also examined the portal, apprehended by the sight. The light dazzled him before it soon turned into a black vortex shrouded in shadow. Little light came through as the void swallowed it. Through the void, dark eyes caught Mason's attention. They had a powerful gaze as they shared with Mason their vision. Mason tried to reach out, but the machine turned sporadic, spewing harmful energy into the room.

The machine began to exhaust and burst. The overhaul pushed to its limits. Forced to look away, Jimmy climbed to the kill switch and pulled it before more damage could be done.

As the light faded, Jimmy caught a glimpse of someone looking back. The figure had an old, familiar face. Jimmy felt a connection as the whole thing came to a close. The machine spat a few more sparks as it shut down. Then, it released a final burst of energy that slammed Jimmy and Mason to the ground. The swirls dissipated, and the whole machine went quiet. The darkness left them stranded, hair disheveled and bones shaken. Mason's mouth was wide open, and he was almost unresponsive.

For what felt like minutes, Jimmy managed to awaken Mason from his malefic thoughts. Mason had no more doubts; his world had fallen from under him. He had seen the true power.

"Mason!" Jimmy cried, shaking him. "Please, listen to me!"

Mason shook his head, relieving the pain. "What?"

"I think I saw him! I saw Tommy!"

"You did?"

"He called out to me! I know he did!"

Standing and looking over the time machine Mason turned to Jimmy. "How bad is it?"

"Hmm?" Jimmy pondered, walking around the device, trying to get a good look and checking the Source Crystal once again. Jimmy confirmed the machine was only slightly damaged from that test.

"What does it need?"

"It needs much more power."

"Like electricity?" Mason grimaced in pain but continued overlooking the problem area. "What does that mean?"

"The generator is bad, but Tommy said he thought it wouldn't give as much power as we needed. He started building something that would help if the generator would not be enough."

"What would that be?"

Jimmy pulled Mason aside to reveal a machine on the floor. It had arms that sprawled out like a trap, and a thick black wire that ran from it to connect to the generator.

"It was a bad idea," Jimmy mumbled.

"What does it do?"

"Tommy said it would use the combustion from a Hellhound to ignite the time machine. He called it Dog Bite. But he was too afraid to use it. He decided the generator would be enough." Jimmy looked over the schematic of Tommy's design. He measured all the pieces he needed and wrote down any extra parts Mason would need to collect. Once settled, Jimmy and Mason returned home.

The next days were excruciating. More storms ravaged the land. Hellhounds chased the chaos coming closer. But, unappalled, they still continued with their plan. Emily was still under Mason's spell, while Jimmy built Tommy's machine.

On the day of the test, Mason scavenged through his food storage. It was depleted most of the way as he smashed the empty jars on the pantry floor in a fury. A nervous Jimmy entered, asking if he was all right, but Mason didn't pay him any attention.

"This has to work," Mason said. "We are out of food. You have to hope that it will."

"I want it too! I followed everything Tommy told me. Did all that my father wrote down."

Mason took Jimmy's hands. He could feel his sweaty palms, panicked and shaken.

"We need to leave this place today."

Jimmy looked at his mother still sleeping.

"This is the last day we have to struggle," Mason told him.

Jimmy gathered his things in a small bag and made his way to the ladder. Mason went up first and opened the hatch. The air was hot and rough outside as a breeze blew open the bunker. The howling sands pummeled Mason as his grip slipped. He caught himself, but the hatch made a horrific bang as it slammed open.

Abruptly, the trouble woke Emily. Her senses caught up as her mind snapped to alertness. The scene became clear.

"Get down from that ladder!" Emily shouted. "It's not safe! Mason!" she called out, furious. "Bring Jimmy back down!"

"Don't worry, Mom!" Jimmy shouted back as he climbed out of the hole. "Mason is keeping me safe. The time machine is working! We will come back for you!"

"The time machine?" Emily gasped. "Mason, you bastard! Bring him back down here now! It's too dangerous!"

"He is safe with me, Emily. We have no more food and we have…"

"Shut your mouth, Mason!" she snapped. "Jimmy, Mason has been poisoning your mind. Come down from there!"

"But mom!" Jimmy cried. "I saw Tommy! He needs me!"

"I'm coming up there to get you, and we are leaving at once."

"Where would you go?" Mason questioned.

But Emily didn't respond. Instead, she began ascending the metal ladder. The cold pierced her feet, her hands were weak, and her mind was ill. She did not quite have the strength to make it to the top. The harsh and violent winds rushed against the three of them. Mason took hold of Jimmy as Emily tried to keep her strength. Inevitably, she lost her grip. Emily fell backward, reaching out to Jimmy as she fell. The table broke her fall, but the damage had been done. Blood poured from her head coating the concrete floor.

Mason acted, leading Jimmy back down into the bunker. He wrapped his shirt around her and placed her back in the bed. There was a loss of color on her face, and her skin ran cold. Her breath was soft, but only mirrored her faint heartbeat. "We have to go, Jimmy!"

"Will my mom be okay?" he cried. "We can't just leave her."

"She will not make it without help. Only Tommy can save her. We'll be back when the time machine is working." Mason was stern with his words but offered Jimmy a comforting hug. "Be strong."

Mason and Jimmy made their way to the abandoned barn. The shifting dust overhead signaling the return of the storms. The wind howled around them, carrying with it the ominous promise of chaos. As they approached, Jimmy took another look at the machine. This time, it stood more robust, its structure reinforced and slightly larger. It exuded a newfound strength, capable of withstanding the immense pressure from within. The unpredictable outbursts from the void would have little effect.

The barn creaked under the strain of the approaching storm. But the machine remained steadfast. Jimmy's eyes reflected determination as he and Mason prepared for the uprising of the machine.

"I'll fix this for you Mom, don't worry," he said under his breath.

Jimmy knelt down and welded the last parts together. Mason moved the heavy pillars in place and laid the flaps outward in a star pattern. They pounded the dirt, kicking up the dust as they were set in place. The cord stretched back into the barn connecting to the time machine.

Jimmy asked for help as they hooked it up to what Tommy called Dog Bite. He flipped the switch as the generator powered the chaotic machine. Jimmy's cheerful outburst became overshadowed by the whirling noises of the device.

"Tell me how this works again," Mason asked.

"Well, you need to lead a Hellhound onto the harvester," Jimmy began. "That's the part that looks like a star. I will hit the lever and activate the Dog Bite. When the Hellhound dies, the explosion should be enough to superheat the conductors and channel the power into the machine."

"For an eight-year-old, you are quite some kid."

"This is it?" Jimmy asked. "Will we save my mom?"

"I know we can," Mason said whilst giving one last encouraging hug. "You can do it! I'll get on my bike."

The engine rumbled like always, and Mason rode off in search of a Hellhound. He never had to go very far, as they were plentiful and always starving. The only problem was they hunted in packs. Mason counted the bullets in his gun, too few for a real fight. The heat waves made him sweat as the bike emitted a sickening noise. Revving, the bike kicked up dust as the wheels spun.

As Mason planned, he came across a pack of the demonic creatures. He counted four large beasts with fire upon their breath and putrid fur. Mason covered his nostrils with a rag, avoiding breathing the sulfur smell.

The roar of the engine kicked off the chase with a violent burst. Their dry mouths released sickening howls and their claws propelled them forward. The wolves closed in, shrinking the distance. Mason swerved, their fangs snapping empty air.

The barn was in sight, but Mason knew he needed to thin them out before bringing them back that way. He pulled the shotgun, and fired back. The first shots rang out more like a warning, giving him distance to safely deal with them one at a time. Four became three. Three became two.

Conniving as the creatures were, they learned from the death of the pack. Splitting from the dead, they moved to the flank from opposing sides. Mason pushed the bike into high gear, twisting on the throttle to give it the last of the gasoline it had.

Relentless. Hateful. Hungry. The Hellhounds charged once more. Mason dodged the clenching teeth. His clothes escaped the snares of their fangs as he raised the gun. Mason had to steady his hand. He pulled it up once again, but the beast reacted with an unpredictable maneuver.

The teeth shredded a bike tire, throwing Mason from the bike, rolling in the dust. Mason scrambled, rushing to the cover of the shed, as Jimmy watched in horror.

The Eight Heroes of Old

"Don't do it Jimmy!" Mason shouted as he ran toward the boy, but his voice fell short.

With a flare in his hand, Jimmy set it off and threw it to distract the wolves. For a moment, it worked, giving Mason enough time to mount the bike once again. But like all hope in this world, it died as a Hellhound rushed the shed.

Mason kick started the bike and sped faster than he had ever before. By this time, the second Hellhound was upon Jimmy as the poor boy stumbled to find a safe place to hide. Inside the shed was not an option, so he climbed above it. The wolves were barking at his feet, out of reach.

The Hellhounds stood on their hind legs, sniffing the air to sense his fear. Their combined weight bent the structure beneath them. A long tongue with protruding thorns emerged from one of their mouths. It licked the sweat that fell from Jimmy. The taste fueled their motivation.

The roof of the shed, already compromised, began to collapse. The rusted paneling gave way as Jimmy's leg fell through. The beasts, eyes glowing with hunger, spotted the movement. One of them circled around, searching for a way to get inside and reach Jimmy.

Mason fired more shots into the air as he rode faster. Snatching an extra cord from Dog Bite, Mason made a makeshift lasso and dragged a Hellhound away. The second beast showed no interest in Mason and felt no pity for the other Hellhound being dragged away. A more savory meal awaited as it climbed the shed in search of Jimmy.

Red eyes peaked over the roof, gushing with flames. Its mouth and claws scrambling to get a grip to climb up. Jimmy was backing away. The beast found its footing and made its way on top. A shift in the wind and wobble of the shed threw both Jimmy and the hound to the dust, as a part of the roof collapsed.

By the neck, Mason dragged the Hellhound until it was set loose by him. Its hatred knew no bounds as it leaped for the man on the bike. With a burst of flame, the beast erupted into a violent storm, echoing the rampage above. Mason stood victorious over the beast as he rode through the burst of flame. In front of him, the Hellhound was upon Jimmy.

Jimmy and the beast were now face to face as the dust settled. The hound's eyes locked onto him, freezing Jimmy in place with fear, his legs stuck like glue. He felt his light dim, staring into those malevolent eyes, a void of darkness and evil. Hope seemed lost, and pain crept into his heart, making him weak. The beast's power brought him to his knees as it stepped forward, mouth widening. Its growl blew acidic air towards him. His heart stood still.

Mason put himself between Jimmy and the beast, locking eyes with the creature. "Don't be afraid!" he shouted. "Go for the lever!" Mason revved his engine, taunting the Hellhound and slashing at it with his knife as he drove past. He slowed down with intent, allowing the beast to take a bite at him, but protected himself with the cord. As the beast latched on, Mason pulled it into the Dog Bite, leaping from the bike at the last moment.

With a snap of the lever, lightning shot up from Dog Bite as it trapped the beast within. Mason pulled his gun taking aim with his last bullet and ended the beast. The machine did as intended, absorbing the blast.

Jimmy sprang into action, pulling all the switches and levers. He worked frantically, as the faint swirl of the machine began to sound. He gasped as the lights turned bright and the machine roared back to life.

"It's working!" Jimmy said. "It's working!" His face was bright and full of tears.

Mason stumbled into the shed to witness the magnitude of the time machine. He tied off his bleeding wounds, congratulating the small boy on his accomplishments.

Emily lay in the bed, her lips parched and dreaming of water. Her consciousness wavered, drifting in and out. She uttered words for Jimmy, but he didn't answer. Whispering the softest words her voice could manage, she offered a final prayer for her son. She wished the best for Jimmy, feeling the cold creep around her. If Jimmy was coming back, it might be too late.

Summoning her strength, Emily gripped the bed frame. Stumbled to her feet, she avoided slipping on the bloody floor. The weather outside had turned violent as the storm returned. Something felt terribly wrong. She grabbed the shotgun and held it close as she waited. She could hear the howls outside, drawing nearer. Closing her eyes, she braced herself for what was to come.

23 Back Home

A gasp and a fall. The eight heroes turned to face the closing portal as it threw Tommy like a bag of sand. Tommy coughed and spat out the gravel that ground against his teeth. Christana and Owen helped him gain his footing, as the other heroes tried to set up a stone for him to sit.

"What's happened to you?" Christana asked, taking the handkerchief from Arnold and wiping the beaded sweat upon his brow. "You look like you've seen a ghost!"

Tommy's mind was swirling. The clouds and faces became mixed, but he shook the feeling as best as he could. Gorn stepped forward, pulling him up with a firm grip, against the wishes of the others.

"He should rest, Gorn!" Marcus snapped, but Gorn pushed back.

"He is stronger than you believe," Gorn replied. "He needs to know it."

"I... I saw him..." Tommy whispered. Before he could speak, his eyes welded tight. He could not contain the flow of tears as he tried to keep whatever flashes he had fresh in his mind. The soft smile upon the innocent face of his brother was fading. "I saw my brother..." Tommy continued, the agony was apparent in his voice. "I miss my family." He gripped the shoulder of Gorn, and he pulled himself closer. "My home, as dark as it was—it's where my mom is. Where my father was."

"You will find them again," Gorn reassured. "By my strength you will."

"How is it that you saw them?" Arnold asked. "I thought you were forbidden to see back to your time."

"I peered too long into the void..." Tommy said, fixing himself up right and straightening his jacket. "I saw flashes through the vortex of time and through the void, I dared myself to see further." With a breath of fresh air, Tommy took sight over the city. "I thought I saw someone staring back at me. I tried calling out to him, but he could not hear me. Who else could have been staring back. My brother Jimmy is tampering where he shouldn't."

"That doesn't sound good to me," Marcus said. "What happens if Jimmy fixes the time machine?"

"It won't work," Tommy said, his tone grim. "If he tries to use the machine, it may kill him. It was a miracle what happened to me. I doubt it will happen a second time."

"Why is he even trying? I thought you said it was too dangerous."

"Mason must be helping him. I don't know why. Maybe there is trouble back home. They might be looking for a way out."

"Does this change the mission?" Jin asked. "Do we need to find a way to help your brother?"

"No. We still have to stop Manson. It's the only way. Maybe…Once my part in this is over, I can return to my time. Or better yet, my era would not be so desolate." Tommy held up the paper with the Convergencer on it. "This will be our key. Once we build this…"

"We will, Tommy," Owen said. "Whatever you need. We are here to serve you."

"Marcus, is there anywhere we could build this? Is there someplace that would have all the parts we need?" Arnold asked.

"I know where…" Marcus sighed. "My father's old company. They still have a small workshop here. I can call in a favor from them."

"You know they won't give you access."

"They will for me as the hero, not as Marcus..." Marcus furrowed his brow. "One way or another."

"I like the way you think, Marcus," D said, smiling over his shoulder.

"Very well!" Arnold exclaimed. "Let's get moving! I am also very much excited to see all these contraptions you have and all these wild innovations."

"Lead the way, Marcus," Christana said.

It was a far walk, but Marcus showed delight in every step, eager to take in the wonders of the city. From atop the skyscraper Tommy had placed them, getting down was the first step. The elevator was an awkward ride as just seeing lights was a first for many of the heroes, let alone all the buttons and mechanisms that decorated the inside.

Outside, the city unfolded before them like a spectrum of wonders and fears. A place both awe-inspiring and unsettling. The buildings towered into the sky, steel and glass giants that seemed to defy the very laws of nature. The sheer scale of the metropolis was beyond anything they could have imagined. An endless hive of activity where the streets pulsed with life. Like an active anthill teeming with people.

The roar of engines and the flash of passing cars both frightened and intrigued the group. The vehicles moved with a mechanical precision that seemed almost unnatural to those not accustomed to such sights. Owen and Gorn, veterans of battles in far simpler lands, were ready to draw their weapons at the slightest provocation. The world they now found themselves in was alien and overwhelming.

Their nerves reached a breaking point when a plane roared overhead. Its sleek form cut through the cyan sky. Owen and Gorn instinctively called out, bringing for the swords and glow of their magic. Their hands gripped their weapons with such fury as their eyes scanned the skies.

"It's not a dragon!" Marcus shouted, using D to pull down their weapons. "Keep yourselves in line or you will have the police on us. New York already doesn't like citizens arming themselves in public. I don't want the added distraction of the NYPD on us. Just stay calm, nothing will harm us here."

"Oh, come on, Marcus, you know that's not true," D said. "There are plenty of worries in this city. Plenty of thrills."

"Not now, D."

Gorn pulled his sword from D's grasp and stowed it in his scabbard.

"I see you kept that blade. Does it still ring in your ear when you swing it? Does it still sing your uncle's name?"

"Look how far you've fallen," Gorn spat.

"D!" Marcus shouted, calling him back within his shadow, but the laugher still hung in the air.

"Let's keep walking," Tommy continued. "We need to get this finished. Marcus is right. We don't want any more distractions."

As the heroes continued, Frutuoso and George stayed side by side, taking in the scenery. Frutuoso expressed himself to Gorn and George, taking note of the absence of greenery. "Where are the flowers?" Gorn asked Marcus. "The Cactus wants to know. Why do the trees have too little space to grow?"

"There are areas for the flowers," Marcus replied. "This part of the city however, not so much. They call it a concrete jungle."

"This doesn't look like a jungle," Jin said.

"Concrete is the foundation of what we use to build. It's like the stone that you use to build your castles."

The sprawling metropolis, with its steel and glass structures, offered little in the way of nature's beauty. And Frutuoso expressed with his movements of yearning for the familiar colors and scents of blooming flowers. George was supportive and offered him a firm pat on the shoulder as he rode on top of the Cactus.

With a smirk, Marcus told everybody to follow him. Not too far off the path they came upon a hidden gem amidst the urban sprawl. A haven of green where nature still thrived. "This is one of my favorite spots," Marcus cheerfully said. "We aren't too much further from our destination, this is a nice detour."

It was here, in this peaceful oasis, that Tommy had first met Marcus. Where Marcus had once glimpsed at Diana among the trees. The memories of that day flooded back to Marcus as he stepped onto the familiar paths. His hand instinctively reached into his pocket, pulling out his phone. The screen remained dark. The battery long dead. But the weight of it in his hand reminded him of all the connections he had left behind. He stared at the lifeless phone, a small frown creasing.

"You're curious, I see," Tommy said.

"I just have so many questions. How many messages have I missed? I wonder how my mom is doing," Marcus responded. "Just how far along are we from when we left?"

"From the day I arrive to take you away? About five months. It's been a long while since this city has not had its hero," Tommy said.

"What do you mean?" Marcus asked. Tommy's words threw him for a loop. "Aren't I still here?"

"I'm afraid not, I made it so we would not be running into your future self. When you left this world, time moved on without you."

"How does that work?"

"As for you, the future isn't written yet as it was for me. Changing things in your life now affects the outcome of the future."

"Diana!" Marcus was quick to realize. "Does she...? Has she been trying to reach me?"

"Marcus, there will be a time for that, but not now. Guide us to the place where we can build this."

"All right..." Marcus said. "Have any of you had coffee? My favorite café is here and I really need one!"

"Do we have time?" Arnold asked.

"What's coffee?" Owen stuttered.

"It will be quick!" Marcus shouted, already making his move towards the café.

Each hero ordered a coffee that suited their own taste. Marcus, Christana, and Arnold all ordered it black. Gorn, Owen, and Jin all smiled at the copious amounts of sugar in their cappuccinos with what they considered wild or exotic flavors. But in all actuality, they ordered mocha and hazelnut. Marcus smiled at their simple choices but marveled at their excitement.

Once happy with his salted caramel, Tommy dabbed his finger in the foam and drizzle that topped it. The taste sweeter than he could enjoy, but never tired of it. Afterwards, they rushed to the building where Marcus's name was read on the front.

"Stone and Steel," Arnold read out loud.

"My father's company," Marcus said. "It started out as a machining factory that delved into the marketing aspect. It blew up, skyrocketing in shares and profits. They ended up selling it overseas after... Well at least they kept the home factory..."

"This will be fine," Tommy remarked, and he watched Marcus break into the building. "You're a master at this."

"D, silence the alarms," Marcus ordered the demon. And before they could even ring, the devices went offline. "Yeah, I'm not proud of it."

Entering the workshop, Tommy rummaged through the old parts. He found exactly what he needed, producing a smile. "I suppose we don't need all of you here, just a few hands to help out. If the others would like to go for a walk back at the park, we can manage alone."

Unwrapping the schematic upon a station, Christana set some pieces down on top of it. Aligning it with what they needed, Arnold laid out the tools. With D's help, Marcus started up the machines. Soon, the workshop buzzed with creativity and ideas.

Owen stood by the window, his expression flat and unamused as he watched the bustling city below. The alien landscape—so far removed from the world he knew—left him feeling uneasy. Turning to Tommy, he muttered, "I think I'll take you up on that offer to walk to the park."

Gorn had been silently observing the machines ready to strike if the magic that consumed them stepped out of line. With a furrowed brow, nodded in agreement. George and Jin, sensing the need for some fresh air and familiarity, joined them. Together, they met Frutuoso outside the building and made their way to the park. The group gravitated toward the pond, where they watched the ducks gliding across the water. Their presence was a small comfort amidst the unfamiliar surroundings.

Gorn, feeling the weariness of this strange new world, found a bench and sank into it with a heavy sigh. The bench was cold and hard, a stark contrast to the warm, earthy seats he was accustomed to back home. Owen, seeking a place of his own, found a spot beneath a large tree. Its shade offered a brief respite from the overwhelming city.

As they watched the people passing by, Owen couldn't shake the feeling of being in a foreign land. The people's clothing was strange, far too tight or too loose, and their behaviors baffled him. Some walked with brisk steps, heads down, seemingly in a hurry to get nowhere in particular. Others jogged past, sweat dripping from their brows. Owen's eyes narrowed in confusion. *What were they running from?* he wondered.

Gorn's thoughts mirrored Owen's, but with an added layer of discomfort. The air here felt thin, devoid of the rich, invigorating essence he was used to. Back home, the atmosphere had a tangible quality, filled with the hum of magic. But here, in this modern world, that sensation was gone, replaced by something cold and mechanical.

"It's the loss of magic," Owen said, breaking the silence. "The good kind of magic."

Gorn turned to him, his eyes searching Owen's face. "You can feel it too?" he asked, his voice echoing the concern that rumbled deep in his heart.

"We all can. I can feel it in their hearts. No one cares for magic," Jin added. "It takes some time to be comfortable with this feeling."

"It's worse even. The love of the Allfather seems faint here. Distant and dark. I don't want to be comfortable with it," Gorn said.

"With hope, you won't have to. Isn't that why we are here?" Owen continued. "To fix this whole catastrophe?"

"Tommy says it gets a lot worse," Jin said as he threw a rock down the water. He watched the ripples wash back and forth.

Frutuoso spoke to Gorn, reassuring him of the powers at work.

"I suppose you are right, Cactus," Gorn replied. "Even if you feel that way, the Lady of Light was right to choose you. Both of you seem to be more pure than all of us."

"Well, I hope we can get this all settled soon. I do wish to return to my home," Owen said, as he laid his head down. He closed his eyes, seeking a brief moment of peace amidst the chaos. The weight of their mission hung heavy on him. But the longing for the familiar comforts of home was even stronger.

As Owen rested, the others busied themselves with whatever distractions they could find. The park was a hub of activity, filled with city goers and park walkers. Yet, the heroes were conspicuously avoided by everyone who passed by. To the people of the city, they were just another group of strangers among the countless faces. Here, in this city, they were another oddity, one of the many peculiarities in a city that had seen it all.

24 Fear of Destiny

With harsh scrapes, drawers were opened. The junk inside them rumbled about in a jerky motion. A hand rummaged through them, discarding unwanted items, yet remained dissatisfied. They searched more desks and other compartments until a long black cord emerged from the rubbish.

"USB-C," Marcus said. "Finally!" He walked back to Arnold and Christana that were going over the notes one last time. In his other hand, he continued to sip on his coffee. Savoring the taste he missed. "Now if only I could find a block. You mean to tell me no one in the workshop has a block?!"

"What's wrong, Marcus?" Christana asked. Her perplexed face did not stray from the design upon the pages.

"I just wanted to charge my phone. My mom must be worried. And Diana…"

"Diagnostics are done!" Arnold exclaimed. Placing the half welded part upon the table, he pulled the crystal from his pocket. "If I set this in here, it should give us a small demo of the conversion process. Marcus, I must say, technology in your time is far superior than I could have ever imagined. This is…"

"Tu es un homme extraordinaire, Arnold," Christana said. She took his hand and watched the crystal glow as the magic flowed through the device. "It's beautiful," she said as the soft blue light made her eyes dazzle.

"If only I could give it a little more power. It would help it set faster. It needs a spark, so to speak. Marcus, do you have anything like a large battery?"

The words fell short in the room as Marcus hardly paid attention. "Ahh, found it!" Marcus exclaimed. "I'm sorry, what do you need?"

In the corner of the room by the break table, a small, red, greasy sofa sat. Tommy lay upon it, tossing a ball in the air. He didn't want to disturb his comfort. But, he listened to Arnold and Christana with the support. "An idea has come to mind!" He shouted, sitting up with a sudden force.

He took the phone charger from Marcus, and plugged it into the wall.

"Hey! I needed to charge my phone!" Marcus detested.

"Not now, Marcus. We have to get Arnold's creation sorted out. You can have it when I am done."

But Marcus's feelings weren't still. "Take it. I'll find another."

"We still have a multitude of calculations to make," Arnold said, getting back to his notebook and scribbling with his lush pen. "And a fine amount of machining to do."

"Marcus!" Tommy said. "We have more work to do."

"My hands have blisters! I can't stay put here anymore. I already have an uneasy feeling about being here."

"No time for whining Marcus. Help cut out the last pieces."

Tommy took to his torch, dropping his goggles over his eyes and carefully soldering wires together. He cut pieces at the bandsaw and worked in perfect unison with Marcus. Lost in the blue sparks, Tommy reached for the next piece to weld, but Marcus hadn't finished it yet. "Jimmy, could you hand me the…" Removing his goggles, Tommy felt strange. "I'm sorry. For a moment, it was like I was back home building the time machine with my brother."

"It's fine Tommy, it happens," Marcus replied, handing him the last piece.

With a deep sigh, Tommy pulled the plug on the device and handed the charger over to Marcus. "Go ahead. Charge your phone. You missed your home. Like I do. And your family. Help me machine these last parts and insert the wires and I'll let you go. The evening will be yours. However you wish to spend it. I'll look after everyone, I promise."

"Thank you, Tommy." Marcus offered his hand, and the two met with a firm shake. Marcus set his phone up, the buzz gave him a sigh of relief as it began to charge. But the moment of calm was short-lived. From around the corner, the creak of a door echoed through the hallway, followed by the sound of voices. The noise grew louder, punctuated by the slamming of doors and the clatter of footsteps. Marcus quickly alerted the others.

"I think we've been found out!" he shouted, moving to brace the door.

The sounds from the other side of the wall grew closer. Laughter and the metallic jingle of what could only be toolboxes accompanied the approaching men.

"Weekend workers?" Tommy asked, his brow furrowed.

"Maybe they're trying to get ahead," Marcus replied, gripping the doorknob tightly to prevent it from turning.

"Well, Marcus, do your thing!" Tommy urged.

"D, don't harm them," Marcus ordered, but even as the words left his mouth, the building began to tremble. The lights above flickered erratically, casting eerie shadows across the room. The doors rattled with stricken violence in their frames, and from the other side of the wall, the clattering of tools hitting the floor was followed by startled shouts. Objects flew off shelves and tables, as if propelled by an unseen force.

Arnold and Christana moved with haste, covering their design. And protecting it from the chaotic rampage unfolding around them. Arnold held down the mechanism on the table, his muscles straining to keep it steady. Christana placed her hand over his, shutting her eyes tightly until the room began to settle. The lights returned to their normal fluorescent glow at a steady pace.

As the chaos subsided, Tommy began to tidy the room in a calm manner. Picking up scattered tools and pieces of junk and placing them back in their designated locations.

"That's how it's done, Marcus!" Tommy said, clapping his hands with a grin. "What a show!"

"It's not something to be encouraged," Marcus scolded.

"Well, we are nearly finished! That's all we need is someone snooping around here and drawing unwanted attention. How much longer, Arnold?"

"I can finish assembling the final pieces if you and Marcus are done. Then the calibration needs to happen and a test run. Maybe seven hours at the most."

"Come on, Marcus. The sooner we have this the better!"

Marcus picked up his phone from the ground, checking the charge it had. "Eleven percent," he whispered. The screen lit up at the touch of his fingertips. His face tilted inward to see his messages, scrolling to read everything he had missed. "Mom…" He mouthed the words.

"Marcus!" Tommy called again.

Setting it down, he returned to business and once it was all said and done, Marcus returned to business, focusing intently on the task at hand. As soon as everything was in place, he watched with bated breath as Arnold began to bring the device to life. After a tense silence, Tommy, ever resourceful, grabbed a charging cable one of the workers had dropped outside. He connected it to the machine, giving it the spark it needed.

A small hum of energy filled the room as the device flickered to life, its lights blinking on in sequence. Marcus exhaled, the tension easing from his shoulders as the realization set in that they had succeeded.

"See? It all worked out!" Tommy said with a triumphant grin, his eyes gleaming with satisfaction.

"I can go now?" Marcus asked. "I really need to do this."

Without waiting for the signal, Marcus grabbed his sweater and phone and ran out the building. He hailed a taxi and set the destination on his phone. Marcus continued to scroll. His thumb hovered over the call button. Diana's name on the screen. His favorite picture of her was behind the text and keypad.

"I feel awful," Marcus spoke to D. "I have so much on my mind. Is Diana okay? Will the others be all right without me in this big city?"

"Just focus on what you want to say," D responded.

The taxi driver gave Marcus a look, but continued driving. Marcus watched the passing building and people unsuspecting to the impending doom. "I hope it isn't as bad as what Tommy describes."

Miles away, in a small but cozy home nestled in the suburbs of New York City, Diana was busy helping her mother with chores around the house. It was before noon, and the warm sunlight streamed through the kitchen window, casting a gentle glow on the worn, familiar surfaces. The house was modest but comfortable away from the mess. Although it meant a longer commute for Diana, it was the best option she had for now.

As Diana dried the last of the dishes, her mother left the kitchen to check on her father resting in the living room. Despite being young, his health had taken a downturn. His heart condition was growing more serious with each passing day. He sat in his favorite recliner, staring at the television. The TV was low, and nothing good was on. But, its hum was a comforting background noise.

The afternoon news began its broadcast, the anchors' voices cutting through the quiet atmosphere of the room. The host displayed their trust by reporting on Manson Herold's remarkable strides. His name was now on everyone's lips, his influence growing with each passing day. The upcoming celebration in his honor was the main topic of discussion. A highly anticipated event that had the city alight with excitement.

Diana's father was usually uninterested in such news. But found himself drawn to the screen as the anchor announced an exclusive interview with Manson himself. The reporter, unable to hide her excitement, promised the interview would reveal Manson's future plans. A future that seemed increasingly shaped by his vision. The anticipation in the air was palpable. The broadcast shifted, preparing to showcase the man who had become a symbol of hope. And perhaps something more for the world.

Diana's mother walked into the living room, drawn by the sound of the television. She paused, listening to the familiar voice of Manson as it filled the room. Her husband, sensing the importance of the moment, reached for the remote and turned up the volume. The reverence in Manson's tone was unmistakable. And Diana's mother found herself captivated by his words. There was something magnetic about him, a charm that was impossible to ignore.

Even from the kitchen, Diana could hear Manson's voice clearly. She paused in her work, the dish towel still in her hands, and made her way into the living room. She stood at the doorway, her curiosity piqued as she watched the man on the screen. Manson was impeccably dressed, his suit tailored to perfection, a clear symbol of his rising status. His hair was precision-groomed, each strand carefully aligned. His smile made his teeth glimmer under the studio lights. It showed a polished image of power and control.

"Broadcasting to you today from City Heights Network Station, we have Mister Manson Herald!" The reporter's tone was reverent. She sat back in her chair, but leaned forward as she couldn't contain her fascination. "Welcome to the show! We are honored to have you!"

"Thank you. It is good to be here to speak to the people of this wonderful city, and the world," Manson Said.

"Mr. Herald."

"Please, call me Manson."

"All right! Manson, never has someone united the world like you have! Not a single soul out there seems to doubt your potential. We have nations ceasing wars just by visiting. How do you explain your success in this?"

"With all the destruction we've seen," Manson began, solemn in his words, but truthful. "It's difficult not to see the danger in front of us. No doubt Marcus is our hero, but he caused a great deal of damage. Everybody knows what happened that day. When a world changing event occurs, the world seems to fall into place. I just happened to be the man everyone loved when I began raising the question."

"What are going to be your first plans for this new world?" the reporter asked.

"I am just pleased to help with solving our problems and to unify our world. Doesn't that make you sleep easier at night? You won't have to worry about war, or conflict. Just peace. Food on the table for everyone."

"It does!" the reporter said with such enthusiasm. "And you've managed to get the whole world to understand each other. They can all agree to be a part of this... This... Utopia, I suppose you could call it."

"It amazes me what humans can do when they come together. Once they see there aren't any differences. Just lines in the sand we put in place. Surely, anyone wouldn't want another catastrophe as we saw before with our previous hero. United against an evil like that is a sure way to motivate people. They would be begging for it, even if I didn't offer it."

"You are right. The world will never forget. Are you nervous about things not going to plan? How could you be sure the whole world will come together?"

"On that day, I was terrified, but I saw true light in that darkness, one that could save us all. And in this light, I cannot be nervous. I am honored to be beholden to the world."

As Diana watched the TV, she felt her gut twisting. Her spine ran cold but she was also eerily moved by Manson's words. They had a certain cadence to them and a harmonious flow that was addicting and fascinating. She sat comfortable on the sofa next to her father, dropping the dish towel on the floor. Mesmerized by what was on screen.

"As I see it, the era of heroes must end," Manson continued with the interviewer. "The fate of humanity cannot be left up to such falsehoods. The destruction that was caused cannot be risked again. It's time we stop believing in foolish prophecies and fabled magic. We need more grounded rules and a basis of true identities. This magic is born in us and bleeds into our laws and countries. It deludes us into believing that violence is the key to survival. We wield this magic to battle the darkness—but what if that darkness didn't exist? The darkness feeds on this magic, and as long as we cling to it, it will continue to return, hungering for more."

"You're right... If this magic wasn't here..." The interviewer's voice trailed off, her thoughts ensnared by Manson's words. His beliefs seeped into her mind, as they did for everyone watching. This broadcast was a global event. Countless viewers tuned in to see the man they all admired. His golden rhetoric twisted their perceptions. Even Diana found herself caught in its web.

"Don't place hope in heroes, but place hope in me. Together, we can build a better world, a stronger one. Stop waiting for a hero because no one is coming to save you."

"These are powerful words, Manson," she said, nodding her head and taking in a large breath. Her tone was obvious. She changed her voice. Even her appearance had her in an upright position. "We can take care of ourselves."

Manson was the picture of perfection—clean-shaven, with skin free of blemishes. There was little to fault in his appearance; his strong, umber eyes stared into the camera with an intensity that seemed to reach through the screen.

"I hope everyone is ready for a better world because one is coming," he declared, a confident smile spreading across his face. "Our world will never know darkness again, only light. And by the end of this curse that has plagued us, there will be no more conflict over this magic. Rest well, New York—prepare for a new beginning!"

As the broadcast neared its end, the interviewer was speechless. The screen faded to a color test pattern and tone, filling the room with its monotonous hum. Diana and her parents sat frozen, the sound ringing in their ears. Manson's golden lies had ensnared them, holding them captive. It was only the insistent thumping on the door that finally broke the spell. She shook her head, the trance lifting as she heard a voice from outside call out.

"Is anyone home?"

She sprang to her feet, her parents laboring to clear their minds. The knocking continued, growing more urgent. The voice was familiar, but it took her a moment to place it.

"Diana, please!" Marcus's voice called out from the other side. The doorbell had been broken for months, but the parts still lay untouched on the small table nearby. Marcus raised his hand to knock once more. But stopped as he heard the sound of the locks turning and the door creaking open.

Marcus exclaimed her name once again, his eyes tracing every familiar feature of her face, as if committing them to memory all over again.

"Marcus?" Diana said with disbelief. Her body froze, inches from embracing Marcus, as shock set in. Instead, she closed the door behind her and stood on the front porch with him. The sun was beginning to set. They both stood bathed in the warm hues of the horizon, the orange sky casting a soft glow over their faces. Words failed her, and her heart fluttered, pounding in her chest. The pain she thought she had buried surged back, chilling her to the core. Here he was—the man she once loved, standing before her after all this time.

"It's me…" Marcus said, quivering in his tone, uneasy to reach out to take her hand.

"I know…" she murmured, still reeling from the whirlwind of emotions that the broadcast had stirred within her.

"I…I just wanted to…"

"What are you doing here, Marcus? Where have you been?" Her words grew vicious as her eyes burned.

"I can explain. Please. Let me speak to you."

"Who's at the door?" her mother called out from inside.

Diana didn't respond, her focus locked on Marcus. "I was worried sick about you! I thought you died or something. It's been months since I saw you!"

"I know…I know…" Marcus stammered, his hands shaking as he struggled to find the right words. He hadn't anticipated how difficult it would be to face her, to see the pain he had caused. He wanted to save their marriage. But, her sight left him speechless, emotions choking his voice. Diana's patience wore thin; the wounds of his absence were too fresh, too deep.

"You never returned my calls. You just vanished," Diana continued. "I thought you gave up on us…"

"No, it's not like that…"

"And now you are back." Her voice began to crack now as well. Confusion and hurt intertwined as she tried to gather the strength to say what needed to be said. Marcus took a deep breath, trying to calm himself.

"Honey, I…"

"Don't call me that."

Heartbroken, he continued. "I left, yes… Well. I was taken, actually… I'm all right. I didn't leave."

"Where could you have possibly gone, where you could not have at least called? You left me alone…"

"I wanted to, but I was far away. I went…How can I tell you this so I don't sound crazy?" Marcus scoffed. "You have to believe me, but I was picked up by a time traveler!"

"A time traveler?" Her eyes rolled, not believing Marcus's lies. "Am I supposed to believe that? I suppose you went and saw all the great heroes with him too?"

"I just wanted to see you. I wanted to make sure you are all right. I missed you…"

"Don't start! I was just beginning to heal! I don't want this! Not again. I can't be hurt by you anymore. I don't want you to lie to me!"

"I'm not lying! My part to play isn't over. I'm still the hero and Manson Herold…"

"Manson Herald has done nothing but good in this world!" Diana snapped. "He has united us! He has done more than any hero has ever done! Especially you."

"Diana... That's not fair... I..."

"You ruined this great marriage we had. All for what? Powers? Money?"

"Diana, this isn't like you..." Marcus's voice faltered as the sky above them darkened, clouds rolling in ominously. Thunder rumbled in the distance, and the light seemed to drain from the world around them. From the shadows, the darkness that lived within Marcus emerged, taking shape beside him.

D tried to intervene with as soft of a tone as he could. "Marcus is telling the truth. You must understand the powers that are at hand. Evil things are in this world that are trying to take hold. Believe Marcus."

Diana's heart raced with fear, but it was a fear she had known before. She had seen the face of this demon once, and had sworn never to see it again. Now, here it was, standing before her.

"The only evil I see is right here," she scolded, her voice trembling with both fear and fury. She turned to gaze, grabbing the doorknob to retreat into her home. "You promised me I would never see him again. But I see you would rather keep your powers over our marriage."

"Diana!" Marcus begged, desperation seeping into his voice. "You have to trust me. Manson is evil!"

"No... He is right. This world would be better without that thing. Marcus, you've broken my heart too much. Get away from me!"

Marcus tried to catch the door, but D stopped him.

"Go away!" she said from behind the door. "Please leave me alone!."

"Marcus..." D tried calling to him. "Let her be...We cannot worry ourselves with..."

"Why did you have to show yourself?" Marcus hissed, anger boiling over him. "I could have explained!"

"She wouldn't have listened." D dragged Marcus from the house. He held him with a firm grip, despite the kicking and shouting.

"Listen to me," he said, sitting Marcus on the ground. "Manson has her under his spell. I can break her out of it."

"No! You will never touch her!"

"You're a fool! You're losing yourself, Marcus. You've been losing yourself ever since I met you. It is why you were so easy to overtake!"

"How dare you! Everything that happened is your fault!" Marcus stood, shoving D back.

"You are just as much to blame for our own losses!" D pushed back harder, slamming Marcus down. "You have problems, Marcus, but you don't let me help."

"Every time you help, you mess it up!" Marcus shouted and wiped the dirt from his face. "I really wish I didn't have you."

The demon's fury simmered, his voice turning venomous. "And so it all comes to this. The world you promised me. You swore it wouldn't come to this. That this wasn't our fate. Are you going to abandon me now? Then what? Will you face Manson without me? You would follow that foolish Time Warden to get your bitter life back. It's just as he said. You are just trying to get rid of me."

Marcus's voice faltered as he whispered, "No, D…" The guilt was evident. "I didn't mean it…"

"This fate cannot be changed. The world pulls back to how things are supposed to be…"

"Then why are we here?"

"Don't stare into the darkness, Marcus."

"What does that mean?"

The silence was a blur.

"What do you mean, D?" Unamused by D's silence, Marcus turned away from him. "You just don't want to go back to the void. You are selfish."

"Selfish?" D chuckled. "Well, you aren't wrong. But you have to understand I do what is in the best interest for both of us."

"I'm sorry…"

The Eight Heroes of Old

"It's this magic spell Manson has in this world. I can feel the strong pull of the darkness. It calls for me to return."

"What kind of magic is Manson using?"

"I'm not even sure it is magic, but it's strong. You just felt yourself losing your grip. You want to be lost to this darkness. Remember, Marcus. Remember how badly you wished to be a hero. Don't forget that."

"You're right. We need to get back to others now. It's nearly dark."

"I'm on your side, Marcus," D reassured with his sinister slithering voice.

Joe Cordova

25 Hidden Stars

City lights flickered. The neon screens painted the sky. Shadows bent around the pillars and bricks. High beams blessed the sidewalk and streets. Marcus watched his shadow escape him as he made his way back to the workshop. The building towered over the city as he read names upon the marquee one last time.

The shade of night hid him well as he snuck back through the doors. Within the halls and empty rooms, silence had taken over. Tommy, Arnold and Christana were nowhere to be found. Everything was put back as they were.

"They sure did a good job cleaning up." Marcus laughed. "Where could they have gone?"

The Eight Heroes of Old

"No notes, no clues left behind," D responded, searching the place with Marcus.

A sense of unease crept over Marcus as he realized he had no way to contact them. Searching the entire city might take forever. Then, a thought struck him. "The park!" he remembered. But when he reached the park, they were already gone. The heroes were nowhere to be found.

The city, however, was alive. The packed bars filled the streets with an overabundance of joy. Marcus observed the scene, his spirits lifting as he took in the energy of the night. The city was breathing, vibrant, and alive. It was hard to believe that darkness was looming over the horizon. For a moment, even he could almost convince himself that what Manson was doing seemed right. As he walked through the downtown he decided to stop into the café and order another coffee. Something to warm him as the night grew colder. Marcus stepped outside with coffee in hand and resumed his search. The steam curled around his face in the chilly air.

"I can sense them!" D spoke. "They aren't far!"

"Where?" Marcus said, aimlessly wandering in circles waiting for D to speak again.

"Not far, they are in a bar just a few blocks away."

Following the D's guidance, Marcus made his way to a place called the Viking's Horns. A bar with food and drink, its décor influenced by the hero, Gorn. A massive, colorful mural adorned the place, exaggerating its portrayal of heroic deeds. As Marcus walked past the painting, he spotted Gorn and Arnold sitting at a small table, sharing a drink and a laugh. Though he still hadn't found everyone, relief washed over him at the sight of familiar faces.

Marcus called out, weaving through the crowded room. The bar was alive with heavy music, dark and full of guitar riffs that rattled the walls. Neither Arnold nor Gorn had heard music like this before, but Gorn seemed to enjoy it.

"Marcus!" Gorn shouted, greeting him as he took a seat next to the two. "We have just been discussing this whole affair with everyone. We think this plan is going to work!"

"You're drunk?!" Marcus asked.

"He is quite drunk," Arnold replied. "But it makes this all the funnier! Watch!"

"Gorn, do that thing again!"

Gorn, with a dramatic flair, struck a pose mirroring the mural and sent bolts of lightning from his fingertips. The bar erupted in cheers, the crowd thrilled by the spectacle. It was the kind of place that thrived on chaos and danger, and Gorn fit right in.

"Gorn has already made himself known to everyone here as the hero of old. Whether or not they believe him is something else entirely," Arnold continued.

The Eight Heroes of Old

"I'm surprised I found you in a place like this. Where are the others?"

"Well. Tommy and I had a bit of an argument. And we went our separate way, at least for now."

"An argument? Like how? What could you have argued over?"

"Well, it's like this. I... We...Christana and I felt like we were not achieving the results we wanted. There were parts we needed and other tools. It was beginning to be frustrating, but Tommy had an idea. He left for a minute and came back with the part already made."

"What is the problem?"

"Well. I asked him where he went, but he would not tell me."

"Why wouldn't he tell you?"

"He said it was a secret."

"A secret? You've got to be kidding me? I thought we were past all these games!"

"I thought so too, but it happened again. We were lacking things we needed, and Tommy left and came back with the items assembled and ready to be put together."

"So did you build the device?"

"This is where we had our disagreement. Christana and I wanted to be of more use, so we asked if we could go along with him to this isolated location. He would not reveal where he went. He said it was a place only for him to go. But I believe he has a secret work area. That is how he built these helmets he gave us. He goes and spends time there. It could be days or weeks. I'm not sure, but he came back with everything we needed."

"What does it matter if he has a secret place or not, as long as we get the device built and we fix everything?"

"My thoughts exactly, Marcus, however, I recognized the tools and parts he was bringing back. They were of my design. I made the slightest slip of mentioning something I wished I had back in my own estate."

"He was stealing from you?"

"I suppose it isn't stealing if I have no use for those things anymore. But I felt guilty putting my faith into the machine again. He used the very devices I tried to hide away from the world."

"Magic shouldn't be used!" Gorn said, bringing another ale to the table.

"I agree," Arnold said, taking the ale away from Gorn. "Where is he?"

"He finished the device," Arnold began with sipping the ale. "Gorn brought the machine to life with his spell, and he placed it over his arm. Fit like a glove!" Arnold chuckled at his own pun.

"I shouldn't have done it," Gorn started again. He dropped his head down, catching it on the table.

"Don't mind him." Arnold drew Marcus's attention. Shaking his head, he continued. "And then he vanished. He left and he took Christana with him. I've been sitting in this bar with Gorn since. I am fairly upset with him. This project was supposed to take a few days. I know he is a smart man, but I wanted to double check everything. Just to make sure it would work. It needed calculations! So many calculations before a test run!"

"He's impatient..." Marcus said, brushing off the server that asked if he needed anything.

"He said he had to make things right."

"Do you know when he will be back?"

"No. He did not say."

"And the others? Do you know where they are?"

Arnold took the last sip of his ale. "This is not like the stuff we have back home. Not at all."

"Where are they?"

"Tommy... sent them... to your place."

"My place?!"

"You know, Marcus," Gorn said with a hiccup in his speech. "The future isn't too bad. You have good ale, fine music, and the people are easy to entertain."

"Glad you like it, I guess." Marcus took Gorn by the shoulder and encouraged him to leave. Arnold stood and gave reassurance.

Gorn's expression turned defiant, a wild look in his eye. "You want to fight in this tavern, boy? 'Cause that's what you're askin'."

"Gorn, what's gotten into you? This isn't like you!" Marcus rebuked.

"Calm down. I'm only fooling you," Gorn uttered a gentle denial, a sly smile on his face.

"How did you even buy this? I doubt you have cash."

"People here are very generous. They just kept giving him one after another. Especially with all the tricks he did. I don't think he realized exactly how much he had."

"Let's just get him home," Marcus said, shaking his head.

Arnold joined Marcus in helping Gorn out of the bar. The cold night air hit them as they stepped outside, the chill sobering Gorn. Taxis were hard to come by at this hour, and Gorn still wasn't comfortable with the idea of riding in a car. So, they walked. Marcus lived on the other side of the city. And this time of night was usually when he'd be out patrolling, keeping the people safe. But the weight of the night's events pressed on him, and he trudged on, his feet aching with every step. His shoes had worn thin, allowing the wet streets to soak through to his socks.

As they walked, Gorn's mood shifted. The energy from the bar faded, replaced by a growing sorrow. He looked around at the world he had once fought so hard to protect, and a deep sense of failure washed over him. "How has this evil become so powerful?" he muttered, more to himself than to anyone else. He shared his feelings with Marcus and Arnold, his grief heavy in the air. The magic within him, sensing his despair, worked to sober him. And by the time they reached Marcus's apartment, Gorn was more himself again.

"Does it always feel like this?" Gorn asked quietly.

"Like what?"

"Don't you feel it? This world has lost the touch of the Allfather. I must have failed him. I must not have chosen correctly. I can no longer feel his light. Devoid of all love."

"I'm sorry..." Marcus, unsure of how to respond to Gorn's confession, let him keep walking. The stairway leading up to the apartment reached for the night sky. The dark blue contrasted with the building lights as they climbed to the top.

Gorn had his eyes fixed upwards. "Where are they?" Gorn asked. "Where are the stars?"

"They are hidden," Marcus replied.

"Even they cannot shine past this darkness. What a shame."

"It's just the light pollution," Marcus tried to explain.

"Don't try to make excuses," Gorn argued. "The sky has lost its beauty." He leaned over the balcony and began to pray, hoping the Allfather could hear him.

Marcus lived on the sixth floor and after climbing all those stairs, he did not wish to debate with Gorn. He took his keys and inserted them into the tumbler only to find the door was already open.

Inside, Jin, Owen and George had already made themselves at home. They had raided his cupboards and fridge, leaving a mess in their wake. The three of them sprawled on the gray couches. Their muddy boots trekked dirt everywhere. They scattered their armor in the corner.

"This is a very small place, Marcus," Jin remarked. "Do you have any other rooms?"

"I have just one bedroom and a kitchen. The living room is very small." Marcus looking through the house totaled the damage in his mind. "Great! I'm definitely not getting my deposit back…"

"How are we going to stay here?" Jin continued.

"I never said any of you could stay here."

"Well, I don't wish to sleep on the floor."

"We aren't going to," Owen interjected. "Marcus, do you have a castle we could stay? Maybe your lord or king or serf would provide that to us."

"I don't have any of that!" Marcus responded, becoming annoyed.

"Well, where are we going to sleep?"

"Come on, all of you. I'm taking you to a hotel!"

"What's that?" Gorn asked.

The Eight Heroes of Old

"If you are interested. I'll have Arnold explain. I'm sure he had read about them in books or something."

"I have done more than that, Marcus," Arnold said cheerfully.

Gathering the group, Marcus led them back down the stairs and into the night once more. "Where's the Cactus?" Marcus asked.

"He's around back in the pool," Arnold said.

"There isn't a pool."

For a second time, Marcus gathered the heroes and began leading them to the nearby hotel. The sores on his feet throbbed with each step. Despite his weariness, he pressed on until they reached a small hotel where they could finally rest. Marcus led them inside, showed them the lobby while he checked in at the front desk.

"I purchased a few rooms," Marcus said, handing out keycards. "You may have to share some. I'm not made of money."

Everything was new for the heroes from the elevator to the carpet and wall art. The rooms seemed to have magical water spring from the wall but were only showers. Settling into his room that he shared with Gorn, Marcus laid on the soft bed. His head hit the pillow as he wanted to fall asleep right there and then.

Pulling his phone, he used the complimentary charger the receptionist gave him. Checking his bank account, he feared a negative balance, and worried about paying for the rooms. At least the fresh sheets were comforting to him. He rubbed his hands over his face trying to shake off the feelings. His eyes ached almost as much as his feet.

"This place must have cost a fortune," Gorn said. "Does a lord stay here often?"

"We don't have lords or kings."

"You don't have kings? Chieftains? I followed a few in my time." Gorn laughed. "Who leads you? Do the heroes lead your nations?"

"I don't feel like giving you a school lesson. Here, just watch some TV."

"Oh, it's those magic boxes like they had at the tavern. A stranger appeared inside it. He spoke of troubling times. His words were evil. He wants to forsake the prophecy! I wouldn't let him say such things in front of me. I have heard too much blasphemy in my lifetime."

"I don't want to talk right now, Gorn. I have a lot on my mind." Marcus was trying to focus. But, Gorn's constant dictations made him uneasy. The AC turned on and a cold breeze pushed through the room. Gorn, startled, drew his ax as he asked Marcus what that machine was. "It's just the air conditioning. It blows cold air."

Gorn felt the wind blowing from the vent. He felt the tingle in his hands, and he welcomed the refreshing feeling. "I like it!" He smiled.

"Gorn. Please. I don't mean to be rude, but I need some time to myself. Maybe go see what Owen is doing."

"Very well, Marcus. I'll leave you to your nice air machine."

Gorn wandered the hotel, snapping keycards in half after each use, convinced they were some kind of enchanted trinket. He eventually found Owen and Jin in another room, sitting with Arnold and George. The Professor had been explaining the various modern marvels around them. Owen was still baffled by the TV. Jin remained indifferent, finding no beauty in the technology.

"Gorn, we have been learning much about these things Arnold is telling us about. I still don't understand it, but I never thought the world would become this complex," Owen said.

"I still cannot believe it either," Gorn replied.

"All of this still excites me!" Arnold said.

"Do you think this distracts from the Allfather?"

"On the contrary!" Arnold reassured. "What better way to understand the Creator's world than to learn and piece together what is given to us! If only Christana was here to share in seeing these marvels!"

As if on cue, a flash of purple light illuminated the room, the telltale sign of time travel. Arnold was the first to rush outside. The sight of Tommy and Christana, laughing and radiant, made Arnold smile.

"You're back..." Arnold said.

Christana's face brightened as she called to him. She rushed over, flinging her arms around his body in a warm, heartfelt embrace. The feel of her soft skin, the scent of her hair, made his heart swell. "Oui, nous sommes de retour!" Peaceful eyes met his. "And it worked!" she said. "Ça a marché!" Her voice was a symphony in his ears.

"Where did you go?" Arnold asked, pulling back to look at her, his hands still resting gently around her back.

"I'm sorry about earlier, Arnold," Tommy addressed. "I didn't want to tell you until I was certain Christana saw it first."

"What? Where? And how did the machine perform? Did it struggle?"

"Arnold, it's fine!" Christana said in a comforting tone.

The others emerged from the hotel, their faces lighting up at the sight of Tommy and Christana. They gathered around, their voices filled with relief and joy. But for Arnold, the world had narrowed to him and Christana. The noise of the city faded into the background, and all he could hear was the steady rhythm of her breathing. The softness of her voice, the warmth of her gaze.

"I kept my secret because I did not want to upset Christana," Tommy spoke again. "But it was actually your home."

"My home? My study? That's what I reasoned." Arnold's brow furrowed in confusion. But not wishing to leave Christana's arm as he would have done, he questioned Tommy

"Yes. Well, let me explain. Marlon had to sell your property after you left. I may have been the one to purchase it."

"Arnold, it was beautiful!" Christana said. "I almost began to cry when I saw it. I had not been there for a long time. I missed it. Tommy had made many changes to it, but it was still the same."

"You know I wanted to make a visit back to my place. I could have done a lot of research there!" Arnold admitted, his voice tinged with regret. "Why do I feel different?" Arnold turned his attention back to Christana. Her elegant smile was his only focus.

"We had to test it on something small," Tommy said. "To change time is tricky. I've tried to do it before, but it all goes horribly wrong. But with your invention, my powers are more focused. I took Christana back to your time and changed the outcome a bit."

"What did you change?" Gorn asked, his curiosity breaking the intimate moment.

"Many of the books that were lost to time are now in your possession. They are all neatly arranged back in your study."

"I can remember them..." Arnold said. "Like holding a fresh book in my hand, the memory is clear to me."

"There is also one more thing," Christana said, her voice soft as she took Arnold's hand in hers. She turned his palm over, revealing a ring he hadn't noticed before. It was a simple, elegant band, but it felt as though it had always been there. "I married you," she said, her eyes locked with his. She gave a smile, her laugh slipping through. "You married me! I should say. Tommy went back and arranged it. You found love a bit sooner, with a little nudge."

"We're married!?" Arnold asked, his voice filled with wonder as he stared into Christana's eyes. Memories began to flood his mind of a day he hadn't known he'd lived. He saw her standing before him, dazzling in a white dress that seemed to glow in the sunlight. Her smile was brighter than the world around them. It was their wedding day, and it was perfect in every way.

"This is a thank you, for everything you two have done for me," Tommy said, but realized his words were falling on deaf ears.

At that moment, time seemed to stand still. The world around them faded. The love that had always been there, simmering beneath the surface, now blossomed fully. Arnold's heart swelled with a joy so profound that it brought tears to his eyes. He cherished Christana beyond his own reason, his feelings unfolding in unexpected ways.

And now, that love was real, tangible, and it was everything he had ever dreamed it could be.

Christana smiled, her own tears slipping down her cheeks and took his hand with a gentle touch. "C'est réel, Arnold," she whispered, as if reading his thoughts.

Frutuoso grew flowers around the couple through the cracks in the pavement, as Jin picked a few to give to theme. One by one the heroes congratulated them.

Marcus finally stepped outside, shivering off the cold from the AC. He saw the group gathered around Christana and Arnold, all celebrating their reunion. Despite the heaviness in his heart, Marcus felt a small flicker of hope.

"What's going on?" Marcus asked.

"Marcus!" Christana ran to him, exerting her excitement and showing him her ring. She gave him an embrace. "Arnold and I are married! Arnold's device worked! He can change time for good!"

"I'm happy for you!" Marcus cheered. "That's wonderful!"

"You're a good friend, Marcus."

After the commotion and celebration died down, the heroes retired to their rooms. All except for Arnold and Christana, who stayed up talking. Their hands clasped as they sat on a bench, watching the moon. A tradition of late-night, deep conversations back home. But now, there was a deeper connection between them. The chirping of crickets filled the night air. The city sounds became a soothing background as they lost themselves in each other's company.

Tommy returned to his room, preparing for bed. He ran a hot shower, letting the warmth ease his tense muscles. The luxury of modern amenities was something he hadn't known as a child in the desolate wastes. The unforgiving world of his youth had been harsh. Yet, he couldn't help but worry about his brother, who shouldn't be working on the time machine. A knock at the door interrupted his thoughts. Still dripping wet, Tommy shuffled over, peeking through the peephole. He wasn't surprised to see who it was. He dressed in his towel, clothes in the wash, but answered the door nonetheless.

"What brings you by, Marcus?" Tommy questioned.

"I saw what you did for Arnold and Christana…"

"You wish for a better outcome for you?"

"I do… More than anything I want to save my marriage."

"I can't go fixing everything, Marcus. What I did for them was a small test for the machine. To see if it really worked. Changing fate too much could be detrimental."

"You're trying to save your future. Can't we do the same for me?"

"It's not that simple, Marcus." Tommy sighed. "Time is too complex. You and Diana can never be as long as you're the hero. She just can't accept him. You know how your fate ends. I told you it would drive you mad. Christana and Arnold's story had not changed. They still need to part ways when this is over. Arnold will need to return to his time and Christana will meet fate as it reads in the history books. Some say the only way to escape fate is to die."

"But isn't that always the case?"

"Yes." Tommy sat down on the bed. "Marcus, do you know how many times I've tried to change the world? How many times I have tried to fix every mistake within my power?"

"I could only imagine."

"Five..."

"Wait, that's it?"

"I stopped counting after that," Tommy admitted, his voice heavy with the weight of his failures. "No matter how many times I tried, time always corrected itself. Every split eventually rejoined the main flow of events. To be honest, I'm not sure why this time would be any different."

"So, you don't think we can change fate?"

"I believe we can, but that is lost to me. It is a powerful force, but that is why I believed I could not do it alone. It would take an equally powerful force to change it. That is us. All of us. The magic that is in us can ignite this world back, I believe."

"Well, I hope so, otherwise this has been really depressing."

"I don't mean to be, Marcus. I have a lot on my mind. I am so uncertain at times. As I know you all are."

"All of us do, as I am finding out... You've really helped surface a lot of our issues. Like a therapist."

"Oof, I hope I haven't dampened their spirits."

"I have an idea. Tomorrow, join me in my room."

"After continental breakfast?" Tommy asked cheerfully.

"After breakfast." Marcus smiled.

26 Pizza Night

In the morning light, Marcus awoke to a soft golden glow spilling into his room. The sun's rays creeped up the walls and cast warm patterns across the floor. He stretched, sinking deeper into the sheets and pillows. He savored the comfort of a modern bed. At least, until Gorn's thunderous snoring shattered the silence like a boulder rolling down a hill. Marcus sighed, trying to return to his dreams.

The peaceful moment would not last as the sharp shrill of his alarm clock beckoned his turmoil. It rang out like a war cry, startling Gorn awake. The warrior bolted upright; his eyes wild with sleep-induced fury. With a roar that could have made mountains tremble, Gorn smashed his ax down on the clock, reducing it to a pile of shattered plastic and twisted gears.

"Gorn! I have to pay for that!" Marcus shouted. "I just wanted a moment longer. I was actually getting a good night's sleep."

"Why have such trinkets in a room?"

"It was so we wouldn't miss breakfast."

"How does this work?" Gorn grumbled, as he squinted at the broken pieces scattered on the floor. He wasn't used to such fragile objects. He tried to piece the clock back together as best as he could, seeing Marcus's disapproval. But his broad shoulders slumped in a display of guilt.

"They're serving breakfast downstairs. Could you wake the others?" Letting out a long breath, Marcus took the broken clock from Gorn. "I'll go tell the front desk."

The scent of fresh pancakes and crispy bacon wafted into the hall from the dining area downstairs. The heat lamps buzzed. Overfilled waffle irons dripped. Twists of knobs released cereal into the bowls of the hotel guests. The fridge held drinks from milk to orange juice. A worker was stocking yogurts with berries beside it.

Warmers full of golden scrambled eggs, perfectly crisped bacon, and stacks of fluffy pancakes spread across the table. Gorn, per Marcus's instructions, escorted the other heroes to the welcoming sight. Owen and Jin eyed the unfamiliar foods with suspicion. Their warrior instincts alert in this strange new environment. The rich scents, so different from their homeland's hearty stews and roasted meats, made them hesitate.

Christana and Arnold found themselves hovering over the coffee pot as the hot liquid finished its drip. Marcus greeted them with George by his side, pulling him away from the bellhop's cart. George sat next to Jin, taking hold of his own cutlery made of plastic, and tucked in the paper napkin. He motioned with Jin as he ate the bacon and eggs, though no food was in front of him.

"For us, this is just a simple breakfast," Marcus said as he poured himself a cup of coffee and offered the creamer to Christana and Arnold. The steam rose in lazy spirals, but the first bitter sip made him grimace. "But I imagine for you all, it must be quite something."

"Not to burst your bubble, Marcus, but this coffee is horrible!" Arnold replied.

"That's why I added the cream," Marcus laughed, offering it once more, with sugar this time.

"More cream it is!" Christana smiled.

"I enjoyed your breakfast, Marcus," Owen said. "You have a fine royal cook. Who is the lord of this house?"

Owen, ever the adventurer, picked up a cup of Marcus's coffee, mimicking the way he saw Marcus drink it. But the bitter taste hit him like a slap. His face twisted in disgust, and he spat the liquid out, splattering the floor. "That's foul," he declared, wiping his mouth with the back of his hand. His usually composed demeanor cracked for a moment.

"I could have warned you," Arnold said.

"Try it this way," Marcus said, fixing it with the chocolate and caramel sauce near the coffee machine and topping it with whipped cream.

Of everything in the hotel, the whipped cream in a can fascinated all of them the most as Marcus made Owen's coffee extraordinary.

"This would be more like you had yesterday,"

"It's...better..." Owen replied, still wincing at the burnt aftertaste.

Marcus was going to reply, but he saw Tommy was already at the waffle station. His boyish enthusiasm was infectious as he piled his plate high with waffles. Then, he poured syrup over the melted butter that topped them, dripping onto the carpet. His face lit up as the glistening dribble fell. Around them, the other hotel guests ignored the colorful fruit display, but Tommy eyed it. His fingers itching to try everything.

"It says one waffle per person!" Marcus exclaimed. "I hope they don't say anything!"

After breakfast, Marcus pulled Jin aside, his expression turning serious. "Would you join me and Tommy in the room? I think he could use the same meditation session you gave me." His eyes darted to Tommy, who was still munching on his breakfast, blissfully unaware. "I promised him I would help him. I think you're the man for the job."

"As my duty and my honor," Jin replied.

"Great, I'll go grab him. He can't actually eat all those waffles by himself."

"I'll finish them!" Gorn interrupted, splashing his coffee around from his Styrofoam cup.

"You look as if you could use meditation yourself, Marcus," Jin taunted.

"I need a whole lot more than that…"

As the others lingered in the dining area, caught up in their conversations and the novelty of the food, Marcus, Jin, and Tommy retreated upstairs. Jin moved with a fluid grace, every step measured. His long fingers deftly lit incense sticks. The room soon filled with the rich, earthy scent of sandalwood. Wispy smoke tendrils rose, forming gentle curves towards the ceiling. Marcus, usually mindful of rules, didn't care about the no-smoking policy. The damage they'd already done to the hotel was enough to guarantee a hefty bill—what was a little more at this point?

"I welcome you to have a seat, Tommy," Jin said as he settled into a cross-legged position on the floor. His movements were slow and deliberate. Jin's voice, when he spoke, was calm and steady, each word a soothing balm to Marcus's frayed nerves. Marcus followed suit, though his mind was still racing with worries. He closed his eyes, trying to focus on Jin's voice, to push away the rising tide of frustration.

"I like to think to myself," Jin started. "Of how the Creator melded this world. His peaceful thoughts coming together. His love brightening our world. Focus on this."

Tommy, however, found it impossible to concentrate. His mind was a storm of worries. Thoughts crashing against each other like waves against jagged rocks. He shifted and squirmed, his hands fidgeting in his lap. Jin, sensing Tommy's turmoil, opened his eyes and reached out, placing a firm but gentle hand on Tommy's shoulder.

"Breathe," Jin instructed, his voice a soft command. He began to apply pressure to specific points on Tommy's shoulder and neck. His fingers moved with practiced precision. The tension in Tommy's body melted away, like ice thawing under a warm sun.

Tommy's mind became flooded with memories he hadn't revisited in years. He saw his mother's face, the kind smile that always made the harsh world around them seem a little brighter. He remembered her voice, soft but strong, and the way her hugs felt like a shield against all the cruelty they faced. The memories were bittersweet, filling his chest with a warmth that was both comforting and painful.

Jin could still feel the tension under Tommy's skin. Something did not sit right with him, as he pressured for answers. Tommy, sinking deeper into his regret, leaving his brother home alone, dared not dive any further into those memories.

"I can feel something angering you, or is it fear?" Jin asked. "What makes you afraid?"

Tommy turned away from the red eyes, abruptly standing and forcing himself away from Jin. "I can't do this."

"You'll be fine, Tommy," Marcus reassured.

"You don't know Marcus… The beasts…I can't"

"He fears them," D said, growling through Marcus's shadow. "They breathe the hatred of the one true denier."

"It's difficult to imagine something so terrifying when I am literally the shadow hero," Marcus replied.

"Find your inner peace, Tommy," Jin said once again, fluffing the pillow next to him in encouragement.

As Tommy's breathing steadied, the chaotic noise in his mind quieted to a whisper. The room seemed to settle into a deeper silence, the city's usual clamor fading into the background. There were no honking horns, no blaring sirens—only the gentle cooing of pigeons by the window. The quiet was a relief, a cure for the wounds Tommy hadn't even realized he was carrying.

"I see them running away from me," Tommy said. "In my mind, I can choose to make them fear me."

"Let it go…" Jin said, taking a deep breath. "My master… He told me the same thing. I should have listened to him. I felt anger. I felt fear. I wanted nothing more than to let loose all my aggression. If I had just let it go, and not let my emotions control my decisions. Name what it is you wish the most."

"I wish to see my mother…" Tommy replied. "More than anything, I want to hold her and thank her for being so strong."

"Let go of those emotions. Your fears will no longer control you."

"Let go of my mother?"

"I understand," Marcus said with a deep inhale. "The fear of losing your desires."

"I…" Tommy's words faltered, synchronizing with the others' exhalations, deceiving with each breath. "I set you free…"

"I feel it melting away from you. Let the Allfather replace those fears."

"Thank you, Jin," Tommy said, hiding the nervous tone behind his smile. "And thank you Marcus. This was a great idea… I have a feeling things will work out."

"You are most welcome, my friend," Jin said. "I have been practicing this art since I was a child. The dragons taught us. My master helped me stage my wild instincts."

Marcus nodded, feeling a renewed sense of determination. "Let's do this again tomorrow," he

The Eight Heroes of Old

suggested. "It'll help us stay calm before the storm we're about to face. It's going to be a party!"

"Marcus, I need you to educate everyone today." Tommy's face grew serious. The boyishness from breakfast was gone. And replaced by the hardened resolve of the Time Warden. "Make sure they understand the dangers ahead. The real danger. Modern weaponry and everything. Do you understand?"

"I know exactly what to do," Marcus replied, his voice firm, leaving no room for doubt.

"Good," Tommy said, turning to Jin with a nod of approval. "Listen to Marcus. He'll help you understand this world better."

"I will learn," Jin replied. "What is your plan?"

"I'm heading to D.C. with Christana. We need to scope out the place where Manson will be. His coronation is soon, and we need to be prepared. She wants to develop our plan further after seeing the layout of the event."

As Tommy left the room, Jin remained on the bed, letting out a deep breath. He sank into the mattress, marveling at its softness. The bed was a far cry from the stiff, wool-covered wooden boards he slept on back home. He ran his fingers over the fine fabric of the sheets, tightly bound, yet so soft they felt almost unreal. The scent of fresh flowers lingered in the linens, and for a moment, Jin allowed himself to savor the luxury.

Meanwhile, Marcus went to gather the others. Christana entered the room, her hand resting around Arnold's arm. They looked every bit of a picture Marcus would have seen in an old movie or photo in an era long ago.

"Did you enjoy your breakfast, Christana?" Marcus asked, as he stopped them at the door.

"I did, Marcus, merci!" Christana replied, smiling at her dear friend.

Marcus couldn't help but feel a pang of regret as he approached them. "Christana," he said, his tone gentle but firm, "Tommy needs you. You'll be going on the journey with him."

Christana's expression shifted. A brief flicker of concern crossed her face as she glanced at Arnold. She gave his arm a reassuring squeeze before nodding to Marcus. "Of course. Duty calls."

"Arnold, if I may, I would like to talk to Christana before she leaves. Help yourself to the sodas in the fridge and take a seat in the room."

Arnold stepped away, accepting Marcus' invitation with gratitude. He found a seat next to George and adjusted himself in his place.

"I believe Tommy is waiting outside," Marcus said. He guided Christana to the balcony that overlooked the parking lot. It wasn't the most compelling of places to be, but Marcus leaned over the rail. His sweater protected his elbows from the cold metal.

"What's wrong?" Christana asked, taking Marcus's side.

"It seems things are going well between you and Arnold."

"I try not to think about the bad times."

Silence hummed between then as Marcus gazed over the city, teeming with energy and an exotic glow.

"It's a beautiful city, Marcus," Christana tried to say. "Why did you bring me out here?"

"I spoke to her…To Diana… I feel just the same as the day I hurt her. That day everything came crashing down. I miss the woman I love. I miss my wife."

"I know how you feel, Marcus." Christana peered into the distance as if remembering all the days of grief that unfolded before her.

"I don't mean to be a buzzkill, but I feel trapped. Diana is the most beautiful girl I've ever met. I don't think things will be fine. I know you must be feeling the same sort of…"

"Dread…" Christana whispered.

"Exactly…" Marcus exhaled.

"It does spoil the happiness. I know Arnold feels it too."

"How do you make it look so easy? I feel like I can't see past this darkness."

"Hope can save us. I know it will only break my soul further when it crumbles."

"I've been trying…" Marcus rolled over, bending his back against the rail. He tried to hide the grief that was beginning to amass.

"I won't stop hoping if you don't. At least we will know the pain together."

"It's at least comforting knowing I am not alone." Marcus adjusted his sweater, zipping it up further to fight the cold. "Thank you, Christana."

She leaned in to offer a comforting hug, warm and tender, as their fears solidified in their soul.

"You've become a good friend, Marcus. I can see why Tommy speaks of you so highly."

"When we return to our times, I'll look to the past to remember you."

As they pulled away from each other, Christana wiped the tear that shed from her eye, and pulled her jacket together.

"There you are!" Tommy announced himself coming up the stairs. "I was waiting in the lobby for you, Christana."

"Sorry, we were talking for a moment," Christana responded, reading herself.

"Oh, I hope I wasn't interrupting anything."

"We're fine," Marcus reassured him and offered Christana his credit card. "Buy yourself a souvenir. You'll understand when you visit D.C."

"Are you ready, then?" Tommy asked, skipping his step with eagerness.

"Oui!" She smiled, holding on to Tommy as he ripped open time.

"Enjoy your movies, Marcus!" Tommy said, waving goodbye.

With a blink of an eye, they were gone and the portal closed with a snap. Marcus returned to the room, in hand were movies from the front desk, and a guide to all the channels on the TV. Settling in his seat, he began scrolling through the channels. Fighting the static and poor signal from the satellite.

"We're short on time," Marcus began, his voice carrying an edge of urgency. "I'm going to show you some movies—lots of movies. They'll give you a sense of what life is like here in New York and what our enemies are capable of."

"What's a movie?" Gorn asked.

"Think of it like a play," Marcus explained, trying to be patient, but also trying to find the right words. "But instead of actors on a stage, it's captured on this screen." He gestured to the TV, a large flat screen that dominated the wall. "We'll start with some action films." Scrolling through the guide, he found a movie halfway through to the end. "Perfect! This one has gunfights, car chases, explosions. And it's just getting to the good part! Don't be alarmed; none of it is real. It's just camera magic."

"Magic!?" Gorn questioned with a raged tone.

"Not real magic," Marcus clarified quickly. Rolling his eyes, he stopped Gorn before he did any more damage to the hotel's property. "It's just a way of saying it's all tricks and illusions. Nothing that can harm you and there is no magic involved."

"I don't like being fooled," Owen muttered, crossing his arms over his chest.

"It's not that kind of foolery," Marcus replied, frustration taking a toll on him. But he caught Jin's eye, who gave him a subtle nod, reminding him to breathe and stay calm. Marcus drew a full breath, before continuing. "Just think of it as a way to learn more about this world. And it can be enjoyable, too."

Arnold, who had been silently observing, finally spoke up. "I've seen movies before," he said, his voice carrying a note of nostalgia. "They're just fancy lights and good acting. I'm sure what Marcus has in store will be quite fascinating."

"Thank you. Now everyone is seated, just enjoy the movie."

The microwave door had become loose over the mishandled use of the hotel guests. But the warm light and rotating hum brought the bag of popcorn to life. The steamy bag puffed with excitement and soon emitted demanding beeps to announce its completion. Marcus pulled the bag out from inside and shared the snack around with the heroes.

The group settled in; curiosity mingled with skepticism. The first movie began, and the room was soon filled with the sounds of rapid gunfire, roaring engines, and explosive impacts. Owen and Jin found the exaggerated Brooklyn accents amusing. Their laughter rang out as they mimicked the actors' lines with surprising accuracy. Jin, usually so composed, allowed himself to enjoy the absurdity. His laughter was a rare and pleasant sound.

Gorn and Arnold, however, were less amused. The fast-paced camera work and intense action sequences left them wide-eyed and tense. The sight of characters leaping from buildings and dodging fireballs was a far cry from the battles they witnessed. This was chaos, and it unnerved them.

As the movies played on, Marcus noticed a shift in the room. The heroes were beginning to grasp the scale of destruction ahead. Even Geroge and Frutuoso, who watched from the window, seemed to absorb the lessons, at least in their own way. The movies served as a stark reminder of how dangerous the world had become. How deadly man had become.

By the end of the marathon, Gorn's knuckles were white as he gripped the sword upon his belt. Owen, cross-armed and stomping his foot. Jin remained calm, though his demeanor displayed heavy thoughts. Arnold and George took careful notes, planning to avoid danger wherever possible.

As the credits rolled, Marcus stood, feeling the weight of leadership settle back onto his shoulders. "Now that you've seen what we're up against, we'll start planning," he said, his voice firm. "I need everyone to focus. Things are about to get real."

Tommy and Christana walked through the field, feeling nature's glow. The sky was very much alive with birds in flight, singing their songs. The air was crisp and clear, a sharp contrast to the bustling city they had left behind. D.C. hadn't changed much since Christana was last here—a place of both triumph and sorrow for her. She took a deep breath. The cool air filled her lungs. It grounded her in the familiar sights and sounds.

Tommy wandered over to the throne Manson was having built. It stood half-finished, a grotesque monument to the man's arrogance. The gilded edges glinted in the sunlight. And Tommy could almost see Manson sitting there, lording over the world with a smug sense of

The Eight Heroes of Old

superiority. The thought made Tommy's jaw clench, his hands balling into fists at his sides. He could already see the confrontation playing out in his mind. What he would say, how he would end Manson's reign of terror.

Christana, meanwhile, lost herself in thought. She could feel the rhythm of the city, the pulse of life all around her. Her instincts spoke to her.

"Marcus up there," she whispered to herself, pointing to the area of interest. "Gorn here. I presume an intense battle will take place. I sense chaos." She ran her fingers across the walls of the building, hiding herself from the secret service that were patrolling the area. "There is something evil growing." The sunlight reflected off the white walls, and she observed the cold concrete underfoot. In her mind, she perceived everything, a heed to the warnings. She steadied herself as she made plans, writing down what she was feeling. Every shot, every footstep, every soul present. "Tommy!" she called out, approaching him.

Snapping back to the present, she found Tommy seated on Manson's unfinished throne, a grim, solemn look on his face. His eyes were empty as if no one was home. His fingers traced the intricate patterns carved into the armrests up to the device upon his arm.

"Manson won't win," Tommy declared, his voice firm, breaking the silence. He looked up at Christana, his eyes playful as he smirked. "I've already claimed his throne, if only for a moment. He thinks he has a hold over this world, but Marcus is going to shatter that delusion."

"I have a good feeling about this," Christana said in a soft tone. She spoke to match Tommy's playfulness. She approached him and sat on the arm of the throne that was large enough for another to sit. "My instincts tell me we can do this."

"Good. I have faith in you, Christana."

"Can you see it? Our victory?"

"I wish I could. I want it to be true. I've learned something from each of you. I have faith, determination, and temperament. But I still can't see what the future has in store for me."

"I can see it," she said with a solemn tone.

"You can?" Tommy asked, baffled by her statement.

Christana reached out, taking his hand in hers, guiding it to rest over his heart. "It's not a power. It's something you can feel, right here. Your feelings won't lie to you. You can feel the magic being restored. Just our very presence here has changed that. I can feel the strong change in the wind, the good overcoming the darkness, and the light returning." She paused, her gaze unwavering. "We don't have to be blind. We are the heroes. Time does not make mistakes. The prophecy goes, as time calls, a hero will come. You are that hero, Tommy. You will make things right."

Christana and Tommy spent the rest of the day walking through every building. Examining every corner, every shadow. The security team would fortify and protect the premises with vigilance. Determined to leave no stone unturned, they continued.

Tommy explored the common areas where people would come and visit, with props and D.C. memorabilia. From hats to shirts, and posters and flags, the store had everything. What caught Christana's eye was a small book about the heroes time had called. Within the pages contained pictures and descriptions of every hero. *Now including Marcus!*, as the new revised edition claimed with excitement. But deep within, it had a perfect picture of Arnold, and a well-drawn out caption of how brave the man had been. Christana read every line, down to the last period.

"Thank you, Marcus," she whispered.

As the sun dipped low in the sky, casting long shadows across the green field, they knew they had done all they could for now. When they returned to the hotel, the others were coming back from a coffee outing Marcus had arranged. The smell of pizza filled the air—a welcome change after the day's heavy planning. Marcus had ordered from a local favorite, and the table piled high with boxes.

"Pepperoni, my personal favorite," Christana said with a grin, reaching for a slice. The cheese stretched as she pulled it from the box, and she took a bite, savoring the rich flavors.

"I ordered a mushroom one, just for you, Tommy," Marcus said, nudging a box toward him. "I know how much you like them."

They all ate, sharing stories and laughter as the evening wore on. The pizza was hot and fresh, the crust perfectly crisp, the sauce tangy and rich. Gorn, true to form, devoured the meat covered slices. Owen marveled at the amount of cheese that oozed from each slice. Good food and good company eased their worries about the upcoming confrontation.

"Marcus, my friend," Owen said, raising his soda in a mock toast, "this has been a wonderful evening. The whole day, in fact. I thank you, good sir. I would knight you if I could."

Marcus chuckled, raising his own drink. "Thank you, Owen. I appreciate that."

The evening set, and a single star shone in the New York sky, perfectly visible from the balcony. The heroes held their last conversations under that single beauty until Arnold gave a yawn that spread like a virus to the others. They all retreated to their rooms to answer the nightly call.

The next day, they knew, would be even more demanding. The morning dawned much the same as before. Marcus and Tommy spent it with Jin, meditating and centering themselves. While Christana, and the rest, perfected her plan. She clued them in on her findings and set the markers on the map. Arnold stayed in his room, pouring over notes and preparing for the challenges ahead. The day drifted by in stillness, fear intensifying, yet all anticipated tomorrow. They could feel the loom of dread.

The sun rose that morning, bright and clear, with no clouds to a barren sky. The wind was gentle, stirring the branches outside Marcus's bedroom window. He was already awake, the remnants of nightmares clinging to the edges of his mind. Even with the meditation, the burden he carried was heavy, almost too much to bear. He gathered his belongings and made his way to Jin's room, knocking on the door with a gentle rap.

"Hey," Marcus said, his voice subdued. "I thought we could do some meditation today. You know, to help clear our minds and keep us under control."

Jin was hardly asleep, far from it as Marcus walked into the intense scene. Jin seemed to be fighting with himself, concentrating and sweating.

"Are you all right?" Marcus asked as he cautioned into the room.

"Stay away," Jin muttered. "I don't want to hurt you."

But Marcus remained firm, his feet not moving an inch, nor did his face flinch. After a moment, Jin's symptoms subsided.

"You were losing control, weren't you?"

"The beast is hungry," Jin replied, picking himself up. "But that's not a worry." His voice was steady but with an undercurrent of something darker. "Today, we may need to lose a little control."

27 Convergence

A fogged mirror hid the aged face that stood before it. A pair of polished goggles on an old leather strap held back some frayed, stray hairs. Wiping away the condensation, droplets of water rolled down the glass, bleeding onto the counter. The same hand roughed the stubble upon the chin. Tommy took a deep breath, trying to practice what he learned, clearing his mind of the tangled threads.

"You can do this," Tommy whispered to himself, trying to gain inspiration. "Everything has led to this point. As long as I stop Manson, the Hellhounds won't return. If Marcus brings back hope to the heroes, If he…" The droplet on the mirror sank in unison as if his reflection was shedding them as tears. "That's a really big if…"

"Tommy?" A knock at the door startled him, with the accompanying voice of Owen. "We are all waiting. Are you all right?"

Tommy straightened his coat and answered the door. His cheerful demeanor, he wore as a mask.

"It will be a challenging day, but we are here for you," Owen said to greet Tommy, walking in the room accompanied by George. "What's holding you back?"

"I was preparing myself," Tommy replied then walked back to his bed where the Convergencer sat. He played with the dials and switched before sliding it over his arm, fine tuning the device.

George glanced at Owen. The expression didn't change, nor did he speak. But, Owen knew exactly what he meant.

"Listen to me, Tommy," Owen said, stepping up to him. "We have all had our struggles, including me. Failure is who we are. I know that more than anyone. But it's our failure that makes us come back stronger than before."

"I can't fail, Owen. I fear the Hellhound that haunts my mind. If I can't complete my mission, my worst nightmares are unleashed upon the world."

"If we don't succeed, then we will try again."

"We will be victorious," Tommy said to them.

The Eight Heroes of Old

The Doll sat on the bed, looking over the schematic of the device, his eyes were drawn to the detail put on the paper.

"He says, nothing is stronger than the bonds we choose to create," Owen said, listening to the echoes in his soul that resonated from George. "Nothing is stronger than the team you have made. It was unlikely the heroes would have grown to get along, but you united them." Owen placed a hand on Tommy's shoulder and looked him dead in the eye. "He is right. You did this, Tommy. You succeeded in this. Your time will come, and your bravery will be written in history books. They will sing of your great achievement. You will save the world from this darkness."

"By the prophecy, it will be true."

"Because of you, Tommy. I will follow you into the darkest battle, and so will all the other heroes outside this door."

"Have they had breakfast?"

"They have, and they wait for you."

"I suppose I won't keep them waiting any longer."

The stairs leading down to the lobby felt like small steps before the monument of a climb the day would be. But Tommy, Owen and George all met with the others. The room was silent, waiting Christana's order. She looked over each and every one of them, like a sergeant would for her battalion.

"We each have our part?" Christana asked, and they all nodded in response. She looked to Tommy, signaling the team was ready.

With a gust of foul wind, Tommy motioned in hands, pulling from the void to rip open a portal. The vortex and light and smoke, cast in like a radiant sunset over a stormy day. With a cracking response, the portal burst wide open. The heroes geared up with their helmets and walked through one at a time. Then finally, Tommy stepped through with George by his side.

With a heavy stomp, Frutuoso was the first to land on the lush grass. He knelt down to feel the nature of the ground. The other heroes slipped in, as the Cactus prepared a garden around them, to hide their presence.

"Thank you for the cover, Frutuoso!" Tommy rewarded as he stepped through. "Christana and I have a room where we can establish a base of contact. From there, once our threshold has been met, starts with the next phases of our plan."

"Follow me but stay close. If you don't, we will be seen too early," Christana said, ushering the heroes to move. She made a series of turns and halts, while they waited for men in suits to pass. Through doors and upstairs, led to the room that contained a balcony and a small courtyard. The building was not far and was a clear sight to Manson. The constructed throne to devise his evil plan, sat in the open.

Frutuoso climbed the siding using a series of vines that he grew. Ascending his way to the courtyard, he marveled at the view. With the cover of trees, the balcony was a good place to overlook the crowd below. Well hidden from the circling helicopters above.

"Are there really this many people in favor of this one man?" Christana asked, and she used her rifle to gain a better view. She aimed the crosshairs at Manson. He was in the throne room, a few meters from his balcony that overlooked the people below.

"I've seen this event a million times before," Tommy replied. "Thirteen million people attended his coronation. People from all over the world came to worship this one man. It would have been more if they had the room."

Christana slung her rifle over her shoulder. Then, proceeded to walk back inside the building. Marcus turned on the small TV mounted to the wall, playing the events. He pulled up a chair for himself and Christana as she watched. Arnold took a chair, and sat himself, placing his helmet upon another seat. The other heroes did the same, preparing themselves in their own way.

With a brisk pace, Tommy moved around the room, trying to get a feel for the area. Owen removed his helmet to gain a better view of the outside through the shades in the window. Gorn's steady hand pulled him back as more men in black suits rushed past.

"Those are evil men," D snarled through the shadows of the room and showed himself behind Gorn. "I can feel it in their hearts."

"You'll have to wait here, Tommy, while they clear out," Christana said. "Arnold, let's go." Christana placed her helmet next to his, and readied herself with rifle in hand, and braced for combat. "Marcus, are you ready?"

"Come on, D." Marcus nodded.

George pulled up his sleeves and stabled his top hat upon his head. He gave his best nod to Marcus. The Doll rolled onto the floor, fighting. He moved through the empty halls, scouting for Marcus.

"Wish us luck!" Christana said, chambering a round.

"Take this with you," Tommy said, handing her a small earpiece. "It's a radio so we can stay in touch. There are more in the other room. I give them to everybody."

"Don't be seen," Marcus whispered to George, who had scrambled too far.

"I'll be in and out before you know it. They won't even know." Tommy placed it in her hand, holding on a while longer. "Be safe."

"I feel it," she replied. "This will be a good day."

As Marcus, Christana and Arnold moved together, leaving the other heroes behind, George stopped them as more men rushed by.

The Eight Heroes of Old

"Keep us hidden, D," Marcus ordered. The shadows and corners grew darker, as the heroes stayed within them. Anywhere the sunlight missed, they moved in silence.

Frutuoso motioned like he wanted to help Christana and Marcus before they got caught. Instead, Tommy stopped him. He and the others watched them make their way down through the mix of buildings. Tommy put his hand on the Cactus's leg, giving a reassured pat. "Don't worry, my big friend, we will set you free in just a moment," Tommy said to him. "We need a way to clear out all these people, but we cannot scare off Manson."

Upon the balcony of Manson's throne room, an announcer proclaimed to all present. The loudspeakers carried his voice to all corners of the city. His face plastered on every screen. The heroes watched as the people praised Manson's name. Behind the man, Manson, in a quality suit, was visible and whispering into the ear of another.

"He is alerting them of our presence," Christana said over the radio.

"As I feared," Tommy replied.

"We are almost to our position."

Turning to Jin, Tommy spoke, "You're up."

Transforming before them, Jin's fur glistened with golden fury. Silently he moved. Catlike and paws landing flat as he chased down the men in suits. Their earpieces of echoing voices made them easy prey for the Tiger. They fell in silent numbers. The swipe of claws moved with invisible speed, cutting down men before they could scream.

"This area is clear," Jin said through his earpiece. "No one follows."

The crowd cheered and roared, as the announcer welcomed Manson. Jin made a face in disgust. A man he would love to tear apart. But with the oncoming threat of more of his henchmen, Jin moved to a better position and waited to ambush.

Through the halls, Marcus and George made their way up the stairs, forsaking the elevator in an effort to stay hidden. The building had a nice view from the windows inside, making it perfect to televise the event. But Marcus did not have any time to spare gaze upon the crowd.

Ahead, the console room awaited, the nerve center of Manson's propaganda machine. The locked doors slowed their progression. But Arnold, with his immense power, had no trouble breaking them apart. The metal crumpling under his mere touch. Inside, the room buzzed with activity. News teams worked, guarded by police and operatives. They stood ready to defend Manson's broadcast.

As they approached the final door, Arnold prepared to break it open. But Christana placed a hand on his arm, pulling him back. She took in a deep breath, her senses sharp. "There's danger ahead," she warned.

Without a moment's hesitation, George sprang into action, darting down the hallway. He took cover by a corner as Manson's men rounded it, guns drawn. The air filled with the sharp crack of gunfire, sending nearby workers into a panicked frenzy.

George, ever the agile fighter, fixed his sleeves and suit after each opponent fell. He did it with a calm, almost indifferent air. His movements were unpredictable. His limbs swung like a ragdoll, delivering punches and kicks with a speed that left his foes disoriented. Marcus held firm, shielding Christana and Arnold. Bullets ricocheted off the walls around them.

As one of the men tried to call for help, his earpiece irritated his mind. The static came through clawing and screeching. Voices came through, demonic cries as Marcus commanded D and set him loose upon the suits. D's torment and flickering lights proved most effective, even frightening George in the process.

The corrupted man's movements became erratic, his eyes darkening as he fell under D's influence.

"Don't hurt him, D" Marcus ordered, his voice reflecting the tension.

But more men arrived, guns raised, unaware that one of their own had been compromised. With a sinister grin, D unleashed a barrage of bullets, the room erupting in chaos. The counterattack left the men scrambled. The loud blasts untamed by the walls, echoes through them.

"That's enough D!" Marcus shouted. "I said no more killing. We are past all of that!"

"They are evil at heart, Marcus. Their assault will never cease."

"Not if we can't make others believe in us again."

With a frustrated kick, Marcus slammed the man D controlled to the ground. D stood before him, a shadow unphased by the kick as the body fell.

"There's more, Marcus!" Christana shouted.

"You know, for someone who is loved by everyone, he sure does need a lot of protection!" Marcus muttered, taking cover behind a small table. The makeshift shield offered little safety, but it was all they had. The Doll, gaining his composure, leapt into action, creating a distraction as Marcus allowed D to continue his work.

D looked back at Marcus, who watched as concern etched across his face. The demon's twisted talons hovered inches from a man's trembling face. But D held back, exercising restraint.

"I won't kill them," D scoffed, a hint of disdain in his voice.

Marcus exhaled, relieved. "Thanks, D."

Christana stepped forward, her eyes scanning the path ahead. "This is where we split up, Marcus. The staircase to the balcony is up ahead, and the control room is a few rooms down."

"Got it," Marcus nodded. He braced himself by the door, ready to hold off any guards that might come as Christana and Arnold slipped past him. They sprinted toward the reinforced door accessing the balcony.

"Do your thing, Arnold," Christana instructed, her voice firm yet calm. She readied herself with her rifle, steady upon her shoulder.

Arnold stepped up to the door, placing his massive hands against the metal. With a quick, powerful motion, he shattered it into pieces, the fragments scattering across the floor. Inside, two guards had little time to react before Christana. With lightning-fast reflexes, she took them down, her movements precise and efficient.

Together, they moved into position, gaining a clear view of the entire area from their vantage point. Across the way, Manson stood on a platform, addressing the crowd below. Despite the fear evident in many of the people's faces, Manson's voice carried a chilling calm. He assured them his protection would keep them safe. His control over the crowd was unsettling, as if he had woven a spell of obedience around them.

"This is where you go back to Tommy," Christana said, her voice laced with concern. She grabbed a radio from one of the fallen guards and handed it to Arnold.

"Take care of yourself," Arnold replied with a kindhearted tone. He leaned in to kiss her before turning to leave. He made his way back down to the lower level, passing Marcus and the Doll as they engaged more guards.

"I'm in my location," Christana radioed to Tommy.

"Copy that," Tommy replied, then signaled to Owen and Frutuoso.

Owen nodded, determination in his eyes as he broke through the ceiling and soared into the sky. The saguaro, now freed, stretched his massive form, preparing to defend the heroes. He saw the danger and positioned himself like a living barrier between the threat and his allies.

Gorn, standing tall amidst the chaos, drew his sword in one hand and retrieved a stone from his bag with the other. Whispering an ancient spell, he called forth a mighty storm. Lightning cracked the sky, and a fierce tempest began to howl. He attempted to clear the crowd of Manson's enthralled followers. But despite the ferocity of the storm, the people remained, unmoved and unfaltering. Their minds were held captive by Manson's malevolent influence.

"Do not harm them!" Tommy commanded Gorn and Frutuoso as they charged into the fight.

Owen, with his crystal wings, turned his attention to the oncoming choppers. They opened fire with miniguns that shattered his skin. His size was still enough to withstand the fire. In a blaze of destruction, he crashed the choppers in the fields below. Many more came forth with a volley of missiles targeting the ground. Owen gave cover to those below taking tremendous amounts of damage. His wings cracked and broke off; gravity pulled him back down.

Through the thick smoke and crumbling rubble, Tommy slipped forward. His movements were cautious but determined. Gorn led the way, his keen eyes scanning the chaotic battlefield. They watched Frutuoso's deadly dance of kicks and swings. He dispatched enemies with brutal efficiency.

The air was thick with ash, providing a temporary cover that Jin used to his advantage. With the stealth of a predator, he pounced on the men in suits, taking them down with little effort.

But their victory was short-lived as reinforcements arrived. Soldiers in full combat gear, their weapons at the ready. Jin, a guardian of silence, navigated through the haze, forging a path to Tommy. As the smoke began to clear, Jin emerged, his fur bristling, with Arnold close behind.

"This way, Tommy," Jin growled. "I can smell Manson. I will lead you to him."

Tommy nodded, his heart pounding as he reached for his earpiece to contact Marcus. "Marcus, are you in position? It's starting to get chaotic down here!"

"Working on it!" Marcus shouted back, his voice strained as he rejoined the fray alongside George.

George, an eerie yet agile figure, was a blur of movement. He wrapped himself around a soldier, his iron hands striking with mechanical precision. The soldier struggled in vain. His cries cut short as the Doll choked him into unconsciousness. Marcus, surprised when he caught sight of George's efficiency out of the corner of his eye, applauded. He was far more formidable than he had anticipated. Bullets ricocheted off his metallic hands, leaving him unscathed. He dodged and rolled with uncanny agility. Another soldier fell, pleading for help as George overwhelmed him with relentless strikes.

With the last of the guards subdued, Marcus cleared the next room of any threat, though there was little. As he turned back, he saw George standing amidst the aftermath, his coat full of bullet holes. His once-pristine hat was too tattered to wear. The Doll looked almost… forlorn.

"You'll be okay, right?" Marcus asked, a note of concern in his voice. "It's time for us to move again."

As he started to leave, George tugged on his sleeve, stopping him.

"What? More bad guys?" Marcus was quick to survey the area. But George wasn't indicating danger. Instead, he began undressing one of the fallen soldiers.

"What are you doing!?" Marcus asked, baffled.

George glanced up at him, his expression, if it could be called that, showing determination as he motioned toward the soldier's uniform.

"You need his clothes? All right, but hurry!" Marcus urged, turning his attention back to the door. More guards were attempting to break through. D, had already begun barricading the entrance with desks and chairs, moving them like a poltergeist. He rejected their advances, his dark presence filling the room with an ominous aura.

The guards finally breached the door and encountered D's malevolent grin. The demon tore into them with savage glee, his attacks swift and brutal. The guards, choking on the thick, acrid smoke D emitted, were too terrified to fight back.

"Are you finished yet?" Marcus called over his shoulder. Glancing back, he saw George wearing a green soldier's uniform, with body armor and a helmet. The transformation was almost comical, but the Doll wore the uniform with an air of grim purpose.

"Did you really have to take his underwear too?" Marcus sighed while shaking his head. "I did not have to see that."

The Doll merely shrugged, his expression inscrutable.

One last room lay ahead. Its entrance lay guarded by a formidable number of soldiers. All holding their ground with grim determination. George, now embracing his new uniform, charged in with fierce enthusiasm. His hands moved with precision, every swing a flawless execution. The fluidity he had mastered from observing Frutuoso's deadly grace.

George tore through their ranks with precision. D intensified the chaos, flickering lights, and hurling objects. But George needed little help; his strength alone brought the soldiers to their knees. One by one, they fell under the relentless onslaught of George's powerful strikes. The room became a battlefield strewn with defeated foes.

"Geez, that's brutal, even for me," Marcus commented.

"They'll live." D chuckled, his voice carrying a hint of satisfaction. "George is quite the fighter."

"All right, George, the camera room is just inside," Marcus said, giving the door a forceful shove. The door creaked open, revealing an empty room. The crew had already evacuated, leaving the camera unattended. George continued his rolling movements into the room. His enthusiasm to assist was evident. Marcus had no time for games and began explaining the basics of operating the instrument.

"Just keep it centered and focused on me," Marcus instructed. He spoke into his radio, alerting Tommy of his success.

"Did you read that, Christana?" Tommy asked.

"Loud and clear," she responded from the balcony looking through her scope. "Manson isn't moving. It's like he was expecting us. His secret service is still around him."

"Even with all the trouble, Manson still stays put?" Tommy questioned. "How many does he have with him?"

"At least a dozen that I can see. I feel uneasy."

"As do I," Arnold said. "Just give us the path to take."

Christana took precise shots to protect Gorn and Frutuoso as they battled below. She gave direct instructions to Arnold as he led Tommy to Manson's throne room. Jin was in her sights, as she aided him from anyone drawing their weapons upon them. Her eyes were sharp and her fingers faster. Not a single target escaped her. She saw everything from that height.

Meanwhile, from beneath the rubble, Owen shook off the dust, his powerful form rising as he grew new wings. These wings, composed of fine crystal-like stained glass, shimmered with a myriad of colors as he took flight. Circling the heroes below, Owen unleashed torrents of fire. Blazing barriers obstructed any who dared approach Tommy or the other fighters. Owen's presence in the sky was both protective and commanding. He ensured that no enemy could advance without facing his wrath.

"Tommy is almost to Manson," Christana exclaimed over the radio, taking shots between and reloading. "Marcus, you'd better relay your message now."

"The camera is set," Marcus responded. "George, are we rolling?"

The Doll nodded in response, raising his thumb and holding the boom.

"Okay, here it goes," Marcus began, turning to face the camera. "Hello, everyone. Hello, world. This is your hero speaking... I have an important message for all of you. Don't give up hope on the heroes. Don't lose hope in yourselves. I come with a warning. Manson is not the man he seems to be. He is deceiving us all. Put faith in the prophecy and believe."

Turning away from the camera for a moment, Marcus called into the radio. "How do I know if it's working?"

"I'll know. Just keep talking," Christana replied.

"Uh... Well... Uh... People of this earth," Marcus continued, his voice wavering before gaining strength. "We have been given a special blessing, protected by the Allfather with his prophecy. A hero will always come. A hero will always save the people... I know it's hard to believe right now, but you have to trust in that."

"Just keep talking, Marcus. Speak from your heart," Christana urged him with a concentrated voice.

With a heavy sigh, Marcus shook his head and looked into the camera once again. "I'm deeply sorry... to the world, to those I've hurt. I know the destruction I caused, the lives I took, the evil I unleashed. There's nothing I want more than to make things right. Please, forgive me. From the bottom of my heart. I am sorry. Especially to you, Diana. I know you are listening. Please accept my apology. As sincere as I can be, please forgive me."

Marcus choked on his tears, holding them back and composing himself, he continued. "But I'm here now, doing what's right. If there's any part of you that still understands, please, listen to my words. Don't believe Manson. He's been lying to you, lying to all of us. He's going to bring great harm to this world. You have to stop trusting him."

In the small home far from the chaos, Diana sat with her parents, her cat curled up on her lap. She stroked it absentmindedly as she watched the events unfold on the television. When Marcus appeared on the screen, her breath caught in her throat. It felt as though a light had ignited inside her, a spark of life she thought long extinguished. "Marcus?" she whispered. Her heart skipping a beat, doubt creeping in as she questioned everything Manson had told her. The man on the screen seemed so different from the lies she'd heard.

"It's working!" Christana declared with a cheer! "I can feel it, can't you?"

"I can feel it," Gorn said. "The tides turn, and our sails are flying high on these winds. Carrying us forth to victory, thy Allfather!"

"I know this is going to sound bizarre and strange, but I've been on a wild journey," Marcus continued. "And right now, the man down there in that chaos. The one fighting for our salvation, needs us to believe in heroes again. His name is Tommy Kent, and he comes from the future with a warning. He brought us here. All of the heroes are together, working to end the evil works of Manson. We have one last chance to fix everything, you can count on that. Awaken from this spell. Pray for our safety and that of the world."

"Marcus, you have to come out here," Christana called through the radio. "Tommy is going to need us. He just reached Manson's throne."

"Come on!" Marcus commanded, a fire of determination blazing in his eyes. He and George returned to Christana with remarkable pace. The remaining soldiers on their level already retreated in disarray, their morale shattered.

Arnold approached a heavy door, cracking it open just enough to peer inside. "There are three of them," he reported to Tommy.

"Stand back!" Tommy instructed, using the Convergencer to control his powers. The men inside began to weaken. Time seemed to slow around them as Tommy and Arnold walked past. Using his power, Tommy

The Eight Heroes of Old

disorientated the guards. They crumpled to the ground, coughing and choking before losing consciousness.

"Just up those stairs," Christana guided over the radio.

They ascended to the door of Manson's throne room. Its heavy locks and massive doors crumbled from Arnold's touch. As they stepped inside, they found Manson seated on his throne. A crown encrusted with jewels resting upon his head, matching the opulence of the throne beneath him.

"Manson!" Tommy shouted. His fist shook with rage, confidence finally finding itself within his resolve. "I've come to take you down!"

Manson looked up at Tommy and laughed, a cold, chilling sound that sent a shiver down Tommy's spine. As Tommy took in Manson's appearance, the man's almost otherworldly presence struck him. Like a drop of pure gold in a crystal-clear river. Yet, beneath that surface shimmered a darkness as profound as the demon Marcus commanded. Manson's gaze, cold and malevolent, froze Tommy in his tracks.

"You're too late, Tommy," Manson said,

Christana tried calling out on the radio but was only receiving static.

"Something is wrong, Christana," Arnold called out as he watched from behind the broken doors. "He is just standing there."

"Did you really think it would be this easy?" Manson sneered, his voice dripping with condescension. "You're still just a child."

"Do you know me?" Tommy stammered, his confidence faltering under the weight of Manson's presence.

"I'm surprised you haven't recognized me after all this time. Any of the times," Manson replied, a sinister smile curling at his lips.

Tommy's lips trembled as he uttered the name he feared most, his hands quivering with dread. "Mason?"

28 Convergence Part II

Hellhounds gathered on the horizon as Jimmy activated the machine. The earth trembled beneath their feet. And the sky above darkened into a swirling mass of storms, blocking out the light. Sand whipped through the air, forcing everyone to shield their eyes. Jimmy, his heart pounding, adjusted his goggles and peered into the machine's depths.

"I can see them! I can see them!" Jimmy shouted, unable to contain his excitement in his tiny body. He adjusted the controls to focus the time machine for a clearer picture. The light shined blinding his wincing eyes. Jimmy donned his goggles and flicked the final switch, stabilizing the vortex.

The distant howls grew louder. The Hellhounds' hunger was palpable as they closed in, eager to feast on the souls in the valley. The machine roared. Its cacophony drowned out all other sounds as it hummed with dark, unfathomable energy.

Mason gripped Jimmy's shoulder, his voice a low, menacing whisper. "Now is our chance."

* * *

In the courtyard, the battle raged on. Frutuoso and Gorn fought with relentless determination. The Cactus used every ounce of his strength. Bullets sank into his thick skin, useless against his massive, crushing arms.

Gorn watched in awe as the Cactus moved. The sight was almost a mesmerizing grace, cutting down wave after wave of soldiers. His massive arms swung with precision. And despite the relentless assault, he remained unharmed. Gorn glanced down at himself, noticing the blood seeping from his wounds. It wasn't the first time his skin had been pierced, and he knew he was close to his limit. Tightening his belt, he wiped the blood from his mouth and summoned the last of his strength to cast more spells.

"Allfather, forgive me," Gorn prayed, kneeling on the ground. "This enemy is too strong for me but let me help my friends."

The Eight Heroes of Old

The ground beneath the soldiers quaked, causing them to stumble and fall. But as Gorn cast his spells, he couldn't help but marvel at Frutuoso's unwavering composure. He moved with his *ginga* undeterred by the tremors. Crushing kicks continued to batter the fallen soldiers.

"That's a powerful spell," Jin marveled.

"It wasn't right of me," Gorn responded.

"Why? You cleared the way. We can make it to help Tommy now."

"It's a grave sin to cast against another man."

With a consoling hand upon Gorn's shoulder, Jin helped him to his feet. "I understand, but this is no ordinary enemy. We will do what we must."

"There are so many of them," Owen said on the approach. He landed himself with gripping claws, and a thunderous flap of his wings. "My crystals can only regrow so much. I feel the magic falter."

"We stand here catching our breath," Gorn rebutted. "But in the sunlight, Fructuoso still fights."

"He has heart," Jin stated.

"He fights because he doesn't want to lose those who he loves," Gorn said, coughing and bringing in a large intake of air.

"Not again…" Jin muttered, sharpening his claws and charging forward."

"More units on the left flank!" Christana called out over the radio, her voice steady despite the chaos. She braced her rifle, eyes darting as she searched for Mason and Tommy through the bodies. But the frantic motion around her made it impossible to line up a clear shot. Her gaze shifted, catching the glint of rifles on the neighboring rooftops.

"Snipers," she mumbled.

Her heart pounded in her chest, each beat echoing in her ears as her finger tightened on the trigger. Sweat gathered at the tip, making her grip slick, but she held firm. With practiced precision, she squeezed the trigger. One shot, then another, and another—each one finding its mark. The enemy snipers dropped in rapid succession, their threat neutralized.

Marcus stepped onto the balcony; spotting Christana focused through her scope. She turned at the sound of his approach, her rifle snapped up in his direction. Finger twitching on the trigger as her eyes widened in surprise.

"Easy, Christana," Marcus said in a soothing manner, his hands raised in a calming gesture.

"Sorry, Marcus," Christana replied, the guilt was evident.

"Things seem to be going well," Marcus said, looking over the balcony.

"Manson has an army," Christana admitted with a shaken voice. Her eyes continued to survey the battlefield. "Something's wrong. I don't feel the same as I did yesterday. Something has changed."

"What do you mean?" Marcus's concern deepened.

"I don't know. I think our best course of action would be to leave. Fight another day."

"Leave? Back to New York?"

"I don't know. Tommy isn't responding, and Arnold is with him. I just have a bad feeling."

"Are you sure about this?"

"Yes, Marcus, you have to go to Tommy."

"All right. I'll go find him, and we'll regroup. George, stay here with her. Keep her safe, okay?"

George nodded solemnly, his silent agreement clear.

Marcus, D's voice echoed in his mind, a dark whisper. *This is a lost fight. Don't waste your time finding Tommy.*

"We have to do something! I can't leave him." Marcus's frustration boiled over, his voice tense.

"What?" Christana looked at him as she did not understand Marcus speaking to himself.

"It's D," Marcus muttered before turning to leave, his mind racing. "Something is terribly wrong." Marcus leaped from the building, impacting the concrete. But remained unscathed by the power of the demon.

You're a fool, Marcus. I told you to be weary of him. I told you not to follow him.

"Shut up!" Marcus ran as fast as he could.

"Owen, are you there?" Christana asked. "Does anyone have eyes on Owen? He needs to fly us out of here! Everybody, if you can hear me, pull back!"

Not a single word from Christana reached the heroes below. The battle was too fierce, the cries of combat drowning out any chance of communication. Whether the radio had been lost in the mayhem, or the distortion too much, Christana was cut off. Above her, the mighty form of Owen soared through the darkening sky.

"The metal dragons are back," Owen shouted, setting fire to the sky. Owen tried to intercept the missiles from the F22s and choppers. But they were too fast. The explosions rocked the battlefield, throwing Gorn back. Frutuoso, already battered by the assault, absorbed the blast, imposing a severe penalty. Staggered and bruised, Frutuoso found his footing. He was all collected except for an arm that lay before him.

Jin, sensing the danger, warped out of the blast radius just in time. The heroes, though shaken, remained on their feet, with Gorn's fury igniting a new, brutal resolve in him.

Owen, seeing the devastation below, drew in a deep breath. Concentrating his power, he unleashed a torrent of blue flame at the helicopters and F22s still swarming above.

The Eight Heroes of Old

The flames crystallized them mid-air. Engines froze and the flying machines plummeted to the earth. The impacts echoed for miles, a distant rumble against the darkening sky. Owen gazed upwards. The clouds twisted and tangled, a harbinger of the storm to come.

* * *

"Pull them back," Mason whispered into Jimmy's ear, his voice dripping with malevolence. "Start with the dragon."

* * *

Marcus finally reached Tommy, only to find him frozen in shock as Manson loomed over him.

"Manson!" Marcus shouted, his voice cutting through the chaos. But before he could act, Arnold yanked him aside.

"Wait, look behind him," Arnold urged, his tone grave.

Marcus's eyes widened. Behind Manson's throne was a machine with an ominous vortex. It emanated a sickly green glow, shrouded in a ghastly black haze. The energy pulsing from it was palpable. A dark force they could only observe, powerless to enter the room where Tommy stood.

"Mason," Tommy questioned. "How did you…?"

"Silence!" Mason commanded, his voice cold and vengeful. "You've failed, and my true authority is already granted. I have fulfilled my destiny."

"My father? You killed him on purpose..." Tommy's voice trembled with a mixture of rage and disbelief.

"If he hadn't died, it never would have worked. The time machine needed someone with a pure heart. You were the only one who could accomplish that. And your brother—the Source Crystal would never have obeyed me or your father. We had done too much in the name of survival."

"So, that's what this is about? Survival?" Tommy asked, his voice filled with bitter confusion.

"Not anymore," Mason sneered. "It's about power now. He made me an offer I couldn't refuse. I gain the world, and I will never have to 'survive' again."

"Who?" Tommy demanded.

"It's too late, Tommy." Mason laughed. "You are powerless to stop it."

"I won't allow this!" Tommy shouted, his resolve hardening. He raised his hand, opening his palm wide. The glow of the crystal that powered the Convergencer illuminated Tommy's face.

"You still don't understand," Mason replied with a condescending smirk.

The ground beneath Marcus and Arnold began to tremble. The tremors grew more intense with each passing second. Fissures snaked across the earth. The building around them collapsed into the open crevices. Only a portion of the structure remained, containing their surrounding area with Tommy and Manson. At the mercy of the world around, retreat was the only option. Fractured earth separated the heroes.

From outside the collapsing structure, Christana watched in horror as a cascade of debris pinned Arnold. His pained cries echoed through the crumbling walls.

Driven by desperation, Marcus tried to reach Tommy, but encountered a blocked path. A Hellhound, born from the darkness of the chasm, pulled itself up. Its eyes glowing with otherworldly fire, daring Marcus to come closer.

Tommy's eyes widened, the sight of a snarling Hellhound at the forefront of the battle, began to rage a storm in his mind. "Stop this, Mason!" Tommy screamed, but his own throat froze.

"You haven't even seen my greatest invention yet," Mason taunted, with a wicked grin. With a wave of his hand, the throne shifted, revealing the time machine behind it. Corrupted, twisted, and in violent turmoil. "I have all of your powers," Mason continued, his tone dripping with arrogance. "You think you're the only one who can manipulate time? You're a fool."

From the crumbled debris, Arnold stumbled forward. His vision cleared in time to see Marcus locked in a deadly confrontation with a Hellhound. Shock and fear gripped him as he watched Marcus unleash his devastating power. With a ferocity that left Arnold stunned, Marcus tore the Hellhound apart. The evil energy coursing through him pulverized the creature until it exploded in a wild burst of dark energy. In the chaotic aftermath, Arnold called out to Marcus. But before he could respond, the silhouette of Tommy emerged through the haze.

Understanding the fear and confusion in Tommy's eyes, Arnold shouted. His voice was strong despite the turmoil around them. "Don't let them control you, Tommy! We're here for you—all of us!"

Arnold's words struck a chord deep within Tommy, giving him the strength he needed to break free from Mason's sinister hold. Summoning his power, Tommy adjusted the dials on his device, channeling energy to close the gaping chasm that had torn open the ground. But Mason, seizing the moment, charged at Tommy with a savage fury. The two clashed in a brutal battle, fists flying each one trying to overpower the other.

Pulling from the vortex of time, Tommy unleashed a torrent of temporal energy, forcing eons to surge through Mason's body. The power of the spell was devastating, aging and unraveling his foe as time itself tore at Mason's essence. As the spell reached its climax, Tommy didn't relent; he summoned another surge of power, attempting to drag Mason into the same vortex.

But Mason, fueled by desperation and dark whispers from the void, fought back. He channeled his own time spell, attempting to force Tommy into the abyss of nothingness. Their powers collided. The clash created violent tremors that shook the ground. And distorted the very air around them. The atmosphere grew heavy and oppressive. Each breath a struggle as their minds teetered on the brink of madness.

In a final, desperate effort, Tommy dialed up the Convergencer once more. Pushing every ounce of his power into subduing Mason, he held firm. The two engaged in a battle that transcended time itself. Determined, Tommy looked to the sky. The vortex swirled above. His heart gave into despair.

High above, Owen had finished off the last of the metal dragons. Spotting the fierce struggle below, and Christana signaling to him to engage. He tucked his wings and dove with lightning speed. He displayed his ferocity, traveling to aid Tommy in this confrontation.

* * *

"Bring them all back," Mason whispered again to Jimmy. "We need them here. Save your mother."

Jimmy, terrified and obedient, focused the machine, creating a swirling cyclone. The darkened skies tore open, revealing purple swirls of smoke and ash. In perfect unison, it mirrored the storm in both timelines.

The whirlpool of air and cloud engulfed Owen, who made a desperate bid to escape. But without the protective power of Tommy's helmet, Owen was defenseless against the malevolent force. The void mutilated him, warping his form as he screamed in agony. Time dragged the Crystal Dragon in, turning his powerful body to stone as it drained the life from him. The storm spat him out into a barren field, where he landed as nothing more than a statue—a hero frozen in time.

"I'm sorry, Jimmy," Mason said, hiding his cruel smirk. "I guess dragons don't do well with time travel."

Jimmy felt appalled by the horror, but unsure of what to do next, he listened to Mason.

* * *

Frutuoso's *ginga* came to a halt due to the loss of his arm. He could not fight as well as he could, but he fought, nonetheless. Gorn, who stood by him in battle the whole time, fell to his knees. Unwilling to let Gorn suffer defeat,

The Eight Heroes of Old

Frutuoso stood him up by the pelt on Gorn's back and gave a supportive pat on the shoulder. As the Cactus returned to the fight, the vortex from above swallowed him. Time accelerated without mercy, forcing the Cactus to grow at an unnatural rate. Branching limbs burst forth, contorting and coiling in swift succession. In an instant, he withered and died. Reduced to a brittle, lifeless skeleton.

Both sides had many casualties. Seeing two of his best friends whipped up by the vortex, George leaped into battle. He met Gorn, pulling him to safety and packing his wound with medical gauze. He left Gorn to rest for a moment, while rushing to find Marcus and Jin. The battlefield was a mess of bodies. The enemy was as scarce as his friends, but he persisted. Gazing upward, George saw Arnold assisting Marcus with the debris. Tommy was nearby, and it could only assume they were on their way to assist. Stowing his fear, he began his ascension over the wreckage.

Twisted clouds hailed above, a swirl of purple touched the earth like a tornado. Ensnared by the vortex's grip, George scrambled, limbs flailing in a futile attempt to escape. The pull was too strong. Though time and the void had no power over him, George hurled through unscathed. With a violent outburst, George reached terrifying speed. When he struck the ground, his delicate porcelain head shattered into countless pieces. The Doll, once resilient, lay in ruins, broken beyond repair.

"Keep trying, Jimmy," Mason urged. His voice was a twisted mixture of encouragement and menace. "We will get one of them. Don't worry."

Through the crackle of the radio, Christana's voice broke with urgency. Her heart was pounding in her chest. "Arnold, don't go in there!" she shouted, her eyes scanning the battlefield below. The once mighty heroes had fallen. Gorn, bruised and bloodied, lay motionless. Jin had disappeared into the chaos, his fate uncertain. A deep sense of dread settled in her gut, but there was no time to think. Gripping her rifle tighter, the cold metal pressed against her chest. She descended the staircase, risking everything.

The forces arrayed against Marcus and Arnold were formidable. But Tommy's efforts kept them protected, his powers shielding them from the worst of Mason's wrath. Desperate to gain the upper hand, Marcus sent D to confront Mason. Yet even with the demon by his side, they were no match for Mason's power. Mason wielded the vortex of time like a weapon. Its energy limited D's abilities and forced the demon out of the fight. Frustration boiled within Marcus as he watched. Fists clenched and ready to charge into the fray.

"Don't do it, Marcus," Arnold urged, sensing his friend's growing impatience. "I have another idea. The time machine—Mason draws power from it. Maybe I can find a way to shut it down."

Tommy signaled to them, giving the distraction needed. The Professor and Marcus took the opportunity to sneak around the back. Arnold extracted a compact pouch of tools, his hands stable in turmoil. Opening the control panel, he examined the makeshift wiring and haphazard connections within.

"This thing's held together with tape and bubblegum," Arnold muttered, letting out a nervous laugh. "It's highly unstable. I'm not sure I can do anything without setting it off."

"We don't have time to be careful!" Marcus shouted as a pack of Hellhounds spotted them. Their eyes glowed with malevolent intent.

"This is my design. My life's work," Arnold said in his despair. "Have I doomed humanity?"

"What?" Marcus questioned, baffled by Arnold's statement. "Professor, we have to go!"

With a strong pull, Marcus yanked Arnold from the machine. They both sprinted as the Hellhounds closed the gap. They took a few steps before a wolf sprang, jaws agape. D's sudden appearance and attack obliterated the Hellhound. The force sent Marcus and Arnold tumbling aside and knocked the wind out of them. Both writhed in pain as D urged Marcus to his feet.

Christana screamed into her radio for Marcus, her voice raw with desperation. Marcus, locked in his own battle, surged the demon within him. D snarled at the Hellhounds that dared to approach. The creatures faltered, unwilling to challenge the demon. But Marcus couldn't tear himself away, standing guard over Arnold.

Hellhounds swarmed from every direction. Christana found herself trapped, no escape in sight and nowhere left to run or hide. She steeled herself, Locking eyes with the feral creature advancing toward her. The same darkness she had faced before stood to haunt her. With a determined breath, she pulled the rifle's bolt, loading a round. The Hellhound charged, its snarls echoing with malevolence, but she didn't flinch.

Her bullet struck true, piercing between the creature's eyes. Christana winced as the Hellhound exploded into a blaze of fire and ash. But from the flames emerged more beasts, snarling with even greater fury. She stepped back, thoughts swirling for an alternative, as the situation darkened.

Nearby, Gorn found his second wind. Pulling his weapons, he fought with savage determination. His ax a blur as he cleaved through the Hellhounds with brutal efficiency. The searing heat of their fiery breath filled the air. But the ancient runes on his armor flared to life, glowing brighter with each strike. His spell shifted the metal

The Eight Heroes of Old

as he moved, warding off the flames from the void. The evil powerless against him.

"Go, Christana!" I'll hold them off!" Gorn shouted, scaling his voice to compete with the Hellhounds.

Christana, grateful for the brief reprieve, turned to thank Gorn for his timely intervention. But as her gaze swept the battlefield, Gorn was absent. Panic surged as her eyes shot to the sky. The clouds twisted in a violent spiral, clawing at the heavens with terrifying force. The vortex had claimed him, pulling Gorn into its grip and hurling him upward. Tearing him through the very fabric of time.

Gorn faced his new fate without fear. He closed his eyes, focusing inward, his thoughts steady as he began to pray. The runes upon his armor ignited with a soft glow, casting a protective shield around him. For a fleeting moment, he felt the grip of the swirling storm loosen. The crushing force was easing as if he were breaking free. The sensation of falling slowed, and hope flickered in his mind. But it was too late. The vortex's power surged once more, and its chaotic embrace swallowed him.

Though the vortex could no longer claim him, Gorn found himself lost between worlds, trapped in the endless void. The silence was absolute, the emptiness vast. No human could survive in such a place, suspended between existence and oblivion. Yet Gorn remained, a warrior spirit undaunted, fighting against a fate that sought to erase him from time itself.

Marcus rushed over to Christana with Arnold close behind. Shielding them both from the onslaught, he could feel D's power begin to diminish.

"You have to leave them," D said to Marcus. "This fight is lost."

"I won't," Marcus said, steadying himself for another fight.

"You're not alone, Marcus," Jin said, finding his place with the heroes. The four of them stood back-to-back, facing off against the gnarly teeth and acidic drool.

"We have to get Tommy out of here!" Christana shouted.

"That's going to be a problem," Marcus replied. "I don't think we can even get ourselves out of here."

"There has to be a way," Jin muttered, launching himself into the fray. His warping ability kept him ahead of the Hellhounds' scorching flames. Flickering in and out of their reach. But as they closed in, their numbers grew. Each strike became more perilous. And the risk of becoming overwhelmed grew with each moment that passed.

Above the beleaguered heroes, the sky churned once more with ominous force. The clouds swirled faster as the vortex returned, hungering for yet another victim. Its relentless pull focused on Jin. The hero leaped and dodged with his cat-like agility, evading the grasp of time itself. But even Jin's incredible speed and instinct were not enough to escape the vortex's reach. He could feel its pull growing stronger, tugging at the very essence of his being.

The vortex, unsatisfied, turned its attention to Christana and Arnold. The winds howled as it descended upon them, their fates sealed. Christana, her heart full with dread and love, looked into Arnold's eyes. Time seemed to slow as she gently took his head in her hands, her gaze locking with his. Despite the chaos swirling around them, they shared a moment of profound peace.

"I love you," they whispered in unison, their voices entwined in a final declaration of their bond.

The vortex spared nothing. In an instant, the whirlpool pulled them in. Their bodies spiraled upward into its depths. They clung to each other as their forms faded, their last embrace echoing in the storm. Moments later, their skeletons fell together, lifeless, into the ash at Jimmy's feet.

Tears streamed down Jimmy's face as he stared at the tragic scene before him. Confusion and panic overwhelmed his young mind. He could hardly grasp the horror of it. His heart broke with every breath.

"Jimmy, I know how this looks, but Marcus is strong," Mason's voice slithered into his ear, cold and deceitful. "He will survive. He can save them."

Jimmy, lost in his grief and fear, clung to Mason's words, not realizing the true cause of the devastation before him. He couldn't see that Mason was the architect of this nightmare. The man he trusted was leading him deeper into despair.

Marcus, consumed by the dark power of the demon, let it take full control. With the D's strength, he covered vast distances in moments. He leaped over the snarling Hellhounds and the treacherous fissures in the battlefield.

In a desperate struggle against Mason, Tommy saw Marcus's terrifying change. The grim fate of the heroes was for him to witness. He shed tears to himself, as his powers weakened. "I couldn't save you," he whispered. Tommy tightened his fist, trying with all his might to stop the vortex from absorbing what remained of his comrades. But Mason, relentless and merciless, thwarted his every attempt.

Mason fought with cold fury, draining Tommy's strength with each blow. Tommy, though determined, struggled to keep up, his power no match for Mason's. He needed Marcus's help. But as Marcus rushed to join the fight, a barrier of purified light blocked his path. D roared in frustration, powerless to break through the glowing wall.

"I've found every one of your weaknesses," Mason sneered, tightening his grip around Tommy's throat.

"Mason, you have to stop," Tommy gasped, struggling to break free.

"My name is no longer Mason," he hissed, his voice dripping with malice. "I am the Herald of the Defier. The Earth's reckoning is here, and from the ashes, I will rule this world. Everything does my bidding."

Seeing Tommy in dire straits, Marcus tried to help. But Mason's power struck him down, knocking the wind from his lungs. Mason turned his attention to the device strapped to Tommy's arm, reaching for it with a wicked grin. His strength waning, fought with all he had to keep the device out of Mason's grasp. In a final act of defiance, Tommy overloaded the Convergencer, creating a shockwave that sent both combatants reeling.

"Marcus, get out of here!" Tommy shouted, his voice strained and desperate, every word filled with urgency. With a trembling hand, he managed to open a portal, offering Marcus a chance to escape. The swirling light beckoned, but Marcus hesitated, knowing the dangers that lay ahead. He couldn't survive the journey without his helmet. Without its protection, the portal was a gateway to certain death.

Sensing the impending doom, the demon surged forward. His presence wrapped around Marcus like a shadowy cloak. But before they could act, the vortex descended upon them. Its hunger was insatiable and unstoppable. The air around them twisted and churned, pulling at their very essence as the dark maw of the twister loomed closer.

As the storm began to pull them in, Marcus reached out to the demon, trying to hold on. But D fixed his gaze on the swirling abyss.

"My home," D whispered, a twisted sense of longing in his voice.

"D! Don't let me go!" Marcus shouted, desperation tinging his words.

"It's calling to me, Marcus," D replied, the pull of the void too strong to resist.

"D, don't do this!" Marcus pleaded, but the demon was resolute.

"You would have done the same for me. Your freedom," D said, as the longing turned melancholy.

"D! No!" Marcus cried, but it was too late.

"It's too powerful. I see my own freedom. I would no longer have to take orders from you," D said, with a sense of finality.

"Listen to me, demon…" Marcus began, his voice bursting with anger.

"Goodbye, Marcus," D said, watching as Marcus began to fade into the abyss.

"I'll make you pay for this, Mason," Tommy growled, pulling himself up with the last of his strength. "I'm not going to let this end this way. I can change fate."

"You cannot change fate, Tommy. It was mine to rule all along," Mason said, throwing his hands in the air, readying to call upon his powers to finish off Tommy.

Beaten and bloody, Tommy mustered the last of his strength. His battered body trembled as he raised his fists. He knew this might be his final stand. With a desperate resolve, he tried to summon the energy to activate the device once more, hoping it could turn the tide. But as he locked eyes with Mason, a cold, cruel smile played across his enemy's lips.

Before Tommy could suspect anything, the time machine's wrath surged forward. It was a violent, malevolent force that wrapped around him like the grasp of death. He wasn't meant to return home—not yet. The vortex tore at him, pulling him through the fabric of time with an unforgiving brutality. His mind assaulted by the relentless force that shoved him deeper and deeper into the void.

Tommy could feel his strength failing, his energy draining every moment. The world around him blurred into a whirlwind of chaos and confusion. As he struggled to control it, the vortex's weight pressed down, threatening to crush his spirit. He knew he was running out of time, and with each breath, he could feel his grip on reality slipping away.

Jimmy, panicked and desperate, used the time machine to pull Tommy back. But when Tommy emerged, he was a shadow of his former self—a frail, shaking man, unsteady on his feet.

"Tommy?" Jimmy's voice trembled with fear and sorrow as he looked at the broken man before him.

"Why, Tommy, you're so old," Mason taunted.

Deep lines carved into Tommy's face, and the weight of age clouded his eyes. His senses dulled, leaving him almost blind and deaf to the world around him. But he did gasp as the cold blade of Mason's knife plunged into his heart. Tommy crumpled to the ground, his lifeblood pooling beneath him like a dark, tragic flower. His breaths grew shallow until there was nothing left but the haunting stillness of his final moments.

Jimmy, stricken with grief, looked up at Mason and saw the true depth of the evil in his eyes. Panic and confusion gripped him as he realized the extent of the betrayal. With trembling hands, he snatched key components from the time machine, including the Source Crystal, and ran. He ran as fast as his little legs could carry him, tears blurring his vision. He stumbled, he cried, but he kept running.

Mason's laughter echoed behind him as he claimed his victory over Tommy. He watched the boy fleeing in terror, kicking up dust in the distance.

"Hunt him," he commanded. His words cruel. His voice cold. His breath fierce and vengeful. As promised, Hellhounds were his to command as they surged forward, their snarls promising a wicked and relentless pursuit.

Joe Cordova

Marcus will return in book II The Possessor.

Letter from the Author

Hey friends,

Thank you so much for picking up my book and diving into the world I've created. My hope is that something within these pages resonated with you, as I truly believe each character has a little piece of all of us. This story came to me after waking from a dream that unfolded like a vivid movie—every scene rich with detail and emotion. I've done my best to bring that dream to life in this novel, and I hope you experienced it as fully as I did, right down to the very last page.

I'm already hard at work on the next book in the series, where you'll get to explore the stories of each hero and discover what shaped their journeys to this point. I'd love for you to join me as we continue the adventure together.

To stay connected, follow me on Facebook, Instagram, and YouTube, where I'll be regularly sharing updates and content. And if you'd like to support me further, leaving a review would mean the world—it truly helps more than you know.

Thanks again!

And remember: when time calls, a hero will come!

Acknowledgements

I am deeply grateful to my incredible test readers, Danny, Hans, and Juan. Your dedication, insightful feedback, and unwavering support helped shape this story into what it is today. A special thank you goes to my wonderful wife, Kacey—your belief in me, your endless encouragement, and your invaluable input were the pillars that kept me going. To Belle, my brilliant editor, thank you for your keen eye and for polishing this work with such care. And finally, to Lou, whose remarkable artistry brought this novel to life—your cover art has given my story the face it deserves. I am beyond fortunate to have had such a talented and dedicated team behind me.

Made in the USA
Middletown, DE
19 January 2025

68599069R00300